BAD DAY
IN THE LATE WISCONSIN

by

D. M. SEARS

BOOKS BY D. M. SEARS

Under the author name **D. M. Sears,**
The Untimely Journey of Veronica T. Boone series:
Laurentide
The Jeremy Bentham
The White City

Under the author name **Michael Bleriot**:
Flying Naked
Flying Naked 2
The Jungle Express
Wings of Blue
Memories of an Emerald World

BAD DAY
IN THE LATE WISCONSIN

D.M. Sears

MacGregor Books

Washington DC MMXXIII

Cover art by 100 Covers

ISBN: 0-9962315-8-7

ISBN-13: 978-0-9962315-8-9

For my father,

who loves a good western

CONTENTS

BAD DAY

IN THE LATE WISCONSIN

1

The day dawned cold, and the growing light put a pause on the killing.

A blinding gold from the moment it breached the horizon, the sun bounced rays off the distant glacier and skipped them in flashes across still-thawing ground. They glanced off the watering hole and its overflow, and off pools that collected in deep footprints in the broken mud. They brightened strips of snow that lingered upslope from the water, and sparkled in ice that clung to branches of larch and birch reaching naked into the sky.

More snow dusted a pile of boulders lying midway to the trees, huge erratics dropped from the glacier. Past the boulders stood a vast plain scattered with juniper shrubs and tall grass. Steam from the earth rose and drifted through the juniper, making the needles appear to tremble.

The season was advancing. The air warmed. Cropped grass showed signs of herds moving through the valley. The watering hole had been savaged, its shallow banks crushed from use. Even the trees showed damage, with aspen standing in broken clusters and the lower trunks of birch devoid of branches.

The man hiding in the boulders needed no lesson in muddy prints or the changing seasons. He had been trapped in the rocks since midnight and knew well enough that wildlife was on the move. He was in a desperate hurry to leave for that reason and more. With a grim face and piercing eyes he watched the forest for signs of life. When nothing moved he crawled to a position where he could look back across the valley, too.

Wedged between stones twice his height he gazed east. Nothing...yet. But it was only a matter of time. They would figure out soon enough where he was going. He needed to be gone before they did because he was in no shape to fight. He would have been gone by now if not for...

Just thinking of it made him shiver. Where was it? He twisted in the rocks to look out without exposing himself. The movement was too much and he slid onto his butt, briefly dropping his carbine. The SOCOM 16 was a weapon he had carried for years, long enough for his name engraved above the trigger to be smooth and flush. *M Kurtz,* it read in tight, confident script. But if the engraving was confident, its namesake no longer was, for at the moment the gun was unwieldy. Kurtz picked it up and with his other hand pressed the bandage into his side. The bleeding there had stopped but the gauze was soaked.

Kurtz struggled to one knee. This was serious, he knew. He had been shot before but had never lost this much blood.

He leaned out once more. A mile away – finally – there was movement. They were coming, emerging from a peninsula of forest that shoved itself onto the valley from the northeast. But in the land between him and them the valley was clear.

He slid between the rocks and dropped onto his left side to shimmy through a low passage. Coming out the other end he rose again and squeezed through another gap to survey the western edge of the pile. The first of two carcasses greeted him, looking just as nasty and foul as when he had killed the creatures hours before. Kurtz had never seen a wolf like that, either in size or viciousness. He remembered the terror he had felt as the pack moved in before dawn. He did not scare easily but these things sent a chill down his spine. Two fell to the .308 but that wasn't why the others left. He had had nothing to do with that.

Beyond the carcasses the land was clear.

He stretched and looked back again. Sure enough, there they were. Five men had crossed the gulley downstream where it bent out of sight. They moved warily through the brush but they were not tracking Kurtz. They knew already where he was going so did not bother to search for his trail. Any caution on their part was not due to him.

Which brought Kurtz's attention back to the west. Now or never, he decided. Steeling himself he stepped clear of the rocks and began jogging across the broken ground that stretched away from the watering hole. The ground there sloped away from what he called the southern forest, that closer stand of dense wood from which the beast had emerged and scattered the wolves. Running between the hole and the forest he headed for a lone pine a hundred yards away, his first real cover. Beyond the pine was a wash that housed a dry streambed; another football field past that was a smaller jumble of rocks: his goal.

Kurtz was halfway to the pine before they saw him. The report of a rifle echoed in the morning air. A wild shot. He never even heard the bullet but the sound bounced off the trees and lingered in the open – long enough to announce to everything nearby that something was afoot. Sure enough, he had gone only ten yards more before he heard crashing in the forest. The movement of something big.

He reached the pine and stopped to rest, masking himself from the men but also from the forest. The crashing there died away, or at least became intermittent. In its place he heard something like the huffing of a locomotive.

Kurtz raised his carbine but the men were too far for a reliable shot. Besides, he was dizzy. He lowered the gun and tried to focus. Get to the wash, he told himself. Get to the wash and hold them from there if you have to.

He moved off in a straight line, now southwest, using a huge boulder at the edge of the wash as his goal. That exposed him to the distant men but even the closest pursuer held his fire now, perhaps having been berated by his companions for wasting a round already. They did not have ammo to spare.

Kurtz was ten yards from the boulder, head down watching his footing on the uneven terrain, when he sensed as much as heard movement forward and to his left. He slid to a halt and pivoted toward the noise. As he did a blur shot past his face and clipped his right arm. The motion more than the impact spun him back to the right as the spear tore off part of his triceps and pulled his hand from the bandage. But with a growl of pain and adrenalin he twisted back and fired the carbine with his left hand.

It was one of them, the weaselly guy called Breen. He had risen from the wash and launched his spear with the help of an atlatl. Now the bullet from the carbine caught him in the same stance from which he had thrown the spear, lunged forward like a major league pitcher putting everything into his fast ball. It picked Breen up and threw him backward into the streambed where he disappeared from sight.

Kurtz hurried to the gully's edge prepared to shoot again but saw it was unnecessary. The .308 is a big round and his shot had caught Breen square in the chest. Breen was now flat on his back, staring at the sky, his signature mat of greasy hair splayed around his head. One foot moved, digging a small trench in the soft sand, and Breen's mouth made gulping motions as though he could not believe what just happened. Soon both motions stopped.

Kurtz scanned the bed but had no time to delay. His own shot awakened more crashing in the forest and the pursuers from the north were almost in range. Ignoring the fire in his arm he sat down and swung his legs over the frozen lip of the gully, then dropped onto the eroding walls below. The wash was six feet deep and the dirt gave way, making him stumble. He crossed the sand and reached up to climb the other side.

He should have searched the wash first. That thought occurred to Kurtz just before he was hit again. The streambed did not lead to or from the watering hole. It curved around in a great loop as its seasonal flow took runoff from the north forest out onto the plain and eventually to the larger prairies in the south. Over the decades it had carved a wide gash in the moraine that was a decent way to approach his position unseen from the north if one had the guts to cross the open ground before dawn.

Obviously someone besides Breen had the guts because Kurtz was halfway up the far wall of the gully when a second spear slammed into his back, high up behind the left shoulder. He cried out and dropped back into the sand. The blow was paralyzing. The .308 fell again, his left side freezing up as though delivered an electric shock. But as he toppled backward he could still move his right hand. Releasing the bandage he grabbed the Glock 40 pistol tucked inside his belt. The thrower had spun on her heel and was sprinting around the turn twenty yards down. He saw it was one of the women – Elke or Zee, he could not tell – and fired two rounds even as he was hitting the sand. One at least got her. Kurtz saw his attacker knocked off her feet as though punched. She could still move, though, and before he lifted himself up to fire again she crawled out of sight.

How he cursed. He was not used to being hunted. It was supposed to be the other way around. He rolled onto all fours and reached behind him to grab the spear shaft. That was not difficult. It was five feet long and already hanging down under its own weight. The woman was not strong enough to skewer him and fortunately had not mastered the atlatl, either. But she had been good enough. The point had glanced off his shoulder blade and penetrated the muscle; already it hurt like hell.

Kurtz worked the shaft loose and threw it aside, then staggered to his feet. These damned Progs. He wanted to hunt down and kill every last one of them. He thought about going after the woman to make sure she was dead. She was vulnerable: if she had another weapon she would have used it first instead of throwing a spear...a spear! He could not believe it. He should go after her and put her down for good...

But he did not have the time. He was fading. The blow to his shoulder was the last straw. Besides, he could not see over the wall of the wash now and did not know how close the men chasing him were.

He heard a shout. Then another. Then a bellow that sounded unlike anything he had heard before. Well, not quite. Kurtz had heard it the night before and knew exactly what it was. It was a frightening sound and it ignited his adrenaline. Ignoring the pain he grabbed his rifle and scrabbled one-handed up the south wall of the wash. Rolling over the lip he looked back.

His five pursuers had passed the boulders and reached the watering hole. Three were beyond the pond, in fact, but two had turned back to seek cover. The reason was obvious: the beast had broken from the forest and was charging across the open ground at them. The third hunter paused, not wanting to give up the chase.

When the beast turned and stampeded toward his partners, he made up his mind. With a rifle of his own, he took off at a full sprint in pursuit of Kurtz.

Kurtz cursed again but expected nothing less. He reached for the Glock – he could not shoulder the carbine anymore – but then remembered he had only a hundred yards to go. Besides, his hands were shaking. Run, he told himself. Run.

He struggled to his feet and pushed on, heading for the small pile of rocks that stood above the growth on that side of the wash. Behind him there was a shout, then another shot. He ignored both and drove forward.

The cylinder he sought was white and tubular, like a small fire extinguisher or a thermos. Kurtz had hidden it in a hole no bigger than the canister itself. Find it, he muttered as he closed on the rocks. Get it, open it, hit the switch...

There was another shot. He looked back. The beast was still at the rocks and the lone hunter coming after him had reached the gully. He disappeared as he dropped into the wash but seconds later his hands were clawing at the brush on the near side.

Kurtz reached the rocks and dropped to his knees. Letting the carbine fall he crawled forward. It had been only forty-eight hours. The grass and twigs he used as cover were still green. He pulled them away – there! The cylinder gleamed – anyone seeing it from even a few feet away would mistake it for another patch of snow. He grabbed it, pulled it clear, and wrenched at the top.

Two more shots sounded behind him. One caromed off the rocks and penetrated Kurtz's thigh. He cried out in pain and this time, trembling or no, he raised the Glock and emptied its magazine at the man behind him. It was a good hundred feet and he could not tell if he scored a hit. Still, the pursuer dropped to take cover.

One more twist...it was open. The guard on top of the cylinder snapped up, revealing a blue light and the simplest, least hi-tech button imaginable. With a final effort the man reached to push it...

"No!" came a yell. Kurtz's pursuer jumped up and raised his rifle.

He was too late. There was a flash of light and an ear-splitting detonation. The shock wave knocked the pursuer off his feet. Even the beast, rampaging on the far side of the wash, staggered sideways.

The noise echoed off the trees and carried down the plain. It shocked birds out of the juniper and sent ripples across the watering hole. Anyone who heard it hunkered down until the sound ran out of things to hit and exhausted itself in the wide open space.

When the pursuer looked up, Kurtz was gone.

In western Wyoming at the top end of the mountain valley known as Jackson Hole, the Snake River forms from a trio of streams dropping down from peaks inside the Bridger-Teton National Forest. The headwaters of the Snake collect at the bottom of a long slope and wander east for miles before turning into the valley proper adjacent to the town of Moran. Where it turns it is met and fed by the Buffalo Fork, a steady but unassuming stream of water so clear one can count the ripples on its sandy bottom. The Fork comes from the southeast, flowing off the continental divide and draining hundreds of miles of watershed around Togwotee Pass. Its rich waters are home to the best fly fishing in Wyoming and pass through some of the most beautiful meadows and forests in North America.

State Highway 287 parallels the Fork until just past Burro Hill. There the road and water diverge, which on this day was just as well since a rockslide had cut the road anyway on the far side of the hill. A good driver could get around the slide by driving into the fields but there were no longer many drivers, good or bad, in the area.

An exception to this dearth of human activity lay east of the slide. There a well-trafficked dirt track led off the highway to the north, tracing the Fork's upstream flow and flanking a field of alfalfa and an irrigation line that chugged its way optimistically around a sixty-acre circle. Highway 287 continued east, its neglected pavement accentuating the loneliness of the land.

The dirt track wound into a canyon below Mount Rudolph, passed north of the Turpin Meadows, then carved a wide loop to head back west. At the peak of the loop leaned a signpost marking a private driveway. An expensive gate had been knocked down and pushed aside and the driveway led into national forest from then on. It ended miles later at a luxurious compound ringed by three buildings.

The smallest structure was an exquisite log cabin. Framed in rustic alder that gleamed in the sun, it had a stone chimney at one end and a wide porch across the front that faced the drive. Floor to ceiling windows on the west wall looked out at the Tetons. Behind the cabin the land stretched for miles until the hills began again. Where they did, forest trimmed the slopes in all directions. A canyon gouged by a long-extinct glacier led up into the Absaroka mountains, trailing a rocky moraine. A mile east of that was a more promising gap that looked to be a pass through the range.

The next larger building was the sprawling main house a few score yards away, across a landscaped but overgrown lawn. Another mountain-traditional construction, the center of the building had an A-frame while the wings spread low and wide in shiplap luxury along a ridge. The building could have been a private home or a hunting lodge for the rich and famous: at the moment it looked deserted.

The last structure was on the edge of a dry wash whose only notable feature was a bus-sized chunk of granite that leaned over it a hundred yards to the north. The building resembled a hangar for light aircraft and in fact an orange windsock stood on the lawn outside although there was no runway and no stretch of land level enough for a plane to touch down. It was two stories of corrugated tin thirty yards long with a wide sliding door at one end. A smaller doorway was cut into the corner. Near the door several SUVs sat in the grass.

Inside the hangar four men crouched before a row of computer terminals. Two others lounged nearby, playing games on their phones. The terminals formed a half-circle facing the center of the hangar. Behind them were stacks of servers, a bank of cubicles, two conference tables, three desks, and a weapons rack secured to the wall and stocked with a dozen semi-automatic rifles. The servers were piled on wheeled dollies and secured loosely to the floor with flexible bands. On the far side of the hangar an ambulance and a fire engine sat by the wide door.

The middle of the hangar was filled by a wooden stage. Round and thirty feet in diameter, its perimeter hosted a Plexiglas wall that angled outward, then straight up, then inward as it pointed toward a hole in the roof. It looked as though two-thirds of a geodesic dome had been sawed off and laid inverted on the concrete floor. The floor of the stage had a rubber wrestling mat; four feet up and all the way around separate foam mats pressed against the Plexiglas. A single door was built into the glass.

In the middle of the stage was a cheap table that could have been purloined from any tavern. On it and held in place by a steel rack was a white cylinder the size of a thermos. The top few inches of the cylinder were bare steel and revealed a crystal arch over a glass tube. With no warning the gas inside the tube began to glow blue. At the same time a buzzer sounded.

The six men looked up. The two playing games jumped up and drew rifles from the rack. A third hit an intercom switch.

"Inbound, inbound," he said.

The guards took positions at converging angles to the stage. The rest of the men also drew weapons but stood well clear. Everyone donned riot helmets with face masks. The blue light on the thermos grew brighter.

The door to the hangar flew open and two more men burst in.

"What is it?" the first demanded. He wore an Allis Chalmers jacket and had gone days without a shave.

Before anyone could answer the blue light flared and an explosion rocked the stage. A detonation powerful enough to shake the building blew outward from the thermos. Everyone staggered. The servers rattled in their shackles.

The shock wave ricocheted off the Plexiglas and burst upward. A blast of dust accompanied it so thick it was unclear at first what damage had been done. But in moments air jets at the stage edge activated. The dust cleared. The thermos was still there, the blue light now extinguished. Its twin lay on the floor, near the body of the grim man who sprawled where he had been thrown against the mats. His weapons lay about him and blood stained his clothes.

"Kurtz," the Allis Chalmers man gasped. "Damn." He dashed for the stage even as others raced to the ambulance.

The second man through the door was more deliberate. Medium height and solid as a steer, he surveyed the scene. As one of the computer techs dashed by he grabbed the man by the arm and pointed to the monitors. "Back to your station."

"Yes, Mr. Galt," the tech complied.

"And get Cooper on the phone," Galt added. "We'll need him."

An older man climbed out of the ambulance. He had black skin and graying hair and a look of concern that could have been a permanent expression. He walked deliberately to the stage door where Allis Chalmers and one of the techs were dragging Kurtz out into the hangar.

"Careful, Neal. He's bleeding everywhere. Let me treat him where he is."

"No!" the man in the jacket snapped. "Out of the chamber, that's the first priority." He barked orders as they lay Kurtz on the concrete floor.

More people came into the hangar. The ambulance pulled around and a trauma team assembled.

"He's alive, Jerry," Neal insisted, backing up to give the older man room. He removed the company jacket, now soaked in Kurtz' blood. "I saw his eyes move."

"He's alive," the doctor agreed. "Angie, he's got a wound behind that shoulder and he's bleeding from his leg. Banks, make sure that's not an artery."

"It's not," a paramedic announced, cradling Kurtz's knee.

"We'll stabilize him here. If we can stop all this blood we can stabilize him here. We'll operate next door if we have to. Call the chopper just in case."

"It's on its way. We'll notify Salt Lake."

"Hope we won't need to...damn it, Banks, stop that bleeding!"

"It's not the femoral, Doctor Campbell. This is superficial. Most of this blood's from his hip."

"Is it now?" The doctor's fingers flew over the patient's torso as he sought to find and stanch the damage to the man's side. "Oh, I see. That's what we've got.

Tears everywhere. There's a bullet wound here but that's not what did this. The round went in and out ...he was hit with something else. Ripped. It looks like he's been gored."

"What?"

"Tore him right open. More Celox, Angie, here and here. We have to get this stopped."

"Can he talk?"

The question came from Galt, who stayed out of the way but loomed over the crowd.

Dr. Campbell ignored the question. His team worked for fifteen minutes before he moved aside.

"We'll take him next door," he announced. "We've got everything the Regional Center does. Ian, get hold of Srivna and Eddleston – they're the best surgeons this side of the Rockies and we can use them."

"They might have gone down to Denver," one of the techs replied doubtfully. "To help with the casualties there. The governor declared it a disaster zone."

"Then get them back, " Neal barked. "This takes priority. Have the governor call me if he doesn't like it."

As Campbell's team slid Kurtz onto a stretcher his eyes flickered. Neal dropped to his knees and crawled forward. Kurtz's lips moved.

"Kurtz," Neal whispered. "Matteus Kurtzen, can you hear me? You're alright, man. You're safe. We've got you now. We've got you back."

Kurtz tried to reply. The muscles around his eyes tightened.

"What happened, Kurtz? What did you see?"

Kurtz's lips moved but Neal had to put his ear to the man's mouth to make out the words. The techs stopped working to allow them silence. But when Kurtz' head dropped back Campbell pushed Neal away.

"He can't talk if he dies. I've got him from here."

"What'd he say?" Galt demanded as the aides bore Kurtz's limp figure to the ambulance.

Neal slapped the floor. "Nothing that made sense, damn it. Something about him being the wrong guy. Or being wrong. Maybe he killed the wrong guy, I don't know."

"How could he kill the wrong guy? They're all targets."

"I don't know. I'm guessing."

"Nothing about, you know..."

"No, just that bit about being wrong. And something about a bad day."

"A bad day? Are you kidding?"

"He said it twice," Neal affirmed. He looked around the room at the bloody floor, the dusty stage, the overturned chairs, and the ambulance rolling out the far door. "A bad day? Yeah, he sure got that right."

2

Seven hundred miles northwest of where Matt Kurtz struggled for his life, Leonard Day inched forward in a stand of tall grass and re-established his sight picture. Day was not a sniper and he did not have a sniper rifle but he could still make the shot he needed if the shadow in the trees across the meadow moved five feet either left or right. Day did not care who the shadow belonged to, he just wanted its owner to move.

The trees that fronted the meadow were mostly white alder but it was a few stubby pines that were in the way. Day could not just shift to get a clear shot. If he did he might give up his position and he did not want to do that. There were likely only three people within thirty miles and the last thing he wanted was for the other two to know he was here. He would hold his position and wait for the other guy to move first. Until dark if necessary. He had that kind of patience.

The meadow was a narrow triangle. It sloped down toward Day where he lay concealed in a thatch of sedge and mountain phlox. Even without the grass he could not see the top of the clearing. A trickle of a stream ran through it but it was nothing. Sufficient to draw from but Day doubted that was why the man across the meadow was there. From the shadow's size he was sure the man was Theodore Grapstein, known to his fellow travelers as Todor. To Day and the rest of the Settlers he was Little Head Ted.

Day knew Ted's file as well as he knew any of the West Central Progs. Ted was big, violent, and not particularly bright, a loyalist to the Prog movement even before their bloody attempt to overthrow the government, what Progs called the Occupation. A ne'er-do-well who nevertheless had a gift for logistics, he had moved high enough in the Progs to have his opinion heard. It was he who had pushed for and organized the school massacres in Davis and Sacramento, the tipping point for so much later mayhem in northern California.

But Ted was not an ideologue like so many of the Progs. He just liked the violence. With a branch of the movement from the Cascades he had fled north after the Occupation collapsed, escaping into the forests along the Canada border and finding refuge in the vast "burned-over" area from Missoula to Seattle that people had abandoned in droves during the brief insurgency. Most of the band had been rooted out in Spokane. Others had drifted back into populated areas farther south and been picked up there. But Little Head Ted and his survivalist companion Philby were one of the scattered elements still unaccounted for. Now it was Day's intention to account for them.

Day had been in the woods two weeks, having entered west of Kettle Falls and worked his way north. He had gathered enough clues about the pair's whereabouts to guess a general location. Philby had hidden in the old Colville National Forest once before, years back when he was fleeing arson charges in Utah and Nevada. He seemed to like being near the border. Crossing a border did not help Progs anymore but maybe he was nostalgic for the days when it did. And maybe, Day figured, Philby just liked this part of the country. The Colville was rough and beautiful. While it was not the middle of nowhere it was partway along that path. It was a good place to disappear.

The population of eastern Washington state was now only a tenth of what it had been before the violence. Most people had fled at the beginning of the Occupation as the middle and upper west turned into a twenty-first century version of Bleeding Kansas. Spokane still had some people but was eerie in its silence. Coeur d'Alene was a ghost town. Kettle Falls was no more than an encampment. It had become a home of only the truly committed. Fortunately they were committed to each other and not to the Progs, which is how the Settlers had heard there might be two strangers in the area. Nobody had spotted the two men but someone had seen signs. The problem with the middle of nowhere is you have to get there, and in getting there Little Head and Philby had left tracks.

Two hours went by. The day warmed into late morning. The man across the meadow moved several times but never enough to give Day a clear shot. He stayed in the shadow of the trees. For a while Day could not see anything and wondered if Ted might have left the area altogether. Then just as he was getting ready to back out of his site he caught a glimpse of the big man again.

It was no surprise Ted was wary. He knew the Settlers were after him. Day and others had been hunting down Progs one by one for months. It was no secret. The federal government denied using bounty hunters but nobody believed that and nobody cared, either. That's what launching a mindless, bloody assault on society did for you. When it failed, everyone hated you.

So Ted and Philby clearly were being careful. Day had scouted the area and he knew the measures they had taken to hide. He knew they had a cabin hidden in the trees a quarter-mile behind the meadow. He knew there was a spring in the rocks near the cabin – another reason Ted would not be going to the meadow for water. He knew the three trails the men used most often, which is how Day had discovered the meadow in the first place. He knew where they dug their latrine and he knew about the traps.

Lots of traps. Traps everywhere. In four days of reconnaissance Day had counted four Vietnamese foot traps, three deadfalls, seven swing-arm kill traps, and one feather spear device that was strong enough to break a man's leg as well as skewer it. Even the trails Ted and Philby used were guarded by hidden hazards. Day had been an outdoorsman all his life and had never seen such a profusion of lethal snares. That told him Philby was around, for most of the traps were delicately designed and well-hidden; Ted did not have that expertise. And it told him that months after the Occupation's failure the men were still on their guard.

The problem was, Day did not know Philby's location. Aside from the traps, Day knew from tracks that Ted was not alone. That meant Philby had to be around. But in a week of stalking Day had not seen the woodsman. And that worried him. Philby was smarter than Little Head on many levels. In addition, he was crafty and at home in the forest. Precisely because of Philby, Day, a decent tracker himself, had taken special care to conceal his movements as he trailed the two men. And Philby's unexplained whereabouts were part of the reason Day was willing to be so patient with Ted. If Ted was not waiting just to make sure the meadow was clear, then maybe he was waiting for Philby to join him. So Day would wait, too.

So it went until early afternoon. There was no movement in the meadow except for one doe white-tail who came out of the forest, wandered to the creek, and departed again. There was no sound but the buzzing of locusts and the chattering of a flock of goldfinches that descended on one patch of the meadow after another without ever shutting up. It was a quiet, beautiful day.

Not until after two o'clock did Day realize Little Head was not waiting for Philby. The revelation came when he heard the plane.

It was a small aircraft. The sound, a light drone just lower in pitch than the locusts, arrived thirty seconds before the plane itself. In that half minute Day realized he had a problem.

He had not considered a plane. He had surmised that Little Head and Philby received supplies from time to time but assumed those came by road. The highway that split the Colville was still in use. It ran north from Spokane about ten miles east of the meadow. Just over the border it met up with another from Grand Forks and together the two roads gave Little Head and Philby options for connecting with sympathizers – there were some in Canada – or just moving around if they so chose. Day had figured that any support came that way.

It did not. Not today, anyway. Day had not heard or seen an aircraft in weeks but now one was going to fly right over where he lay in the meadow. He turned to look behind him. It was two dozen yards back to the trees, too far to back up fast with any stealth. He would have to hope the pilot did not see him.

The Super Cub appeared over the trees, a small plane moving so slow that at first it did not seem to move at all. It looked like it was hanging on a string, flat wings stretched high over cantilever struts. Day could see the pilot behind the spinning nose prop. The man wore a ball cap and was twisted in his seat, flying with his left hand while groping behind with the right.

Halfway down the meadow a large bag tumbled out the side hatch. It was floppy and loose and rolled as it fell like a pack falling off Santa's sleigh. But the plane was not high to begin with so the bag did not fall far. It plopped into the meadow on Ted's side of the stream, barely visible above the waving columbine and early black-eyed Susans.

Twisting to push the bag the pilot must have let the control stick move with him, for the plane banked as the bag tumbled out. Now instead of flying right over Day it went closer to the opposite trees. When the pilot corrected he pulled up on the stick and turned back left, giving him a clear view straight down. Like a kite in a stiff breeze, the tiny plane drifted effortlessly over the clearing. Day pressed his cheek into the soft soil and lay still, praying to be missed. But as the plane passed over he could see it in his peripheral vision and knew he was in trouble – the pilot was directly above him. At that angle the forest-green cammies that made Day invisible against the trees stood out like a shadow on the pale sedge.

Sure enough, the Cub's engine gunned suddenly and the Cub leveled out. Day wondered if the pilot and Ted were in radio contact. Whether they were or not, that was not the pilot's plan. He had a better way to advertise Day's presence. Before he even passed over the meadow he banked the plane again so he could see Day through his open window. And he held a pistol.

The pilot opened fire. Day cursed. There was always something that did not go according to plan but this one took the cake. He was under aerial assault!

The pistol was a semi-automatic and the way the pilot kept shooting it held 10-15 rounds. The range was not unreasonable, either. Day found himself twisting and rolling as bullets spattered into the dirt around him.

The shooting paused as the Cub overflew Day's position. The pilot rolled right to set up for another pass. Day scrambled into a position to see where Ted had gone. He was just in time to see the big man exiting the meadow with the dropped bag slung over his shoulder. Day raised his rifle but Ted disappeared into the trees.

The Cub pilot fired again. Angry now, Day rolled over and shot back. His Bushmaster did not fire a particularly heavy round but it was more than enough for the sheet metal and fabric of a Super Cub. His first shots tore into the engine cowling. Within seconds the cheery buzz of the engine began to sputter. The pilot banked away but Day shifted his aim and sent half a dozen rounds into the bottom of the fuselage just below the cockpit. The Cub rolled out on a heading toward the top of the meadow and then banked again to the right. Its engine seized. With the drone and the shooting stopped, the meadow became quiet as the plane nosed over and crashed into the trees.

Day slung the rifle over his shoulder and speed-crawled backwards into the forest. The ground dipped there and gave him cover, so reaching it he jumped to his feet and ran around the perimeter of the clearing to where Ted had disappeared. The gig was up: Ted and Philby knew he was here now so he had to keep them on the defensive and not let them flee or make a plan to fight back.

Inside the treeline he paused. The nearest trail was forward and to the left, not far from where the stream ran into the forest. The sound of footsteps came from that direction. It was a quarter-mile in a straight line to the cabin and the noise headed that way.

Day broke into a run, wanting to keep pressure on his quarry. He stuck with the trail for the same reason: he wanted Ted to keep to the path, too. Ted would try to lead Day into one of the traps and on that score at least Day was two steps ahead of him.

Sure enough, Ted held to the trail, increasing his distance but not swerving off into the trees. They raced down one side of a ravine and up the other, through a stand of aspen and deep into a spruce wood where light faded and the soil was spongy and soft. At the entrance to the wood Day leaped over the first foot-trap, a long, covered hole masked by the spreading branches of a snowberry bush. Then a hundred yards on he skirted a log deadfall, a scaled-up version of a simple Paiute trap that was as intricate as any Day had seen. It would have crushed him beneath the trunk of a leaning mountain ash had he not discovered it the day before. Philby might be a nutcase but he was a craftsman, for sure.

Beyond the spruce the trail leveled out and entered a mix of fir and cedar. Day followed it as it turned east. He knew the cabin was close, built against a rocky hill and almost hidden in trees, and that the trail would jink again as it came near. He slowed and listened, hoping that Ted stuck to the trail.

He did. Just as the limestone formations of the hill came into view there was a cry from ahead. It was followed by thrashing in the undergrowth. Day sprang forward.

He found Ted lying dazed on the ground at the foot of a lodgepole pine, arms flung wide. One foot was caught in a nylon line that stretched to the top of a young maple nearby. Day had set the snare as best he could, knowing the maple was not big enough to hoist a man but confident it was strong enough to knock someone off his feet. That it had done, yanking Ted's foot out from under him and throwing him almost upside down against the trunk of the pine. The bag he carried broke open and spilled its contents on the forest floor.

Day leaped upon Ted, dropping a knee on his chest and clubbing him hard against the side of the head with the butt of the Bushmaster. Ted's own rifle had fallen into the pine needles. Day pushed it out of reach, then removed a revolver and a Bowie knife from the big man's belt. Ted had lost weight: he was thinner than in the pictures Day had, the ones that showed him leaving a bank robbery in Eugene the previous summer, but he still tipped the scales at over 240 pounds. The Settler was taking no chances. He left Ted's foot bound as it was and zip-tied his hands, then took two more ties and secured the loose foot to the first. It was fast work but left Ted trussed and inverted with the blood rushing to his head.

"Where's Philby?" Day demanded when he had finished.

Ted barely heard him. He gazed blankly at Day.

Day did not care. "Philby," he repeated, keeping his voice low but raising the butt of Ted's own pistol for emphasis.

Through his fog Ted got the message. He could not turn his head but his eyes looked left toward the cabin. Day glanced that way and then back at Ted to determine if the man was telling the truth. Deciding he was, he swung the pistol against Ted's temple. It was like hitting a grizzly with a paperweight but Ted's eyes rolled back and he went still.

Day took up his rifle again and tossed Ted's revolver into the brush. He backed away from the snare and for a while stood in the shadow of the pine, assessing the situation. On a good day he stood only five-feet-eight and his build was stocky, so in the gloom of the forest with the rifle held close he looked like nothing so much as an old tree stump.

If he stood on his tiptoes he could see the cabin through the trees, a one-room hunter's shack flush against the rock. The roof sloped away from the hill and into the clearing, its edge dipping past the wall to cover a shelf below. On the shelf was a propane tank, two animal traps, and some milk crates. Hanging on nails below the overhang were a coil of rope and a pair of snowshoes. A wisp of smoke drifted from the chimney. A cook stove, Day surmised, and one with a dying fire. Logs were stacked by the tank. Another half cord was piled against the hill.

Was Philby inside the cabin? If he was there, he should have heard Ted hit the ground – the big man made more noise than the bag dropped from the airplane. So why did Philby not react?

Without moving, Day glanced down and studied the objects that had spilled from Ted's bag. There were boxes of ammunition, bags of freeze-dried food, a sheaf of letters bound in a rubber band, and a bundle of money. There was a metal flask, probably alcohol, and two plastic bottles of a clear liquid. Strewn around them were smaller white boxes.

Day looked around and listened, then stepped to the bag. He knelt and studied the boxes. Medicine. Antibiotics, corticosteroids, and pain relievers, mostly, but also bandages, gauze, tape, and other accoutrements of advanced first aid. Still inside the canvas sack were IV bags filled with a saline solution. Day glanced back to the cabin.

Working through the trees he moved closer. A blue jay screamed somewhere but otherwise all was still. The smoke from the chimney grew faint. The door to the cabin was on the far side of the building, away from Day and beyond his sight, and that worried him, but the only window was just above the propane tank so as he approached the clearing he comforted himself that he was as invisible to anyone inside as they were from him. He crossed the clearing without incident, staying behind the cabin and moving up next to the hill. The only movement besides his own was an angry chipmunk who scampered up the rocks to a tiny ledge and stared at Day from there, chattering his disapproval.

Day waited until the chipmunk shut up. Then with the Bushmaster at the ready he dashed across the clearing, ducked below the window and turned the corner of the cabin ready to fire.

He need not have bothered. The door was open and through it Day could see a bunk. On it lay Philby, motionless, breathing weakly, with his hands in clear view.

Day nudged the door with his foot, pushing it wide. Keeping his rifle forward he stepped inside.

The place was spare and neat. Surprisingly neat. Two bunks, a pot-belly stove, a wood table with folding chairs, and half a dozen shelves hammered into the wall. The shelves were stocked with canned food and boxes of ammunition. Two rifles leaned in the corner by the stove; a pistol in a holster was on the floor by Philby's cot. There were incense candles burning on the table alongside a kerosene lamp; a dog-eared Louis L'Amour western lay on the empty bed. How about that, Day thought. Ted can read.

Philby was covered in sweat. His eyes followed Day but that was the only movement he made. His face was drawn, his skin pallid. His breathing was so shallow that his whole body seemed deflated. The man was so sick he no longer cared about being caught.

"Bummer," Day observed. *"Take heed, Sickness, what you do. I shall fear you'll surfeit, too."*

Philby blinked.

"Well, Ted got your medicine," Day said. "The problem is, he did not..."

Outside the chipmunk abruptly started barking again. Day stopped himself in mid-sentence. He listened – and then instinctively dropped to the floor, barely making it before a fusillade of bullets exploded through the wall behind him. The rounds tore across the top shelf, blowing apart cans of Dinty Moore stew and showering their contents around the cabin. They ripped through the chimney stack as well, shredding it midway to the ceiling and knocking it over to crash onto the table where it crushed the lamp and threw sparks across the floor.

Philby moaned but did not budge. His eyes barely widened. Day kept an eye on him but scooted across the floor to put the stove between himself and the back wall. The shooting paused but then started again, with the bullets coming on an angle this time through the corner of the room. They stitched a second line through the back wall and tore apart another shelf, this one stacked high with cans of chili. The cabin began to smell like a lunchroom.

Day rolled to the back wall, staying low and trying to gauge an angle from which to shoot back. But the shooter was on the move, running apparently because the next burst came through the side wall. Again he aimed high, shattering the window and blowing apart the frame it sat in. Glass rained down in the cabin with pieces landing on Philby who weakly raised a hand to brush them off. Smoke began to rise where the spilled kerosene caught fire. It joined with what already drifted out of the broken stove.

Again the shooting stopped. Huddled behind the stove, Day cursed and listened, trying to hear footsteps or some indication of where the shooter might be. But then the chimney stack which had fallen onto the table rolled off it, clattering to the floor. The shooter outside took that for a sign of life and opened up again, this time blasting through the boards below the window frame and splintering the table top. Rounds flew across the cabin and tore apart the far wall only inches above Philby's chest. Philby made a futile effort to roll off his cot.

Day grabbed the holster and pistol at the head of Philby's cot and slid them out of reach, then he took hold of Philby himself. The woodsman was not nearly the brute Ted was, so with one heave Day rolled him out of the bed and onto the floor. Philby hit with a thud, which prompted yet another burst of fire from outside. This one crashed into the traps stacked outside and caromed off the propane tank. Within seconds there was the smell of leaking gas. Day edged toward the door, realizing he needed to get out of this trap.

"Philby!" came a cry from outside. "Philby! Are you okay?"

That was not Ted's voice. Day did not recognize it at all. It was high-pitched, like a woman. He swore to himself. His intel had been bad. Ted and Philby were not alone. But who was this new shooter? Where had he come from? Day had been all around the area for a week and there had been no sign of a third Prog.

"Philby!" came the cry again.

"He's alright!" Day yelled back, not knowing what else to do. "He's alive but if you…"

His words were cut off by another burst of fire on full automatic. Bullets tore through the cabin from left to right about three feet above the floor. The table collapsed and rounds ricocheted off the stove. The bottom two shelves fell off the wall. Day hugged the floor, keeping his rifle trained on the door. The firing was working its way toward that wall of the cabin and pretty soon the shooter would be in a position to see inside.

Yet that was not the worst of Day's problems. The kerosene on the floor of the cabin burned and its dirty smoke mixed with dust and ash to obscure the top half of the room. Flames worked their way to the wall and started climbing. It was getting hard to breath.

But just as Day was hoping the smoke might somehow give him cover for an escape the propane pouring out of the tank outside found an open flame. An explosion ripped the air, gas and dust erupting into flame that filled the room, blew out every port, and scorched the back of Day's body from his head to his boots. The detonation was fast and hot and almost noiseless, but when it was gone everything in the room from the cots upward was on fire.

Now Day was scared. He did not want to be shot but he sure as hell did not want to burn to death and for the moment he could barely breathe. He flipped over and snapped the switch on his own rifle to automatic. Pointing it at the back wall, he opened fire, blasting a line below where the first round of firing had come through from the other direction. Bits of wood flew in every direction. Behind him and above the sound of the flames he heard answering shots from outside but now he had no time to note where the bullets went. With the flames and the smoke it was getting hard to see much of the cabin anyway. At this point, as long as they were not hitting him he did not care.

He got to his knees and dragged Philby to him. The Prog did not resist: he was limp and his face bled from hitting the floor. Day pulled him into a sitting position and then slung him into a fireman's-carry. Taking the Bushmaster in his free hand, he backed up and then charged at the back wall to hit it with everything he had.

The boards there were two-by-sixes but they were old and dry and now they had been shot up and set on fire. Day and his burden crashed through and sprawled into the clearing.

Behind him the cabin ceiling collapsed. The propane tank fed gas into the conflagration and flames leaped above the eaves to the tar paper roof. Black smoke poured up through the trees.

Day landed on Philby. He dropped his rifle but managed to keep the Prog in front of him to break his own fall. Philby lay spread-eagled in the dirt, out cold, looking more dead than alive.

The Bushmaster was a yard away. Day was reaching for it when a bullet ricocheted off the rocks and a voice behind him shrieked, "Freeze! Don't touch that!"

Day gave up on his rifle but instead of freezing he spun around and grabbed Philby by the collar, pulling him up to use as a shield. He did not carry a pistol but he had a small hunting knife at his belt; that was at Philby's throat before he turned to face the source of all the shooting.

The source was a complete surprise. The shooter was a thin man, short and bald with a gray ponytail pulled tight at the back of his head. The pony tail matched a scraggly goatee and moustache that clung to a dirt-streaked face. The man's eyes were wild, his pants torn, his sweatshirt caked with dirt. Only his jacket was in decent shape. It was an oversized corduroy blazer complete with leather elbows, making its owner look like a feral college professor. The man's eyes were wild with anger as he leaped into the clearing.

"Get away from him! Get away!"

"Back off or I'll slit his throat," Day barked.

"The hell you will!" the man screamed but he hesitated. He carried an M-4 and wagged the barrel back and forth in sync with his words. When Day did not respond he wagged the barrel faster, and finally in frustration pointed the gun straight up and fired another burst through the trees. "Let him go!"

Day crouched lower behind Philby. "Back off," he repeated. He tried to sound calm but he could see the man's finger was locked so tight on the trigger that he might fire whether he meant to or not.

Pony Tail's features twisted. His face burned. Instead of backing up he lowered the barrel and stepped forward. "You'll do it, you'll do it, you'll do it..." he chanted. He looked ready to shoot right through Philby and Day was at a loss how to stop him. Then a voice from the back of the clearing spoke up.

"Back off, Doc."

Day's blood went cold. Keeping Philby in front of him he glanced back.

Little Head Ted was awake. Awake and loose from his bindings. He stood behind Day at the edge of the trees, dazed but angry. More than angry. He held his revolver in one hand and the Bowie knife in the other and glared at Day with the same savage expression that campus security cameras had caught on tape at the Davis killings. The damned zip ties, Day thought.

"He lets Philby go right now or I'll kill them both!" Pony Tail demanded.

"You shut up," Ted replied, his voice low, his eyes on Day. "You watch how I handle a Settler." He started across the clearing.

Day struggled to his feet while keeping Philby as a shield. He tried to back toward his rifle but Pony Tail hurried to cut him off. They were now on either side of him.

"You're going to die, Mr. Bounty Hunter," Ted snarled. "And you're going to die slow. Slow so you can watch while – watch out!"

Ted's warning was directed at his companion but Pony Tail never saw what hit him. A great, gray mass flew across the clearing and tackled him even as he turned. The rifle fired one reflex burst that almost took off Philby's nose before Day could launch both himself and his captive backwards into the dirt to get out of the way.

Pony Tail screamed but the cry dissolved into a bloody gurgle as the animal drove for his throat.

Day scrabbled in the dust for his Bushmaster, taking forever to find it and expecting a bullet in the back every second. But when he finally got his hand on the stock and spun around to face Ted, the big Prog was down. He had taken Pony Tail's final shots square in the chest and lay now like a fallen oak, eyes vacant and mouth wide in surprise.

Day staggered to his feet. "Get off!" he yelled at the creature savaging Pony Tail. The beast ignored him so he grabbed a log from the pile and threw it as hard as he could, striking the animal in its side. The great wolf leaped aside and spun around in fury but Day advanced on it with another piece of timber.

"Get off! Get away, dammit!"

The animal backed off, its muzzle soaked in blood and its eyes wild from the attack. It looked ready to launch itself at Day but the Settler was mad as hell himself and ready for a fight. He hurled another log and kicked dust in his frustration.

"Where the hell were you? Huh?! You took your sweet time!"

Pony Tail was dead – or almost. His neck was broken from being shaken like a rag doll and his throat was gone. His eyes still showed life but they were unfocused, and there was so much blood in the sand that Day could do nothing for the man even if he were so inclined. As he watched, the shooter's eyes glazed over and he stopped breathing.

Day turned in a circle, his rifle leading him, half-expecting something else to appear from the woods. When nothing did he stood still, letting the adrenalin drain away. Then he sat down.

The great beast with the bloody jaws kept its distance. It stretched out in the dirt close to the trees, keeping a wary eye on Day but also watching Ted's prone body with suspicion, as though hoping the big man would move just so it could leap on him.

The cabin fire blazed. The roof fell into the flames and one wall collapsed, throwing up sparks and another cloud of sooty smoke. It could have been worse.

Most of the boxes of ammunition lay scattered in the clearing, and now the propane tank fell off its shelf and rolled away. That left the rest of the structure to fuel the fire which it did for the rest of the afternoon. For much of that time Day sat in the dust and watched it burn.

3

The pickup came into sight five miles out, topping a rise on the valley road and disappearing again when the ground dipped. Day watched it approach, never moving from his seat on the porch, his hands gliding over the pieces of a hydraulic pump spread across his work bench. A short-barrel shotgun lay on the table. Music played inside the cabin but not so loud as to mask the noise of the approaching truck. In the dirt at the bottom of the steps the huge beast that could have been a dog lifted its head and listened.

The truck turned into the canyon. There was a gate there but Day rarely closed it since the fence on either side was in such disrepair that it would not have stopped a determined ground squirrel. The truck drove through without stopping. It bounced over the cattle guard, passed a stand of birch that guarded one of three freshwater springs in the canyon, then forded the creek. Finally it started up the hill that led to Day's cabin. The driver never hesitated. Though the road turned to gravel and then to dirt with washboards that would rattle a chassis, he seemed to know where he was going. And since there was no one else within five miles, that meant he was coming to see Day.

Only when the truck pulled into the clearing did it slow down, downshifting loudly as though to ensure no one was surprised by its arrival. A small cloud of dust caught up with it, settling into the dirt that formed an oval before the cabin.

The huge dog rose. He stood tall and straight, his wide feet planted in the dirt. His chest was broad and the torso behind it did not taper. The huge frame was draped in thick fur that curled and matted. The animal's head was rectangular with oversized jaws and one stray tooth outside the lip. One eye was brown, the other red; one ear folded over to point forward. The eyes focused on the truck as it rolled to a stop. When it did the animal moved, walking a slow circle to a point forward of the right front tire. There he halted, his nose level with the hood.

The truck had four doors and a dual axle. Day relaxed somewhat seeing the bed was empty and all the windows rolled down. The pump for his water mill was still in pieces and he continued picking through them with his left hand as the driver parked.

The visitor got out, holding his hands where they could be seen.

"Mr. Day," he said, conversationally. "I'm from Shell. Just here to talk."

He was medium-height and thin, maybe fifty years old. His tone was level and his expression calm; neither changed even when he saw the shotgun. He wore blue jeans and a Pendleton shirt and moved like someone used to honest work. If he was armed it was not obvious.

The man came around the back of the truck but stopped when he saw the enormous dog on the other side. He eyed the animal. The dog stared back.

"Never seen a hound like that," the man said carefully. "What is he?"

"Big," Day answered.

"I'll say," the man replied, not moving. "Like a wolfhound crossed with a water buffalo. You sure it's even a dog?"

"No."

"Well, if he is, he's the ugliest one I've ever seen "

Day shrugged off the insult. It was not an inaccurate statement.

The driver stepped warily along the truck as though thinking of offering to pet the dog as a friendly gesture. About the time he reached the doors he seemed to change his mind. The dog crouched.

"Don Galt sent me," the man continued, transferring his gaze to the porch. "He has an offer." When Day did not respond he added, "More like an assignment. If you're interested. Mr. Galt thinks you'll be interested."

"Where's Cooper?" Day asked "I always deal with Cooper."

"He was promoted. I'm the new Cooper."

With no warning the dog sprang. His crouch was slight but the power in his legs was incredible, launching his long body in a lightning attack. From a standing start he erupted off the ground and threw himself at the man's chest.

Just as fast the driver flung open the back door of the pickup. His left hand rested on the handle so all he had to do was flip it up and swing the door wide, twisting his hips into the motion. The panel swung forward and met the skull of the charging dog at peak momentum. There was a heavy thud and the beast dropped into the dust.

The driver closed the door and stepped forward, ready to deliver an insurance kick to the dog's muzzle. There was a *click* from the porch. He looked up to see Day level the shotgun at him.

"That's enough," Day said tersely. "He got the message."

The dog rolled over, shaking its head. It tottered to its feet, fell, and tottered up again. With halting steps it stumbled to the porch and lay down.

The driver crossed his arms.

"He's ugly *and* dumb," he commented.

"He learns quick," Day countered. "And he never forgets. Don't try that again." He set the shotgun back on the table. "Alright, Mr. Cooper. What have you got?"

Cooper motioned to the porch. "May I come up?"

"No."

"Are we the only ones here?"

"Yes."

Cooper studied Day. "Galt told me you weren't much for small talk. But then none of you Settlers are. Alright then. I'll get straight to business. Some Progs have turned up who we thought were taken care of. Mr. Galt wants you to take care of them."

"What do you mean, 'turned up?' Did they escape from somewhere?"

"No. If they had escaped from somewhere that would mean they were in prison. If they were in prison instead of dead that means they wouldn't have been important to begin with. Not important enough for a Settler, anyway."

"So how did they just turn up?"

Cooper took a deep breath. "I'm not really the one to go into the details," he stalled. "I know what they told me but Galt said I should let him explain it to you. He said if I tried you would either tell me to go to hell or shoot me."

"I might do both," Day pointed out. "And not in that order. Alright, if you can't tell me how it happened maybe you can tell me how many Progs we're talking about."

"It was twenty-two to start. Were not sure now," said Cooper.

"Twenty-two? Who does Galt think I am, the Terminator? I'm not going after twenty-two people."

"Well, the circumstances are unique. They're likely not at their best."

"What does that mean? Where are they? Urban or field?"

"Field. Definitely field."

"High-ranking or low?"

"HVTs, for the most part, with some foot soldiers."

"High Value Targets? How high?"

"Very high."

"Give me names."

Cooper hesitated again. "Galt told me to leave that to him, too."

Day frowned. "For somebody who's trying to get me to take a job, Galt's being pretty cagey. I just came off an assignment. Why don't you get someone else?"

"We did. It didn't work out so well."

Day's eyes narrowed. "Who?" he asked.

"Kurtz."

"Matt Kurtzen? That doesn't check. You said they were in the field. Matt's a cop, a city guy. The best in a city. Put him in population and he'll smoke you out no matter where you hide. Put him in the woods and he's a weekend warrior. He's out of his element and he would be the first to tell you. Why did you send him and why did he go?"

"Well, we didn't know we were sending him to the field. We thought we were sending him to Dallas."

"You're not making sense. You didn't know where you were sending him? He didn't know where he was going?" Day paused. "How is he?"

"He died two weeks ago."

Day stared at Cooper, who met his gaze.

"Why me?" Day asked.

"Galt said he wanted the best."

Day scoffed. "If he wanted the best for tracking someone in the wilderness he would have called Sid Evans in Steamboat, or Kruehler in Mobile, or Big Mountain Dave down in Apache Spring."

"Evans is in Mexico looking for the Caesar brothers. Kruehler is laid up from a broken leg he got going after Eric Dafoe, and Big Mountain said no."

"So I'm the best of what's left."

"As you said, you just got back from an assignment," Cooper explained. "We all thought you were still in the Northwest. He might have called you before now if you were around."

"Not likely."

"More likely than you think. He knows you'll want this assignment. And you have the kind of record he's looking for."

"What's that supposed to mean?"

"It means," Cooper said, "that you don't tend to bring Progs back. And there's no one in this particular group that we want back."

Day stopped sorting pieces on the table. "Mr. Cooper," he said in a voice that could have carved stone, "every assignment says Dead or Alive. That's your policy, not mine. And every assignment I do my best to bring in these sons of bitches alive. I'm not a contract killer. The government has been just as ruthless with captured Progs as any Settler. The only difference is they hold a trial before killing them. I would just as soon see a Prog fry as shoot him myself and I do the best I can to deliver them for just that destination."

"You may try, Mr. Day," Cooper countered, "but something always seems to happen. None of your Progs make it to the courts."

"If you're talking about Little Head Ted, that was an accident. I didn't kill him."

"He still died," Cooper pointed out. "As did Philby, and Rory Strauss in the Wasatch, and Crazy Mary Lee down in Texas, and both of the Shettleman twins over in Goldfield."

"Strauss I killed," Day conceded. "I didn't want to but it was a tight spot and it was either him or me. But Crazy Mary jumped in front of a train, for god's sake. And the Shettleman twins were killed in an avalanche. I was five miles away – you can't blame that on me."

"They were running from you," Cooper reminded him.

"Well, they shouldn't have been."

"That doesn't change the facts."

Day scowled. "Philby was alive all the way to Salt Lake," he muttered.

"Where he died," Cooper added. "Before any court could see him."

"He had the hanta virus! I had nothing to do with that."

"The point is," said Cooper, "that he died. As does every Prog you go after. That's how you got your nickname, isn't it? Look, I'm not here to argue with you. Shell wants you for this group and I've come to see if you'll go after them."

Day was angry but he had no right to be and knew it. It was true that every Prog he had tracked in the year he had been a Settler was dead. It was also true that he made an honest effort to bring them in alive. He had nothing to feel guilty about, if one could feel guilty about the death of people who had caused so much misery. He considered his options as Cooper leaned against the truck and waited. The music from inside the cabin changed. It had been classical; now the cd switched to 60's pop. The Four Seasons.

"What happened to Kurtz?" he asked.

"He was shot. And mauled. We're not sure by what."

"Mauled? Like, by a bear?"

"We don't know. Maybe a wolf."

"In four hundred years of American history wolves have attacked men maybe two dozen times," Day informed his visitor. "You're not telling me something, Mr. Cooper."

"You have no idea."

"How many did you say he went after?"

"Twenty-two. It should be lower now. Kurtz said he killed three."

"Then it is lower. If he said he killed them, they're dead. Kurtz was one of the best."

"Yes, and one of the last things he told us before he died was that we should call you."

"Bull," was Day's response.

"No bull," Cooper countered. "He said 'Get Bad Day.' We asked him why. He just repeated, 'Get Bad Day.'"

Day went back to sorting wires on his table. He picked up a circuit panel and studied it. "And why would Kurtz say that?" he asked. "We never met. I knew of him: we've all been hunting Progs since the people crushed their insurrection. But we never worked together. There's no reason he would know me from Adam."

"You sell yourself short. When you killed Rory Strauss that was huge. #6 in the Prog leadership, the leader of the Prog assassination division, the one who planned and directed the attack on Congress. Except for Jeff Reed himself Strauss was the man everyone in America hated and wanted dead. Taking him down made you famous – at least in Settler circles. Kurtz would have known about that. And, of course, he knew about your kids..."

The circuit panel splintered into a dozen pieces under Day's grip. Cooper shut up, realizing he had overreached. Even the dog looked up. He had never taken his eyes off the visitor and now, detecting a charge in the atmosphere, he rallied. A low growl built in his throat.

For thirty seconds neither man said a word. Day stared at Cooper but he wasn't seeing him. Cooper pursed his lips. He tried to think of a way to continue. Not succeeding and deciding the conversation was over, he moved to get back in the truck. But at the door he paused.

"I know you're angry, Day," he said quietly. "I know how it feels. You're not the only one who lost someone. You're not the only one who's hunted them. I hate them all. I hate them, I've killed a few, and I want them dead. I would go after these guys myself but I'm not that good."

Day didn't respond. He was watching remembered smoke rise into the air.

"You want the whole story, Day? It'll be my ass with Galt but I'll tell you. He isn't holding back for fun. He knows you won't believe it so he wants to tell you in person. But I'll tell you. You'll shoot me but I'll tell you." He came back around the truck. "These Progs weren't in prison. They weren't on the run. They were – they are – in Wyoming. If Galt is right they're not ten miles from their old compound near Jackson. And who is it? It's Blake Reed and his Cadre."

Day woke from his reverie. "You lie," he spat the words. "Reed's dead."

"No, he isn't," Cooper retorted. "We've been telling people that for six months. 'Died in the Teton Inferno, surrounded by the military with no way out. Waco revisited.' Not hardly. It never happened."

Day's hand was bleeding. "You lie," he repeated. "It was all over the news."

"Lots of things are all over the news. That doesn't make them true. And if I'm lying so was Kurtz. He *saw* Reed. He said so. That's why he told us to get you. He knew you would go to hell to get the man."

In his mind Day saw smoke and explosions that rippled from one building to the next. How could he go to hell when he was already there?

"Ten miles...where?" he demanded. "And how is it nobody reported them?"

"They were in Jackson Hole. South of Yellowstone. They never left."

"Impossible. The Mormon Brigades scoured that whole region. That tri-state area was one of the first declared clean. That wasn't the feds talking – the Brigades said so, the Settlers said so, the locals said so. Hell, there was even an Indian tribe up there that killed two hundred Progs on their own. Reed had no base there. They couldn't have been hiding there. There's nothing to hide behind but the mountains, and Reed's not a mountain man."

"The tribes were farther south, on the Colorado border," Cooper corrected him. "And the Progs *did* have a base there. Not big, but they had supporters. There was a lot of West Coast money in Jackson Hole. His band has been there ever since Ganesh drove them into the compound."

"The compound?" Day repeated, his patience wearing thin. "You just said that never happened..." He picked up the shotgun and pointed it at his visitor. "Quit playing Twenty Questions and tell me what you came to say."

"They went into the compound but they never came out. There was no fire. There was an explosion but when the feds stormed it they found only Ganesh."

"So where were the others?"

Cooper wavered again, trying to find words. Day swung the shotgun and pulled the trigger. One barrel shot flame – the blast accompanied the sound of glass shattering as the front passenger window of the truck exploded and the panel below it was peppered with shot. The dog leaped to his feet.

Cooper flinched but stayed put.

"They're...in...Wyoming," he enunciated, holding his voice level. "It's just not Wyoming yet..."

Day swung the barrel back toward his visitor. His patience was gone. "I've got one more barrel, Mr. Cooper," he said. "And I'll use it."

Beads of sweat appeared on Cooper's forehead. "Ganesh Subramaneya was their scientist," he persisted. "Recruited from India by Reed himself and set up in a lab at Cornell. A PhD in quantum physics and another in network engineering, he ran their cyber units, he designed their bombs, he helped them get the nuke they used in Houston. The man is a sick genius. He's got the brain of a Cray computer and the conscience of a Nazi."

"So? They caught him. He was the only one to survive the fire. Or so they said. Are you changing that part of the story, too?"

"No, except that like I said there was no fire. Yes, they caught him. That's how we know what happened. Ganesh had a hobby: teleportation. Moving somebody from here to there in an instant. I know, I know...hold your trigger finger a minute! He got it to work. Or he thought he did. He put things in a box, hit the button, and boom...the things vanished and appeared on the other side of the room. But he only got that far before the Prog revolution kicked off. The country went to hell and the whole Cadre was so busy he never got to test beyond that. He kept tinkering with it and moved his lab out of Ithaca and to the middle of nowhere so nobody would bother him. That was his compound north of Jackson, not Reed's. A place they borrowed from some Silicon Valley backer. And when the movement failed and they had nowhere else to run, Ganesh told Reed he could get him away. Why else would they go there?"

Day listened. He didn't believe a word Cooper was saying but every one of his senses told him that Cooper believed it. And in truth he had always wondered why Reed had fled to Wyoming. The Prog mastermind was a spoiled left-coaster, born and bred to money in San Francisco. His support was on the coasts and in the big cities. Anything between Las Vegas and the Appalachians was flyover country to elitists like him. Retreating to a ranch on the edge of the plains, in the foothills of the Rockies, never had made sense to Day.

"So Reed and twenty of his closest allies jumped into a box and were teleported to Dallas?" Day scoffed. "Is that what you're telling me?"

"No," Cooper replied. "We don't know where they meant to go. The Dallas theory came up later when Shell tried to repeat the experiment. They teleported a beacon using Ganesh's equipment and a signal came in from Dallas. But it was a false alarm. The actual beacon they never found."

"But you're telling me this thing actually worked?" Day pressed. "These Progs teleported somewhere?"

"Yes."

"Where?"

Cooper took another breath and braced for a shotgun blast. "You're asking the wrong question," he told Day. "Where they went is not the problem. It's when."

After Cooper left Day rose from his workbench and stood at the steps, watching the truck get smaller on the valley road. He had almost shot the man just to send a message. Just how dumb and desperate did Shell think he was?

Yes, he was angry. That was an understatement. His anger knew no limits. He was livid, furious, consumed by his loathing of Progs. Anger was what had kept him alive these last two years. It's what had turned him from a college professor who paid scant attention to politics into a remorseless pursuer of men.

When his children died he had fallen apart. It was his wife who got him through it. As devastated as she was, she was strong when he was not and she pulled them through together. But in the year that followed she died, too, another victim of the chaos that rose with the Prog movement as extremists in every American city strove for power through relentless and vicious violence. Two hundred thousand people died in the unrest and she was one. Anger became his escape: cold anger that let him face each day and continue, even if it was only to track down the people who had taken his family, his country, and his life.

"Do you believe any of that crap?" a voice behind him asked.

Day didn't turn. "No."

"Time travel, escaping from the feds by jumping back ten thousand years?"

"Fourteen," Day corrected her. "He said fourteen thousand years."

The woman snorted in derision. "I don't know what's more ridiculous: that he said it, or that he expected you to believe it."

"He didn't expect me to believe it."

The sun drifted below the hills and threw shadows off the sage. Far up the gulch that led off his property a timber wolf appeared and jogged through the scrub. Rare this far south before the insurrection, wolves had spread as towns in the near West emptied. Their loping gate and insouciant gaze from a triangular face were now a common site in the Rockies. Day took it as a sign that civilization was regressing. Going backward in every way. The huge dog saw the wolf, too, but showed no interest in giving chase. He had killed a couple in the past and the wolves had learned not to come into the gulch or approach the cabin. Sure enough, this one turned around before long and disappeared over the hill.

The woman propped a Beretta carbine against the wall and dragged a rocking chair over to the work bench. She produced antiseptic and bandages and cleaned and wrapped Day's hand. He let her do it but paid more attention to moving around pieces of the pump again. At the rate he was going it would take him five years to fix the damned thing.

The woman finished and dragged her chair back to the other side of the porch where she settled down with the rifle across her lap. She was taller than Day and lean. Despite the rural setting she wore cargo pants and combat boots and a leather vest over a black t-shirt. She didn't seem angry at Day necessarily but still moved as though she were two seconds from kicking someone's ass.

"So what are they pushing?" she asked.

"You heard him."

"To go after them? Through time?"

"That's what it sounded like. *O, call back yesterday, bid time return.*"

"Save your poetry. What do they really want?"

"I don't know."

Looking vaguely across the clearing, Day assembled the pieces of the pump except for the circuit board.

"What a scary thought, though," he muttered. "To turn back time. *Tomorrow and tomorrow and tomorrow, creeps in this petty pace...* But everything is moving fast now, not creeping. The Progs chose their great leap forward and we let them drag us along. When we finally got wise and stopped them, we had to run ourselves. Now it's not clear how we slow down again. It's funny, they wanted to shove us all into their future and now – if Shell is right – they've trapped themselves in our past."

"What are you babbling about?"

"Why not *yesterday and yesterday and yesterday,*" he continued. "Those are the days that creep in a petty pace. Yesterdays don't even move. Macbeth should have worried more about his past than his future. If a guy could creep back a few yesterdays maybe he wouldn't have to worry about those damned tomorrows..."

She waited. The sky turned pink and then purple until off at the end of the valley it sank to gun metal blue. Nighthawks swooped overhead.

"They're setting you up for something," she said.

"Why?"

"I don't know. But if Big Mountain said no, that should be a warning."

"A warning of what?"

"That he didn't trust Shell."

"But why not? Shell isn't some cabal. It's a clearinghouse – five guys and a bunch of techies who get leads and pass them on. They haven't screwed anybody that I know of. Hell, a year ago most Settlers were so anxious to kill someone they were begging Shell for assignments. Some still are."

"If guys are begging for assignments, why are they turning this one down?"

"I don't know."

"But you're still thinking about it. Damn it, Day! I don't mind you being stubborn but I do mind you being stupid. I should have shot Cooper myself. I'm telling you, they're setting you up."

Day put a foot up on the railing and rested his chin on his fist. "And if it has anything to do with Reed," he said in a tone that ended the conversation, "I'll go."

Inside the cabin the music stopped. Above the canyon a star appeared. The great dog left his place by the porch and wandered off into the brush, vanishing after a few steps. For a long while Day and the woman sat in silence, listening to the evening come awake and watching a crescent moon rise into the sky.

4

Day pulled off the interstate and drove north. The Oklahoma landscape passed windswept and clean, with hedges tilting in a common direction and the cordgrass along the road looking like it had been combed. There were farms and homesteads but few were occupied. The farther Day drove the more isolated it got.

The land rolled. It was open country with scattered hedgerows and trees. The trees were native, the hedges were not. They stood watch on property lines, holding fast against the wind and catching soil that might otherwise blow off into Kansas. Though even on the abandoned farms that was unlikely. The once-tilled earth had adapted to the absence of crops by spreading clover and bittersweet to lock down the earth. Bluestem prairie grass joined the effort. So did the trees, cottonwood and elm that stood in mature islands and younger clumps that sprang up where a farmer's plow might once have turned over seedlings.

All the foliage was full. It leaned downwind in a casual nod to circumstance. Nature on the Great Plains accepted a hard life and to Day's eye it did not seem to miss the dwindling population.

He found the turnoff and headed west. Ten miles later he slowed. There was a house near the road but he didn't want that one. The feeling was mutual: a woman appeared on the porch with a rifle in her hands. Day tipped his hat but she just watched him pass.

A cairn approached, a dirt road beside it that led onto the prairie. In the distance was a homestead. In the sun's glare it was hard to make out more than a couple of buildings and what looked like a flagpole but Day angled his truck off the pavement and headed that way.

The house improved in appearance the closer he got. It was a rambler in a z-shape, set inside a circle of barbed wire. There was no lawn. The place seemed to grow right out of the soil. Except for the tire tracks the whole setting could have been lowered into place by a helicopter. The flagpole turned out to be an HF radio antennae. There was a U.S. flag but it hung from a pole by the door. A greenhouse joined two other structures out back.

Two windmills turned at the western edge of the property. One had an electrical cable running from it while the other powered a water pump. The pump fed a horse trough that was full. To the pumping rod was attached a crude drawing of a hand with an upraised middle finger. In the light breeze as the fan turned and the rod rose and fell, the finger rode slowly down and then up again, flipping off the world. The roof of the house was blanketed in solar panels.

A gate blocked the driveway. Day opened it and drove through, then hopped out to close it. Out of nowhere a pack of dogs charged, snarling and barking. There were at least eight and they had Day dead to rights.

But suddenly the dogs spun away, yelping and racing toward the house as though they had received an electric shock.

"Thanks," Day muttered toward the back of the truck.

The great beast standing in the pickup bed watched the dogs run, then lay down again. Day drove on up to the door.

No one greeted him. The ranch was quiet. Enough that Day heard the creak of the pump and the tapping of a dream catcher that blew gently against the clapboard siding. Day parked where the tracks stopped and studied the setting, then got out and walked around back.

Behind the house was a chicken coop, the greenhouse, and a small machine shed. The coop sported a blue and silver waterbird painted on one side, the only colors in sight.

Beside the shed was a huge pile of logs: someone had cut down a cottonwood tree. Except for one tall log that stood on end like a totem pole, the whole stack now awaited a chain saw and axe and someone with a couple of weeks to use them. There was also a garden plot, a work table, a blackened fire ring, and a trio of hay bundles set up for an archery range. The only movement came from hens that pecked around the logs and from light ashes in the ring that rose like smoke on the breeze. At least here the soil was well-trod.

"I thought Comanche never left tracks," Day mused aloud.

"I'm in my own damned house," a voice behind him said. "And you're trespassing."

Day turned and looked eye-level at the tip of an arrow held steady in a drawn bow. He was thirty feet from the nearest cover and the ground was strewn with twigs from the cottonwood, yet somehow the man had gotten behind him without making a sound. "But at least you're quiet," he added.

The man held his aim and studied Day's face, then relaxed.

"Bad Day," he growled, lowering the bow. "It's been a while. You're lucky I have a good memory. You ought to know better than to sneak onto a man's property unannounced."

"I drove up in a diesel truck," Day replied.

"What if I was listening to music? I could have just opened fire. You assume I don't listen to music?"

"Yes. I also assume you would want to know who you were killing before you killed him."

"Don't assume. If I wanted visitors I would live in town. Anyone out here is fair game. And where are my damned dogs?"

"They met me," Day reassured him.

"Why didn't they rip you apart?"

"Guess they didn't find me appealing."

The owner studied Day. He was eight inches taller than the Settler and as solid as one of the logs. Faded jeans and a t-shirt with a waterbird logo draped his olive skin; black hair fell to his shoulders. An amulet in the shape of a bear hung from a leather necklace. His eyes were the color of the fire ring and they peered out over high cheekbones that could have been carved from teff. Lean, strong, and hard-featured, he could have been a roadhouse bouncer, or the kind of guy who liked to fight with roadhouse bouncers.

"More likely you're so short they didn't think you worth the effort. I'll deal with them later. You want a drink?"

"Sure."

The man waved him over to the house but they did not go inside. Instead he dragged two lawn chairs to a wide tree stump shorn at knee-level that sat near the bottom of the z. He went away and came back with a pitcher and two glasses.

"Water?" Day asked.

"It's all I have," the man replied.

"If I had known that, I would have brought beer."

"You should have."

They sat for a while without talking. It was warm in the sun and the house blocked the breeze. In the distance the Black Kettle Grasslands stretched to the horizon. The owner of the house stretched out his long legs and peered at the prairie over his toes like a farmer inspecting his crops. His feet were shod in moccasins that Day could not help but notice: not flashy or colorful, they were nevertheless hand-stitched with exquisite care and decorated on the instep with the outline of a bear.

"You make that bow?" Day asked.

"Of course."

"It's nice. Osage?"

"Hickory. Osage is better but it's hard to find and the hickory is local. I'm going back to my roots the older I get."

"What qualifies as local?"

The man shrugged. "Kansas, Oklahoma, northwest Texas. I'm not a purist. My grandmother was Kiowa so I'm not even pure Comanche. Both tribes are only a few hundred years old anyway and they came from the Shoshone up north, so I'm not going to quibble over details. If I found good wood in Missouri I would use it. But I try to stay closer than that. And don't get me wrong...I still like technology: I have a compound bow inside that cost two thousand dollars. Looks like something NASA designed."

"You make the fish trap, too?" Day pointed to a reed box leaning against the stump.

"Yeah. The Washita is a short walk from here. I hunt for everything these days."

"You're a survivalist."

"I'm a survivor," the man replied. "What's on your mind, Day?"

Day sipped his water and watched the hens scratch through the garden plot. A half-dozen chicks clustered around one, running back and forth under her feet.

"I want to run something past you, Roland. It'll sound odd."

"It must be if you drove all the way out here to ask me."

"Well, I wanted to ask a fellow Settler but I couldn't think of anyone who had the kind of background that would help. Our group has its skill sets but higher education usually isn't one of them."

"This is coming from a PhD in English literature?" the man replied. "You're not exactly a hick, Day."

"No, but you know what I mean. Most Settlers are cops or military."

"And cops and military guys are dumb?"

"I didn't say anyone was dumb," Day said calmly. "I said *higher* education. Formal. And I need someone to approach this problem differently than a typical shooter would."

"But someone who also hunts down people and kills them."

"Someone who also has experience tracking and killing Progs, yes. That includes you. You're a little unusual. Your group, the Pahnah, singlehandedly cleared out half of Oklahoma and most of North Texas."

"We had help."

"Not much. Not from the Settlers and none from the feds. And you hunted these guys into pretty vacant land."

"We hunted them wherever they went," Roland affirmed in a hard voice. "They came here treating us as victims, trying to buy us off as wards of the state. They had some song-and-dance about all the tribes getting their land back: the

Kiowa, the Comanche, the Arapahoe. All we had to do was sign up for their demented scheme to overthrow the government."

"But you didn't buy it."

"Some did. The usual lot. Most didn't. And when the majority pushed back, the Progs turned to violence." Roland looked out across the grasslands. "One of the first people they killed was a friend of mine. A teacher in Anadarko. A smart lady who thought for herself. When the Progs talked about fairness she saw they really meant taking away our freedom. When they talked about justice she recognized they meant the rule of emotion in place of the rule of law. She organized anti-Prog rallies where people talked instead about Indian culture and tradition. Native values. Personal responsibility, the importance of family... So they killed her. Shot her during the annual Expo, right in front of her children."

"That was before the bombing of Congress or after?"

"Before," Roland said. "Long before. Almost a year. The Progs were spreading their mayhem in the states and counties before they ever attacked Washington: controlling the media, putting their politicians in office, taking private property. We were fighting them in the courts long before the federal government ever got involved. They might have been successful if they'd been patient. But they weren't. They got overconfident. So once they attacked Congress it was open war as far as the government was concerned. And with those massacres in the schools they stirred up everybody else who had been sleeping until then."

Day said nothing.

"Anyway," Roland continued. "At some point people here had had enough. We had been doing things the legal way and not getting anywhere. The Progs had been trying to get us to rise up so once the gloves were off we did, just not the way they planned."

"And you led the fight. Because of your friend?"

"Because of our people. The Comanche were never meant to be slaves, not to white men and not to a government. We Indians are finally getting on our feet in the modern world and we don't need some utopian fantasy to push us back down. Hell, between that and the epidemics that have been hitting us we're under pressure like we haven't been in a hundred years."

A prairie king snake appeared from under the log pile and moved toward the garden plot. It was tan with black markings and blended well with the dry grass.

"You call yourself an Indian," Day noted, refilling his water. "I thought the politically correct term was Native American."

"For the white man. We call ourselves whatever we please."

"I call you educated."

"So you said. You call me that because I have a doctorate in anthropology. But that's more of a trade sometimes than an education. Culture in my world often means what someone ten thousand years ago ate and how they killed it, not the music they created or the literature they wrote. You want to know how to gather pine nuts or track elk or weave tule reeds, I'm your man. You want to know what prehistoric people talked about or how they entertained guests, your guess is as good as mine."

"I want to know," Day said slowly, "what they would do if a dozen people with semi-automatic weapons suddenly dropped into their world and started killing them."

Roland looked over the rim of his glass. "And you call me unusual."

Day adjusted the brim of his hat and studied the king snake's progress. The chicks had followed their mother up a two-by-four that leaned against the chicken coop so the snake, now exposed, froze.

"Three days ago Shell sent a guy to talk to me. He said they've found Jeff Reed and want me to go after him."

Roland's eyes narrowed. "I thought Reed was dead."

"So did everyone else. The government said so. Shell said so. Shell now says they lied."

"Why?"

"Because the truth was unbelievable. This messenger said Reed and two dozen companions escaped the Teton Massacre by teleporting fourteen thousand years into the past, to the end of the last Ice Age and a period known as the Late Wisconsin Glaciation."

Roland studied Day a long while.

"I do have some beer," he said finally. He walked to the trough, thrust his arm into the cold water, and retrieved a six-pack of home brew. He came back to the stump and popped the tops off two of them. "Don't worry if your vision gets a little fuzzy after drinking this," he said, handing one to Day. "A guy down the road makes it using a sand grass that turns out to be hallucinogenic. Given what you're talking about, though, you shouldn't mind."

Day eyed the bottle with suspicion but drank it nonetheless.

"Whether or not the story is true, the messenger believed it. And he said Shell has already sent one Settler to go after Reed."

"Who?"

"Matt Kurtz."

"And?"

"Kurtz is dead. He got back from wherever they sent him but died from a gunshot wound and some animal attack. They didn't get much out of him other than that he saw Reed."

"They teleported Kurtz?"

"So they said."

"Teleported? Like 'beam me up' teleported?"

"I don't know if it was up, down, or sideways."

"Have you checked this with anyone who's not with Shell?"

"Like who? Who do you ask about time travel? I checked on Kurtz: he's dead. Shell also approached a few Settlers before me and I checked with them, too. They didn't get all the details I did but they confirmed that Cooper – that's the messenger – had been to see them about a mission to go after Reed. Only one agreed to consider it and he backed out after going to Shell and hearing what I just told you."

"Who was that?"

"Dave Dahtes. Down near Tucson. Goes by Big Mountain."

"I've met him. He's not a bad guy for an Apache."

"He's a very bad guy when he wants to be. Apparently this time he didn't want to be, or he was smart enough to smell a rat when they told him this cockamamie story."

"And you're not?"

"Not yet. I haven't talked to Galt but his messenger sure was on board with what they're selling. I held a shotgun in his face and he never deviated from the script."

Roland traced a finger along the stump, following a ring. "You've never struck me as crazy, Day," he mused. "Or dumb. What drives you to believe things you normally would dismiss out of hand?"

"What do you think?"

The king snake moved again. It slithered into the shade of the chicken coop and approached the two-by-four out of sight of the chicks above.

Roland settled back in his chair. "Well, at least you're honest. Fourteen thousand years, huh? Sheesh. How's that for irony? A bunch of latte-sipping elitist sociopaths got zapped into the Stone Age. Think of what they're going through. Think of the sitcom possibilities."

"Shell isn't laughing," Day said. "According to them, there has been contact between Reed's party and whoever was around back then. Natives. And Progs being Progs they've killed a few."

"How do we know that? If any of this has actually happened – and look, I'm playing along just for fun – how does Shell know anything about what Reed's party might be doing? And why would we care?"

"I don't know how they know. Kurtz maybe, or maybe they're seeing something happening now that wasn't a problem until these guys disappeared. Why do we care? I know why I care: because I want Reed dead. Not dead because he got old or sick or because he starved to death, but dead because someone killed him. Preferably me and preferably in a way that gives him time to think about it."

Roland's face went flat again. His eyes looked to the horizon.

"The Late Wisconsin was the final stage of the most recent glaciation in North America," he reflected. "It was the end of the last ice age. The ice sheets were around for about 70,000 years but the period you're talking about was 12,000 B.C. or so. Most of the glaciers by then had retreated into the northern plains and Canada. Summers were shorter but the Great Plains, the Great Lakes, the forests, rivers, and topography of the central United States looked like something we would recognize."

"How much like it?"

"The plains were here but not as open. More trees, more rocks, some canyons. There was tundra. The glaciers were still close and they carved hell out of the land wherever they surged and retreated. You would feel at home except for a few key differences."

"Like what?"

"The weather for one. Summer in the plains was probably no more than ten weeks. Temperatures in the sixties were probably the norm. Lower in the spring and fall, of course. Winters might not have been that bad once the glaciers pulled back. Cold, but not the swings in temperature between seasons that we see now."

"What else?"

"Well, it would have been pretty quiet. Sounds basic but quiet is elusive these days. There were people but not many. It was only during the early Wisconsin that the Bering Land Bridge formed and nomads moved into North America from Asia. We don't know when exactly but there were probably several migrations over 70,000 years. By 12,000 B.C. there were folks here. Not a lot by today's standards but they got around, following the game herds. How many? I have no idea."

"Cavemen?" Day asked.

Roland shook his head. "No caves, white man. You see any caves around here?" he gestured across the horizon. "There were some in the Great Basin, over in Utah, Nevada, the rest of the southwest. Here and up in the Tetons there would have been plains tribes. Hunter-gatherers, nomads, following food from one season to another."

"Following food...deer? buffalo? Were the buffalo around then?"

"Oh, yeah. The buffalo have been in North America for hundreds of thousands of years. My ancestors came late by comparison."

"Okay, so that's something that would look normal. A buffalo herd, I mean."

"Well, that brings me to difference number three," Roland averred. There was a spark in his eye and he studied the prairie as though seeing into its past. "Besides the weather and the people, the animals were different. Including the buffalo. Two words should sum it up for you: mega fauna."

"Meaning what? There were more animals then?"

"Probably, but mega doesn't mean more. It means bigger."

"We're not talking dinosaurs, are we?" Day asked.

Roland rolled his eyes. "You humanities majors should get out more. No, the dinosaurs died out millions of years back. They never mixed with humans. But up until about 10,000 B.C. there were species of animals in North America that aren't around anymore. Most were variations of what we have today: bison, bear, deer, etc. But they were bigger. A grizzly bear today tops the scale at maybe 800 pounds. A grizzly back then would have been over a thousand. There was something called a short-faced bear that would have been even heavier. Bison would have been a third bigger than they are now, too. There were woolly mammoths, mastodons, lions..."

"Lions?"

"Oh, yeah. Big-ass African-type lions. Tigers, too. The saber-toothed type. Both were eight hundred to a thousand pounds. There were no half-measures back then. There were horses, camels, giant beavers, cheetahs..."

"You're pulling my leg," Day said. "Camels? Cheetah? Here? Then where did they go? Did they just disappear in fourteen thousand years?"

Roland was unfazed. "Most of them disappeared faster than that," he continued. "They were gone by ten thousand years ago. We don't know why but it was likely a combination of changes in the climate and human hunting that either wiped them out or caused them to evolve into the sizes we see today. But they were here, there's no doubt about that. I've seen the fossils. I've seen the bones. They were here."

"You sound nostalgic."

"Yup."

"Because you study the past for a living?"

"I like nature," Roland said simply.

"Why? It's just as brutal as humans, maybe more."

"Yeah, but it's simple. Every morning the deer wakes up and knows it has to run faster than the fastest cougar if it wants to survive. And every morning the cougar wakes up and knows it has to run faster than the slowest deer if it wants to survive. Simple."

Day took a swig of beer and stared at the fire ring.

"Would they act the same?" he asked. "The animals, I mean. You say everything was bigger but was that the only difference? Were they more aggressive?"

Roland shrugged. "We don't know. Take bears, for example. Bears find food by following their nose. A grizzly bear today has a sense of smell about a hundred times more sensitive than a coon hound. He can smell a man coming a mile away, more if a guy is wearing cologne or carrying a hamburger. It makes sense that a grizzly bear ten thousand years ago – or a short-faced bear, which is a grizzly's older, meaner brother – would have at least that capability, but does that mean he followed his nose faster or with more blood in his eyes? Maybe, since there was more competition and the competition was bigger, too. But that's just a guess. We don't have data either way."

"Have you ever imagined living then?" Day asked. "14,000 years ago?"

"No," Roland replied, finding the question funny. "My curiosity extends only to a time just before you palefaces showed up."

"Why?"

In response Roland pointed past a collapsed fence at the back of his lot to a speck of blue that rested on the high grass of the prairie. "Look out there. You see that bird? That's a Western Bluebird, *Sialia Mexicana*. It's native to these parts and there used to be thousands. Now they're rare. Starlings have pushed them out. Immigrants from Europe brought over starlings in the 1800s to remind them of the old country. Not a bad song but they've taken over, pushing out the native birds. There are a hundred other species – I'm just talking birds right now – that have gone extinct or been pushed out of their native habitats in the last five hundred years because of interlopers like the starling, or because of cats and cars and windmills and radio towers."

"You can't stop change."

"Really? What have you and I spent the last two years doing? Trying to stop fanatics who wanted to change the world into a darker, bitter place. It depends on the change, is all I'm saying. As for this," he gestured at the grasslands, "the white man changed this continent forever the first day he showed up. I've always been curious what it looked like before that happened."

"Have you spent any time in Wyoming?"

"I've done digs in Yellowstone and hunted near Cody. I have relatives up there. I told you, my roots are Shoshone."

Day thought for a bit. He felt stupid even discussing this.

"How about wolves?" he asked, remembering what Cooper had said.

"What, in the past? Sure, there were wolves. The worst would have been something called the dire wolf. Larger than modern wolves and half again as heavy. Think of it as a hyena on steroids."

"Reed couldn't survive in an environment like that," Day muttered.

"Are you taking this seriously?" Roland asked. "Come on, Day. It's a conspiracy theory."

"Sure it is. And where do conspiracy theories come from? When people don't have the facts they make up their own. Well, I don't have all the facts so I'll grasp any straw there is. Reed disappeared. There was never a body. The guy behind the worst carnage in U.S. history since the Civil War just up and vanishes and we're supposed to believe he and his buddies are dead because the government said so. Now the government – Shell, anyway – says oops, he's not dead, after all. He's stuck in a time capsule or something and killing people in the past."

"And you believe that?"

"Not yet, but they convinced Matt Kurtz and he wasn't exactly a newbie. And Kurtz – so they say – backed up the story just before he died."

"Okay, so let's say Reed is back in the Pleistocene, camping out with his leftist nutcases and eating roots and berries. So what? They'll die out soon enough. How many women went with him? Two, three? That German chick, the other one from Boulder, I don't remember. Is Shell worried Reed's going to start a new colony to compete with the natives? God, how would that even work? It wouldn't – they're going to run out of bullets eventually and the locals will kill them off."

"We didn't kill them off here," Day reminded him. "For years Reed and every one of his followers showed their stripes but the rest of us never stopped them. Why should a Stone Age tribe be any smarter?"

The hen had her brood on a ledge of the coop. She pecked at cracks in the wall boards while the chicks scratched at blown straw. None saw the king snake move up the two-by-four beneath them.

"So you'll volunteer to follow Kurtz?" Roland summarized. "To keep the tribes from making our mistakes?"

"I'll talk to Shell."

"That means you'll volunteer."

"It means I'll talk to them."

The snake crested the ledge.

"No, it means you'll be teleporting or faxing or microwaving wherever they want you to go," Roland repeated, his tone as level as the horizon his gaze surveyed.

"Really?" Day demanded. "How are you so sure?"

The snake was less than a foot from the nearest chick. It poised to strike.

With one movement Roland rose from his chair, lifted his bow, and shot an arrow thirty yards that hit the snake inches behind its head, pinning it to the two-by-four. The *thonk* of the impact sent the hen fluttering off the ledge and into the grass. The chicks came tumbling after her while the snake writhed in pointless spasms until both tail and head hung lifeless.

"Because with you there are no half-measures, either," Roland replied. "Another beer?"

5

Don Galt had the physique of a bank vault and the face of someone who had collided with one. Neither feature recommended mirth. When he looked at Day, it was with stoicism bordering on unconsciousness. Whether that was for Day, the situation, or something else was unclear.

"It's a mess," he growled in a voice like gravel pouring. "We got information from Kurtz before he died. Not a lot but some. It confirmed – or supported, anyway – what we got out of Ganesh. Reed's alive. Reed and almost twenty others. Here's the list." Galt slid a sheet of paper across the table. "They're in the wild. Jackson Hole and the surrounds. Mountainous, tundra in the lower areas, no assistance from outside. Armed...the weapons Kurtz saw are there, too. That info's two weeks old."

Day settled back in the armchair. He glanced at the page but did not touch it. The fluorescent light overhead hummed like it was filled with bees but otherwise this part of the hangar was quiet. The smell of discarded fast food rose from the wastebaskets.

"From what I hear, it's older than that," he commented. "A lot older."

"Yeah."

"That all you're going to say?"

Galt was imperturbable. His glance at Day could have said anything. Day had known him for two years: Galt was smarter than he looked but since he looked like a washed up boxer Day never knew what the man was hiding and what he only feigned to know.

"Yeah."

"Tell me what you know," Day demanded.

"What I know?" Galt's eyebrows rose. For him it was the equivalent of a somersault. "I don't know squat. I know what Kurtz said. I know what Ganesh said. I know what the scientists say. That's what you'll get, too, and you can do whatever you want with it except share. You share, we'll kill you." He said it with no malice, just a statement of fact.

"What scientists?"

Galt nodded toward the window and the expansive ranch house on the far side of the compound. "We've got a team. Physicists, microbiologists, bacteriologists, chemists, anthropologists, geologists... A few on site, the rest scattered around the country. Compartmentalized: they only see what we give them. They've looked at every stitch of Kurtz' clothes, every seed in his shoes, and every speck of dirt under his fingernails."

"And what'd they find?"

"In small words, evidence to back up what you've already heard. You can get the details from them...if you take the assignment."

"Evidence that Reed is in the Stone Age?"

"You got it."

"I don't believe it."

"It's your call."

Day slammed the table with an open hand. "It's not my call! Give me something more credible than this. What is Shell up to?"

Galt was unmoved. In the past he had had an explosive temper. His staff whispered that he had once killed two men with his fists. They warned the clues to an approaching eruption were subtle: crossing of the arms, a slow rocking on his feet, reddening in the face. But either he had mellowed with time or – more likely – he had already experienced Day's frustration himself, for now he leaned on the table and spoke in a calm voice.

"I've been at this two years," he reminded Day. "Two years of the largest manhunt in history, two years of organizing the tracking and killing of the worst vermin civilized society ever produced. We had a list – you know it; you've crossed off your share of names. It's been getting smaller. We've made progress, enough that we thought the end was in sight. I was within months of wrapping up this operation and getting on with life."

"So what stopped you?"

"The Indian die-offs."

Day hesitated. "That pandemic with the Blackfeet?"

"It's not just the Blackfeet. Cree, Chippewa, Cheyenne, Shoshone,...the list goes on. The Blackfeet hit the news because so many died so quick."

"How is that related to Reed?"

"We didn't think it was." Galt folded his hands. "There was no reason to. It took months for Ganesh to come out of his coma and when he did, nobody believed his story. In the meantime, a few thousand Indians dropped dead for no reason. Others, too, but mostly Native Americans. No disease, no injuries, everyone on the same day at the same time. Some mass ritual was the best guess. Maybe suicide – cultural depression or some such crap stereotype, brought about by the anarchy of the Progs. The media bought that and spread it, as well as talk about another coronavirus. But then it happened six more times. The deaths spread across tribes all over the West and Midwest with random individuals elsewhere. Seven thousand and counting. And not a clue why."

"So..."

"So some wizard in-the-know about Reed guessed it was related. Come on, when was the last time anyone dropped dead for no reason at all?"

"It happens," Day argued.

"Seven thousand times? In a half dozen groups, each at the same moment? No. Even I get religion on that one."

"So the theory is that Reed is killing people in the past and it's affecting, what, their descendants?"

"You got it."

"Now you come on. That's Hollywood garbage."

Galt leaned back. "Cue the scientists," he sighed. "Across the compound we've got more theoretical physicists than a Stanford campus. And they will talk to you all day about non-locality and entanglement theory and wormholes..."

"Which mean what?"

"That time travel is possible. In theory, anyway."

"And they know about Reed?"

"Not exactly. They know less, which is almost nothing except it's a national security priority to understand how the past and present interact. At least in terms of physics."

"How does it work?"

Galt snorted. "The time fairy snaps her fingers...how the hell do I know? Something about quantum mechanics and local reality."

Day pointed to the hangar. "And what is that in there?"

"Do you want the simple answer or the technical one?" a voice asked. A bald man with a walrus moustache appeared in the doorway. He wore blue jeans and a Polo shirt.

"Speaking of theories," Galt said, "this is Dr. Saks. He's a researcher but he speaks English. He interfaces with the rest of the brainiacs on our behalf. We learned soon enough that we needed a translator."

"So translate," Day ordered. "Give me the simple answer first."

"It's a switch," Dr. Saks said. "A bottle with a switch. When the charge in the bottle is sufficient, the switch triggers a signal between the particle on the stage and the one sitting in that exact spot 14,037.4628 years ago. I'm rounding that number, by the way. The particles swap places. Depending on the size of the charge, the particles bring along anything and everything within about five meters of them. The stage is there to contain the violent event that accompanies the particle movement."

"And the technical explanation?"

Dr. Saks took a deep breath. "The bottle is a titanium carbide tokamak device containing a superheated plasma on the edge of thermonuclear fusion. Given the right conditions – some of which we can induce, others are on their own schedule – the magnetic field inside loses control of the fusion process. The energy vents into a single sub-atomic particle that is in communication with a distant partner that it interacted with most recently during the later stages of the geologic period known as the Wisconsin Glaciation. Together the two particles initiate an exchange of time and space. The gravitational forces associated with their movement pull in anything close by, and quickly. The momentary vacuum creates an implosion with the equivalent force of a quarter kilo of dynamite."

Sak's tone was apologetic, his face earnest, like a surgeon explaining why a hangnail required amputation.

"Uh-huh," was all Day said.

"Someone told me you have a PhD of your own, Dr. Day," Saks tried in a collegial tone. "I'm sure the technical aspects won't be…"

"It's in English literature."

"Oh."

Day had long ago mastered the inner sigh. He exercised the skill as he turned back to Galt.

"So it's a switch," he said.

"Do you believe us now?"

"Not in the least."

"So what's your question?"

Day scoffed. "Where do I start? Okay, if it's a time machine, why don't you just transport a SWAT team back to the night Reed and his team got here and kill them all before they go anywhere?"

"It doesn't work that way," Dr. Saks said from the door.

"Why not?"

Saks chewed his lower lip. "We don't know. Well, we know but we don't know. We know the time gap between particles is fixed at the interval I mentioned. Fixed, as in not changeable. We can't dial it up or down and we can't just punch in a new date. 14,037.4628 years – the decimals actually extend another thirty digits – is what we have to work with. Why that number? We don't know. That's the relationship between those two particles and it's not flexible. Compare it to two children of exactly the same weight at the ends of a seesaw: they both have to be in the seats for the seesaw to balance. You can't keep one in a seat and bring the other closer. If you do, there's no balance. We've tried varying the charge but when we do, nothing happens. We've tried manipulating the signal but, well, we don't understand the signal in the first place so that got us nowhere. We're stuck with what we have."

"Well," Day persisted, "why don't they come back when you reactivate it? If they got there through this particle swap, why don't they just teleport back when you trigger it again?"

"The particles appear to be fixed not just in time but in place," Saks repeated. "Let me clarify: the *gaps* between them appear to be fixed. In other words, if we send something today, it gets there today in the Pleistocene. If we send something tomorrow, it gets there tomorrow in the Pleistocene. As for location, we believe it works the same way. So long as the transmitter and its partner particle are in the same geolocation it all should work. But according to Ganesh, Reed and his team went on a one-way ride. They took no means of energizing a transmission with them. And of course they moved away from their arrival site, probably within minutes of arriving. They had no motive to stay there. As for us, we haven't tried moving anything on our end yet. We intend to, though."

"Are there other signals? Other particles?

Saks wagged his head. "We're not sure..."

"Is there another machine?

"No," Galt interrupted. "Stick to what we've got."

Day glared at Saks who shrugged. When there were no more questions he nodded and disappeared back into the hangar.

"You cut him off," Day commented.

"Because I have to stick to what we know," Galt insisted. "Ganesh said a lot of crap when he was delirious. He rambled and mumbled and if you pick and choose the words you want you can come up with machines like this all over the place. But we've scoured the country and this is all there is. There's no evidence of anything else so we need to focus here."

"I don't believe this."

"You said that before."

"Yeah, and before it was a simple trip back to the Stone Age. That's my sarcasm talking, by the way. Now you're telling me there might be another machine so instead of battling cavemen I could run up against Arnold Schwarzenegger in a robot costume."

"I'm telling you the exact opposite."

"But how can I believe you?"

"Believe what you want," Galt said. "Look, I've got a sick genius, a professional killer, and a herd of PhD's telling me the guy we're looking for is on the other side of that crystal. Short of going there myself I can't give you any guarantees. I've also got a timeline which is damned short. I don't want another twenty thousand people dropping dead because some Prog in the Ice Age decides to cap another native. Believe it or don't, but until some Houdini raises the curtain on this side-show it's the only shot at Reed you'll get."

"What if I say no? Who's your backup?"

"We don't have one," Galt confessed with hesitation. "Though one might be forced on us."

"What do you mean?"

"The government might get involved."

"Which one?"

Day's question was not an idle one. The federal government was still in turmoil and most states had had some form of martial law in place for over a year. Shell, the Settlers, and other vigilantes had thrived in part because traditional security institutions – the military, the national guard, police – had had their hands full restoring order and weeding out insurgents in their ranks. But their time was ending and Galt knew it.

"The feds, most likely."

"How much do they know?" Day asked.

Galt's eyes bored into him. "Nothing."

"And when they find out, you'll have a Ranger regiment on your doorstep. Or a squad of SEALs and two hundred people in Washington micro-managing the mission. You'll never keep it a secret."

"It would be an unholy mess," Galt admitted. He scowled and looked at his hands. "Day, this thing, this switch, is dangerous on a level we can't imagine. What politicians would do with it – or academics, or religious fanatics – scares the hell out of me. We can't turn it over to them...they'll think us to death. I need someone to go in there, kill Reed and his team, and get out again as fast as possible. Then we're going to destroy this thing and Ganesh is going to disappear. There won't even be a body. He'll never build one of these again or teach anyone how."

"I'm surprised you haven't killed him already."

"Not 'til we close this down. And not until we're sure this is his only toy. When we know for certain, he's gone."

Day looked past the door into the hangar. The stage was in place, the table and its white thermos in the middle as though awaiting a cheap meal. The whole setup was as plain as a workbench.

"I expected more bells and whistles," he commented.

"We have a buzzer."

"What can I take?"

"What you need and no more. Anything that goes into the past has the potential to change it so your profile has to be as low as possible. If I could send you naked I would."

"I left my biodegradable gun at home," Day said lightly.

"Take a cannon if you want," Galt snapped. "We know Reed's team had an assortment of long guns and pistols, plus some explosives. Ammo...we don't know. They may be out by now, or close to it. Or they may have an armory."

Day glanced at the paper on the table.

"19 guys?" he asked.

"We think that's about right."

"You think... How did you come up with that number? Or rather, how did you come up with 22, since Kurtz eliminated three of them?"

Galt nodded to agree the question was a good one but the way he did it conveyed that his answer would not meet the same standard.

"We have a list of Reed's top advisors and supporters. We know who is still unaccounted for. Subtract one from another and that gives us about fifty. But we know a bunch weren't anywhere near Wyoming when the end came. Also, while Ganesh says he didn't count how many people he transported he did say he filled the stage. We went and filled the stage ourselves to see how many people we could put up there..."

"That's not very scientific."

"...and it was about 30."

"*30?!*"

"We made allowances for ammo and supplies."

"Please tell me you're kidding."

"To tailor that even more...there's a mole."

Day sat up. "A mole?"

"A mole. In the Cadre. That's how the feds were tipped off Reed was headed to Jackson Hole."

Day finally picked up the paper from the table. "Who is it?" he asked, studying the names.

Again Galt appeared uncertain. It was not a natural look for him and it hung on his face like an earring on a pit bull.

"We don't know."

Day dropped the paper and fought the urge to put his forehead on the table.

"You don't know," he repeated, the way a teacher might query a student who cannot remember his name.

"We don't know," Galt persisted. "We don't think it's a turncoat. We think it's an undercover agent on an assignment that preceded the uprising, who somehow got wrapped up in it once it began. The FBI insists it's not their guy..."

"Do you believe them?"

"No. Nobody believes the FBI anymore. But they're usually quick to take credit even when they didn't do anything so they might be telling the truth this time. For my money it's someone from either ATF or the Marshals. Before all hell broke loose ATF was heavy in California trying to stop the gun-running over the border. And the Marshals were all over the west coast because of the assaults on federal buildings. But we just don't know. The mole could also be one of the women or maybe Stevens, the former cop."

"Why?'

"Stevens because he was dirty but he tried to turn state's evidence on the rest of his department. He has a motive – restore his reputation. The women because a couple of them were political, corrupt even before Reed came along. They would sell their soul to save their hides."

"That is so weak I don't know what to say."

"I've got no data to offer on this so I'm guessing," Galt admitted, not apologizing.

Day drummed his fingers on the table. "Let's back up to the guns: specifically, to the weapons they took and what I can take to match them."

Galt spread his palms to indicate he had told all he knew.

"They had what they could carry. Every one is a murderer, most several times over. But what exactly they got on that stage with, we don't know. The only one to see them arrive here was Ganesh and his memory is spotty. As for you, I'll say it again: anything that goes into the past – *anything* – will affect the future and we have to assume that what goes there might not come back. Kurtz came back with everything he took, fortunately."

"Except his life."

"Don't try my patience, Day. This is a cost-benefit analysis like no one has ever seen. Neal and I shouldn't even have responsibility for it. We would pass it off to someone if we could trust anyone not to screw it up even worse. Until we do, we're trying to balance things as tight as possible. You go in light and you go alone and since there's no way for us to know if you get in trouble, you'll have a deadline. Nine days plus a few hours. That's one cycle of the switch. If you're not back by then, we'll make a decision."

"A decision?" Day repeated. "I thought you only had Plan B. What's there to decide?" When Galt did not answer, Day scoffed.

"Decision, hell," he said. "You lying son of a bitch. There's a Plan C and it involves leaving me wherever the hell I'm going."

"Leave you? No, but you might be stuck," Galt shot back. "I told you we don't control everything. You heard Saks: some things about that switch are on their own schedule. As best we can tell, the two particles communicate in phases. Picture two flashlight beams moving over the same wall where sometimes they overlap. Well, they're still overlapping but it's happening less and less. Saks estimates that after the next cycle they won't overlap enough for the charge we can generate to cause a swap. That's why you've got to make the jump, do what you can, and get back out the first chance you get before the phases move beyond what we control. That thing scares me, Day," he hurried to add. "The Indian deaths caused a lot of questions. If word of this switch leaks and it looks like we can't keep this under wraps..."

"...I'll be on my own," Day finished. He had gray eyes that his wife used to say reflected a squall. Now that squall bore down on Galt. "I'll kill every native I find if you leave me in the lurch," he promised.

"No, you won't."

"I will. And I'll find whatever ancestors were cursed with you and kill them, too."

"They would be in Ireland so you would have to swim." Galt stood up. "The switch cycles every ten days. Plus or minus some hours. To work it needs a charge and it needs to be in phase. That happens next at dawn the day after tomorrow. You have until then to decide."

Day remained in his seat. He mumbled something that Galt did not catch.

"What's that?"

The time is out of joint," Day repeated with precision. *"O cursed spite, that ever I was born to set it right!"*

"Uh huh." Galt was unimpressed. "I heard you like poetry. I don't, so what did you say?"

"I've decided," Day said. He felt numb inside. But then he had felt numb for two years.

Galt looked down at him, thinking of a moment like this just two months before when Matt Kurtz had agreed to go after the Progs. He hated sending men into danger. He hated it with a passion.

"I figured," he grunted. "In that case be here early. We're going to move everything a hundred yards in case they've set a trap."

"You can do that?"

"We're not sure. Saks says yes but then he's not going so you'll be the first to find out." Galt went to the door. "Remember, Day," he said. "Light and alone. If you need anything, we've got it here. But don't need anything. Let's keep this simple."

6

"That's not simple," Galt barked two days later. "And what the hell is that?"

He stood in a pre-fab shed thrown up a hundred yards north of the hangar, adjacent to an enormous granite monolith that looked like it had been there since dinosaurs walked the earth. The shed was almost an exact duplicate of the hangar but it was new. It had not been there during Day's first visit and the speed with which it had been built showed in the empty pallets and spare sheets of corrugated tin that lay in the dirt outside its two-story walls. It stood in a rough clearing hacked from the terrain on the edge of the same wash that ran by the hangar. Sawdust was everywhere, outside and in, and great ruts and tire tracks led between the new building and the old, reflecting all the equipment that had been moved from one to the other. A helicopter sat outside. Inside, the same stage was in the middle of the dirt floor with the same Plexiglas panels surrounding it and stretching up to a hole in the roof.

Galt kept his distance as Day stepped through the door. Day carried a Weatherby bolt action rifle and a Colt revolver but it was not the guns that kept Galt at bay. The great beast that might have been a dog did that. It swung along at Day's heels, saliva dripping from the exposed fang while its mismatched eyes noted everyone in the room.

"Not sure," Day replied.

"What part of *alone* did you not understand?" Galt demanded. He crossed his arms and blocked the way. "Not a chance. No animals, that's our rule. Especially not some mutant wolf. There's no control, nothing to stop it from messing with the gene pool. Absolutely not."

"You think something's going to mate with that?" Day scoffed. He went around Galt and threw a canvas duffle onto a table. "Not likely. That's why he's so mean."

The animal prowled the control room and inspected everything before slinking over to the wall to lie down. The techs who dared to move slid back into their seats.

"Goddammit, Day," Galt growled. "The plan..."

"*Your* plan," Day interrupted, "was to get someone stupid enough to go after Reed. My plan is to kill that son of a bitch and come back alive. How I do that is up to me. If you don't like it, get someone else."

Galt's face reddened. On his forehead first one vein, then another, enlarged and receded like bubbling lava. He crossed his arms and began to rock on the balls of his feet.

Neal Davis came through the door. His Allis Chalmers jacket was still in place and if it looked like he had slept in it at least he had slept. He came into the hangar with energy.

"Is he here?" he announced himself. "Security told me he was on his way – where is the crazy...Day! Alright, now we're getting somewhere."

Day shook Neal's hand. He had met Shell's director once the year before but the man had shed weight since then. Stress had made him leaner but he was still tough as rawhide – his grip had lost none of its power.

"You don't have to go," was the next thing Neal said, his eyes boring into Day's. "I mean it. We want you to, we need you to, but this mission is like no other. None of us have been on the other side of that switch and we can't help you once you go. You'll be on your own."

"You're damned right he will," Galt chimed in and jerked his chin toward the wall.

Neal noticed the beast and stopped pumping Day's hand. "What the hell is that?"

"Oh, for Christ's sake," Day muttered. He picked up the duffel.

"Whoa, hang on now," Neal urged.

"Neal, no animals. *None*. We've talked about this," Galt insisted.

Neal grabbed Day and sat him down, then he thought hard for all of five seconds. He pointed to Galt. "Outside."

"Neal..."

"Outside."

Day sat down and crossed his legs and waited while the two men went out into the pre-dawn air to argue. He could hear the rumble of their voices but paid no attention. What they decided meant little to him – he had a clear path either way. The beast on the floor watched him with the same half loyal, half hostile look he always wore. "You're nothing but trouble," Day muttered. The animal yawned in response.

After a while Neal returned alone. He threw a curt nod to the tech team. "We're on track," he said. Then he sat by Day.

"Don't worry about Don. Someone's got to enforce the rules or the whole program falls apart. He's a good man." He looked at the beast. "You really need that thing to go?'

"I don't know what I need," Day replied. "I've had four days to learn what I can about the Ice Age and I still don't know if anything you guys have told me is true. I don't know where I'm going, what I'll need when I get there, or who – or what – will meet me. So I'm taking a big gun, big bullets, and a big dog. Besides, if I leave him here now he'll eat you."

Neal sighed. "Alright. Just bring him back. Or kill him if you can't."

The beast shifted and studied the director. He did it long enough that Neal grew uncomfortable and moved to Day's other side.

"Another thing about Don," he continued, "and don't tell him I said this...he's scared. We all are. What happened to Reed was a joke at first. None of us believed Ganesh – we figured this machine here vaporized the whole Prog top tier. But then we ran tests. And then the die-offs started. All Indians or people with native heritage. Nothing we did..."

"What tests?" Day interrupted.

Neal gestured to the stage. "We had engineers go all over this thing and none of them could figure it out. I mean, they understood the parts but nobody had a clue how it all worked together. And the software...don't get me started. The programming Ganesh came up with makes the F-35 fighter jet look like a toaster. So in the end we just put a GPS transmitter on the stage and powered up the switch. Damned if the transmitter didn't disappear. Not disintegrate, not burn up. Disappear. And we've never found it. The satellite network looked for it for weeks – nothing. So we tried again. We were pressed for time – we still are – so this time we took a risk. We sent a tope."

"A what?"

"A small block of radioactive material. In this case a synthetic form of nickel that doesn't exist in nature. Nothing major, but one with isotope decay that can still be measured after twenty thousand years. See, we figured if this machine really was launching things through time instead of over distance, then if we sent something radioactive we might still be able to track it."

"And?"

Neal ran his fingers through his hair. "We found it," he said, still in awe. "It took us two weeks but we found it. A quarter mile from here."

Day looked up sharply. "What? So this machine is junk?"

Neal shook his head.

"Just the opposite. We found the tope a quarter mile from here, yes. But it wasn't sitting on the ground. It was in an old streambed, a dozen feet below the surface and below a layer of volcanic dust that our scientists dated from an eruption in New Mexico ten thousand years ago."

"Are you saying..."

"In the same area and at the same level were fossilized bones of animals that went extinct earlier than that. Apparently there was a spring there for eons that fed a watering hole. And – don't give me that look, Day – here was the clincher: the tope we used had decayed. Once they dug it up our guys were able to measure how much...within a few hundred years anyway. It's just over fourteen thousand years ago."

Day was good at spotting liars and he decided Neal was not one. Like Cooper, the man believed what he was saying.

"I don't believe it but go on. Anything else?"

Neal nodded. "Once we found the nickel we searched everywhere within a mile of the hangar. We had people crawling on their hands and knees with the most sensitive equipment there is. At first we didn't find much – a belt buckle, some shell casings – but then where the watering hole had been we found two AK-47s and an M4! Rusted, worn, but intact overall. Rifles! And here's the kicker: everything was at least ten feet down, at depths that matched the nickel."

Day was quiet for a while. "I can't grasp it," he admitted. "It's too out there for me."

"Tell me about it. You're a professor, at least. I'm just a retired Marine. Think how my head hurts trying to figure it out. Why do you think we're scared? We need this closed, Day. Closed before it gets messed up any more."

Day stretched. Through the door he saw Jupiter on the horizon. It would be light soon.

"How is it no one has figured out what you're doing here?" he asked. "It's remote but you must have traffic coming in and out. If you had people crawling around the plains surely some cowboy noticed."

Neal shook his head.

"No cowboys here since the revolt. The ranch owners were moved long ago and who knows where the cattle went. Besides, we limit traffic and 90% of the people we drag out here never set foot inside this hangar. They only know what we tell them. And you didn't see it but we've got a perimeter around this location that rivals the NSA. The highway's cut in both directions and it's under surveillance. Ten miles out there's a fence. Five miles out there are live patrols, fixed squads camouflaged in the terrain, drones, electronic sensors. The patrols are 24/7 and cleared to shoot on sight. If some cowboy wandered this way his days punching cows would be over. We would either lock him up indefinitely or kill him. That's the way it is. The control center is in the house next door. With you this morning, for example, we knew you were coming while you were still on the highway. Hell, a jackrabbit doesn't move in this county without us knowing."

"Good to know," said a voice. "I'll consider myself welcome."

Roland Set-ete stood inside the door holding a compound bow and a quiver of arrows. A large knife and a hatchet were on his belt. Like Day he wore pale camouflage under a heavy jacket. Unlike Day his feet were in moccasins instead of boots.

The two guards spun in surprise and grabbed their weapons.

Neal jumped up. "Who the hell are you?"

Roland shrugged. "Call me Tonto," he replied. "In Spanish that means stupid, which I must be if I'm following this guy around." He gestured toward Day who, as surprised as anyone, leaned back in his chair and clasped his hands over his stomach, thinking.

Galt stepped through the door. He had gone for a walk to calm down and had mostly succeeded. The veins in his forehead were smooth and his color was back to normal. Now he stopped short and surveyed the scene. A tall Indian covered by two rifles, Neal on his feet ready to choke someone, and that damned dog-thing still on the floor. Without a word he went back outside.

"His name's Roland," Day explained, closing his eyes in an attempt to relax. "He ran the Pahnah north of Wichita Falls."

"How did you get here?" Neal barked.

"Walked."

"There's no way."

"Not from Oklahoma. You'll find my truck in Moran but I've had a good hike since there."

"Impossible!"

"Because of your security?" Roland replied, his own tone so neutral it was not clear he was asking a question. "It's high-tech, I grant you...and just as effective as these guys."

Galt returned accompanied by a third guard who carried handcuffs and a tranquilizer dart.

"Get him out of here," Neal growled.

"You might rethink that," Roland suggested. "Unless you can hire new guards."

"And fend off the dog," Day added quietly. He opened one eye and looked at Neal. "The Indian's his best friend," he whispered.

Neal's jaw tightened. "Don't push me, Day."

"Not pushing. But the clock is ticking. It's almost dawn. You don't have time for a fight."

"I'm a Marine. I always have time for a fight."

"Not this one. And not one that'll leave Reed alive."

The guard raised his dart. Roland's hand moved to his knife.

"Wait."

The voice was Galt's. Squeezing behind the servers to avoid the line of fire, he circled the room.

"How many more, Day?" he asked.

"More?"

"Yeah, you've surprised us with a dog and now an Indian – what next? You got a robotic horse you want to bring along or maybe a troop of Ninja girl scouts?"

"Galt," Neal interrupted. "This guy can't go."

Galt threw up his hands.

"Oh-ho! Really? Why not? You said it was okay to take the damned dog so why not an Indian? What the hell's the difference?"

"It's a good thing we're all friends here," Roland observed.

"You keep quiet! I don't know how you got here but..."

"Sir," one of the techs spoke up. The man had a doctorate in particle physics so 'tech' was an unfair description but his role at the moment was well below the post-graduate level. He pointed to the stage where the tube at the top of the tokamak device began to glow a light blue color.

"Crap," Neal muttered. He stalked to the bank of computers and studied the images on three screens. "It's early. And it's shifting again. Call Saks. Get his ass over here."

The tech hit a button on his console.

"How much time?" Neal demanded of the scientist.

"8, maybe 10 minutes."

Shell's director put his head in his hands. As a Marine he never expected things to go according to plan but it did get tiring when they *always* went awry. Galt did not like being pushed into a corner, either. He strode across the floor and got right in Roland's face, shoving his boxer's mug two inches from the Indian's nose. The two men were still locked in a stare-down contest when Dr. Saks hurried in. With a quick glance at the confrontation, the physicist rushed to the console and pulled up page after page of data.

"It's almost an hour early," he confirmed. "The shifts are getting larger. But if we want to use this we'll have to charge in six minutes."

Neal dropped his hands and looked at Galt, who was fixed on Roland like a Rottweiler trying to decide if a Doberman was worth eating. Day was not sure how Galt did it: as fierce as he was, Roland's eyes were depthless and his face held the menace of a prairie storm. Trying to stare him down was like trying to stare down Kansas.

"Fine," the bank vault said, dropping his gaze but only due to the press of time. "You want to send a party, send a party. I don't see how they can screw this up any worse than it already is."

"On that note of confidence, let's get moving, shall we?" Day proposed. He threw his duffel onto the stage and climbed up after it. "What do we do: stand, sit, hold hands? You have space suits for us?"

Neal went to a locker at the back of the room as Roland joined Day. The two hunters had not yet spoken a word to each other but the Indian now stood next to Day as nonchalantly as if he had been invited.

"Why are you here?" Day asked.

"Because if I drop dead, I want to see who killed me."

"You said your curiosity about the past extended only to just before palefaces showed up."

Roland shrugged. "It's more of a guideline than a rule."

"You sure you're bringing enough firepower?"

Roland crossed his arms and stared at the far end of the shed. "With this bow I can drop an adult moose at a hundred yards. And I can make more arrows. Can you make more bullets?"

"I'm hoping I won't have to."

Neal returned with two bundles. He tossed one to each of them.

"According to Kurtz, the arrival is pretty violent," he said with no apparent empathy. "Don't expect to keep your feet. We would give you more but everything has to break down."

"Leather helmets?" Day asked, looking at the headgear. "Where did you get these, from the 1947 Chicago Bears?"

"Wear 'em or don't," Neal barked. "But it would suck to travel 10,000 years and end up with a concussion."

Day and Roland sat back-to-back on the stage and reluctantly pulled on the gawky but well-padded covers.

"I look like Snoopy and you look like Michael Dukakis," Roland growled. "We'd better find someone to kill 'cause I'm gettin' in the mood."

"Two minutes," Saks called.

The men gripped their weapons. Day wrapped his sheepskin coat around him and slid the duffel close by his side.

"Aren't you forgetting something?" Galt sneered. He gestured to the great beast still sprawled on the floor. The animal watched Day's every move but so far had shown no inclination to join him.

Day nodded to the dog. "You won't want to miss this."

The beast yawned and got to its feet. With no haste it mounted the steps and prowled the stage, finally settling into a half-squat behind the thermos where he could keep an eye on everyone.

Roland muttered, "That explains my dogs."

Day wanted to crack something about getting the party started but did not. He realized everyone was nervous, including him.

Neal handed him a white thermos identical to the one on the table.

"Hide that container wherever you land. You'll need it to leave and you'll have to do it from the same spot. The particles are in phase every nine days, plus or minus a few hours."

"How long do they stay in phase?" Day asked.

"40 minutes tops but don't push it. When the light turns blue, hit the button as soon as you can. You should come back."

"Should?" Day repeated.

Neal shrugged.

"Thirty seconds!" Saks said from his position at the back of the room.

Day shifted in place and brought his knees in tight, making sure his feet were flat on the floor. Not knowing what to do was excruciating.

"And if the light never turns blue?" he asked. "Or if it goes out again before we can hit the button?"

Galt closed the door to the stage and stepped back.

"Then make yourself comfortable," he advised. "Because we'll see you in fourteen thousand years."

The canister on the table flared. There was an ear-splitting explosion and everything went black.

7

For the briefest of moments, like a dream right before waking, Day felt himself tumble. He had a sense of rolling through space with nothing to grab onto or hold.

Then suddenly he *was* rolling but this time he was on the ground. As though ejected from a speeding car he bounced and tumbled through waist-high juniper, tearing at branches and gouging hairgrass with the butt of his rifle. When he stopped it was with a jolt as his head smacked down on a tree stump overturned in the soil. The leather helmet cushioned the blow and his first thought was to be grateful after all for the stupid headgear.

He lay still to get his bearings. It was cold, it was dark. There were stars and a sharp breeze skimmed the earth. His ears rang so at first he could not hear anything. He did not know if it was from the bump on his head or something else, but the feeling unnerved him. When he sensed movement to his left he rolled over and low-crawled twenty yards, scurrying between the shrubs like a lizard evading the sun. A depression in the land opened and he slipped into it, rifle ready.

There he remained for half an hour, not moving, waiting for the ringing to go away and for whatever had moved to show itself. But whatever he had sensed stayed away.

He had no idea where his duffle bag was, let alone Roland or the dog.

The stars were the same, he noticed. Except for a storm in the distance it was remarkably clear and the sky was full of them, far more than were visible even at his mountain cabin. The Milky Way hung overhead like a cloud. Without moving he saw Arcturus between the stems of a pigweed, still pinned above the horizon as dawn arrived. It had been above and to the left of Jupiter when he arrived at the compound so only an hour or so had passed since then. The air smelled similar, too, though sweeter and wetter. Day wondered if the machine had malfunctioned, maybe exploded, and if he was not just ten feet outside the shed. Or if this was all a joke after all.

The sky lightened. He looked around and saw no shed. No hangar or cars, either. The granite boulder was there but nothing else that looked familiar. Dark trees limned the sky to the south. More stood in the north and northeast, while behind him a skeletal cottonwood tree leaned into a breeze. To the west the land was open, rolling toward distant mountains. As the glow in the east increased, Day saw snow in the northern hills and steam rise near what looked like the entrance to a pass. Probably a stream or small lake, maybe a hot spring...

A hand touched his shoulder. He spun, bringing the rifle around, but Roland grabbed the barrel.

"Easy, white man," his companion said softly, and touched a finger to his lips. "I don't think anyone else is around but I've only searched out fifty yards."

Day fought to get his heart rate under control.

"You scared the hell out of me," he whispered.

"Be grateful," the Indian replied. "I could have cut your throat."

"Did you see my bag?"

"Over there about thirty feet."

"How about the dog?"

"Sitting on the bag."

The two men crouched low as light spread across the rim of the prairie. Roland propped himself on his elbows behind the pigweed and scanned east while Day watched the other way.

"How did you find me?" the Settler asked, his ego bruised.

Roland shrugged. "You're the only thing out here that doesn't smell like Wyoming. Well, you and your dog."

"I would have heard you coming but my ears were ringing. There must have been an explosion."

"There was."

They lay motionless, watching and listening.

"What makes you think we're still in Wyoming?" Day whispered.

"We're definitely in Wyoming. Same place we left."

"Then where did those trees come from? And the snow?"

"Don't know, but this is Shoshone land. I feel it. And that is not just snow. It looks like a glacier."

"A glacier? Then we're definitely not in Wyoming."

"Yes, we are," Roland repeated. "We're in the same place, next to the wash where they put up that shed."

"The wash? How do you know that?"

"Because I went sailing over the side of it when we landed. Just missed that damned big rock. Those Snoopy helmets work – I'll have to thank that guy."

Day fingered his scalp and nodded.

"Anything else?"

"Yeah, a body. Bones, anyway. Bits of clothes. I'll look more when it's light."

The stars winked off one after another. Arcturus dropped below the horizon. Black turned to gray, then gray to dawn. The dog rose and trotted off. Day watched it go. He knew the hound could smell trouble a mile away so he waited to see if the shaggy mane veered left or right or suddenly went to ground. It did neither. The animal explored, moving this way and that, and finally made its way to a watering hole west of the forest near a pile of boulders.

"We're good," he muttered and got to his feet. Roland, less confident, moved off several yards before rising.

Day retrieved his duffel bag. He also picked up the white thermos.

"Your tracks start here," Roland pointed. "Mine here, and the dog's there. That means we dropped in...here." With his toe he drew an X in the soil. There was nothing remarkable about the spot but two feet away was a flat stone the shape of an anvil. Day paced the distance to the granite boulder and then dropped to his knees and dug a hole for the thermos.

"For god's sake, don't go anywhere," he muttered as he filled it in. "If we're not in Wyoming, we're going to need you."

The streambed was sandy and damp. There were animal tracks everywhere but most were muddled from rain. Roland led Day to the remains of a skeleton. It was human but every bone was broken. Crushed. Pieces were spread across the wash while remains of a shirt hung in tufts of needlegrass at the base of the wall.

"Coyotes don't do this," Day observed. "Or wolves. Hogs?"

"Maybe," Roland mused. "Or hyenas."

"There were no hyenas the last time I was in Yellowstone."

"No."

They searched the wash but found little else. The ground was soft and gave way under their feet. They followed its course to the northeast until the bed narrowed and the walls lowered. In places they could see over the walls in both directions: to the west the land was open, the dominant features being the moraine and a stream that came down from the glacier; to the southeast were the watering hole and forest.

After a bit the Settlers left the wash and turned back, going above the wall and stepping through waist-high piñon and juniper. They examined the great boulder but there was nothing remarkable about it other than its size. No marks or scratched messages or arrows pointing one way or another. The cottonwood was old and dropping limbs so Day carried one back to their arrival location and leaned it against a nearby bush, making it easier to mark the spot.

"Where are we?" he asked as they turned to explore the watering hole. The huge dog was already there, prowling the muddy ground.

"Same place, different time," Roland reminded him.

"I don't believe that. I don't know where we are but don't believe that. Do you?"

"Yes." Roland pointed south to a snow-capped peak. "That's Mount Leidy. It hasn't moved. And if we could see around that ridge I have a feeling the Teton Range is still there, too." He knelt and examined a thistle peeking from the dirt. "But you're right, it's not the same. There are plants I don't recognize. There are smells I don't know. And the air...it's clear like I've never seen it."

The dog trotted up to the forest and disappeared, then reappeared a hundred yards down the tree line. That reassured Day: his biggest fear was that they would walk into an ambush, that if they had actually moved somewhere in time or space then Reed and his party would be waiting near the arrival site to shoot anyone who showed up. But so far that was not the case. As far as they could tell there was no one around. He raised his rifle and looked through the scope in all directions. It was a quiet morning.

Still, the dog acted strangely. Day saw him stop and look one way or another, and turn often to sniff the ground. He was trying to get his bearings, too.

Halfway to the watering hole a *crack* from the woods made them drop and take cover. Roland nocked an arrow while Day readied his rifle.

Two mule deer, mother and fawn, moved from a thicket at the edge of the trees. When the men stood the doe saw them and froze. But soon she moved on, browsing as they went.

"That looks normal to me," Day whispered. "Not exactly a saber-toothed tiger."

Roland was unsure. "She's big for a mulie," he observed. "Awful big. And why didn't she run?"

At the watering hole there were tracks aplenty. Despite the rain many were distinguishable. Roland perked up.

"Cattle," Day concluded.

"Nope."

"What do you mean, nope? This is cattle country. A herd must be nearby."

"It's a herd but not cattle. Too round, too big. These are bison, though they're big even for that." Roland scanned the horizon.

"Nobody farms bison out here. It's cattle."

"Uh-uh."

"Why not?"

"Because unless someone is breeding some kind of mutant Angus that's all these tracks can be."

"You're too anxious to see us in the Stone Age. Your curiosity is overcoming your judgment."

"Maybe, but I've spent a lifetime learning to feel the world around me and this morning the world feels strange. So let's stick with bison, otherwise I'll need a drink."

At the rocks they made another discovery when Day found the carcass of a wolf. It was not dismembered like the skeleton in the wash but it had been picked almost clean. The bones and remaining flesh gave an idea of the animal's size. The fur was black with tinges of red. The dog wandered over to sniff at the remains.

"That is definitely not your normal wolf," Roland pointed out.

"Timber wolves get that tall," Day shrugged.

"No, they don't. And they don't have a rib cage that broad or jaws that massive." He dug around the body. "Can't see what killed him but it wasn't old age. Man, this was a brute. Look at that skull. It's as big as your dog."

"So there. Maybe it's not a wolf at all," Day argued. "If I've got a hybrid mess, why shouldn't someone else? This could be a Russian wolfhound or a mastiff..."

"Pumped with steroids? That wandered off the prairie, miles from any road, following a random buffalo herd and a couple of tame deer?"

"Sure."

Roland wandered back down to the water and splashed some on his face. "You're in denial," he said over his shoulder.

"And you're too in touch with your inner shaman."

Roland was going to to reply when another sound came from the tree line. The men turned and aimed their weapons – and then froze, astonished.

Trotting from the forest came a baby elephant. At least it appeared to be an elephant and if not actually an infant it was young. Covered in fur overlaid with long hairs, the animal was the size of a minivan and the color of slate. It had a broad forehead, tiny tusks, and a hairy trunk. Long whiskers hung over its cheeks. Its ears were relatively small but still floppy and broad. Without a care in the world and paying no attention to the men, the creature jogged down the slope straight for the watering hole. Sliding in the mud, it worked its way to the water's edge and proceeded to drink.

Day's stomach sank. Roland set his bow in the weeds and crouched yards from the pachyderm, watching in awe and delight.

The huge dog was exploring the rocks. Now he detected the new smell and came out to see its owner for himself. He kept his distance at first but when the newcomer did nothing but scoop water into its face the dog crept closer, stepping boldly across the mud flats. Day did not stop him. He was still in shock, trying to come up with a remotely plausible reason why a months-old mammoth should be wandering near Jackson Hole. It was only when he asked himself the question a third time that he saw their danger.

"Hey! Get away!" he hissed.

The dog looked at him.

"What's the problem?" Roland asked. "He can't hurt this thing."

"It's a baby...get away, you stupid mutt..."

He waved at the dog but that only spooked the mammoth, who turned and saw the great hound for itself. In surprise it let out a plaintive cry and spun around, slipping in the mud and falling to its knees. As the dog jumped away the baby rose, but at the same time an answering bellow came from the forest followed by great crashing and a trembling in the earth.

"That's mama!" Day warned. He spun on his heels and dashed for the rocks as an adult mammoth burst from the forest and tore down the slope at them. The dog followed him, taking cover in the boulders. Roland, on the wrong side of the water, sprang away in the opposite direction and ran like the wind. The mammoth gave chase in full fury, the ground shaking beneath each booming step. There was nothing for Roland to hide behind so he sprinted for the wash.

Had it been a hundred yards farther the mammoth would have caught him and trampled him into the soil. As it was, Roland threw himself off the wall only a dozen feet in front of the pursuing beast's waving tusks. He landed in the sand, rolled, and in three more steps was going up the opposite bank. The mammoth pulled up short on the near side, bellowing and stomping, eyes wide behind a matted waterfall of hair that cascaded down its face.

Day squeezed inside the rock pile as far as he could. In the process he found another wolf carcass and a handful of .308 rounds. Together they filled in a gap regarding Kurtz's fate but it did not comfort Day at all to know he was trapped in the same refuge as his predecessor.

The mammoth returned, head high and alternating ear-splitting bellows with tender huffing directed at its offspring. It cast a shadow over the boulders along with the sour stench of sweat and grass. Day felt the great dog squeeze behind him, flat on its belly. "Get out there, you coward," Day growled. "You started this." But the dog stayed put.

The mammoth gave a cursory check to the baby and then charged the rocks. Day pulled back, making sure he had cover overhead. The boulders were huge and there was not much even the mammoth could do to dislodge them, but Day found it astonishing and terrifying that the animal knew he was there and was determined to get at him. He watched as the mammoth tested the boulders with its trunk, pushed on a few with its feet, and occasionally scraped its tusks across their surface as though trying to cut through. Day saw the tusks wave over gaps in the rocks. They were ten feet long and curved inward, like alabaster tongs for a giant ice block. He shuddered to think how close he had come to being skewered.

For a quarter hour he endured the assault. The huffing, stomping, and bellowing seemed like it would never end. Finally, frustrated at every turn, the massive beast turned away. It corralled the youngster and led it back up the slope and into the forest.

With great caution Day emerged into the sunshine. Roland returned, working his way down the wash and back to the pool.

"Told you," was all he said.

His mood darkened when he found his bow. He had run with the quiver on his back but the bow lay broken and bent beyond recognition in the weeds where he had dropped it.

"Clearly she wasn't impressed by NASA's work," Day commented, but he was not laughing. They were in the Stone Age and had just lost half their firepower.

Roland picked up the pieces. "It was a he," he glowered. "And you worry about finding Reed. I'll get a weapon."

For two hours the men searched. Before he died, Kurtz had provided little information beyond the number of Progs he had killed and how far he had had to go to find them. Day lacked even a direction to favor so he and Roland split up and scoured the land looking for clues. That is, they looked but only after Day first knelt down and came to grips with what he had just seen.

His life had turned upside down in the last two years: he had gone from being a family man to a near recluse, from being a teacher to a hunter of men. Earnest optimism had burned as on a pyre, leaving a murderous vengeance in its ashes. But even that explosion of his world paled in comparison to the sharp turn from reality this morning had brought. He needed time to collect himself; neither Roland nor the hound disturbed him as he knelt in the dirt and did just that.

Roland went into the forest to reconnoiter there. The great hound wandered and then settled by the rocks, perhaps figuring that was safest if the mammoths returned. They did not. No more sounds came from the forest beyond the chatter and singing of birds.

The birdsong caught Day's attention. Not as sensitive to his surrounds as his Indian companion, he nevertheless recognized when things were unusual and there was an unusual number of birds this morning. A larger variety, that is, than the typical Western landscape supported. Small birds, in particular. Song birds. Birds he had never seen before. Granted, there was water and forest nearby along with plenty of scrub, but the sheer volume of tiny shapes flitting through the air surprised him, as did their colors and calls. Where were they coming from? And why had he never noticed them before today?

He looked past the birds onto the plain. If there was a mammoth and strange birds, what else was out there? The morning was crisp and the air so clear it dazzled but for a while he detected no wildlife at all. He began to doubt again, to wonder if somehow this was all a con. Maybe Shell had set this up – maybe they had only one fake elephant and a baby to make him think this teleport thing worked. But why?? What the hell was their motivation?

When he did see something his confusion only increased. Around mid-morning he detected motion far to the northwest, two miles away along the hills between the glacier and the pass. Through his scope he saw it was a bear but it was unlike any bear he knew. It was darker than a grizzly and half again larger. And the shape was wrong, with a massive body and a smallish head. It also walked with a see-saw gait, an awkward pace that Day could only guess was to compensate for its great size. Even through the scope it was hard to make out more detail. The bear slipped in and out of sight, eventually disappearing for good in the uneven terrain. Another fake? he wondered.

While he tried to re-acquire the bear Day saw movement in the trees directly to the north. That forest was spruce for the most part – which was strange enough this far south. It crowded down onto what looked like a marsh where aster and Indian grass waved so tall it almost hid the animal that emerged. At first he thought it was an elk: it had the same thick shoulders, proud head, and rough neck fur. But this creature was too big, way too big, and its antlers were flat. A moose, then. Okay, but the face on this thing looked more like a caribou. And just like the bear this animal was *huge*, easily eight feet at the shoulder. He recalled what Roland had said about mega-fauna and his stomach sank. However one might decorate an elephant to make it look like a mammoth, could someone fake a bear wandering in the foothills? Would someone pump growth hormones into an elk and push it into the open? Day could deal with a con and he wanted all this somehow to be a sick charade. But that hope was dying fast.

Roland returned carrying a long branch. He dropped it at the forest's edge and came down the slope, moving among the juniper like a shadow, appearing here, disappearing there, until he met Day well east of the pond.

"I believe it," Day greeted him. He removed his neckerchief, folded it, and tucked it into a pocket, doing every motion with care as though it were part of his thought process. "I don't know where we are but we've traveled. That mammoth isn't alone."

"No, he's not," Roland confirmed. "There are four more a mile south of here on the other side of this wood."

"You're kidding."

"I'm not. This wood is about two miles long and a quarter-mile deep but on the other side of it is the head of a plain that stretches as far as you can see to the east and west. Still some trees but a lot of grass and open ground. It rises to the east, toward what I'm going to guess is Togwotee Pass. There's a stream coming down from that way. It might be the Buffalo Fork. There's mammoth out there, deer, some kind of wild hog, and maybe some horse. The horse were far out and it was hard to tell. Saw something else, though, real clear."

"Fred Flintstone?"

"No, bison. A lot of bison." Roland said this with a light in his eye that Day had not seen before. "In the thousands. Tens of thousands, maybe. That plain is mixed-grass prairie stuff, taller than it should be for this part of the country but it's there. It probably flows right on over the pass. Forget the mammoth. Nobody has seen a herd like that since the 1880s. You still want to argue?"

Day shook his head and told Roland about the bear and the elk. "It was an unusually large elk," he admitted, forgetting the illogic of the rest of his morning.

Roland grunted. "If we're in the Pleistocene they'll be that way," he pointed out. "But that might have been a stag-moose. Kind of a cross between moose and wapiti. The mammoth is the real surprise. Even if we're in the Ice Age they're farther south than we ever thought they were."

"When we get home you can write a new thesis."

"Maybe. But lucky for me that's not the only mistake we anthropologists made."

"How's that?"

"I went looking for hickory but found something better: hedgeapple, also called Osage orange. Back home it's rare enough. Even in the pre-Columbian era it was supposed to be limited to east Texas. Uh-uh. There's a stand in that wood back there. One was knocked over but it's green enough to use for a bow."

Day should have been glad to hear that but inside he felt anxious. The clock was ticking. They had been on the ground for hours and so far had no sign of their quarry.

"Any sign of Reed?" he asked.

"One fire pit, inside the trees straight up from the water," Roland pointed.

"That could be natives."

"Nope, too big. It was a white man's fire, made by someone afraid of the dark. Can't blame them if those wolves were about. It's an old site – months old – but it was used more recent than that. Days ago, maybe. The rain and the mammoths have obliterated any tracks but there's evidence of foraging to the west and north." Roland pointed to the forest where Day had seen the elk.

Day considered that, trying to imagine what Reed and his band might have been thinking once they grasped their situation. Though he could not fathom their political ideology, he understood survival instinct. Forests offer shelter but they are claustrophobic. Plains let you breathe but at the risk of being caught in the open. A band of survivors might compromise, finding shelter in a place where they could see the wide open spaces while still staying under cover. If these woods already harbored wolves and ferocious circus acts, the desire to move would be strong.

"The high ground is that direction, too," Roland added. "The first impulse is usually to find a place to look around."

Day studied the land between them and the north forest. From where they knelt the ground sloped down a half mile until it bottomed at a gully fed by overflow from the spring. Then it rose gently the same distance. Thereafter the terrain was level to the north until the trees ran into and over the hills. The gully itself curved east and disappeared around the woods behind them, eventually – Day assumed – feeding into Roland's valley.

"They could be watching us," he said.

"Doubt it."

"Why?"

Roland gestured toward the wash. "If they were going to watch us, they would be closer where they could do something about it when we showed up. What's the point of watching from afar, just to raise the alarm? If they wanted to hide they would just high-tail it out of here. More likely they're a hundred miles from here."

"No." Day shook his head.

"How are you so sure?"

"Because they would have had to cover that distance in the time since Kurtz was here. Or since they built the last fire up there. You said that was recent."

"They could have split up. Maybe some headed south, or east, or anywhere. Maybe the only ones who stuck around were the ones Kurtz killed."

Day had thought about that. He thought about it more now while he crouched in the brush, admiring the landscape before them. The land was wide and deep and unnervingly pure, yet at the same time it held a presence he could sense but not see.

"Yes, they could have split up," he admitted. "But someone's here. You know how you said you could feel this was Wyoming, that it was in your blood? Well, I've had a feeling all morning I can't shake. I thought it was just this craziness, the travel, the explosion, but it's something else." He knew what it was but did not say. It was his anger. Like a sixth sense, it tickled his nerves and was growing in intensity. Something in the very air had awakened it. *Vengeance is in my heart,...blood and revenge are hammering in my head.* "I don't know if it's Reed but someone's near. I feel it."

"So how do you plan to find them?" Roland asked.

Day pulled forward the duffel bag.

"I don't plan to," he said. "They're going to find us."

8

That evening a wraith streaked into the sky. With a hiss it shot from the juniper, going straight up trailing smoke that floated in the dark like a lanyard from heaven until dissipating against the stars. Seconds later the sky flashed. A *boom* rent the night.

Another rocket went up, going even higher than the first. With a *pop!* spokes of green fire burst in all directions. The spokes inscribed a wheel against the black canopy, arms spread wide while emerald sparks flushed the land in an otherworldly light. As the embers cooled they fell, drifting in sparkling rain that hung in the air far longer than their fiery debut.

A dozen more rockets went up over the next hour. In a moonless sky they celebrated the prehistoric world in a dazzling exhibition it had not yet seen.

When the echoes faded and the last sparks sank into the soil, night returned.

"Oooooo, aaaaahhhh," Roland muttered.

He and Day sat twenty yards from where the rockets launched. The great dog was with them. The beast had prowled near the north forest until the fireworks began but after the first explosion he returned to the men. There he sat, growling angrily with each display until Day told him to shut up.

"Fireworks? Is that supposed to bring them to us in a flush of remembered patriotism?"

"No," Day replied. "It's supposed to bring them to us in a state of curiosity and desperation."

"Reed will see right through it."

"So he won't come. But others will. If any saw that show they won't be able to help themselves."

Roland thought about that as he sat cross-legged on the ground with the hedgeapple limb across his lap. He had stripped and carved the branch and now continued to shape it with a piece of pumice as they sat in the darkness, the low rasp of stone on wood barely audible above a light breeze that rustled the chokecherry growing nearby. Every now and then he stopped scraping to feel the bow and gauge his progress, using his fingers to see what his eyes could not.

"Out of curiosity?" he asked.

"And desperation. Mostly desperation, I hope. They've just spent six months in the Stone Age. I'm betting any who are still alive will jump on a chance to go home, even if they suspect it's a trap."

"Why? They know they'll die in the twenty-first century as fast as they'll die here. Maybe faster."

"Home is home," Day insisted. "Some will want to go."

It was too dark to see features so Roland put his skepticism into a whisper. "Don't know if you're a cynic or an optimist, Day, but I hope you're a cynic. Otherwise I'm gonna have to watch your back."

The rest of the night passed quietly for the most part. To the west a storm played over the mountains but the thunder was distant and the rain stayed with it. Once the drama of the fireworks ended, the dumbstruck plain took time to find its own voice. A whip-poor-will finally broke the silence, calling tentatively from the gully as though expecting an explosive response. When none came the bird continued to call until midnight. Besides it and the chirp of insects there was little on the breeze to listen to.

The temperature dropped into the forties. Day rolled out a sleeping bag and lay down. Roland produced a thin poncho with a hood: he wrapped himself in it and closed his eyes. The great dog rolled onto its side.

Then an hour before dawn a blood-curdling cry interrupted their rest. Day sat up; Roland turned his head. The dog looked up as well, perhaps wondering what he was missing.

The cry, more of a scream, stopped abruptly and then repeated moments later. It was a horrible sound, truly terrifying, like a grown woman being eaten alive. Judging distance was difficult but Day guessed it came from less than a quarter mile away. He uncapped a night scope and peered through the lens. The scream came twice more while he looked.

"Fox?" he whispered. "Mountain lion?"

Roland strained his ears. "That's no fox," was all he said.

The night scope revealed a flat tableau of black-on-green, an improvement over the starlight but not enough to make out detail on the ground. To the east the land was open. To the south it dipped, prairie flowing through it like a river. The scream came from somewhere in between but Day saw nothing but a two-dimensional montage of jumbled shapes.

The screams stopped and after a while Day put the scope away, but it was hard to relax from then on. The great dog wandered off and did not come back until light appeared on the horizon.

Around then a new sound rose on the wind. This came from the west, at least a mile distant where the watering hole lay. It was a howl, deep and rough as though gurgling from the earth, and it chilled the blood. At first just one voice, soon others joined to make a throaty paean to the dawn. The hound leaped to its feet and peered into the night. At the same time the men heard hoof beats drum the soil to the east. Day raised his scope again and saw a herd of maybe forty wild horses not two hundred yards away but increasing the distance fast.

"Horses," he said, surprised. "So you weren't kidding."

Roland did not answer. He looked west, his eyes keen to spot the source of the howling. The sound lasted for several minutes and then stopped as though on signal. The Indian made out distant shapes against the western sky but that was all.

"What will your dog do when he encounters a dire wolf?" he asked.

"Probably eat it," Day replied.

"Not likely."

"He's killed wolves before."

"Not these, he hasn't."

If the hound was concerned it did not show. He studied the darkness to the west with professional interest but when ten minutes had gone by and the howling did not recur, he lay down again and licked his paws.

Dawn brought a light rain. After it stopped, steam rose into the air so clean it made even distant objects seem close. The horses were gone, so were the wolves, but the bison Roland had seen the day before were now in sight to the east, a scattering of dots on a grass-trampled horizon.

Near the watering hole vultures circled over the carcass of a deer. Foraging coyotes kept them aloft for a while but when they finally moved on the birds swooped in, hopping onto the remains to tear at whatever was left.

Where the men had spent the night the ground was now empty with no sign of their passing. Almost no sign – a fox wandered near and stopped short, sniffing the air. It spent several seconds prowling back and forth with its nose pressed to the soil, particularly where the great dog had lain, before deciding it wanted no part of whatever these smells were. It disappeared back into the brush.

Twenty yards away a pennant stood tall and rigid on a thin rod. It hung over the empty cardboard rocket tubes.

For hours nothing moved on the plain. Dawn turned to morning, morning to afternoon. The *prrreeep prrreeeep* of a curlew rose from somewhere up by the water but the bird itself stayed out of sight.

Around two o'clock a thin hand pushed aside a sapling at the edge of the spruce forest. The man it belonged to stepped out. Gaunt, in tattered clothes, wearing a fleece jacket and carrying a rifle, he had hard eyes and a lined face beneath an auburn beard. For a long while he stood at the tree line, scanning the plain.

He saw the pennant but he had seen that from the forest. Now he searched for whoever had planted it.

His gaze roved the open land, trying to penetrate the waist-high brush that camouflaged it with frustrating efficiency. The man licked his lips, debating. Finally, curiosity overwhelmed caution: he crouched, moved into the open, and then knelt to disappear behind a willow sage.

Another figure emerged from the trees. Like the first, this one came to the edge of the forest and stopped, allowing his outline to blend with the foliage. He was just as patient and stood still for so long that even a careful study of the woodland would have missed him. Only when the first man moved farther onto the plain did the second follow with quick steps. He never lagged less than a dozen yards and took cover often. In that way the two worked themselves closer to the pennant, moving down the gentle slope toward the gully.

There were in fact two gullies, one carved by overflow from the pond and the other coming from the north. The first joined the second at a ninety-degree angle a hundred yards below the north forest. There the trickles of water merged and became a quiet rivulet overhung with milkweed and wild onion.

The men stopped at the edge of the north gully and knelt again, listening. Then, using hand signals, they moved farther apart.

The gully was narrower than the wash where Roland had found the body but about the same depth. The first man slid gingerly over the edge and down to the bottom. He stepped across the tinkling water, rifle pointed upstream, and listened again. Hearing nothing, he climbed the other side.

The climb did not go as smoothly as he would have liked. The gully's sides were sandy and the chokecherry roots gave him little to hold. With great reluctance he slung the rifle over his shoulder to use both hands. But he made it. With a roll he went over the top and disappeared into the brush.

The second man waited. He expected his companion to reappear to give him a sign but after several minutes of no movement he assumed he had misunderstood the plan. He slid down into the gully himself.

Inside the tree line a third man had not moved. Short with thick hair and a prophet's beard, his eyes peered out from where the undergrowth was thickest, near the edge of the forest where sunlight reached in but trees blocked the wind. Immobile, silent, his clothes so dirty they blended with the ground, he was invisible.

Minutes passed. He lost sight of his companions about the time they reached the gully but still he did not move. From his position he could see little unless he stood up but he was loathe to do that. He knew the value of staying still.

A rustle came from his left. Glancing over he saw a red squirrel scratch in the leaves at the base of a tamarack. The animal was four times the size of a normal squirrel, the kind the man associated with the normal world, the squirrels he knew from back home in Portland. This one easily weighed four pounds. The man's stomach growled. He could not shoot the animal, not now, but he could set up a snare in less than five minutes and with luck maybe nab some dinner. He had eaten enough squirrels over the last several months and had the process down.

But that would require moving. His eyes shifted back to the plain. There was still no sign of his companions. They should have reached the pennant by now. What had they found? It was unlikely to be trouble – the one bounty hunter had come after them but would there be another so soon? Even if there was, nobody hunting them would announce his arrival with fireworks. That was idiotic. It had to be a signal of some kind, a sign.

The man thought back to what they had seen the night before. They were camped in the foothills four miles upstream when the first explosions came but at first none of them went to investigate – moving at night was dangerous. Only after the blasts kept coming and after they saw flashes in the sky did they scramble to a bluff and see the last of the fireworks shoot up into the night. His heart had leaped at the sight, he did not deny it. Out of nowhere had appeared this sign of the real world, a vision of his home, of his past, of something not from the savage survival expedition that they had been on for more than half a year. Bursting in the sky was light, fire, modernity, and celebration. It had been impossible to sleep after that. He had thought of nothing else while they waited for dawn.

It had to be a sign. A signal to them that they should come out.

Another rustle brought him back to reality. This one was behind him. The squirrel must have moved...no, he was still there by the tamarack. Too late the man sensed danger. He turned and in his peripheral vision caught a blur of movement just as something swung at his face.

Day sat near the pennant going through the contents of the first man's pockets. A handful of dry moss, a piece of flint, some piñon nuts, a roll of twine, three twenty-dollar bills, and a Nevada driver's license. On the dirt beside him was a bolt knife with a chipped blade. Beside that was a well-worn AK-47 rifle with a collapsible stock and three 7.62 cartridges.

"Alberto Cruz," he read from the license. "Funny, you don't look Hispanic."

The man who lay in the dirt glared at Day. He was hog-tied with a gag wound so tight that his cheeks flushed white beneath his beard.

"You don't look like the guy in this picture, either. You would need a haircut and a shave. Is this fake or something you stole, or is Alberto Cruz just some guy you killed?"

The man muttered something but Day was pretty sure it was not an answer to his question.

Roland came up from the south, staying low to keep below the tops of the juniper.

"Where's the other one?" Day asked him.

Roland, behind the man on the ground, pointed with his thumb back the way he came. Aloud, he said, "Dead."

Day feigned annoyance.

"Why did you kill him? I told you we just wanted information."

"Yeah, but he wouldn't talk. Nothing useful, anyway. Jittery guy with a foul mouth. Pissed me off so I cut his throat. Bastard can lie there and think about it while he bleeds to death."

The man on the ground erupted in a torrent of profanity that was distinguishable even through his gag. Roland dropped onto him putting a knee into a kidney. The man deflated.

"You have something to say?" Roland asked, removing the gag.

"You mother-f…" was the reply that began and then stopped when Roland leaned again into the man's back.

"Be nice," Roland warned him. "I said I don't like profanity."

The man gasped in pain. "I'll kill you," he moaned. "I'll rip your heart out."

"That's better. Threats but no cursing."

"Judging from your general unfriendliness I'd say you're one of the people we're looking for," Day observed. "Where's Reed?"

"Go to hell."

Roland leaned his full weight onto the man's back. There was the sound of something popping and the man in the dirt howled.

"Where's Reed?" Day repeated.

On the verge of fainting, the man whispered, "I don't know. But he'll know you're here soon enough. And he *will* rip your heart out."

"Who will tell him, your guy in the trees?" Roland asked. He flipped a thin billfold over to Day, who caught it and sorted through the contents.

"John Flute," the Settler read, holding up the driver's license. "No kidding? Crazy John Flute has lasted this long? He's a piece of work: pharmacist gone psycho, responsible for poisoning the municipal water supply in five Midwestern cities. He killed over two hundred people and put another thousand in the hospital. Also spread anthrax through caterers in Las Vegas. That wasn't as successful, though I notice he didn't hit anyplace in Oregon, where his license says he's from. Hmm, a credit card…Diner's Club, some irony there. Starbucks Rewards, that fits; an employee ID from some drug firm; and two…no, two hundred fifty dollars. You guys are hanging onto your cash. Is he dead, too?" Day asked Roland.

Roland bowed his head. "Yeah, sorry."

The man on the ground drooped in resignation. Day slid over and put his boot in the man's face, pushing him back up.

"I don't care about your pals and I don't care about you," he said, throwing aside the billfold. "I want Reed. You want to live another day, start talking."

The man wanted to fight. It was in his eyes. But he was also tired, exhausted beyond measure.

"Up north, I don't know where," he muttered, then yelled as Roland pressed again into his back. "I haven't seen him in a week! We broke up, then he sent us down here to watch for more of you."

"What do you mean, you broke up?"

"King and Reed argued. King and Gromer blame Reed for the whole disaster and when Reed blew a set-up with the slants, King said the hell with it and left. Four others went with him. I shoulda gone, too."

"King? Is that Holden King? The actor?"

"Yeah."

"He and Reed fought over what? Slants? What's a slant?"

"The natives. They look Asian... Elke was the first to meet a group of them at the spring. We had trouble at first but then she worked out some hand signal crap so we could trade with them for food. Reed learned they were fighting with a tribe from the mountains so he tried to team up with them. You know, make a deal to get them on our side so we would have some protection and local muscle. But he must have scared them because they ran off. King got pissed when that happened – he was making moves on some bitch they had and next thing he knows they're gone. He and Gromer and a few others took off, following the slants. He and Reed have fought since the beginning so if it wasn't the slants it would have been something else but King also thinks there are other people out here. He wants to find them."

"Other people besides Indians?"

"Yeah."

"And what do you think?"

The Prog drooped again. "King's an idiot but he's right about one thing," he muttered. There's no one around here. If there was we would have found them by now. Reed's insane; he doesn't care if he gets back to civilization. He wants to run the world, any world, and this one'll do just fine for him. That damned Ganesh dropped us in the middle of some theme park...this place is crazy. When that other bounty hunter showed up last month it was the first time we knew we were still on Planet Earth. Hell, we've lost half the guys already. But you didn't come from nowhere – maybe King was right to go..."

"Where did he go?"

The man hesitated but when Roland made a move toward him he blurted, "East! Somewhere that way. I don't know. Where the hell are we? How do we get out?"

"You said you lost guys...who?" Day demanded. "How?

The man's eyes grew defiant again. "Untie me," he growled. "We can talk."

Roland lunged up and put his knee – and his weight – on the man's head. The man yelled but the sound suffocated in the prairie dirt.

Day leaned in close. "Let's get something straight," he said. "We're here to kill you or bring you back. It's easier if we kill you. So convince me not to do that. Tell us your real name – and if you say Cruz I'll break all your fingers."

A while later they put the man's gag back in place. Roland led Day south through the brush.

When they got to the spot where Roland had left the second Prog they found an empty rifle by the side of the clearing. It was an M4 carbine but the gunman himself was gone.

Day dropped and took cover. Roland merely frowned and studied the disturbed soil. Removing the tomahawk from his belt he followed a trail of drag marks and crushed grass to the edge of the gully. There he looked over the side.

"Huh," he said, and put away the tomahawk.

Day joined him and looked into the gully. The second Prog, still tied at both hands and feet, lay at the bottom, half in the water but with his head at an impossible angle at the base of a rock.

"I thought you were kidding," Day accused.

"I was," Roland insisted. "I left him in perfect health. He must have rolled himself off trying to get away."

Day slid into the wash and checked the man's pulse. With a sigh he hauled the body clear of the stream, then removed the ropes and put them back into his duffle. Finally he went through the man's clothes.

"Sorry," Roland said. "I didn't see that coming."

"He doesn't have any i-d. You recognize him?"

The dead man was young. Latin features, early twenties. Roland studied the face and then stripped off the coat and shirt. The man's torso, front and back, and both arms were covered in tattoos.

"Nope. The guy's a Crip, though."

"How do you know?"

Roland tapped a drawing high on the man's right arm, then another over his heart. The first was a three-pointed crown. The second a trio of letters in Gothic script: IGC.

"While in school I did social work in Tulsa. Some of the neighborhoods had a gang presence." He pointed to the crown. "Three points or six points is a Crip. The letters stand for Insane Gangster Crip."

"There are Crips in Tulsa?"

"Oh, yeah. They're based in L.A. but they spread decades ago."

Day consulted a small notebook he carried that Galt had given him. "Well, the good news is Shell listed a Crip in Reed's inner circle."

"Good. Cross him off."

"No, because the bad news is they have a name for that guy. Raymond Williams."

"Are you saying this isn't Ray?"

"It's not. Ray's black."

Roland glanced down at the body. "So this guy is not on the list at all?"

"Nope. We have a maverick. Crap."

"Is that bad?"

Day nodded. "Yeah. Galt said there's a mole. We don't know who it is so it could be anyone. I would hate to think we just killed a good guy."

"You think a Crip would be a mole?"

"The world's a strange place," Day said. He looked around and added, "Sometimes very strange."

With a pen he made notes in the book and then put it away. "Too bad Sorley wouldn't talk," he sighed.

"He gave you his name," Roland reminded him. "If you had let me break his fingers he might have given us more."

"Maybe."

"But you're not the torturing kind, are you?"

"Don't underestimate me," Day said. "I didn't see the point as long as we still had two more guys we could question. At least I *thought* we had two more. You didn't leave the other guy to roll into a gully and break his neck, did you?"

Roland shrugged. "No, but the way my day is going he might have been eaten by a 400-pound squirrel."

Crazy John Flute was not in a gully. When Day and Roland found him he was still where the Indian had left him, bound and gagged and hanging upside down from the tamarack.

"Good morning," Day greeted him.

Flute twisted to glare at Day. His face was red from the blood rush of being inverted and he had a deep bruise low on his forehead, but it was his eyes that grabbed Day's attention. They blazed with ferocity. The Settler decided that Crazy John was not just a nickname.

"I'm here to kill you or take you back to Oregon," he continued. "Your choice. If I kill you it won't be with a gun or a knife or by breaking your neck. You'll hang here until you're eaten by wolves. So you decide. I know you're a coward but are you stupid?"

Flute exploded in wrath, spittle flying around the gag. He shook and bounced, making biting motions toward Day, his efforts causing him to swing gently below the stout limb where Roland's piggin strings secured him. Day waited, saying nothing. When Flute tired and his swinging tapered to nothing, Roland poked him in the back. The Indian had stayed out of sight so now Flute freaked out again, not knowing Roland was there. The Prog launched into another tirade as he tried to swing about to see the new threat.

Day let him flail into exhaustion. When Flute looked ready to pass out Day jabbed his rifle into the man's gut and yanked off the gag.

"Talk. How many are still alive?"

Flute tried to shout but a whimper came out instead. He began to babble and cry at the same time. Half of it was not even words, just sounds. Some whiny, some guttural. The other half were random, a one-sided conversation. All spewed forth as though under pressure

"...cold...cold...always cold...They shouldn't have said that...You're thirsty? Everyone's thirsty. You want water? I'll give you water. I'll give you water right down your lying, thieving throat!...Oh, my head. Get away from me! I'll kill you!...M aaaaryyyyy.. Oh, Maaaaryyyyy. Come back, Mary, it's okay. I won't hurt you. I'll protect you. They'll hurt you but I won't. Maaaaarryyyyyy..."

Day slapped him. Flute's gibberish stopped and he looked around, his bloodshot eyes gaining focus.

"You're a bounty hunter," he said when they settled on Day. "I can tell. You've got that smug look. What do you call yourselves, Settlers? Why is that? Do you settle for failure?"

Roland knelt and looped a rope around Flute's neck. Pulling it tight he choked off any further speech, making the Prog's whole head turn crimson. His body jerked and danced as he fought to breathe.

"Your pals are dead," Day said when Roland finally released the noose and stepped back. "They wouldn't help. Whether you live another day is up to you. How many are there, and where?"

Flute coughed and spit.

"I have rights," he gasped.

"You did," Day conceded. "But you threw them away. How many and where, or the gag goes back on and we leave you hanging."

Flute hesitated but when Roland made an audible motion toward him he blurted, "In the pass! They're in the pass."

"Which pass? The one near here?"

"Yeah, yeah. There's hot springs. It's warm and there's food. Everyone's there."

"Everyone?"

"Yeah."

"They're not moving farther north? Or going out onto the plains?"

Flute snorted. "No. The plains...been there, done that. The pass is the best."

Day studied the Prog, who looked away. "How many are left?" he demanded.

"How many what?"

"Your buddies in the pass. How many are there?"

"You'll find out," Flute sneered. "You and your little deputy will..."

Roland punched him in a kidney. It was not a hard punch but it was enough on Flute's weakened frame that he turned white and vomited, fluid dripping up his nose and sending him into another coughing fit. Day waited.

"Five," Flute finally gasped. "Reed, Elke, Heather, Rudd, Sorley..."

"Sorley was with you."

"Oh,...Lace, then. I meant to say Lace."

"Lace Stevens? The cop?" Day exchanged a look with Roland.

"I don't know what he did," Flute said.

"What about weapons?"

"Rifles, like us."

"Ammunition? How are they fixed for ammo?"

"We've got plenty." Flute's voice tested defiance again.

"Really?" Day asked. "Then why do you only have three rounds in your gun and it hasn't been fired recently?"

Flute didn't answer.

"Why did he send you at all? Why are you here?"

Flute took a while to answer. "To watch for you," he admitted with reluctance.

"To kill us, you mean."

Flute mumbled something about how they should have been closer. Day strained to hear.

"That's a good point," he pressed. "If you were setting up an ambush why are you waiting over here? Why not back at the spring?"

"We *were* at the spring," Flute snapped. "But then the wolves..." His voice broke and he shuddered. "We almost got eaten the first night. Reuben couldn't take it. He shot his bullets and then wouldn't stay..."

"What about the others? The ones who went with Holden King?"

"They're fools. King's following his dick."

"What?"

"There's a woman, one of the slants. In the group that we scared off. King wants the woman, that's why he left. He goes on about finding other people but he's just chasing tail."

"So he's not at the pass," Day pointed out. "You said everyone was at the pass."

Flute did not answer.

"Who went with King?" Day asked. "Which way did they go?"

Flute shook his head to say he did not know. Roland nudged him.

"I don't know!" the Prog cried out. "I wasn't there when they left. I don't know!"

Thoroughly spent, he began to sob. The man looked as miserable as a human being could: filthy, emaciated, flushed and ready to pass out with vomit streaked through his beard and hair. How far John had fallen. Or maybe, Day thought, this was man's natural state and everything above it was no more than a temporary condition, a vain evasion of reality. *Is man no more than this?* King Lear had asked, and Day now wondered that himself..

He stepped back and considered his options. After a while he made a motion to Roland, who stepped forward and yanked on the piggin strings. Flute dropped to the dirt like a bag of rotten apples.

Roland retreated into the forest where sunlight only filtered through the trees. The afternoon was almost done.

Flute rolled over in the dirt as though reluctant to get up.

"*Maaaaaaryyyyy.. Oh, Maaaaryyyyy..*" he sang into the soil, then muttered incoherently for a while. When he did look up he rasped, "Kill me. Go on, Mr. Settler. Shoot me and put another notch in your gun."

"I wouldn't waste a bullet," Day replied.

Flute's face twisted. "I would waste one on you," he swore.

"I don't doubt that."

"You bastard. You damned Settlers. You're no different than us!"

"I've heard that before," Day said, kneeling to look at Flute straight on. "Even from Shakespeare: *The jury passing on the prisoner's life may in the sworn twelve have a thief or two guiltier than him they try.* The key word, though, is *may*. Sorry, John, but you and your pals are in a class all your own."

"Then KILL ME!"

"I want to, trust me. You killed families, John. Families. Sickened and killed people you didn't even know and for what? Because you could. You're a monster, John. No one would bat an eye if I killed you right here. But you still have choices to make. You can go back to the spring and wait for us…"

"No! I told you…I won't survive the night!"

"You will if you get up into the rocks. There are spaces the wolves can't get to. And if you're still there in three days we'll take you back with us."

"The hell I will!"

"Then you can run to Reed," Day shrugged. "Tell him all about me. Of course, you'll have to explain why you didn't kill me when you had the chance, why none of you even tried. And why you led me right to him. But I'm sure he'll understand."

Flute's eyes went insane again but he had no energy left to sustain his anger. He searched the clearing for an answer.

"Give me my rifle."

"No."

"Give me food, at least," he begged, spying Day's duffel. "You've got it. Give me something to eat!"

Day hesitated but then reached into a pocket and pulled out a trail bar wrapped in heavy paper. He tossed it to Flute who snatched it from the air and held it to his face, sniffing. The smell of cinnamon and sugar brought tears to his eyes. He rolled over and got to his feet, then backed into the woods, as feral as the squirrel he had hungered for earlier.

"I'll kill you," he vowed. Then he turned and ran.

"You're welcome," Day muttered.

Roland emerged from the trees.

"You gave him food?" he asked.

"I did." When Roland glared at him Day added, "It's late. He'll be one step ahead of the wolves and will need all the energy he can get if he's going to lead us to Reed."

"Isn't Reed in the pass?"

Day shook his head. "I don't think so. That answer came too easily. We'll have to follow him."

"I thought that's why we left the ropes loose on the first guy, Sorley. So we could follow *him*."

"It is, but after hearing Crazy John I've changed my mind. Sorley will get free but I don't think he'll go to Reed. You heard him: King this, King that...he'll go east."

"But you fed a mass murderer."

"I did. And he'll hate me for it soon enough. *Mercy is not itself, that oft looks so. Pardon is still the nurse of second woe.*"

Roland waited for an explanation but none came, so he stepped to the treeline and looked east. The bison were gone from the plain but his sharp eyes picked out a band of horses in the distance, as well as something that might have been antelope scattered across the grasslands farther south. The land in that direction was vast.

"Some are north, others east," he considered. "If we split up, I volunteer to go east. Wouldn't mind getting a closer look at those buffalo. To see a herd like that run...I would be the first man in 150 years to see that sight."

"No. We'll stick together."

Roland shrugged. "Okay. So who's the priority, then?" he asked.

Day picked up his duffel. "Reed...for now," he answered. "But let's give it a night and sleep on it."

9

Sorley had in fact worked free of his bonds. He was gone when Day and Roland returned to the ravine. True to Day's prediction, his tracks did not go north. Confusingly, though, they did not go east, either: they led south. The Settlers discussed it and decided Sorley might be heading for the plain where Roland had seen the buffalo. The grass was lush there and eventually would make for easier travel to the east than the juniper field they were in. It was a guess and Day worried that already his quarries were scattering to the four winds, but he did not want to go after Sorley just yet.

They took the three Prog rifles and returned to the watering hole. The water there was deep and Day could not think of a better place to dispose of the weapons so they pitched them in and watched them sink out of sight. Then he and Roland returned to the spruce forest to pick up Crazy John's trail. Again, Day had guessed right. Crazy John's tracks headed north, not west toward the pass.

The forest widened as it spread up into the hills, stretching west to the glacier and east until the land leveled out miles away. Not all spruce, it was a mix of deciduous and evergreens that was thickest on the south-facing slopes. There were varieties that Day was sure did not belong in Wyoming but he reminded himself that he did not belong there, either.

Crazy John had an hour and a half head start but the Settlers took their time following his path. The days were getting longer and they still had decent light. In addition, Day was unsettled and being extra cautious. Eighty, maybe ninety percent of the world around him he recognized: it was the rest that kept him off-balance. He went around every tree half-expecting to find another woolly mammoth or a caveman with a club.

Roland was careful, too, though more at ease. Any trepidation for him came from a concern the land might disappear before he had a chance to see it all.

The great dog bounded forward with abandon. It surprised and killed a grouse, then a squirrel, and then disappeared into the forest. It had been gone a while when the men heard a squeal echo in the trees. After listening and wondering, they resumed their forward trek. Eventually they came across the dog in a clearing. It had killed and eaten much of a collared peccary.

"You on a picnic?" Day demanded. The beast ignored him but growled when Roland moved forward to study what was left of the hog.

"That's a big javelina," the Indian observed, backing away.

"So?"

"Javelina are prey," Roland explained. "In any ecosystem, the bigger the prey, the bigger predators have to be to eat them. All these critters he's killed are big. I'm thinking of the predators that must feed on these things."

An hour later he had reason to think some more. The sun was below the horizon and the land turning gray when the trail dipped into a canyon formed by the same creek that ran below the forest. Beaver had dammed the stream, creating ponds fringed with cattails and flooded timber. The soil was soft and cool. In that soil Roland spotted tracks that made even Day pause.

"You had better get religion," Roland counseled, scanning the canyon walls. "I've hunted on three continents and never seen a cat track that big."

The print was 10 inches across with a trapezoidal pad pressed deep into the turf. The huge dog sniffed at it and followed a scent as far as the top of the ponds. From there he looked upstream but showed no interest in exploring farther. Instead he returned to the men and moved to their downstream side.

"Coward," Day accused, but the beast gave him a look that suggested in this case discretion was the better part of valor.

They back-tracked to a spot above the canyon with a clear view of the creek and made camp. Behind them in the gathering dusk, a wild panorama of tumbling hills and peaks rolled away and lost itself in the crimson and gold ribbons of the western sky. To the east the black mountain overhung them, menacing as shadows grew long on its naked bulk. In a short time it was so dark they could not see each other.

Day was tired, yet it took him a long time to relax. His fatigue came from stress more than exertion, the anxiety of being out of his element and not knowing all the factors in play in this strangest of manhunts. Apprehension over encountering a creature of the Pleistocene also did its part to wear him down. He lay in the chilly night trying to focus on what was familiar to calm his nerves.

There was enough to do the trick. For the most part the sounds, the smells, and the air itself could have been from any century, any time. Breezes from the east sighed across the canyon and brought the comforting perfume of rain-washed sage, while the erratic click and hum of insects was a recognizable soundtrack to the night. The stars were so thick the sky seemed to press down on them but it was a sky Day knew. He picked out planets and constellations with ease, while the Milky Way stretched from horizon to horizon with the eternal glow of celestial energy. It all wafted over him like fog off a lake and helped stabilize his senses. When he fell asleep he was as calm as he had been in days.

If Roland had trouble sleeping it was not obvious. He sat wrapped in his poncho, tomahawk in his lap, as silent as the tree he leaned against.

The great beast flopped onto its side and slept.

For a second night, storms played over the mountains to their west. A few sprinkles fell on their camp but the sky above them stayed clear. There was distant howling near midnight to accompany the thunder, the same full-throated bay of the night before, and then the more familiar yipping of coyotes at dawn, but otherwise the canyon stayed calm as the stars drifted by, its only voice the echo of trickling water.

At daybreak Day scouted forward while Roland worked on his bow. By this time he had transformed the hedgeapple limb into a single-piece recurve almost six feet tall. The riser was supported by the fiberglass grip from his composite bow while the limbs were backed up by strips of birch gathered on their hike.

The limbs tapered delicately as they moved beyond the arrow rest but the design looked anything but fragile. Two bowstrings had survived the mammoth's assault along with the quiver of arrows. So did two of the pulleys from the original bow but Roland had given up trying to leverage those on his new construction. The result was nonetheless a mix of the old and the new, of nature and science: a formidable weapon cobbled together from fourteen millennia of technological evolution.

Day returned and eyed the Rube Goldberg product with doubt. Undeterred, Roland fitted a tiny stabilizer to the top limb, carefully strung the bow, and nocked a primitive birch arrow fletched with feathers from the huge dog's grouse. Down the ravine stood a fat sycamore. Next to it an arm's-length away was the rotting stump of its predecessor. Roland aimed, drew the string part-way, and let the arrow fly. With a *zzzzst* it tore apart the air, flew forty yards, and plunged dead center into the soft wood of the stump.

Day was impressed but Roland frowned.

"I was aiming at the tree," he admitted.

The bow needed work but they had no time for that now. They descended into the ravine instead and picked up Crazy John's trail. Day found where the Prog had spent the night.

"He puked," the Indian commented, studying a mess in the soil. "And he's not walking steady now. What was in that bar you gave him?"

"Sugar and carbs. His system isn't used to it. And those things are dry as dust. You need to drink plenty of water when you eat one. He's probably cramping and constipated as hell."

"Hmm. Maybe you're the torturing type, after all."

They found more cat tracks farther up the canyon, this time crossing a line of snow near a collapsed beaver dam that was turning to meadow.

"What are we talking here?" Day asked. "Saber-tooth tiger? Mountain lion on steroids?"

"I'm not so good on tigers so maybe I'm biased against them," Roland replied, "but this looks similar to an African lion."

"So we're in Africa?"

"Not hardly. No, I told you there were American lions. I'm guessing this is one of them. *Panthera leo atrox*. Roughly translates as, 'really scary lion.' Big. Seven or eight hundred pounds."

"Seven or eight hundred?" Day repeated.

"Yup. Let's not meet him."

"We might have to. That's twice these tracks have crossed Crazy John's trail."

Roland shook his head. "Coincidence. John's heading straight up the canyon. This cat's wandering. And there's beaver here. It probably comes for water or to hunt."

"Would it hunt the same?" Day asked.

"What do you mean?"

"If it's an African lion, does it hunt in a pack? Or if it's American, would it hunt the same as one of our mountain lions? Secretive, standoffish, only attacking a man if it's wounded or sick? How aggressive are these megafauna types? You say this is Wyoming – if they're in the same land would it drive the same behavior?"

Roland shrugged. "You asked me that once before," he reminded Day. "I don't know." Seeing that his response did not suffice, he sighed and pointed at the tracks where they left the marsh. "He oversteps in the grass. I'm saying he, by the way, because I hope to hell the females don't get this big. Once in the snow, though, the rear feet place inside the prints of the front. That's normal."

He moved to the side of the canyon and studied the cat's trail there. "He came down the wall laterally, he didn't come straight. That's normal, too, so we can say he wanders and walks like a twenty-first century cougar. But what that means for his character..." Roland shook his head.

"Wonderful," Day said. He nudged the dog. "You go first from now on." As usual, the great beast ignored him.

All morning they moved up the canyon. By mid-day they had climbed two thousand feet and neared the source of the creek, two springs that trickled out of the rocks and carved their way through the last of the snow until meeting and washing downhill. Just below that the last beaver dam came in sight. Behind it they spotted one of the architects of the ponding.

"You've got to be kidding me," Day muttered.

The beaver was the size of a golf cart. It sat on a lodge in the pond, enjoying the sunlight which had just stretched to that part of the canyon. There was movement in the water which suggested a companion but the animal on top was the only one in sight, and it was enough. Even from a hundred feet away the Settlers could see the rodent's teeth and tail, both longer and wider than on its descendants. No tree they had seen thus far was safe from this creature.

As the men approached the beaver lifted its head and followed their movement but it never dove out of sight, not even when the great dog trotted to the water's edge. Separated by a dozen yards the two animals studied each other. Finally the dog lost interest and moved on.

"Back home he would have dropped into the water the instant he heard us," Roland commented.

"Back home he would be a circus attraction," Day grumbled. He knelt and studied a patch of plants hanging over the water. They were short with white umbels, delicate in structure, and a handful had been torn away at the roots. "Someone has been foraging."

"That's *cicuta*. Water hemlock. John's tracks come here...you suppose he doesn't know what it is?"

Day was doubtful. "He's a druggist. If there's one thing John knows, it's poison. *Put this in any liquid thing you will, and drink it off; and, if you had the strength of twenty men, it would dispatch you straight...* I suppose he might want it as a diuretic if his cramps are bad enough but I don't think so. My guess is he's stockpiling it as a weapon. Keep that in mind if he offers you tea."

The top of the canyon rose onto a sunlit plateau of waist-high grass. The snow vanished. A stand of aspen clustered at the lip of the canyon while aster and goldeneye waved in abundance.

"Elk," Roland said, pointing to markings in the turf. "At least three, big, one favoring a hind leg." He moved around, using the bow to nudge aside the grass. "And here's your cat," he added, finding what he was looking for. "Another huge print. That's the trail he's on, not Crazy John."

The plateau appeared empty. That was good...but it posed a challenge. Crazy John's tracks led straight across the meadow, heading toward a cleft in the terrain a half-mile distant. If the men followed they would be exposed in all directions. There was no telling what awaited them when they reached the other side.

Day crouched in the shade of an aspen and propped his rifle against a tree. He pulled a thick wad of paper from his bag and unfolded it. Roland kept a lookout but glanced over and arched an eyebrow.

"You brought a map?"

"Yup."

"Isn't that cheating?"

"Nope."

Day studied the pages, looking up now and then to note the land around them. When he finished he folded them with care and tucked them back in the bag.

"You're from the panhandle," he told Roland. "You going to tell me you didn't do any research on this area before you came out here?"

"Of course I did. But I didn't bring Rand-McNally with me."

"Neither did I. These are 1:50 topographical charts from the Corps of Engineers."

"And what do they tell you?"

Day picked up his rifle and sighed. "They tell me the land has changed in 14,000 years. This canyon isn't even on the chart. There's a draw but nothing like what we just walked through. We're in the Bridger-Teton National Forest, below Yellowstone. But the forests are more widespread than the map shows so you've got to look instead at geology and contour lines. Even with those it's hard to tell what's what. These hills are on the map as well as this plateau, and it shows a valley on the other side, and that should be Eagle Peak over there, but the rest of it is guesswork. Besides the glaciers, there've been at least two volcanic eruptions in this region in the last ten thousand years and no telling how many floods, earthquakes, rockslides, and storms. This whole corner of the state is volatile, geologically speaking. If we try to use these maps to identify anything other than mountains we'll spend more time deciphering what evolved into what than we will walking...it's not worth the trouble."

"I figured as much when we stood at the watering hole," Roland said. "Once I saw that moraine, I knew we could forget 90% of what the book said."

"Well, I thought it was a good idea at the time."

"No such luck, paleface. We'll have to do this old-school."

One alternative to crossing the plateau in the open was to move to the right, staying masked in the aspen until the land narrowed, which it appeared to do several hundred yards to the east. That would reduce their exposure when they crossed but it also led to a second challenge: something large was moving inside the tree line at the edge of the grass plain.

"What is that?" Day whispered.

Roland peered but the animal went in and out of sight.

"Some kind of bear," he decided. "Let's not find out."

"The wind is from the east," Day noted. "He shouldn't smell us. Let's move away and not let him see us, either."

They moved to the west, looking to cross the meadow where they would be less exposed. They found a spot, a dip where seismic activity had made the land drop and created a ledge that broke their line of sight to the east. It masked their movement from the bear so they took advantage of it and moved out onto the plateau.

Yet they were not alone here, either. Deer grazed in the open, as did several elk. A band of wild turkeys wandered near the forest's edge almost hidden in the grass, while a creature that Day thought might be a llama stood tall above it. All marked the men moving into the meadow but none showed concern. Only when the dog trotted into view did the animals perk up. The deer and elk stopped eating, the turkeys moved off, and the llama, after a careful study, walked away and disappeared into a draw.

"Was that a llama?" Day asked.

"Or a camel. Both are native. Forget that...look at those elk. I've never seen bulls that big."

Day had to concur. The elk before them were twice as large as any he had seen before: taller, broader, and sporting the bulk of beef cattle. Their coats were thick and their antlers wide, even on the youngest bull at the back of the group who appeared to be the one with the limp. Bellies brushing the grass, they were a hunter's dream – except that anybody who shot one would need a forklift to get it back to camp.

The ground was firm beneath their feet and the path easy-going. It was a perfect day to be in the high country. A breeze wandered across the meadow as though on a stroll. Day smelled pollen and dew, leaves and earth, clear air and the musty sweat of his own dog. The sweet mix of a chill morning. Under other circumstances he would have been tempted to sit and soak it all in.

The great dog moved ahead. He was so big that Day could follow his progress even through the soaring stalks of wild rye. But around the time they reached the middle of the plateau he saw the beast stop suddenly and stand tall. Day knew that look – he held up a fist and froze.

They were well into the meadow. The ledge sheltered them from the east but they were exposed in all other directions. And in the grass lay something...

The elk huffed, blowing clouds of vapor in the chill air. A *snap* came from the forest and a few of the deer looked up but not in alarm: a branch had fallen.

There were close to thirty deer overall, mulies for the most part though others were smaller and had a shape like pronghorn antelope. Of the mule deer an adult buck stood aloof. He and the largest herd were at the edge of the plain, near the draw where the llama had disappeared. The elk were closest to the trees. The young bull snatched a mouthful of grass and raised his head toward the Settlers, chewing in a rotary fashion. The great dog was a statue. The men, too, hoped to blend into the terrain.

The dog's head twitched. His bent ear rose as he focused on a spot halfway to the elk. Day hissed to call him back but instead the dog bounded forward.

There was a cry and a man burst from the grass. Short, lithe, wearing hides and superbly camouflaged, he was surprised and terrified by the sudden appearance of something that looked like a great, shaggy wolf. Flushed from cover, his outburst spooked the deer and they scattered. As they did three more figures jumped up and threw spears at the closest doe. She stumbled and let out a plaintive bleat.

The big dog beat a retreat. Whatever he had expected to encounter, it was not this. And anyway, the man he flushed was not a threat.

The herds went in all directions now, each hurrying to the nearest cover. The buck led its group into the draw while others disappeared into the forest. A few raced across the plain in great bounds, soaring over the grass and onto the ledge.

The elk ran for the trees but as they neared them an explosion of movement erupted from the forest's edge. The elk spun around and sprinted into the meadow as a lion burst from the woods. The enormous cat had tracked the herd to the edge of the grass only to have them unexpectedly flushed toward him; now he had the advantage of surprise and proximity. Within seconds he was one leap behind the young bull.

The hunters were caught exposed, especially the fourth man who had raced to get away from the dog. Hurrying after the injured deer they were now charged broadside by the fleeing elk. Three leaped aside and avoided a collision but the fourth was sent flying as the crippled bull, realizing it could not escape, hit the brakes and turned to meet the lion.

The elk never saw the Indian as it whipped its head around. The antlers tore across the lion's flank, opening a great gash just as the cat plowed into the elk. The momentum of the lion's rush sent both animals rolling. The lion was up in a flash. It leaped on the bull as the latter struggled to its feet. The cat was massive: splayed across the elk's back he almost hid it from view. Yet it was a testament to the bull's own great strength that even then it spun again and threw the cat clear. But with a bad leg there was no avoiding the inevitable. The bull made it ten yards before the cat hit him again, knocking him sideways and going for the throat with powerful jaws. The elk bawled and staggered. Together the two went down in a maelstrom of pollen and dust. The bawling continued as did the sounds of struggle.

The Settlers remained frozen, in part because it was not clear where they could go that was safe. Deer had raced to their left while the surviving elk thundered up the ridge to their right. Now the lion downed its prey directly before them. Even the dog had gone to ground, unsure what to do. But as the action settled and the death throes of the bull quickened, the great beast made up its mind. He dashed for the cleft they had been heading for. Day followed, his grip so tight on the Weatherby his knuckles hurt. Roland did likewise, though with reluctance. When he joined Day at the edge of the meadow his granite face was flush with excitement.

"That's no African lion," he declared as though Day had suggested it was. "No mane...and he's alone. Did you see that skull? Like a jaguar: rectangular, *huge* jaws. The books are wrong – it's a separate species."

"Oh, good," Day replied, his heart racing. "Glad to hear it. It's new to science. Was worried I might have missed something about mutant cats."

They peered over a rise, watching the lion tear at the elk.

"Unbelievable...he must be eight feet long. Nine hundred pounds if he's an ounce."

The hunters had disappeared, three at least probably to the south where the injured deer had headed. Day was about to comment on them when something moved at the edge of the meadow. He nudged Roland.

Across the rise the rye gave way to Indian paintbrush and bitterroot that grew waist-high. The stalks shivered as an arm appeared, then a head. Finally the fourth native dragged himself into view. He was trailing blood, his bow was gone, and the grass camouflage that had hidden him so well was in shreds. He made it to the base of the rise and collapsed.

Day studied the scene, thinking. Crazy John's trail was behind them, through the cleft and down the back side of the plateau. The great dog was already exploring there, sniffing and prowling among the trees, unconcerned about the ruckus he had caused. They needed to close the gap on the Prog and follow him into the next valley.

Roland, too, looked down the trail they had to follow. The land stayed level as far as they could see but the shape of the hills suggested it descended soon enough.

"John'll be making good time," Day suggested. "We should get after him."

"Your buddy Galt wouldn't want us to intervene in anything local," Roland agreed.

"On the other hand, that caveman might have been alright except for the damned dog…"

Neither of the men moved. The chitter of cicadas rose again from the meadow, the only sound except for the ripping and tearing of the lion.

But after a bit Day swore. He reached into his duffel and pulled out a canvas roll. Leaving the bag and followed by Roland, he crept around the rise and along the meadow's edge.

The native was on the edge of consciousness. The antler had raked his right arm and shoulder and torn them open, leaving a bloody mess. In addition he had a lump over his right ear that bespoke a concussion. The Settlers dragged him out of the meadow. Day unrolled the canvas to reveal a trauma kit.

"Hope it's complete," Roland commented after examining the man. He grabbed several quick-clot bandages and jammed them into the deepest wounds. "His brachial artery's intact but the rest of this will need sewing."

"If he doesn't die from shock first…"

Day spun a log around to put under the native's feet and raise them off the ground. He checked the pulse and airway, then gave the man a shot of atropine. From the kit he pulled a shiny square that unfolded into a flashy space blanket. Without getting in Roland's way he wrapped and tucked that tight around the native, leaving only the injured area clear.

The native's biceps tendon was torn but they decided there was nothing they could do about that. Once the bleeding had stopped Roland stitched together the smaller ligaments and muscle using needles and sutures. They cleaned the wound and the man's upper torso, then closed the injuries with a combination of tape and aerosol bandage. When they finished Day gave the man a shot of antibiotic. They moved him into the sun still wrapped in the blanket.

"He won't be pitching for the Rangers but he might survive to kill another deer," Roland mused. "Good thing you brought all that. How much is left in case I get shot or gored?"

"So long as you don't do both you'll be alright." Day cleaned and secured his kit. "Now what do we do with him?"

"Leave him," Roland advised. "He's not in shock at least. Not for now, anyway. This blanket should keep him warm until his friends get back."

He studied the native's round and weather-beaten face. The man had brown skin and a low forehead hidden in matted hair. A half-circle opening downward, like a shell or a moon, was daubed in clay on each wrinkled cheek. The Indian could have been any age. He looked strong and his breathing was level, but he was unconscious and they could only guess at his recovery.

Day poured water over the man's head. When he did the man woke so he also poured some into his mouth. The native swallowed and his eyes flickered.

"You'll live," Day told him. "In the long run I don't know if that's good or bad, but I can't keep guessing about the long run. It's too confusing."

Roland found the native's spear close by in the grass. He examined it, keeping a wary eye on the lion.

"This is functional," he allowed, admiring the length and straightness of the shaft, which was made of spruce and about five feet long. He held it in one hand, testing its balance, then studied the point. "And this is not Clovis," he murmured in surprise.

"What's that?"

Roland ran a finger along the spear point, the face of which was as wide as his thumb and shaped like a leaf. "Before the Bronze Age all spear points, arrowheads, and darts were – are – chipped out of rock, like this one," he explained. "The earliest ones we know in North America are the Clovis points, but this isn't one. Clovis points have fine edges and grooves on each side. This one doesn't."

"So another revolution in archeological thought?" Day asked, still kneeling over the Indian and uninterested in spear ballistics.

"No. We know there were other styles before the Clovis point. We just have trouble placing them in the right time frame."

"Well, this guy's time frame should extend past today if the lion doesn't have him for dessert," Day commented. He gave the native a final gulp of water and then stood up. "We need to move."

Roland placed the spear within reach of the injured man. He touched the native's arm and mumbled something in Comanche. "It's a prayer for healing," he explained. "With my luck your descendants will be Crow and I'll regret it, but it's the best I can do."

"I hope you don't regret it," Day muttered. "I also hope we didn't just change history by inspiring his tribe to invent HemCon bandages. Let's go. His buddies may be back soon."

They slipped away but not before Roland took another long look at the native. The man was short; wrapped in the foil blanket he looked like a hairy burrito or a space age papoose. But even broken and bloody there was strength in him. He was a rough-hewn creature of a hard, harsh world, a true American aborigine. Roland was not sure whether to feel inspired or disappointed that this man was his ancestor. For his part, the native looked at the Settler in confusion, struggling to understand what was happening.

"Don't bother," Roland advised. "And don't get eaten." With a tap on his chest as a farewell gesture, he slipped behind the rise and followed Day off the plateau.

10

The cleft was a break in the hills that rimmed the meadow like a lip on a bowl. Once through, the Settlers found a series of smaller fields dotted with trees and boulders that funneled them to the west. These eventually joined up with the draw the llama and deer had used for their escape. They knew it was the same because they spooked the deer again, the buck giving them an annoyed glance before flashing his tail and trotting up and over the opposite ridge. But as Roland had noted before, the herd's departure was almost leisurely: humans did not generate nearly the panic that a four-legged predator did.

Crazy John's tracks turned south with the draw and disappeared but then picked up again when the land flowed into a larger ravine leading back to the west. Day figured that as the crow flies they had traveled no more than ten miles from the watering hole, but had the crow been trudging along with them he would have gone twice as far.

By late afternoon they had lost all the altitude they had gained on the south side of the ridge. The ravine narrowed, forcing them to slow as they watched for an ambush, but John's trail never deviated. When the walls again pushed back they caught glimpses of the valley beyond. The creek in the ravine bottom had run a stepped course until then, with flat stretches interrupted by low falls whose sound echoed off the rock walls; now it matured into a quiet brook. The water's serpentine path showed less urgency and a sense it was nearing its destination.

"He's close," Roland said, kneeling at the water's edge. "Not half an hour ahead. Still not walking great. Looks like he might have twisted his ankle."

"What about these?" Day asked. Yards off the creek were more prints, shallow and less defined. "These are going the same way."

Roland took a look. "They're older," he decided after some study. "A few days. Several individuals...and they're not gringos."

"Not Progs?"

"Not Progs. The step is different. Shorter, softer, with the weight on the ball of the foot. Besides, if the survivors are like John and Sorley, they've still got shoes or boots. These prints are made by hides, and this one here is barefoot."

"So whoever it is, they're not tracking him. They were here first."

"Right. They're just traveling. This ravine leads to the high meadows or across the ridge the way we came so it's probably a common route for any indigenous people."

Day frowned. "But crossing just to cross doesn't makes sense," he said.

"No, it doesn't." Roland nodded toward the setting sun. "The pass is only a few miles that way. Why come here?"

"Exactly."

"Sorley said Reed was teaming up with natives in the pass. But Crazy John seemed to disagree."

"And John didn't use the pass to come to the lake. It would have been easier but he went over the top."

"That he did."

Day studied the tracks. "Let's get out of this ravine and get eyes on the lake," he suggested. "If there's a camp, John will arrive there soon. His story should provoke a reaction and we might get an idea of what we're up against."

Roland pointed with his bow. "Half a mile that way, then right. Another mile to the lake."

"How do you know that?" Day asked.

"Paleface read map, redskin read land," Roland replied. He said it with a straight face.

Yeah, well, redskin can't make a bow that shoots straight, Day wanted to reply but didn't. Instead he shouldered his bag and followed as Roland set off down the ravine. Sure enough, in fifteen minutes they came to the mouth. The walls flared and fell away, flowing into the valley at an angle. The stream turned right as Roland had promised and the lake – a shimmering disk almost hidden in tall reeds – was no more than a mile and a half distant.

"The pass is to the left," Roland explained. "You'll never find a lake at the bottom of a pass."

"But how did you know it was so close?"

"I saw geese headed this way flying low. There's nothing in nature more efficient than a goose and they wouldn't have been low unless they were headed for water."

"Clever," Day allowed. "Remind me to hire you for nature hikes back home. Now let's figure out how many guys are at the camp and how they're armed."

Day crawled through the grass until reaching a rock promontory that stood like a shark's tooth outside the ravine walls. He looked through his rifle scope and scanned the land by the lake. The reeds and sedge obscured the view but there were signs of human activity.

"Somebody's living there," he said. "There's smoke, and three...no, four huts. They don't look new."

"There's John," Roland pointed.

Crazy John was still half a mile from the camp, struggling through marshland that stretched wide across this corner of the valley. The creek itself went to the lake and it was unclear where the excess water came from to cause the marsh but John was having to negotiate it, step by sodden step.

Day set the rifle down and looked around. It felt good to be out of the ravine. The valley curved so only a few miles of it were visible but even that seemed vast after staring at steep walls for hours. The western side of the valley was covered in snow above the tree line, capped with an alpine glacier that sat astride the crest. The ridge opposite was forested and dry. Everywhere between was green and yellow, the colors of a wet summer.

The lake, really a large pond about ten acres in area, sat in the southeast corner of the valley. The lodges behind it stood flush against the forest where the trees grew on rising land until their trunks rose parallel to the slopes themselves.

"We need to get closer," he said. "And we need elevation."

From their present spot it was hard to see what options they had so Roland, staying low, went to the creek and slipped into the water. The course there was shallow but as the creek leveled out in the valley it deepened. Willows grew to nine feet along its banks and formed a canopy overhead, allowing him to disappear even while he moved far from the ravine to survey the adjacent terrain. When he returned he was soaked but triumphant.

"There are two or three places along the valley wall that would be good lookouts," he reported. "We'll get a good view of the camp at any of them."

Day nodded. "Then let's do that. Back about two hundred yards there was a game trail up to the ridge. We can get to the top there and cross over. We'll need to make camp soon anyway and I want to do it with a view that'll give us options."

They re-entered the ravine and found the game trail. It zigzagged up the wall until topping the ridge and entering a rocky field dotted with sage and larkspur. From there they moved across open land parallel to the valley's rim. The great dog led the way, wandering wide and inspecting everything.

The terrain was uneven and slow-going. The sun was below the horizon by the time they reached the most distant outcropping that Roland had spotted from the creek. It was a quarter mile from the lake and a hundred feet above it and provided the last unobstructed view of the camp before forest subsumed the valley walls.

"Just in time," Day commented as they peered out between shrubs that clung to the cliff's edge. "Looks like John arrived."

"And they don't look happy to see him," Roland added.

Day counted six people who emerged from the huts to greet Crazy John, who collapsed in the clearing as he emerged from the marsh. Except for the occasional waving of the arms he did not move after that, while two men came close and spoke to him. The others stood back, listening. Whatever he said caused a flurry of activity. Day watched through his scope.

"I can't tell who's who," he said, studying the figures who now hurried from lodge to lodge. "Nobody looks like their picture. Grooming standards have fallen by the wayside, it seems, and everyone's running for a weapon..."

The huts were of simple construction, stout limbs supporting layers of hides and pine boughs. The camp looked to be a seasonal site rather than a permanent dwelling place. Whatever it was, it was a mess, with tools and firewood and reed baskets in various stages of completion scattered in the dirt. There were two firepits, each with a small fire going. One had a spit suspended over it that held what might have been a rabbit. An improvised drying rack stood next to a hut with a deer hide thrown over it.

The men closest to John alternately quizzed him and berated him. John responded by waving his arms and then curling into a ball in the dirt. The taller of the two men stalked away and disappeared into the trees at the back of the camp. In a while he re-emerged with two more figures.

"Hang on," Day adjusted his scope to its highest magnification. "Those aren't Progs."

Roland lay flat beside him, studying the scene with just his eyes. "No," he agreed. "They're natives."

The natives wore animal hides and each had something in his hair. After a bit, Day confirmed through his scope that the decoration was a feather or feathers, not sticking up but laid flat above the ear.

The tall man led the natives to John. There all three squatted and conversed with much pointing, pantomime, and drawing in the dirt with a stick. The light faded but Day watched until they finished. The tall man seemed frustrated: he appeared to want something from the natives immediately while they spent a lot of time talking between themselves and tapping the ground. In the end the natives rose and disappeared back into the trees behind the camp. Day watched but they did not reappear. The rest of the camp residents dispersed to their lodges, re-emerging frequently to gather and argue and stare up the valley toward the ravine. Nobody helped Crazy John. Eventually he struggled to his feet and staggered to a small hut almost hidden in trees at the end of the clearing. It was dilapidated but intact and he crawled inside.

"I counted two long guns," Day said, laying aside his own rifle. "Whatever the others were carrying looked homemade."

In the twilight Roland's features remained impassive. He moved back from the rim and went to work on his bow, using a tiny reamer to smooth the edges of the small sight window he had cut into the wood. Roland used every available moment to perfect his weapon but Day sensed disquiet.

"I know what you're thinking," he told his companion. "You're worried about the natives."

Roland produced a strip of jerky from somewhere and chewed thoughtfully. Day noticed that for someone who traveled light Roland managed to eat all day, either pulling food from bottomless pockets or foraging berries, roots, and nuts as they walked. He and the huge dog viewed nature as a giant buffet. Even now the shaggy beast wandered off into the brush and scared up a marmot for dinner.

"I'm worried about the natives," Roland agreed. "I don't know what they're doing with these Progs or the limits of their loyalty, but if the Indians will fight for Reed that's a problem."

"We can't kill them," Day pointed out.

"You don't need to tell me," his companion said. "If we choke one of these guys we could wipe out the Assiniboine nation, not to mention me. How would that work? You kill a native and I might drop dead?"

"Let's not find out."

"Make sure you tell your dog."

"He wouldn't listen."

As they spoke the huge beast wandered back into their vicinity, fur from the marmot hanging at his jaw. Day looked at him and said, "Sit." The animal looked at Day like he had two heads. He put his nose to the ground and sniffed around for a bit before finding a scent and trotting away again.

"See?"

Venus and Saturn appeared overhead. Enough light remained to scan the plateau but colors departed and shapes merged. Not for the first time it felt to Day as though they were the only ones left in the world.

"What's his name?" Roland asked.

"Who?"

"That musk ox with fangs that you call a dog."

"Oh. No idea."

"You haven't given him a name?"

"No."

"Why not?"

"He's not mine to name."

Roland lifted an eyebrow. "How Jainistic."

Day slid away from the rim and put the duffel in a position where he could lean against it. He settled in and got as comfortable as the rocky soil allowed.

"I don't own him," he said. "He does his own thing. I don't know why he hangs around. Never have. And he wouldn't answer to anything I called him anyway."

"Where'd you get him?"

Day rubbed his thighs to warm his hands. "Two years ago, just before...everything happened, we were camping in Montana. Cheryl and the kids were at a creek looking for crayfish. They walked up on a black bear, a mama. We never saw the cubs but they must have been nearby because she charged. That dog came out of nowhere and cut her off. He wasn't as big then but he was just as ugly and almost as mean. Scared Cheryl as much as the bear did." Day paused, remembering. "I almost shot both him and the bear but since he was between her and the kids I didn't. That bear quit soon enough. When it was all over he stuck around and we kept him. Believe it or not, he was good with the kids..."

Night fell and stars once again swept across the sky in an endless field. Clouds moved in and a sprinkle of rain passed over. Lightning danced on the horizon.

"You've never asked," Day said softly, one ear always tuned to the sounds of the night, "but my plan was to catch the Progs together and herd them back to where we arrived."

"To transport them back to Shell?"

"Yeah."

Roland considered that and then asked, "How's that plan working?"

"Not well," Day admitted. "We've got two groups so far, King's party in the plains and this one by the lake, but the numbers don't add up. The way Sorley talked, King has a handful of people with him. Add seven here at the lake, including Crazy John, and that makes a dozen or so. Galt's best guess for who escaped the Tri Border raid was twice that. Subtract Kurtz's tally and our unknown tattooed guy and eight or nine are still missing."

"Maybe they're dead."

"Maybe. Or they're in the pass. Crazy John said everyone was there but either he lied or things changed since he left. Most likely he lied. If they're dead, they're no longer our problem. But if they're alive then they're at a third location and we need to find them."

Crazy John had reached the camp around the south end of the lake, which the Settlers perceived was a salt flat that collected discharge from the same creek flowing out of the ravine. Surrounding it were fresh-water marshes and small ponds created by artesian wells that bubbled everywhere the creek did not flow. Though the lake water was undrinkable and probably devoid of much life, the camp's location still made sense from both a practical and defensive standpoint. There was fresh water in abundance from the ponds, as well as waterfowl and – doubtless – fish. Also, any attacker would have to navigate the narrow ridges of dry land running between the ponds to reach the camp.

To avoid being thus exposed, Day proposed an alternate approach. From their ridge the valley walls dropped steeply to the ponds. Climbing down was dangerous, especially in the early morning darkness when they planned to assault the camp. So instead they moved along the plateau rim at just after four in the morning, twining their way through the sage heading for the curve of the valley above the camp. There the slope was more gradual. In addition, it offered concealment in the form of the wide ribbon of birch and aspen that spread up from the camp all the way to the rim. Not only did the trees provide cover but fallen leaves, too, made for a quiet and forgiving descent that would allow the Settlers to drop into the camp from behind and catch its inhabitants unaware.

That was the plan and it was a good plan right up until it fell apart as they neared the descent point. Day was scouting along the rim looking for the best spot to drop down and enter the forest when the great dog suddenly spun and faced into the plateau, a fearsome growl erupting from its throat. At the same moment there was movement to their right. Out of the darkness something charged. The great beast leaped to meet it and against the starry background of the waning night the two shadows met in a tearing, snarling collision.

It happened in seconds. Roland reacted first, pivoting and loosing an arrow at a second shape whose dim silhouette appeared above the horizon. There was a yelp of pain as the arrow found its target.

Day raised his rifle. Its scope was not infrared but it concentrated available light, enough for him to catch a third dire wolf in mid-leap less than fifty feet away. He fired, the crash of the Weatherby splitting the night and echoing across the plateau. An anguished cry followed as the targeted wolf whirled and snapped at the wound delivered by the unseen foe.

"Clear!" Roland hissed, letting Day know his position before the rifleman fired again. He crossed behind Day, another arrow at the ready. But now there was no clear target. A tremendous struggle raged somewhere in the high grass and it was impossible to distinguish exactly where and how many the great dog was fighting. All they could do was wait.

And a terrible wait it was. With only a hint of light on the horizon the men had to rely on sound alone to follow the mortal battle happening yards away. It lasted only moments though it seemed like forever, then suddenly it ended with a howl followed by a *crack*. A shape escaped, stumbling to the left and moving deeper into the meadow. The men held their fire.

"You going to go look?" Roland whispered after a bit.

"Hell, no."

"What if your dog's injured?"

"Then the last place I want to be is anywhere near him."

They retreated to the rim where Day gazed down toward the Prog camp. Fog sat in the valley, its opaque vapors reaching up the treed slope. In the thin light of dawn it looked solid and impenetrable, like a glaze of ice sculpted for the specific purpose of hindering their mission.

"So much for surprise," he muttered. He comforted himself with the knowledge that the Progs, having heard the shot fired, would now be confused as to where or when an attack would come.

He hunkered down and waited. He had been willing to creep through the woods in the darkness when he thought the Progs would be looking the other way but now that they were alerted he and Roland would need to delay until first light. By then they could also find out how the great beast had fared.

After a while another shape hurried away across the plateau. Day's heart sank. As soon as there was enough light he and Roland crept forward. But what they found at the scene of the battle surprised them both.

"Son of a gun..." Roland said softly. A dire wolf, easily a hundred and fifty pounds of canine savagery, lay ripped open in a pool of blood in the matted grass.

Day breathed in relief and studied the tracks.

"There's a second wolf," he pointed. "It's injured and the dog's gone after him. I should have expected that. He's a vindictive bastard."

In the gray dawn Roland searched the ground. "I think that's the one I hit," he said. A moment later he spied a third set of tracks, a bloody spoor leading in the opposite direction. He followed them and after a short distance signaled to

Day. In a fissure where the sage ended and grassland picked up, the third wolf lay bleeding to death behind a boulder. The shell from the Weatherby had hit it somewhere near its right hip and had taken off most of that leg. Yet it was a measure of the power of the animal that it had still been able to crawl so far. The wolf was heavyset with dark red fur, long ears, and a long snout with fangs on both top and bottom jaws. The fangs clicked and the wolf's eyes followed the men as they approached but the animal was fading fast. It had no energy to do anything but gasp for breath. Yet even when lying helpless it was a terrifying creature to behold.

"Let's get down to the camp," Day said.

"You don't want to follow your dog?"

"Nope. If he lives through a second fight, he'll catch up."

11

The camp was empty.

At the bottom of the hill Day and Roland crouched and studied the clearing. Fog smothered everything within a mile of the ponds but it could not hide that the camp was deserted. The fires smoldered, the huts were quiet, the tools gone.

"They went north," Roland reported after studying the tracks. "They followed a game trail between the north pond and the ridge. Maybe three hours ago."

Day explored the huts. He found a few booby-traps but nothing that showed expertise. They were desperate efforts completed in a hurry. The huts themselves were spare and reeked of human poverty: loose reeds thrown down for beds; chewed animal bones; mussel shells piled in the corner. Flute's hut was the worst: cobwebs and a cast off beaver pelt covered in lice.

"They're regressing," Day commented. "They won't last long living like this."

Roland wasn't so sure. "They've lasted months already," he noted. "I told you, I did graduate work in inner cities. On reservations, too... People can survive in filth longer than you think. Civilization is paper thin."

Day studied a clay bowl near one of the fires. It held a small quantity of what looked like petroleum jelly. He held it out to Roland. "Duck?" he asked.

Roland sniffed the bowl and rubbed the fat between his fingers.

"Bear. Oil boiled off the fat. It's smoother and lasts longer. Same as was on Sorley's rifle. Did you notice those guns were clean – not a bit of rust?"

"I noticed."

"Someone in their group knows how to take care of weapons even in an austere environment," Roland concluded.

"Someone also knows how to kill a bear."

"Makes me wonder if they have more ammo than we think."

"I was wondering the same," Day said. "Why put so much effort into keeping your guns clean if you're running out of bullets?"

They delayed to see if the fog would lift but it did not. Instead it thickened, with fresh billows floating in off the ponds. There was no way to tell how long it might last so eventually, with reluctance, Day pointed up the trail.

There in the flat light visibility was minimal. Hearing was excellent, as was smell, but in the moist air neither of those senses was directional and they confused as much as they helped. Both men focused on the ground to follow the trail while letting their ears and nose do what they could to warn of anything coming up. The Indian stepped through the wet grass with no noise and great deliberation, stopping when he found something interesting and using his bow like a divining rod to prod or study clues.

After a hundred yards they heard a splash. A half-mile later they were well into the valley, still enveloped in cloud, when a noise on the trail made them drop and prepare to fight. But out of the gloom appeared their four-legged, erstwhile companion. Wet from his swim, the great dog trotted by with a spring in his step. Patches of fur were absent from one shoulder and at his throat and there was a cut on his muzzle, but those were his only injuries. He barely acknowledged Day but glared at Roland as he passed. Then he vanished again into the swirls of mist.

"Okay," the Indian whispered. "I'm a believer. If that puppy just killed two dire wolves and is still dancing, he's my new best friend."

Day studied the fog where the dog had disappeared and simply shook his head.

The Progs' trail left the game path but soon merged with another. This one held to the side of the valley until the ground began to roll and widen as it curved to the west. The fog thinned and hung in the air in strips.

Knee-high yellow and green grasses spread before them now in muted hues, rising and falling in meadows that rolled down to marshland on their left. Opposite the marshes, lodgepole pines loomed on the hill. Dark spruces and firs grew among them, filling the understory and seeming to grow out of the fog that flowed at their feet. As the sun crested the horizon wrapped in clouds of its own, the ponds and willows fell behind.

Now the valley became a vale, a high-altitude wetland, with the hills lowering on either side and slender courses of spring-fed water snaking through in random patterns. Even without the fog the terrain was damp and the grasses lusher than what had grown on the higher plateau. Poplar and cottonwood trees dotted the land between the hills, dividing the marshes with compact groves that stood like bystanders in a vast park. Not all the vale was visible at once but as they moved north the portions fit into one tableau. In the distance was another pond and behind it stood a knoll awash in clover. After that the hills rose again and the vale curved out of sight.

Day knelt, both to stay hidden in the dissolving fog and to study the trail.

"They're in a hurry," he said, looking at marks in the mud where someone had slipped. "Like they've got a destination and a timeline. This print over here looks like Crazy John...even he's moving quicker than he did yesterday."

Roland lay prone to examine the ground, then moved off to the right and disappeared for several minutes. When he returned he crawled close to Day.

"How many tracks are you counting?" he asked.

"Seven."

"There are eight. A native is in the lead and his tracks get trampled by those behind, but he's there. And look at these two." Roland pointed to prints on opposite sides of the trail. Both were faint, almost invisible, even in the damp soil.

"They're unshod," Day agreed. "But they're Progs. I figured their shoes have given out or they've lost them."

"That's what I thought. But this guy found his all of a sudden. Look: he stopped here, put all his weight on one foot, then again over here but this time it's a boot track, some kind of a day hiker type. And then he splits off from the main party." Roland pointed to a broken spider web and an overturned stone the size of a nickel. "He heads that way along the ridge bottom while everyone else veers west."

"Is the ground rougher over there?"

"No."

"So a guy who's doing a good job masking his trail suddenly pulls on his LL Beans and goes solo. Think they're trying to split us up?"

"Could be, but even with boots he's careful. His trail isn't that obvious. It could be an ambush: the main party leads us into the open while he swings right to snipe from the tree line. Where's your dog?"

"Up ahead somewhere. He won't follow the trail directly. He'll wander left and right and cross it only occasionally to make sure it's still there."

"Smart."

"I don't know if he's smart or just has the attention span of a goldfish, but it's what he does."

Day considered the situation. In his experience only ten percent of hunting depended on action and movement. The other ninety percent relied on out-thinking your prey. What were the Progs up to?

"We can't have someone loose on our flank," he decided. "You take care of him. I'll continue on the trail."

Roland nodded. "Do we need him alive?" he asked.

"I won't tell you how to do your job," Day replied.

The Indian slipped away.

Lace Stevens had a Savage Arms MSR 10 Long Range rifle chambered in .308 Winchester. Even better, he now had a full magazine of 20 rounds, thanks to ammo dropped by Matteus Kurtzen in that Settler's unsuccessful foray into the region. And as a former Los Angeles County sheriff's deputy and experienced hunter, Stevens knew how to use each one of those rounds with lethal accuracy.

He moved north along the bottom of the ridge, staying inside the trees. The ground rolled and he wanted to find a spot that gave him an angle for shooting along the troughs. Enfilade, the infantry called it, recalling his short stint in the Army. He also wanted to be able to look back down his own trail in case he was followed. He did not expect to be but then he did not know who exactly was following them. Crazy John had brought word of the new Settlers but the old hippie had been short on details. John was a physical and mental mess, barely able to string words into a sentence. Stevens was amazed the Oregon psychopath had survived as long as he had but the old man seemed indestructible. He was able to live on berries and roots and no matter how mad he went in his head his body just kept going. Too mean to die, Stevens guessed.

A couple of football fields beyond where Stevens split from the others he found his perch. The forest dipped and reached onto the vale floor where a spring trickled out of the trees. Tall grass grew along the rivulet and offered concealment. Best of all, the spot had an excellent view both back along his trail as well as down the ripples of land that anyone crossing the vale would have to traverse.

He stopped short of the trickling water and listened. The forest was still. Enough that when a mountain chickadee whipped past his head and lighted on a nearby twig, the sound was almost disruptive. That was good. He was alone.

Stevens crept forward, then turned and followed the water's course downhill. Crawling through the grass, he worked his way to a position just past the last tree, a broad Engelmann spruce with long cones that dripped dew in an unhurried rain. From there he could scan 120 degrees of the landscape while keeping himself and his rifle hidden. He estimated the distance to his companions' trail at just under two hundred yards; the drop was maybe thirty feet. It was a good position. If he caught the Settlers in the open he could hit them at that range. His weapon was capable and he was, too. Authorities back in California and Nevada would attest to that.

Back in California... Stevens wondered what was going on in his home state. Probably some massive lockdown and roundup of anyone who had supported the uprising. Even before he and the Progs had teleported out of Jackson – for that is what he was now sure had happened – the whole west coast had been under martial law. He assumed nothing had changed since then. Or had it? Maybe things were getting back to normal. Not everyone in the state was looney; maybe once the wackos had been killed or chased out, life would be alright again.

Stevens shook his head at the irony. Only a few years earlier he had been a respected policeman with a job and a pension pending. Not political himself, he had fallen in with the Progs out of bitterness after his firing from the Highway Patrol. He had been caught stealing from crime scenes – which was a crock because he had done it only twice and nothing he took ever affected an investigation. But that investigation led to a deeper look into his activities, which turned up that he had also been tipping off the local Crips to impending raids. The union never backed him on either charge. Nor did his own colleagues, the bastards. They had turned on him as though they themselves were as pure as the driven snow. He had tried to cop a plea with the prosecutor by naming other dirty cops he knew – guys who were doing a lot worse than tipping off a few drug smugglers – but that only made things worse. Eighteen years in uniform went down the drain.

It was not just the money lost that overturned his world. It was the status, the loss of respect. In uniform he had been somebody. Out of uniform he was just another guy looking for a job. With a rap sheet, no less. That was hard. Harder than he would have imagined.

He realized now that when the uprising happened he should have offered his services back to the CHP, or maybe to the National Guard. But the momentum at the start seemed to be with the Progs. Besides, by then he was so angry at his holier-than-thou former colleagues that he saw the insurrection as a chance to get even. It was Reuben and Ray, his contacts in the Crips, who linked him with the lefties. The gang had made a deal of convenience with the Progs, who were looking for more muscle and firepower to join them. Stevens helped the groups loot a CHP armory, then gave them training in the weapons. After that, it was all downhill. Mayhem, really, kill-or-be-killed as the violence spread. Now Reuben was missing and probably dead and here he was, lying in the mud trying to get revenge against the guys who killed him – guys who might have been cops themselves once upon a time – all while trapped in some alternate reality with no clear way out. Yeah, how was that for irony?

There was movement in the meadow. The fog hid more than it revealed but in a break in the mist Stevens saw the rest of his party moving across the fields at the right of the tableau. They had left the game trail and were cutting a straight line toward a beaver pond that flooded one of the meadows. The Indian, the one they called Puff because of his addiction to smoking sweet grass, was in the lead by many yards. Even from a distance Stevens could make out the tribal markings drawn on the Indian's arms and torso with campfire ash, arrowhead figures that Puff restored and refined each morning. He had short legs but took long strides that carried him steadily across the vale while Eric Wulff and Ray Williams tried to get the others to keep up. Ray was placid as ever but Stevens could tell Wulff was frustrated at his companions' slow pace. Lace sympathized. Wulff was aloof but he was tough and he knew the outdoors, and more than anyone else he and Stevens had kept the rest of the group alive since the beginning. It was hard enough having to coddle these idiots even when they were not being hunted. Now that someone was on their trail the urban Progs were nothing but a burden.

Stevens studied the trail back to the ponds. It was difficult to see anything for certain: the farther south he looked, the thicker the fog hung in the air. But there were gaps, breaches in the vapors where he could make out the yellow-green grass that dominated the land.

He sighted his rifle and squinted through the scope, trying to penetrate the fog. The scope was an old Nikon. It was not powerful but it was good enough and had proven itself hardy in their austere environment. There was a crack in the lens suffered when Stevens fell off a trail a month after their escape from the Wylder Ranch; amazingly, the optics still worked though every time he had to look past the crack he gritted his teeth, remembering the fall.

They had been trekking west of the pass on one of their many early explorations, trying to learn where they were and if any civilization was around, when Noah Abrams had spooked some kind of a moose. The animal was *enormous* and charged down their trail, forcing everyone to scatter. Stevens ran but found himself confronted by a rockslide, the upper levels of a moraine. He leaped into it and saved his life, for the moose had to stop, but Stevens had slipped twice on the unforgiving quartzite. The second time he fell he nearly broke his shoulder in addition to damaging the scope.

That rockslide was cursed. He crossed it a second time some weeks later and fell again. That time he avoided injury but worse, he dropped his favorite weapon, a Ruger .556 that he had had for years. The rifle fell into a gap between boulders and dropped out of reach. He spent days trying to retrieve it – when the sun was overhead, the stock was in sight about ten feet down – but the weapon was jammed. Despite many desperate efforts it remained out of reach.

So now he was left with his .308 with its fraying strap, and a shoulder that woke him up most nights with an arthritic pain. At least the pain was tolerable once he was up and moving. And he could still shoot.

There...something moved down below. Stevens fixed his scope on a hillock shrouded in fog. Something had just run behind it. He tried to...*there it was again*. He squinted hard. What the hell was that? A timber wolf? No, too big. It was the size of those other wolves that had tormented them so much in the early days after their arrival in this strange land, but this creature's fur wasn't as dark. And this one seemed to be alone. Great, he thought. Another mutant carnivore to worry about.

The wolf disappeared again. Its hide was the color of the drifting fog and blended perfectly. Stevens wondered...wolves were not usually on this side of the pass. That was the whole reason the Progs had moved up from the watering hole, to get away from the pack that hunted there. Why was there only one, and why did it appear to be on the trail of the Progs? Or was it alone? Maybe there was a pack...

He peered over the scope. Sure enough, a minute or so later he saw movement farther up the trail. But this time the shape was different. He looked through the Nikon again and saw the outline of a man emerge from the fog. White male, stocky build, approximately five feet-eight inches tall, age unclear...Stevens ran through the standard police descriptive checklist out of habit. Heavy coat, wool cap pulled down over his ears, carrying a bolt action rifle with a scope. Stevens focused on the rifle. It looked nice.

"Definitely a Settler," he murmured. His first thought was whether the man knew there was a wolf not far in front of him. He felt a twinge of comradeship, or was it guilt? The man was a bounty hunter but he was a law enforcement type in his own way. But for a turn of fate their positions might be reversed. He had a sudden urge to try to contact the man. Warn him, even. Maybe they could make a deal...

But Stevens quelled the feeling. He was dreaming: there was no deal to be made. He had killed over twenty people. 23, to be exact. He had never killed a cop, for as bitter as he was toward the CHP he had still drawn a personal line that he would not cross, but he did not suppose that would matter to anyone but him. *In for a dime, in for a dollar,* he muttered, and his finger moved toward the trigger of the .308.

Day did not like his position. The trail ran through the meadows east of the marshes where the ground was elevated and drier and where it rose and fell in gentle waves. The trail thus avoided the wettest areas but there was not enough vegetation to provide cover or concealment. With the fog burning off he was about to be exposed.

He glanced right. The trees on the ridge were becoming visible through the mist, which meant he was becoming visible to whoever was up there. He could not see Roland and had no idea if he had tracked down the Prog yet or not. If Day was going to keep moving forward he had to find a way to do it unseen.

He backed up into the last patch of fog and dropped to his belly. The piebald grasses before him had been cropped by grazers and were not tall enough to hide inside. The marshes, on the other hand, were down the hill to his left and offered more cover. The first stream running through the marshes was only thirty yards away, bordered by bulrushes four feet high. If he kept the fog between him and the trees, he could scoot downslope and drop into cover there. The stream wound in lazy curves so his progress would be slow but its flow still paralleled the Progs' route. Better slow progress than none at all. And better to be alive and out of sight than shot dead when the fog evaporated.

Holding his rifle before him and sliding the duffel around to his back, Day crabbed left into the marsh. By the time he reached the water he was already wet through and slathered in mud. He had also managed to scoop a grasshopper into his sleeve; the insect now hopped irritatingly along his arm. But moments later he was among the rushes and hidden from view.

Up at the tree line, Stevens peered through his scope and waited for Day to re-appear. The patch of fog the Settler had backed into was only ten feet wide and shrinking. He had not come out either the left or the right side so he had to be there still.

"Time's up," Lace muttered as the last fog burned away. But when it did there was nothing behind it. The mists vanished to reveal an empty patch of grass.

Stevens froze. At first he assumed he must have missed the Settler slipping back up the trail. But no, that was impossible. His line of sight to the land behind the fog was clear. It took him a moment to realize what must have happened. The bounty hunter must have gone away from him, using the fog as a cover. That was it. He headed downslope to get into the high grass that flanked the brooks of the marsh. Okay, then. Now it was just a matter of watching the water course for...

Wait a minute... Stevens' mind raced and settled on a paralyzing thought. Why had the Settler done that? Why did he not just follow the trail? Had he seen something up ahead? Was he trying to circle left of Wulff and the others and cut them off? Or did he know that Stevens was up in the tree line hunting *him*?

Stevens had neglected to watch his own trail. He had been so wrapped up in the wolf and then the Settler he had forgotten about the second bounty hunter. But he had not heard anything. The forest was as still as ever, the dew dripping in its random patter. He twisted left and scanned back the way he had come. At the same moment he felt a sharp pain in his neck, a stabbing point just above his collar.

"Time's up," a voice said.

Day worked his way along the stream, staying behind the bulrushes. The stream was just a channel, a ditch two yards wide and one deep, with no edge or shore: the meadow came up to the bulrushes and stopped, then the bulrushes in turn stopped at the water. So once he was through the grass he was in the water where the only way forward was to wade through its icy flow.

The stream carved its way in sluggish oxbows through the soil of the marsh. Day pushed through it against the current, working his way north. He made progress but the water was frigid and he soon lost feeling in his legs. At least the going was easy. Besides being glacier-cold, the water was as clear as a window. He could see every stone on the bottom and every fish that swam past. It occurred to him that fishing in this valley – and era – must be incredible. He also wondered with trepidation if the mega fauna theory applied to creatures in the water.

It was with relief that after much walking he came to a break in the rushes where beaver had trampled the reeds flat. From around the next bend he heard running water: the dam, most likely. Confident he had moved far enough to have lost or confused any sniper, he crawled through the break to get his bearings.

A copse of aspen stood before him; hence the beavers' path. The trees shielded him from the hillside while to the north and northwest was the beaver pond. Sure enough, had he continued in the stream he would have encountered the dam in another minute.

He raised himself to look around. The aspen clustered on an oval patch of ground that was only ten yards across. In places he could see through it to the meadow beyond where his old trail would have taken him. With the stream behind him and the pond serving as a barrier to the north, he figured any Progs lying in ambush would likely be somewhere to his east, out in front of him on the far side of the trees. Together with the shooter on the hillside, they would hope to trap the Settlers in the strip of meadow between the forest and the pond.

Day stashed his duffel and moved left around the grove. It was hard to be stealthy with his legs numb so he took his time. On his elbows and knees he inched across the ground.

He had not gone far when he heard movement ahead, the scrape of cloth on cloth. He stopped.

Before him lay a belt of grass and wildflowers. He studied it, motionless. For a long while he saw and heard nothing. Then came the sound of cloth on cloth again and up from the ground popped a head. It rose as if from the soil itself. The person faced away from him and did not turn around before dropping down and disappearing.

Day waited. Minutes later the head popped up again. It had graying hair down past the shoulders but he could not tell if it belonged to a man or a woman. A hushed voice whispered across the grass. The Prog gestured to someone farther ahead, who whispered something back that sounded like a reprimand. The head disappeared once more.

Day crabbed right and moved into the trees. If he were laying an ambush he would spread his people in a picket line running along the pond's shore. It offered the best concealment from anyone coming up the valley and allowed each shooter to fire without interference. The downside was the escape route: with their backs to the pond the only way to retreat was the way Day had just come, crossing the pond's outflow and heading out into the marsh. But if their ambush was successful that would not matter.

In the shade of the aspen snow lay undisturbed atop the leaf litter. He moved through it on his belly, his face inches from the ground, trying to determine if the Progs had deployed the way he believed. It appeared to be the case. He heard more whispers but only off to his left. He also saw movement in the reeds farther out along the pond.

In the grove itself he saw no sign of a picket. It was hard to do a thorough search while flat on his stomach but he crawled inside the treeline and saw no foxholes or burrows – the only overturned dirt was from a fat poplar that had fallen against a clutch of aspens and toppled them like tenpins. A squirrel ran across one of the jumbled trunks and regarded him with suspicion, flashing its tail in annoyance.

Okay, then. It was a picket line of five or six, running from near the grove to the far end of the beaver pond and arranged at an angle to the game trail where the Progs expected the Settlers to approach. So long as their attention stayed focused on the trail, Day thought he might have a way to deal with that.

He reversed course, slipping backwards through the snow until emerging again from the west side of the grove. He then crawled around to the left as he had before and approached the gray-haired Prog from behind.

There was again the sound of cloth on cloth. The Prog appeared to be in a modified foxhole – literally something an animal had dug that the human had then improved – and rubbing arms and legs to stay warm. Setting his rifle aside, Day drew his Colt and crept within a foot of the hole, close enough to hear the person breathing.

Ahead of them in another hidden position someone else moved. The Prog near Day shifted, listening. Day waited...sure enough, in a few seconds the head popped up. Day lunged and swung the Colt, connecting below the Prog's ear. The person dropped back into the hole without a sound.

Day reached down, ready to strike again, but his caution was unneeded. He now saw that the Prog was a woman. Thin, short, dark skin but not black, south Asian features. He guessed this was Nancy Peal, once a DC lawyer and early activist with the Prog movement. She was married to Bill Galston, a leftist writer for various east coast papers, so Day guessed he might be somewhere nearby and maybe the person to whom she had been whispering. For now, though, she was out cold.

An AK-47 lay at the bottom of the hole, the only weapon in sight. He removed it and hid it near the pond, where tall cattails replaced the bulrushes along the stream. Then he moved forward in search of the next Prog position.

The second Prog was easier to find. This one was also in a hole but whoever it was had scooped out snow from the bottom and thrown it up onto the ground behind. The scattered chunks of ice betrayed the position. Day approached it swiftly, hidden from the farther pickets by a rise in the ground.

In the aspen to his right, the same squirrel had kept an eye on Day. Now he gave a vigorous flash of his tail and dashed off the fallen trunk, leaping to a tree where he could watch the action from a safe distance.

The Prog in the hole rose into view but instead of popping up as the first one had, he – for the build was definitely a man's – craned his neck away from Day, peering through the grass toward the meadows and the expected ambush. He wore a brown trapper's hat with the ear flaps down which both hid his face and restricted his peripheral vision. Day rose to strike but the Prog was just out of reach so he hesitated, hoping the man would turn around to whisper back to the unconscious Nancy Peal.

"Hey!"

The yell came from his right, in the trees. It startled both Day and the Prog, who spun to look and in so doing caught sight of the Settler behind him. A shot echoed across the grass as Day lunged forward and swung his Colt.

The Prog threw up his arm, blocking Day's blow. The butt of the revolver connected on the man's forehead but the impact was further blunted by the hat. The Prog stumbled as a second shot sounded. That bullet ripped a hole through the collar of Day's coat, a blaze of heat flashing across his neck.

Day dropped flat and extended his right arm to return fire, the Colt barking twice as he targeted a figure leaning across the fallen aspen and aiming at him in turn. The figure dropped out of sight.

But now the Prog in the hole re-emerged. The blow from the pistol had stunned him but not knocked him out; he exploded from his hiding spot in desperate fury. With both hands he seized Day's outstretched arm and wrenched it up, almost dislocating Day's shoulder. Coming out of the hole, he pivoted on the ground and whipped a knee forward to strike Day in the face. Day pivoted in turn and took the blow across his shoulders where it lost much of its force, at a cost of putting his back to the Prog.

From beyond the rise came the sound of gunfire. There were shouts, too. Adrenaline coursed through Day as he envisioned the remaining Progs running to help their own.

He twisted right to free his arm and swung at the Prog's face, then pushed hard on the man's chin to get him to break his hold. But the Prog had wrestled somewhere in his background and did not quit so easily. He spun away from the Settler's grip and rolled across Day's back, flipping Day over with him. The two grappled and tumbled toward the pond.

Day had a weight advantage but the Prog was lean and fast. It was like wrestling a cougar – the man even tried to bite him. He had to end the fight before other Progs came to help.

As they crashed into the cattails Day relaxed his right arm. The Prog was pulling on it to get to the gun so now he yanked it down, parallel to both their bodies. Day swung his legs out of the way and pulled the trigger. The Colt barked again, firing a .357 round straight into the Prog's right foot.

The man roared in agony and let go of Day's sleeve. Day rolled away, thinking the Prog had lost interest in the fight, but the man reached down to his foot and came up with a knife. He lunged after Day, who got clear just in time. When the man rose again Day shot him point blank in the chest.

The fight was over.

In the aspen grove, the Prog who called himself Random X picked himself up off the ground. He had had a beautiful hiding spot behind the fallen trees but the downside of its concealment was that his own view to the outside world was limited. Every few minutes he had to rouse himself to stand up and peer over the downed trunks just to survey the ground to the north and east. That was how he had missed the Settler until it was almost too late.

Now Random – whose real name was Simon Pettigrew – rubbed his eyes in panic. Neither of Day's shots had struck him but the second bullet blasted into the poplar and sprayed wood chips into his eyes. He felt slivers behind both eyelids; his eyes burned and his vision was a blur. Worse, there was more shooting nearby and shouting in the distance. He had to get away.

Clutching his rifle, he felt his way to the edge of the aspen and tried to see into the meadow. The Settler had gotten past him somehow…still, he made out other figures running and crouching on the bright green and yellow lawn. Wulff was right: their pursuers had come that way and walked into the ambush. Random heard Wulff now, shouting down the Prog line:

"Come on! Get up here! Move it, move it!"

Random assumed that order was meant for him. He was the farthest from Wulff's position at the top of the pond. Wulff must be trying to bring everyone in for concentrated fire. Either that or he saw that Random was isolated and was trying to bring him to the safety of the other guns. In either case, Random needed to leave his position. He was half-blind and someone had already breached their line on his left. He had to go.

In a crouch, he stumbled out of the trees and across the grass. Behind and to his left there was a shot. Someone yelled, then other rounds ripped overhead. He tried to duck lower, lost his balance, and fell. His eyes teared up, making it harder to see. Crazy John called his name – it sounded like a warning so Random turned to crawl in that direction. Just as he did a blurry figure rose up on his right, from the meadow, and ran toward him. The Prog forgot his eyes. He rolled onto his side and fired his rifle from the hip. His assailant was close enough that he heard the bullet hit. The figure went down hard and did not get up. Random, his last round expended, crawled away as fast as he could.

Day also crawled away from his opponent but unexpectedly found himself under fire from across the pond. Two rounds tore through the crushed cattails and struck close by. One buried itself in the soil only two feet away while the other exploded one of the ice chunks the Prog had excavated from his hole. Day scooted across the grass, intending to drop into the foxhole and take cover, but at the last second jinked left and crawled past it, realizing he would be trapped like a badger if he rolled into the Prog's hide site.

Instead he scurried around the rise of ground on the pond side, chased by gunfire that kicked up dirt and blasted the cattails so their downy spikes exploded and drifted like snow. There was barely room between the rise and the water but the cattails were thick and broke his line of sight to the shooter. Careful not to shake the reeds, he slithered along the embankment, stopped, then moved forward another ten feet and stopped again. He was still in the open but out of sight from whoever was across the pond.

Out of breath, Day reloaded his Colt and listened. The shooting at the top of the pond stopped. So did the shouting. The valley went silent.

How many Progs were there? Day tried to remember...seven plus one Indian? Okay, two were down, maybe three. Roland had the one guy up in the trees. That left three, maybe four, out in front of him or across the rise. So what were they doing?

After a while another two shots sounded behind him but these went high, well over the cattails. Day wondered if they were meant to keep his head down while the Progs at the top of the picket line advanced on his position. He imagined all four terrorists not ten yards away, splitting up so two could approach from either side of the rise to attack. He listened, striving to hear if the vision had substance, but his ears still rang from his own shooting and he could not be sure which sounds were real and which were imagined.

Only one thing was certain. He was trapped.

12

Despite Day's fears, nothing happened.

There was another shot from across the pond but it did not appear to be directed at him. Stillness returned. Unwilling to wait, he moved around the rise, anticipating at any moment to come face to face – or barrel to barrel – with a Prog, but he found nothing. Instead of advancing on his position the Progs had retreated.

The meadow's natural activity returned. Grasshoppers, bees, a distant lark, all resumed their motion and song with the running water of the stream as background. Among it all Day heard a sound that made him perk up his ears. No ornithologist, he nevertheless recognized the short, annoying calls of a starling, a bird that would not appear in Wyoming or anywhere else in North America for another fourteen millennia. Careful to remain screened by the cattails, he raised his head to see the source.

Roland was fifty feet away, stretched on the grass but propped on his elbows as he studied something in the distance. He whistled a starling's call once more, then motioned to Day that it was safe to come over.

"They're smarter than I gave them credit for," he admitted when Day came near. He pointed past the pond and the knoll behind it where the vale disappeared around a curve. The last of the Progs – Crazy John – was just hobbling out of sight.

"They had a shooter on that hill," Day guessed. "He kept our heads down while they retreated."

Roland nodded. "Yeah, but I don't think that was planned. He wasn't there when I started down from the trees with Stevens. If he had been we wouldn't have stayed in the open. He either went ahead and doubled back or was on his way to meet them. If it's the second, it could mean the next camp isn't far away."

"You had Lace Stevens?" Day perked up. "Where is he?"

"Gone, and I blame you."

"Of course you do."

"He was in the trees, as we thought. Nice rifle." Roland gestured to the .308 Savage beside him in the grass. "I should have killed him but a little voice told me to follow your example and spare their lives, bring them in one by one to face the justice system."

"That's not what I said. But it would help, since Stevens might be our mole."

"I don't think so. He would have told me first thing. Anyway, as impractical as showing mercy is given our circumstances, for some reason I didn't cut his throat. My Comanche ancestors would disown me, I'm sure. Instead I tied his hands and walked him down the hill. Never once did he mention he might be on our side. We were hidden in that trough over there until the last hundred yards. Then we popped out and I kept him up front. Thought we might get close enough to bargain with his buds or at least distract them while you came up from behind. I assume that's what you did?"

"More or less," Day said. "I've got two down near the dam. One's still mobile, or should be soon."

"Well, it's the last time I'll listen to you," Roland continued. "Lee Oswald over there on the grassy knoll opened up and almost drilled me." He showed a crease on the handle of his knife. "I dove for cover and Stevens took off. Another sign that he's probably not the mole. Still, he's different, that one. Not angry, doesn't seem like a zealot. Fatalistic. We have a word for it in Comanche: *tenah nu-meni*. It means 'ready for death' or thereabouts."

"So he got away?"

"Yup. I'll pick up his trail in a bit. The rest of them crossed the pond there." He pointed to a spot at the water's edge where the cattails and reeds had been pushed down. "You can't see it at this angle but there's a sand bar where the water is only inches deep. They knew about it because instead of going all the way around the east side of the pond they ran across there. Clever. By the way, did I mention this was the last time I'll listen to you?"

"I didn't tell you to keep him alive. I told you to do things your own way."

"That's what you said. But you used a subtle white man's moral influence to make me follow your lead."

"Oh, please."

"You made me feel bad. I won't make that mistake again."

"Fine."

They searched the area, alert for Progs who might have stayed behind. They found where each of the ambushers had hidden, though none of the sites revealed much. They also found the body of Lace Stevens.

"Guess he was more ready than I thought," Roland commented. "You shoot him?"

"No," Day replied, looking down at the body with some despair. "I never saw him. My guy is over there and there might be a third in the woods."

He knelt and went through the dead man's pockets. The former trooper still carried his Fraternal Order of Police membership card along with his drivers license. Day remembered what Galt had said about Stevens' offer to turn state's evidence. But if he was trying to get back on the right side of the law then why did he run? He sighed and stood up, hoping like hell they had not just killed a good guy.

They examined the body of the Prog Day had killed near the pond and guessed it was Ben Maddox, another sociopath from the Northwest. He had no formal identification on him but he carried a folding pocket knife with "Ben" inscribed on the handle. He also had an OSU beaver tattooed on his arm.

"Galt said he wrestled at Oregon State," Day said, scanning the little book he had brought with him. "I'll vouch for that. The Beavers...how about that for karma? Then he bounced around city jobs in Portland before getting arrested multiple times during the riots up there. Arrested and released like all the others.

Maybe if they had actually charged him he wouldn't be here. He popped onto everyone's radar during the attacks on the federal courthouse. Apparently he had a knack for burning buildings, sometimes with people inside them."

While Day was going through Maddox's effects, Roland went into the grove and prowled around. He followed tracks from there out to the meadow where they came within a few yards of Steven's body, then continued onward to the pond.

"I may know what happened to my boy," he said when Day re-joined him. He pointed out Steven's trail and how it converged with the one from the grove, then held up a shell casing he found in the grass. "The guy from the woods shot him. I will guess it was by mistake. The last I saw Stevens he was barreling toward their line so maybe he surprised them. This guy shot him and then crawled away."

"How about that guy?" Day asked. "Did I wing him?"

"You might have. I don't see any blood but he's not walking right. Look: he dropped down here, before he shot Stevens. Maybe he was taking cover but he could have fallen. Then he crawls forward, shoots, then crawls again. I don't think he was hurt before today because we didn't see it in the tracks from their camp."

A sound from near the pond drew their attention. Nancy Peal was waking up.

They found the DC lawyer still in her hole, holding her head with both hands. Day grabbed her by her collar and pulled her up onto level ground where he bound her wrists with the same rope that had restrained the unfortunate Reuben. Roland removed himself a few yards where he could listen while keeping an eye on the vale.

"Good morning," Day greeted the Prog. "What's your name?"

Peal blinked against the light. "Who the hell are you?"

"I'm the guy asking you questions. What's your name?"

"Go to hell."

Day took out his notebook and a pen and pretended to write. "Elke Neuberg, the prostitute from L.A.," he muttered. "So then where is..."

"I'm not Elke, you idiot!" came the response. "And she's not a prostitute! She's the state's attorney general."

"Some say she was both," Day pointed out. "Wasn't she known as the mayor's bratwurst bun?"

Peal spat at him. Day continued.

"So if you didn't sleep your way upward on the west coast, then who are you?" he asked.

She glared at him. "I'm Nancy Peal, the lawyer."

Day did write in his book this time. "Nancy Peal, *the* lawyer," he repeated as he wrote. "Guess I was right about Elke... You're a long way from K Street. Are you having second thoughts yet about the glories of the socialist revolution?"

"Spare me your arrogant fascist sarcasm."

"She's a Prog," Day affirmed to Roland. "No one talks about fascism as much as a socialist, kindred spirits that they are."

Peal scowled at them. Dirty, her clothes in rags with her matted hair splayed around her, she reminded Day of the witches in *Macbeth*. She was in her early forties but looked twenty years older.

"What are you doing here?" she demanded. "You Nazi stormtroopers! Why don't you leave us alone? Leave and go back wherever you came from."

"*When the hurly-burly's done, when the battle's lost and won,*" he sighed. "Where's your husband, Bill Galston?"

Peal tried to kick him. Day stepped clear and kicked her in the ribs in return. Not hard – she was skin and bones – but hard enough. She cried out and gasped for breath.

"We're not in DC and I don't have time for your tantrums," he told her. "Whether you stay alive and return to face the legal system you treated with such contempt, or die here in the mud, is all the same to me. It'll depend on your answers to my questions. First, where's Galston? Why did he leave you behind?"

Peal's eyes flashed with anger. "Because he's a coward and a weakling!" she snapped.

"Where did he go? Where did they escape to just now?"

"What do you mean, just now? He didn't..." Peal stopped. Her eyes focused as she gathered her thoughts. "You don't even know who you're after," she said in sudden comprehension. "You're stormtroopers alright. Typical men, blundering into a situation with violence and guns. He's dead!" she shouted as Day stepped forward again.

"Dead? How? Where?"

Peal glared but her face softened. "Bill couldn't take it here," she answered. "If you didn't know Bill was dead you probably don't know much else about him, but Bill was a kind and gentle man. He was sensitive. A writer, a dreamer, a humanitarian. You probably can't even read, otherwise you might have seen his columns and known what a good man he was."

"Let's see," Day pursed his lips, thinking. "Bill Galston...yes, a real philan-thropist. I remember a charming piece he wrote two years ago – someone had to read it to me, of course. It was called "In Search of the Perfect Omelet," in which Kind and Gentle Bill praised the urban riots going on. As I recall, he agreed with certain politicians that despite the burning, looting, and assaults, the riots were 'mostly peaceful.' Not only that, he said they were justified because we couldn't achieve a new, just world without destroying the old one. You know, the old Walter Duranty apology for Stalin, that you need to crack a few eggs now and then. Clearly he wasn't a cop in the hospital. It wasn't his life being ruined, his property destroyed, his family's home attacked. Clearly he didn't live in those neighborhoods or go to those schools or hold those jobs. But he was kind and gentle as he ignored the people it was happening to. A real peach, your hubby."

"You didn't know him!"

"I think I did. But where is he now, your doting patron of culture and humanity?"

Peal looked like she wanted to sob but no tears came. "He's dead," she said simply. Her eyes scanned the hills flanking the vale and the snow-capped peaks of the Tetons that loomed behind them. "He wasn't built for this. After two months of not finding any civilization, of starving and scrounging for food, of sleeping in the open, he gave up. He couldn't take it. He...jumped off a cliff."

"Where?"

"At the pass. Above the hot springs."

Day thought back to the pass as he had viewed it from the watering hole.

"I wouldn't think those hills were high enough to commit suicide," he said.

Peal sighed, her cheek in the dirt. "They aren't. He lived for two days before... I told you, he wasn't cut out for this."

Day chewed his lip.

"And you, are you cut out for this? How have you survived?"

Peal did not answer at first, as though she had not heard the questions. She lay on the ground looking straight in front of her. Finally she said in a tired voice, "I've lost probably thirty pounds. I haven't showered in five months, I'm eating rats for dinner, and you just pulled me out of a hole where I was hiding so I could shoot someone. We're a long way from Bryn Mawr."

"That's for sure," Day responded. "Where's Reed?"

The change in his voice made her look up. The lawyer in her awoke. "So that's it. You want Blake. The rest of us are just rungs on the ladder."

"More like stepping stones than rungs. We're here to bring in everyone who escaped from Jackson Hole. So where did the others just head off to, and where is Reed?"

Peal struggled to sit up. When she did she stared at Day, sizing him up. "You're here to bring us in?" she repeated. "Am I the first one you've caught? What if I don't cooperate? You don't look like the kind of guy who would kill someone in cold blood."

"I'll work on it. But he would," Day jerked a thumb over his shoulder.

Peal looked past him at Roland, who turned and stared back.

"Yeah, I believe he would," she agreed. "Okay, let's negotiate."

With his foot, Day pushed her back over. "There's no negotiation. You tell us what you know or your days end right here in this hole. Who's left, how are they armed, and where are they? You can start with this guy." He walked away and came back dragging the body of Ben Maddox. "Who is this?"

Peal was shocked to see the body of her fellow Prog, though her grief seemed less personal than practical: "Damn," she said. "He was strong. Why did you kill him?"

"Because he tried to rip off my arm and beat me to death with it. What's his name?"

Peal hesitated. "Marchetti. Sly Marchetti. He was from New Jersey somewhere."

Day lifted an eyebrow. "Funny, he doesn't look Italian. And why would a New Jersey furniture salesman go to OSU? You're a rotten lawyer if you lie without a strategy. My notes say you have a photographic memory but apparently it didn't come with good judgment. Let's try again." He pulled her to her feet and hauled her across the grass until they reached the body of Lace Stevens. In contrast to Maddox, her response to seeing the policeman was more dramatic. Peal let out a cry and fell to the ground, this time crying for real.

"Oh, Lace...Lace..."

Day and Roland exchanged glances.

"Something going on there..." the Indian muttered.

Day cleared his throat. "Okay," he said. "Looks like you've changed your tune. You agree with us this is Lace Stevens."

Peal sobbed, overcome with grief. "You bastards," she wailed. "You fascists, you tied him up and then murdered him."

"No, we tied him up and he ran. Your own guys shot him by mistake."

"You lie."

"Not often, counselor. That's your world. Now start talking."

The former acting deputy attorney general cried but eventually opened up. Stevens' death was a crushing blow and for a time the will to resist departed her. Day was sure she would rebound so he tried to get as much information from her before that happened.

"So," he summarized, "You say that besides Galston, Sly Marchetti is dead. The real Marchetti, the one from New Jersey?"

Peal nodded. "He froze to death," she mumbled. "Not long after we got here."

"Why?"

"What do you mean, why? It was cold."

"But why didn't anyone help him?"

"He fell off the trail and went in the water. Zee was there but she couldn't build a fire. By the time the rest of us got to him he was sick..." she held up her hands..."and he died."

Day made a notation. "And what about Zee? Where is she?"

Peal's eyes blazed. "You killed her," she rasped.

"Me?"

"Your kind. That first killer that came after us."

"Ah, that was Matt Kurtzen. So it was Zee he shot. He said he had injured one of the women."

"He shot her in the back, the coward!"

"While she was on her way to the library, no doubt. And she died? Did you bury her somewhere?"

"I don't know. She didn't make it back to camp."

"Who else did Kurtzen kill?"

Peal looked at the ground but not to evade the question. Remembering names brought back the enormity of everything that had happened in the last six months, and now Lace was gone... A wave of helplessness washed over her.

"Doctor Abrams was one," she mumbled.

"You had a doctor here?"

"He was a professor of constitutional law."

"Oh, Jeff Abrams..." Day searched through his notes. "His name I know. He was another lawyer, not a doctor. From Atlanta. If I remember right, he didn't even practice law, he just ran for office."

"He guest-lectured at Emory University on race and gender law," Peal argued. "He was an African-American genius!"

"Why can't he just be a genius? Why do you guys always have to bring skin color into it?"

"You're a racist," she snapped. "I told you. He lectured at university."

"At *a* university. And in your mind that makes him a professor – of constitutional law, no less? Your standards are low."

"You're a barbarian. You don't respect the accomplishments of others."

"Says a woman who pulls down statues. Look, if it makes you feel better, my companion and I both have our PhD's. No, really. You can call us *doctor*, too, if you would like."

"Not me," Roland spoke up. "Not 'til I deliver a baby."

"Back to the roster," Day moved on. "Who else? How about Tim Breen? Where is he?"

"Your assassin killed him, too."

Day knew that already from Kurtz' report but it was good to hear her confirm it. The DC lawyer also mentioned a few other names of Progs who had succumbed to the environment: Hitch Riley, a Teamster from Vegas, had been mauled by a bear, while dire wolves killed Juan Pablo di Savin.

"How did that happen?" Day wanted to know.

"What do you mean?"

"Was he by himself? Was it night or day? Over at the watering hole?"

Peal shook her head. "It was early morning. That's when they're most active. A couple of days after we moved into the pass. He got up early, I don't know why. To go hunting, someone said. He was gay and he wanted to prove he could handle himself out here. We heard shots and then Eric and Lace found him by the hot springs. What was left of him, anyway. That caused a fight."

"What fight?"

She sighed. "Not a fight. An argument. One of the first rules Blake had ordered was to save ammunition so he only let us carry three bullets each. Lace said Juan Pablo had turned out to be a good shot but he had only three bullets so the wolves eventually got him. There was a big argument over the bullets after that."

"But Reed got his way?"

"Blake always gets his way."

"And Riley? Where did he run into a bear? The pass, too?"

Peal nodded.

Day thought for a minute. The Progs had had it rougher than he thought. By his calculations, ten of them were now dead, almost half by the elements.

"Is that why you moved out of the pass?"

Peal laughed bitterly. "That was just one reason. There were Indians living there that didn't like us. We chased them out but anyway, that place is evil. First, Bill killed himself. Then there was an earthquake and rockslide. Then Juan Pablo and Hitch. And the buffalo migrated through...we all had to climb up onto the rocks to get out of the way. Those things don't stop for anything and they're skittish. The slightest noise makes them run. They're as scary as the wolves."

"Why did you go to the pass in the first place?"

"To get away from the watering hole, idiot! There were too many animals there, too: the wolves but also that insane elephant. But then it turned out there was just as much trouble in the pass. Eric says it's a natural corridor for game to travel. So even though it has the hot springs and fresh water, we had to move again."

"Eric Wulff is your outdoor expert, then?"

"He and Kimmel, and Lace..." Peal's glance flickered over toward where Stevens' body lay in the grass.

"Oh, yes, Vin Kimmel," Day flipped a page. "The antifa celebrity. A bit of a weird one, always making videos of himself saying the Bill of Rights needs to be ripped up but he's always holding a gun. Not consistent but he's probably surviving alright out here. How's he doing?"

"He's dead." Peal's tone was flat and final.

"Kimmel's dead, too? Wolves again?"

Her eyes flashed and her anger rose. "Not hardly. He could handle the wildlife. It was the domestic life that got him." When Day just looked at her, she exploded. "He was an ass! Oh, he could hunt and get food. The original Neanderthal. And he never let anyone forget it, always telling us how much he was doing and how little everyone else did. He razzed Juan Pablo so much I think that's why JP went out that morning. And when JP died, Kimmel flaunted it like it was inevitable and we had to depend on him more than ever."

"So what happened? One of the other guys kill him?"

"No, none of the guys were going to fight him. He didn't bother them. Once Juan Pablo was dead it was the women Kimmel wouldn't leave alone. And that's what did him in: he couldn't keep it in his pants."

Day kept silent again, unsure if he was expected to say something but anticipating another outburst about barbarian behavior. He was not disappointed.

"You men, what the hell is wrong with you?! You've got to stick it somewhere all the time! You all belong out here. It's amazing civilization ever developed, when all you can think about is getting laid!"

Day glanced over at Roland, who stood apart with his back turned. The Indian did not say anything but he appeared to be stifling laughter.

"What are you talking about?" he turned back to Peal. "What happened to Kimmel?"

The woman settled back in smug satisfaction. "He tried to rape Elke," she explained. "The *attorney general*. She wasn't having it. She stabbed him. Six times. Six! I love that girl. He messed with the wrong bitch. He should have gone with Holden King instead. King's dumb as a rock but he had the sense to look elsewhere for his joy ride."

"King's the one who went east? Following some Indian woman across the plains, right?"

Peal laughed. "He's looking for his squaw alright but he's not going across any plains. Oh, please. He and those others actually go exploring? They don't have the guts. He only left because he thinks he knows where he is."

"And where is that?" Day asked, surprised.

"Wyoming, you moron!" she snapped. "King thinks he's still in Wyoming. Hell, we all *know* we're in Wyoming. It's not the real Wyoming – you guys have done something to it and us – but come on, those are the Grand Tetons over there. Even a Washington lawyer knows that. You can't fake those. King used to have a ranch on Jenny Lake and he thinks he knows how to get there. That's where he's going, over to Jackson Hole. And yes, the tribe from the pass went that way and they had women. So if he's right, he wins on both counts. And enough of the guys were so desperate to get laid that they went with him. Men are pathetic..."

Peal stopped talking after that. Remembering Kimmel and King reignited her hostility toward the male gender and she sulked, refusing to answer more questions. Accepting the information he had gained, Day left her alone.

"It appears nature has done much of our work for us," he commented to Roland as they huddled by the pond. "They're down eleven: four by the elements, three by Kurtz, two by us, and two by themselves."

Roland grunted. "But we don't know how many are left."

"No. Shell said twenty-two but Galt admitted there might be two or three more. That guy in the gully didn't match anyone on his list, for example. Crazy John said his name was Reuben but that doesn't help."

"It sounds like four or five went with Holden King."

"Who went south, not east."

"I know Jenny Lake," Roland offered. "Where it is, anyway. I passed the turnoff on the way to Shell's compound. It's north of Jackson, maybe twenty miles from here. We would have to get back to the watering hole and then go southwest. I would bet he went that way unless there's another route on the other side of these hills."

"Leaving out King's group, that means only six from the list are still in front of us. Five now that we have Miss LA Law over there. Five that we know of."

"So add three or four as a buffer...that means maybe nine here and five running around the plains looking for tail."

"Ballpark figures, but yeah."

Roland looked toward Peal who had cried herself out and was now shivering in the grass.

"And how do you propose we go forward now that we have her? You going to let her go, like you did with Crazy John?"

Day shrugged. "I was thinking of it."

"You're not serious."

"Well, I don't want to guard her and neither do you. She's a burden at this point; why not give the burden back to Reed?"

"So she can man the next ambush?" Roland argued. "She's frail but an AK-47 makes a great equalizer. She can pull a trigger as well as the next guy."

"True, but how many triggers do they have left to pull? Between pistols and long guns they've lost almost a dozen weapons in the last two days."

"All it takes is one. My time in the Army was short and long ago but I don't think my platoon sergeant would have endorsed turning her loose."

Day nodded in agreement. "You're right, but given that we're outnumbered we've got to keep them on their toes somehow. If we let her go she'll find them for us and they'll wonder what we're up to. And by showing up there unharmed – mostly – she might do something for us that she's professionally suited for but would never do on her own."

Roland was skeptical. "What's that?"

"She'll plead our case."

13

Eric Wulff considered himself a patient man. He hated being trapped in a pre-historic theme park, he did not want to be banished from civilization, and he had never enjoyed the company of his fellow Progs, most of whom he now regarded as effete twits who were nothing more than parasites on any productive society. But he had dealt calmly with those setbacks ever since they arrived in the wilderness. He had done his best to keep the group alive: he hunted, he explored, he protected them from wildlife when he could. And he ignored the factional infighting and petty squabbles that developed as each person struggled to deal with the mess they were in. As much as some members of the band provoked his contempt and even anger, he had not yet killed any of them.

So he considered himself patient when it came to his fellow travelers' weaknesses. What he had trouble dealing with – what he really could not put up with – was stupidity, especially when it came from people who thought themselves smart.

Nancy Peal was now Exhibit A in this category. Missing in action after the fight at the beaver pond, she reappeared hours later, blithely wandering down the western tip of the vale, the curve of land where the shallowing valley turned south like a shepherd's crook to avoid thick deposits of magnetite and iron ore in the hills above. Walking in the open like she was lost in Central Park, she shouted their names, calling for them to show themselves so she could re-join the band. She showed no concern that she was being followed – as she undoubtedly was, though Wulff had not yet sighted the Settlers. She displayed no effort to hide her tracks, no worry about being exposed, no concern that she was leading the bounty hunters right to the Progs' final hide-out. She was as oblivious as she was self-absorbed, a microcosm of the movement itself.

Wulff did not consider himself a member of the Prog movement or any other movement, for that matter. Until the last couple of years he had spent his life working too hard to care about politics. From eastern Oregon, he had moved to Alaska after high school to work on fishing boats. Half the ring finger on his left hand was missing as a testament to that experience, a reminder of the time he forgot to let go of a line as they ran out the nets. Later he moved back to the northwest and worked as a roofer, then as a hunting guide and back-country packer in the Cascades, and finally as a logger, driving a skidder to pull trees out of the cutting zone to where they could be loaded onto trucks. He would tell people he was a lumberjack if they asked because he liked the term, but in truth the work was seasonal and sporadic and he knew he was destined to be a jack of another kind – a jack of all trades – if he was going to get by.

The first time he had felt poor was when he led guided hunts around Mount Baker, "high hunts" where his outfit used horses to take affluent professionals from the city into remote regions where they could be manly for a few days and get away from their urban routine. Most of the city slickers were not bad guys, Wulff felt, but often they had more money than they knew what to do with and were happy to demonstrate it. They usually carried expensive but useless gear that they wanted him to pack onto a horse, and showed off high-end rifles that they dragged out of the closet once a year. Yet they wanted to shoot something anyway – anything, but preferably a 4-point buck, at least, so they could brag about it later in the boardroom.

The city guys were friendly enough but there was an aloofness about them, too. Wulff guessed they were uncomfortable being out of their element and dependent on someone so financially their inferior as Wulff. Much of the time they hung around in camp talking about money. Wulff did the scouting and the cooking and the tracking and would guide them to a spot where they were likeliest to get a good shot. Then, if they actually hit a blacktail, Wulff would dress and hang the animal and prep it for the pack out – assuming of course the first shot was mortal and he did not have to track the deer through the forest to finish it off. He was easy-going by nature and worked hard so the money (and tips) he made as a guide were good, but he never felt so much like hired help as he did in that job. The disparity of wealth was too great to ignore, even for him. After a couple of seasons, when the opportunity arose to take the logging job, he had no regrets about moving on.

Yet he only began to sympathize with the looters after a trip to Seattle, of all places, when he saw the mansions and yachts of the millionaires and billionaires along Lake Union. It was this antipathy toward the tech tycoons that pushed him to support the so-called anarchists of the Prog movement. But when he learned the tech titans were bankrolling the very rioters who claimed to want change, he began to feel he was being used, that no matter how hard he worked he was never going to get ahead, never going to own a yacht himself, never going to own a mansion on a lake. It was not that he needed to be wealthy to be happy but he wanted to believe that it was at least possible. Thinking the system was rigged against him was too much. So when the Progs started their uprising he tacitly supported it, willing to watch the whole system convulse in the hopes that whatever came next would give him a better chance at getting a leg up in life.

To this day he had never killed anyone. He had always watched from the sidelines, occasionally helping at rallies or offering shelter and a place to hide to radicals being sought by the authorities. That was how he ended up at the Moran ranch. He had agreed to hide a group of Progs at a logging camp near Bend, not knowing who it was. When Jeff Reed and his cadre showed up, Wulff found himself wrapped into the remains of the Prog leadership. And when they escaped east into Idaho and then over to Yellowstone, Wulff went along. Partly because he had no other plans and partly because Reed encouraged him to come, the latter being smoothly persuasive and also not wanting anyone left behind to tell the authorities where he had gone. A hell of a way to end up in the Ice Age, Wulf thought. He heard the joke once that life was what happened while you were making plans, and that certainly seemed to be the case with him.

"What's that noise?"

The whisper came from above where Wulff crouched in the hills. Pebbles rattled down to his feet as one of the parasites he was musing about slid down an embankment to take a position at his side. It was Carlos, the software writer and self-described martial arts expert from Chico who Wulff was pretty confident he could knock unconscious with one punch.

"What's she doing?" he demanded, watching Peal cup her hands to her mouth and shout again.

"She's lost," Wulff replied.

"Well, Jesus. She's making too much noise. Those trackers will hear her. Shut her up."

"And how do you propose I do that?"

"Shoot her!"

Wulff did not budge. He had a good position on a ridge twenty feet up from where the valley ended in a cul de sac. The ground climbed from there into hills that gave way to conifer forests and alpine meadows. The hills continued for miles, rolling ever higher until they joined the Tetons proper. There were ponds and at least one lake tucked into the hills before that point, fed by numberless mountain streams stocked with more fish than a man could imagine. Wulff had never seen country more beautiful, not even in Alaska.

"You don't think a gunshot would be louder than her yelling?" he replied, letting his tone convey what he thought of the suggestion. Once again he was shepherding urban warriors in the wild. Shooting was their answer to everything.

The two men watched Peal make her way clumsily toward them. The ground she crossed was level and lush but she limped and the soles on her boots flopped loose.

Suddenly her image jumped and shook. The whole valley shimmered. A low roar, like waves on a distant beach, reached their ears from somewhere. Wulff felt himself jerk side to side. Carlos fell against him. Down in the valley, Nancy Peal toppled over.

The earthquake was over in ten seconds but it was disorienting. This was the third one Wulff had felt since they arrived in the wilderness but it was the first time he had been caught out in the open. With no frame of reference nearby such as a tree or a campsite, it was indescribably weird to see a valley and hills jump about.

Carlos swore and picked himself up. In the meadow below Nancy Peal began screaming.

"Go get her," Wulff ordered Carlos.

"What?"

"Go along the ridge and get her attention. Take her through the gap in the south corner and up to camp that way."

"Why?"

"Because we need to get her quick or she'll lie there for hours yelling at the sky," Wulff explained, not taking his eyes off the curve in the valley far behind Peal. "Worse, if she finds her way to the north trail," – he gestured to his left where a switchback game path climbed into the hills – "she'll be visible for twenty minutes and we won't be able to do squat to help her. If you go south you can get her out of sight."

"I don't see why I..." Carlos began to argue.

Wulff fought the urge to club the man with his rifle butt. Instead he gave up watching for the Settlers and jumped to his feet to get Peal himself. Slipping around Carlos and dropping below the crest, he ran down the length of the ridge. He went all the way to the end where the ridge eroded into a gorge that in turn sloped into the valley. He eased himself down the erosion to the rocky bottom where a trickle of water flowed, then hurried to its end and looked out. Nancy was thirty yards away, on her feet again and heading north.

"Pssst!!" he hissed. "Nancy!"

Peal looked up and around, trying to locate the sound. He hissed again, then stepped into the open and waved.

"Oh, thank god," she cried, and stumbled toward him. Another rumble in the earth caused her to fall again but it passed and she crawled forward. Wulff dragged her into the cover of a dozen aspen that screened the gorge's mouth. From there he scanned the valley again. Nothing.

"I was lost," Peal explained. "You guys left and those bastards grabbed me. Lace, they killed Lace!"

"Shut up," Wulff cut her off. He held a finger to his lips. "Yeah, they grabbed you and then they let you go so you could lead them right to us, yelling all the way. Thanks a lot."

Peal was exhausted. It took her a moment to grasp what he said. When she did she collapsed against the side of the passage, her boots digging into the leaves that matted its entrance. She started to explain but Wulff again cut her short.

"Get up to camp. Tell Reed. Follow this dumb bastard if you don't remember the way." He pointed to Carlos, who had followed Wulff and was now standing there looking at Peal with disdain.

"I don't take orders from you," Carlos protested.

"Then don't. Stay here and fight." Wulff brushed past him without waiting for a response and climbed back up the hill.

⸙

The great dog returned as Day and Roland crawled into a position where they could peer into the cul de sac. He trotted into view as though he had been with them all along, wet from tip to tail but showing nothing to offer a hint to where he had been. Day wondered if the shaggy beast had felt the earthquake long before them and run off to hide as many animals do, or if he had just gone wandering. Day had long since grown resigned to the great dog's independent ways. He tried to look at the bright side: if the animal was not at their side he was likely out somewhere in front or along their flanks, and that offered protection of its own.

They were in time to see Nancy Peal disappear into the aspen at the corner of the valley. They waited but she did not reappear.

"Anyone else?" Day inquired, studying the hills.

Roland nodded toward the west slope. "There was movement up there. Could have been from the earthquake. Not sure."

Day studied the situation. The cul de sac was covered in meadow as was the vale that led to it. Its surface was rounded like a bowl and the grass rose on gentle slopes as it approached the walls along the sides. The walls themselves were not high but they were steep. Hills climbed behind them, swathed in short grass and scrub and occasional open rock, rolling highest as they went west. Day thought it would be hard and maybe not worth the effort to get up there in order to circle the bowl.

"What do you suppose is back there?" he asked, nodding down Nancy Peal's trail.

"Water," Roland guessed. He examined the land beyond the aspen. "Those hills rise quick. A ravine or gorge, something bringing water down from the hills. There's a spring high up on the right and there could be one or two on the left. Something wide enough for a trail."

It was mid-day and though the sun was behind clouds it was as high as it was going to get. Since it was in the south, a thin shadow bordered that side of the valley. That's where they advanced, staying out of the light and keeping a cautious eye on the slopes above. Roland now carried both his bow and Stevens' .308 Savage, loath as he was to throw away such a fine weapon. They reached the aspen an hour after Nancy.

Roland studied the ground under the trees and signaled "two, maybe three" with his fingers. The great dog prowled up the ravine, decided he did not like it, and retraced his steps to lie down among the aspen.

Day studied the streambed while Roland explored far enough to find where Eric Wulff had slid down from the ridge. The Indian climbed up and looked around but enough tracks went in both directions to make it unclear where the Progs might be now. He dropped back into the gorge.

"Somebody met her," he said softly. "There's a trail. Looks like lots of somebodies have used it."

Day continued poking among the stones of the stream. The gorge was deep and narrow with vertical walls and it was wider than the current flow of water justified. Rocks away from the center were polished smooth. New grass grew where water had once run.

"Water's down," he noted.

"Yeah."

"Why is that, do you think? There has been rain in the hills the last few nights."

"Don't know," the Indian said.

Day explored up the trail. The gorge was thirty feet across at the entrance but narrowed farther in, in some places to twice shoulder width. A slot canyon, its walls rose steeply and then bent away at a shallow angle. On top of the walls, trees grew right to the edge. Some leaned over while others locked onto the rocky substrata and sent roots exploring down the walls. It would be almost impossible to see anyone up there who might be lying in ambush; on the other hand, it would be equally difficult for any such person to shoot down on them. As he went on, the passage bulged, contracted, or turned every dozen yards or so. There was no way to know what was around each corner. It would be a hell of a place to have a gunfight if anyone was waiting for them. It was also their only trail.

He returned to the entrance and nodded unenthusiastically to Roland. With an expansive gesture, the Indian waved Day forward to take the lead.

Eric Wulff moved to the north wall of the cul de sac, high up on a bench formed in the hill when the overlying soil eroded off the iron ore. From this aerie, lying prone in a spread of larkspur and lupine, he watched the Settlers enter the meadow and creep along its southern edge. He studied them with anxiety and confusion. Anxiety because they were tracking him – and the others; confusion because he was not sure what to do about it. He was neither a cop nor a terrorist and he had never hunted men. He was not even armed to do it. Unlike most of the Progs who carried some version of an assault rifle, Wulff still carried the Henry lever action that he had used as a guide in Sisters County. It was a great gun but the Settlers were about 200 yards distant; even if he wanted to shoot them – and he did not – that was a long shot for a .30-30 with iron sights. He could move closer, he supposed, but the reality was that he did not want to kill anyone if he could avoid it.

It was fascinating watching the two men move through the grass. Wulff had been exploring east during the summer when the previous Settler had shown up so he had missed that encounter. These two guys were the first people he had seen in months who were not crazy, half-starved ideologues. Part of him wanted just to rush out and say hello.

When the Settlers disappeared into the aspen, Wulff waited to see if they would come back out. They did not. The tall one appeared on the ridge where Wulff and Carlos had crouched earlier; he prowled back and forth, studying the ground. Wulff half-expected the man to continue up the slope toward where he lay but the man did not. He scanned the hills with a searching gaze that Wulff could almost feel, but in the end he turned and disappeared back into the gorge.

When he did, Wulff did not delay. He jumped up and cut to his right along the hill. At the west end of the bench he intercepted a game trail and followed it into a forest of whitebark pine. That trail climbed north before arcing around in a large semi-circle far back in the hills. In a mile or so it would circle over to the gorge where the Settlers now walked and then parallel that passage on the gorge's high wall. Before then Wulff hoped to run into another of the Prog band since both trails converged on the same spot, the high meadow where Reed and the others had established a new camp. Everyone from the valley should be up there by now and he hoped they would be putting out scouts. It was looking to Wulff like that was where the Progs would have to make a stand.

Wulff's trail was the one the Progs had used the first time they left the valley. It was twice as long as the gorge path but they still used it from time to time anyway because the ground in the pine forest was softer and also free of the claustrophobia of the gorge. Wulff avoided the gorge trail for another reason – it was because he could never stop thinking of the contraption at the top of it. All it would take was for that thing to fail and anyone on the trail below would be in a world of hurt.

A mile into the forest he slowed his pace to catch his breath. The hills were quiet. Only a breeze riffling through the pines broke the silence. He breathed easily, listening.

It was ironic how healthy he was despite the situation. The lean existence since they arrived in Wyoming had been good to him overall. He had lost twenty pounds but he had needed to lose it anyway. Hunting was easy – while their bullets lasted – and wild game and fish were plentiful. A real paleo diet, he had joked early on though none of the Progs found it funny. Getting enough Vitamin C had been a challenge until the huckleberry season started but once it did, everyone had noticed a difference in their energy. Lace had discovered an acre of bushes not far from their current camp: it was the main reason Reed had decided to move there while the weather was good. There had been a couple of scares with grizzlies and the massive short-faced bears – who also loved the huckleberries – but so far no one had been hurt. Reed had dictated that they conserve ammunition so the Progs always beat a speedy retreat whenever a bear appeared.

Besides the food, Wulff attributed his excellent physical condition to fresh air, exercise, and sleep. He slept now more than he ever did in the 21st century. The Progs always built campfires at night but otherwise when it grew dark out there it grew *really* dark. The fires were mostly to ward off the wolves anyway. Once the sun went down there was nothing else to do and no light to do it with, so he usually turned in pretty quick. Though the days were hard he was getting the best rest of his life.

The sound of running footsteps reached his ears. It was Ruud Rohanson – Wulff could tell from the heavy step. The stocky Swede from Wisconsin appeared on a crossing trail off to Wulff's right, breathing hard and sweating despite the crisp air. He wore a wool shirt, blue jeans, and Keen hiking boots, and a second shirt tied by its sleeves around his waist. For a weapon he carried only a pistol, a Glock 9mm, which probably contributed to the tension on his face. The stress dissolved into relief when he caught sight of Wulff.

"Thank god," he muttered, working his way over to the main trail. "I thought I would have to go all the way to the ridge to find you."

"They're in the gorge," Wulff related. "Or they were 20 minutes ago. I was coming up to warn Reed."

"How many?"

"Two is all I saw. They have a dog, too."

"You sure they're in the gorge?"

"I saw them go in. It'll take them an hour to get to the top, maybe more. If we hurry, we'll have time to set an ambush."

Wulff went around Ruud to head up the trail but the Swede did not move. Instead he untied the shirt at his waist and tossed it after Wulff. It had been bright red at some point but now was dirty and blood-stained. Wulff recognized it as something Juan Pablo had worn.

"What's this?"

"Reed already has a plan," Ruud explained. He leaned on his knees, catching his breath. "Take that and get to the overlook. When you see them in the Narrows, wave that to let me and Bern know they're still in the gorge. We'll be at the top."

"At the dam?" Wulff asked.

"Yeah."

"That's a long way."

"Tie it to a stick. I'll see it if you get it high enough. Keep waving until you see me wave back."

Wulff took the shirt and tied it around his own waist, giving a thought to Juan Pablo as he did. JP had been alright. A bit on the effeminate side but he was tougher than some of the guys gave him credit for and he never complained. It was Wulff's impression that had JP not known Reed from way back, he would never have gotten mixed up with the Progs.

"What if I don't see them?" he asked. "There's only that one stretch where you can look down into the gorge – they might have passed it by the time I get there."

"Then make sure they don't," Ruud snapped. "Stop talking and move your ass."

It was a fair point, Wulff admitted. He turned to go.

"Wait," he said, "you've haven't told me the plan. It'll be tricky to shoot down from the dam. What are you going to do there?"

Ruud had a blocky head and square features that were handsome in a classic, Nordic way but the paleo lifestyle that Wulff chuckled over had not been as kind to him. He had chipped a tooth eating pine nuts and had gained a scar across his nose pushing through brush at the pass. He did not sleep well just because it got dark and there were deep bags under his eyes. The toll of being hungry, dirty, tired, and scared for six months had weighed on his mind until it was all he could think about. He was gaunt and unshaven and his blond hair had grown long and unruly, hanging across his face in matted strands that made him look like a wild man of the fjords. Any expression of his was bound to look half-savage, and now he offered a manic, gap-toothed grin.

"What are we going to do?" he repeated as though it were obvious. "You'll see, *pojke*. You'll just see."

14

Day moved up the gorge, hating every step but confident he had made the least-bad choice to be inside the geological feature rather than above it. The Progs' tracks were easy to follow – there were sandy stretches between the rocks along with patches of grass and no one seemed to make an effort to mask their trail.

The streambed rose as they walked but not much. To account for the gorge and the lost elevation he guessed there had to be a waterfall ahead. In the meantime the walls remained steep. If the trail was not going to be a dead end, there had to be either a merging ravine or a switchback leading up the walls somewhere in front of them. Otherwise there was no obvious way out.

Animal tracks littered the sand but they were small: bobcat, porcupine, rock squirrel. There was only one set of deer tracks and Day was relieved to see they headed downstream. Not only did that imply there was an exit ahead, it also meant he was less likely to find himself stuck in close quarters with an excitable stag wielding an over-sized rack.

They entered a part of the gorge where the passage narrowed to the width of a man's outstretched hands. High above, maybe twelve feet up, a lintel of sorts hung over them in the form of a tangle of dry brush caught between the walls, jammed there by a flash flood. Day added it to the list of reasons why he wanted out of the gorge.

They had gone half a mile when Roland hissed and ducked against the north wall. Day found cover under a granite outcropping. They waited in silence until Roland worked his way over to Day's position.

"Shadow up top," he explained.

"Human?"

"No. Looked like a flag."

"A flag?"

"Something waving."

They waited.

"Could it have been a bird?" Day asked. "A tree?"

"No."

"A signal?"

"Yeah. It was quick."

Day felt sure it was nothing good. Roland's senses were too acute to lead them astray.

"Any sign we're being followed?"

"None," Roland replied.

Day considered their options.

"They can't ambush us," he argued. "Not unless this place opens up. Most of these walls you can't climb and except for that one spot back there you can't even see the top."

"Do they have explosives?" Roland asked.

Day thought back to what Shell had told him. "Galt said they *might*," he answered. "The Progs used dynamite in some of their assaults. What are you thinking...a rockslide?" He looked at the walls. The walls seemed too solid to cave in even using dynamite. An avalanche did not seem likely.

"I don't know. Just wondering what they're up to."

"Our best bet is to get out of this canyon, and the best way to do that is to move up and find out where they left it. If they're going to bring the fight to us it'll have to be there."

A mile ahead of the Settlers Ruud Rohanson stood on a cliff high above the gorge and marveled at the view. Not just in front of him, where he could see down into the last hundred yards of the cut and also along its walls as far as the trees permitted. Not just behind him, where a twenty-acre pond stretched across what had been a sprawling meadow. The sight also included the construction at his feet, which Bern Jones was just climbing out of, trailing a wire on a spool.

"It's ready," he panted as Ruud grabbed his hand and pulled him up to solid ground.

"You sure?"

Jones waved a hand. "You're welcome to go out there and check. Be my guest."

Ruud looked at the beaver dam that stretched away before them. A massive and ingeniously placed pile of rock, mud, sand, brush, sticks, tree limbs, tree trunks, and even chunks of sod broken away from the shores of the now flooded meadow, it extended seventy yards along the eastern edge of the pond, reaching from one wall of the gorge to the other and beyond as the intrepid architects fell victim to their own success and extended the barrier to plug additional outlets as the water rose. Even now water lapped near the top of the dam. The only reason it did not overflow is because the excess had found an escape elsewhere in the meadow.

On the gorge side of the dam where Ruud stood was a drop of sixty feet, the first twelve of which was the earthen dam and the remainder the actual wall of the canyon. That had been the focus of the beavers' work, where the original stream left the meadow and dropped into the gorge. They had stopped up the waterfall using trees so large that Ruud never imagined an animal felling them, let alone dragging or even floating them into position. The dam cut off the stream and for months now only a misty, seepage-fed cataract fell into the gorge to feed the trickle below. Jones had spent the last half hour clinging to the slippery sticks and rocks around that seepage. He had almost fallen twice. Ruud had no desire to climb out there himself.

"It had better work," he contented himself to say.

"It'll work," Jones insisted, out of professional pride rather than because he cared what Rohanson thought. He was Canadian, medically retired from the military, and had a light British accent that to American ears lent credibility to anything he said. He had been around the Swede long enough to know that Ruud was great for criticizing others even when – especially when – he had no expertise himself in the project.

"Isn't it getting wet?" Ruud demanded.

"Probably. It's a dam."

"Don't give me any lip," Ruud warned.

"Then don't ask dumbass questions," Jones shot back. "That's PE4 out there. Plastic explosive. It doesn't care about getting wet. If it was good enough for the Canadian army it's good enough for you."

"I didn't know Canada had an army," Ruud sneered.

"A good one," Jones replied, nonplussed. "Small, but capable. Better than any you Danes can field."

"I'm Swedish, you idiot."

"Whatever. I'll put our sappers up against anybody's. And you know what makes us different? We *like* blowing up stuff. At least this one does." He grinned.

"Good for you. Just remember, that's all we have so I don't want you wasting it."

Jones unrolled the wire around the edge of the rocks to a spot where he could take cover. He tugged gently on the spool. "Why, were you saving it for your birthday?" he asked. "Or maybe Norway's national day?"

"I told you I'm Swedish!"

"Whatever. Sorry, but you're going to have to find your own candles for a cake because this package is about to turn RDX into a crapload of noise. And a couple of bounty hunters into bottom feeders."

Ruud craned his neck to see where the wires led. Jones had secured the package as deep inside the dam's base as he could, directly above the gorge and approximately one-third of the way up from the surface of the pond. The PE4 was wrapped around a hand grenade that Lace Stevens had stolen from a National Guard armory. Stevens had had two grenades when they arrived but Ben Maddox, the moron, had taken one early on to catch fish. The PE4 needed an explosion to ignite and this grenade was now their only option. It had better work.

"Hey, genius," Jones said from behind him. Ruud turned to snap a reply but Jones held up the wire and wiggled it. "If you don't want to miss your birthday altogether," he advised, "you might want to take cover."

Day and Roland closed the distance between them while the Narrows lasted. No more shadows moved up top; down below the gorge remained tranquil and still. In time the Narrows ended and the walls moved back. The streambed widened. The broader opening allowed in light so grass grew thicker on the bottom, making it easier to walk.

They rounded a curve. Day glimpsed ahead what looked like a slash in the south wall, a V with its own moraine of eroded rock and soil that angled down toward the water. He breathed a sigh of relief – this might be the exit.

He was pointing out the moraine to Roland when the ground trembled. Day's first thought was of an aftershock to the earlier quake but then a distant explosion reached their ears. Echoes ricocheted off the walls, loosing waterfalls of sand and rock. The Settlers ducked, preparing for an attack even as they tried to divine the meaning of this surprise.

"I'd say that answers the explosives question," Roland muttered.

Day wondered what could have exploded. Was it an accident? That would be quite a coincidence and as a bounty hunter he did not believe in coincidences. So what was this? What could...?

The echoes faded. Now something else emerged: muted but growing louder, it was hard to pin down. It sounded like wind.

"We need to get out of here," Roland said.

Day nodded to the moraine. "Let's get up there and..."

Roland grabbed his arm and pointed at the ground. The stream, the gurgling brook that had accompanied them on their hike up the gorge, no longer looked calm. The water was surging, rippling, and spreading among the rocks. The Indian recognized their danger in an instant.

"Flood!" he hissed, and turned and ran.

Day's first instinct was to run forward, not back down the gorge. If it was a flash flood they needed to climb and the moraine was only fifty yards away. He jumped up but had taken only a few steps when there was a crash from up ahead. A wall of water caromed off a curve in the gorge just beyond the moraine. There was no way he would make it to the rocks in time. Panic seized him as he realized the valley was half a mile behind them. Yet he had no other choice. He turned and ran after Roland.

✦ ✦ ✦

Ruud Rohanson and Bern Jones were lucky to be alive. The PE4 they had used was the size of a shoe box and – Bern's claims of expertise notwithstanding – they had let the size of the package influence their expectations of its power. That was a mistake.

The explosion ripped outward from the dam with stunning ferocity, throwing logs the size of telephone poles twenty feet in the air. Two of those landed within feet of where the two men cowered on the wall. Seconds later the dam breached. First in the middle, then wider as the structure crumbled and four million gallons of water began to pour through the opening. The cascade grew as the breach widened, the water carrying away whole trees whose branches tore at the remaining wall, ripping out the beavers' intricate design. Water that rushed through the gap leaped ten yards before thundering straight down, carving chunks from the walls and slamming into the floor with a force that shook the earth. The soil beneath the precipice on which Ruud and Bern lay began to give way. They scrambled to safety, first higher on the wall and then around its corner into the meadow.

"Holy crap!" Ruud exclaimed at the disaster they had unleashed.

Overwhelmed by their success and brush with disaster, the two high-fived each other. They whooped and hollered in horror and delight, their voices lost beneath the roar of the flood.

Day could run. He was stocky and could not cover ground like Roland – who had already disappeared down the gorge – but when motivated he could move like a cornerback on a mission. At the moment he was highly motivated. He raced through the gorge as fast as he could.

But it was not enough. He heard the water coming – the roiling boil of a flash flood – and knew that even if he ditched his pack and rifle he could not escape it. He tripped on the rocks, scrambled to his feet, and resumed running without looking back. A rock flew over his head and landed in the stream ahead of him. He would not drown, he knew, at least not right away. He would be crushed first, thrown against the walls and pulverized by the debris washing down the gorge.

He raced through the Narrows, the barrel of his rifle scraping on rock as he zig-zagged through the passage. The water stalled behind him as it encountered this constriction but not for long. As he emerged into the open onto a gravel-strewn clearing the water topped the Narrows and began falling about him. He had seconds to live.

The walls of the gorge were steep. They were also rough, with chinks and cracks and even small ledges here and there. A man could climb out if he were nimble, careful, and had time to scout a route. But Day was not nimble and he had no time. Time, the thief, was stealing on him by night and day, the Bard told him, and now also by flood. Yet his only bid for survival lay in getting high enough on a wall that it might not carry him with it.

Had he been thinking faster he would stopped at the end of the Narrows and tried to climb its back wall as water poured through the gap. Too late for that. He was past it and with water now striking at his knees he could not turn back. He had to find another wall.

A wave drenched him. He staggered free and sprinted downstream. Suddenly the gorge bulged inward from the left side. It fell back immediately, leaving an outcropping that stood like a flying buttress against the north wall, an outpost of granite and rhyolite lava that remained after the limestone had eroded away. As Day sprinted past he saw that its downstream side flared at the bottom. Better, a jack pine on the ridge above had sent its roots down the outcrop in an effort to find purchase in the rock. The nearest root was only a dozen feet up. If he could climb that high...without another thought Day spun to his left.

A wave hit him and threw him sideways across the gravel. Behind the wave a boiling mass of water and timber thundered forward in a follow-on assault, rolling over itself in massive crests as it lurched and bounced from one wall to the next. Day fought to his feet and leaped for the outcrop just as the topmost crest collapsed on itself and smashed into the streambed where he had been thrown.

The flare in the gorge wall was four feet high. Day scrabbled at the wall to haul himself higher. His fingers grabbed for any protrusion, any crack in the rock. A promising first stone tore from the wall as soon as he gripped it, almost toppling him into the waters that now washed over his feet. But his other hand found a gap between two boulders and held on long enough for him to reach higher and find a new hold. Adrenalin racing, he pulled himself up. He did that again and again, pawing left and right with hands and feet as the water rose with him, feeling for anything that would keep him from being pulled away from the wall.

And the water tried to pull him. It grasped like a living thing, splashing and slapping and tugging at his body and clothes. It roared like an animal and followed him up the wall. The noise was deafening. He would have covered his ears if he could have spared either hand. But he could not. The water swirled about him until he worried as much about drowning right there on the wall as he did about being battered by the debris it carried. It rose faster than he could climb. It was not until he reached the tree roots that he finally thought he stood a chance to make the top of the wall. The water by then had reached his shoulders. He gripped the first root: it held, and with a surge of hope he pulled himself free of the waves.

The front wall of the flood was now hundreds of yards beyond Day. It was marked by a cloud of spray as the cataract blasted its way toward the valley. It would not stop until it drowned the aspen at the mouth and expended its energy in the meadows beyond. Behind it, water backed up and the foam and waves rose so high that the understory of the Narrows disappeared. From where Day perched, everything was now water. He saw no sign of Roland.

He rested but soon the water lapped at his boots again. His initial thought had been to get high enough and wait for the flood to recede but now he decided the best thing to do was to go all the way to the top if he could. He looked up...another fifteen feet to the rim. Gritting his teeth and trying to forget his fear of heights, he reached out for another handhold, following the tree roots. Hand over hand he worked his way up the wall, his feet assisting at any purchase they could find. His forearms began to cramp, his fingers bled, and his toes ached as they often bore his full weight jammed into crevices in the rock, but finally he came within a few feet of the top.

And then the wall gave way. The outcropping on which he climbed finally yielded to the pounding of the waves. The buttress shifted and fractured. In the blink of an eye great pieces of rock fell right out from under his feet. The whole wall crumbled. The tree above and its roots held so Day lunged for them. They kept him above the water and as long as he held on he was not in danger of being crushed. But now he dangled in the open, a few feet above a faster, angrier flood.

The roots were wet. So were his hands. He began to slip. He reached higher but that wood was wet, too. The tighter he squeezed the faster his grip failed and the more the roots slid from under his palms. Day looked down as his grip gave way. Damn. He was going to drown after all.

Then suddenly a hand grasped his right wrist. He looked up. A bearded man had stretched over the ledge and locked onto Day's arm.

"Climb!" the man yelled above the roar of the flood.

Day needed no encouragement. With his left hand he lunged and grabbed the man's coat. He yelled "Okay!" and the man let go of his wrist. Day crawled over the man's outstretched body until he could reach the ledge itself. Swinging a leg over, he got secure and reached to assist his savior. The man needed no help, however. Once Day was off his back he rolled clear of the cliff and scrambled away. By the time Day's exhausted arms could push himself from the edge, the man had his back to the jack pine and was pointing a lever-action rifle at Day's head.

15

Day saw the rifle but there was nothing he could do about it. He was spent with exhaustion in the aftermath of his narrow escape. Unbeknownst to him, it was a feeling he shared with two Progs high-fiving each other half a mile away, but unlike them he had the energy only to lie panting with his face in the dirt.

"You should be dead," his rescuer said, reading his thoughts. "What you just did, you couldn't have planned that if you tried."

"*Fortune brings in some boats that are not steered*," Day mumbled.

"What's that?"

"Thank you," he said louder.

"You're welcome. Maybe. I might regret what I just did."

The man came over and – careful to cover Day with his rifle – stripped the Settler of his pistol, rifle, and pack. He did not take Day's boot knife, either because he did not see it or did not care to.

"Nice rifle," he said, hefting the Weatherby. "A Mark V, right?"

Day nodded.

"You a big game hunter?"

Day shivered. He was soaking wet. The temperature was about sixty degrees but it felt colder. Worse, he knew it would drop in a few hours.

"No," he answered, his eyes closed.

"But you've hunted. You look like a hunter."

"Elk, sometimes," Day admitted. "But it's been a while."

"Where did you hunt elk?"

"New Mexico. The Jemez Mountains."

"Cool. I used to get a tag every year in Idaho myself, in Unit 19 north of Riggins. It's remote but not a lot of guys hunt there so it's easy to have the area to yourself." The man looked around. "Kind of like this place," he added.

The man fell silent, as though waiting for Day to carry on the conversation. After a while the Settler pushed himself up on his elbows and looked at his rescuer. For the moment it was all he could do.

"What's your name?" Day asked.

"Eric Wulff," the man said.

"Wulff?"

"Yeah, why?"

Day hesitated and then risked replying, "You're not on my list."

"List? What, of the people you're after? Well, that's probably good, huh?"

Day rolled over and looked at the sky, then with an effort pushed himself up. Wulff's rifle stayed on him.

"No," he sighed. "It doesn't matter. I'm supposed to bring all of you back."

Wulff studied Day's face.

"And who are you?" he asked.

"The name's Day."

"Well, Mr. Day. Nancy Peal said you killed Lace Stevens. And John Flute said you killed Aron and Reuben. You must not have wanted to bring *them* back."

Day shook his head. "Aron Sorley was alive and well the last I saw him. Reuben...that's the guy with the tattoos? He fell off a ledge, we didn't kill him. As for Stevens, somebody on your side shot him, not me. In the confusion down in the valley. Nice ambush, by the way. Was that your doing?"

"I was there but Lace set it up. Where's Ben Maddox? He didn't come back."

Day shrugged. "He's dead," he admitted. "I did kill him. But only because he was about to skewer me with a boot knife."

"A boot knife like yours?" Wulff asked, gesturing with the Henry. So he had noticed it after all.

"Yes."

"So you're trying not to kill people but bad things just happen, huh?" Wulff summed it up, his tone falling short of an accusation.

"Welcome to my world," Day shrugged.

"Welcome to mine."

They sat looking at each other, sizing each other up. Day saw that Wulff's clothes, though worn thin, were in better shape than some of the other Progs'. They hung loose and Day guessed his rescuer had lost weight in recent months, though he still had broad shoulders and a solid build. Wulff had a beard, too, but he lacked the malnourished, sunken-eyed look of Sorley or Crazy John. And his rifle was clean.

"Unlike you, I haven't killed anybody," Wulff said, breaking the silence. He announced it as though it was something he had to get off his chest. "Not here, not back home. I'm not a Prog."

"Then why are you here?"

Wulff hesitated.

"Bad choices," he admitted. "I gave guys a place to stay when they were on the run. That makes me an accomplice to all the crap they did, I know. I'm sorry. But I didn't hurt anybody or even try to. And here...well, they were on the run and I didn't have anywhere to go so I went along. Little did I know. But I don't want anyone back home to think I was one of them."

"Anyone like who?"

"Anyone. I have a daughter...she lives with her mom outside Bend. At least they did."

Carefully, keeping his hands where they could be seen, Day pulled a handkerchief from his pocket and wrapped his bloody fingers. "So what do you want from me?" he asked.

Wulff shook his head. "I just want to go home."

"Is that why you pulled me out of the flood?"

"I pulled you out because it wasn't right to drown you guys like rats. I'm not going to watch a guy die if I can do something about it."

"But you caused it," Day insisted. "I assume there was a dam up top. You blew it up."

"I didn't. That was Ruud Rohanson. I thought they were going to trap you, or maybe we were going to fight it out at the camp."

"So you're willing to kill me in a gunfight but not with a flood?"

"I don't want to kill you at all," Wulff insisted. "If I did, I could have shot you in the valley. I had you in my sights." To himself he admitted he would have been lucky to make the shot, but the point was still valid.

"So what now, then?" Day asked.

Wulff did not answer right away. He glanced toward the gorge, considering his options. The roar of water was still loud. Spray threw itself above the ledge. It would be hours before the gorge cleared, maybe days before it was passable. Not that it mattered. He did not expect his band would come back this way for a while, not as long as they were being hunted. They would stay in the high country. Even if they decided to leave there were other ways down the mountain, ways that Wulff and others had explored earlier. Reed would decide.

Reed... Wulff wondered what he would tell the Prog leader about the flood. Reed and the others would expect him to know something about it, about whether it trapped the Settlers, about the damage it did. It was pure luck that Wulff had glimpsed even the one man once the water started flowing but they would not understand that. Because he could hunt and track they thought he was some kind of mountain man who could do anything. He sighed. It would be easiest to tell them nothing.

Wulff stood and shouldered his rifle.

"I need to get to the camp before they come looking for me," he said. "You need to find your friend. He's probably dead but who knows...maybe he's got a guardian angel just like you."

Day was incredulous. He was escaping certain death once again. Wulff was not only sparing his life, he made it clear he would leave Day his weapons.

Seeing Day's eyes glance over the guns, Wulff added, "That's a nice rifle. If you don't kill me with it, maybe you'll let me shoot it sometime." He turned to go.

"Where's the camp?" Day asked quickly.

Wulff stopped and pointed west. "We call it the high camp, as opposed to the lake camp down in the valley. At the top of the gorge, on the far side of the pond. Course, there probably is no pond anymore but that direction anyway. You can't miss it."

"Reed's there?"

"He was when I left."

"You're sure?"

Wulff nodded. "I imagine you want him most of all," he said.

"Yes, I do."

Wulff studied him. "Is it personal?" he asked.

Day said nothing but his look spoke volumes.

"I don't blame you," Wolff offered, with a slight tilt of his head as though he had considered the matter at length. "He can come across as normal when he wants...but he doesn't normally want to. He's a nutcase if ever there was one."

"What about the others? Will any go back if we give them the chance?"

"Some will, I think," Wulff answered, thinking as he looked up the gorge. "Random, Nancy, Heather. Maybe Ray. Maybe Carlos, I don't know. He's an idiot but I don't think he's really into their cause. Probably not Elke. She's committed to Reed. Watch yourself around her. In fact, the others I wouldn't trust, either, if I were you. Holden, Trace, the other guys. And Ruud Rohanson. Especially Ruud."

Day stood up, testing his bruises and feeling for anything worse. He did not go near his guns.

"I will take back anyone who wants to go," he promised, looking Wulff in the eye. "Alive. You have my word on that. And so you know, I don't trust any of you."

Wulff shrugged. "The feeling's mutual," he said. "Good luck finding your friend."

With that, he backed away and slipped into the trees. In seconds he was out of sight.

16

The camp at the high meadow was a work in progress, a half-built longhouse with a lean-to next to it along with a dilapidated smaller structure similar to the one Crazy John had inhabited in the valley. Before the dam gave way, all three shelters sat on the west shore of the beaver pond on a slope of fescue and muhly cropped short by mountain sheep. There was forest to the north and northwest while the area behind the camp rose in meadow for another two miles. From there the land undulated in hills to the west and south. To the west the hills led to the Teton range, to the south they lay covered in snow, including part of the glacier that loomed over the previous valley. In between was a wide gap through which the nutrient-rich steppe flowed to lower elevations, ending miles later and thousands of feet below in a glacier-gouged basin at the foot of the massif.

Before the dam's construction, that grassland had begun in a shallow depression at the top of the gorge, a swale where a highland meadow flourished. But once the four-legged engineers had done their work, the pond they created was larger by far than the body of water down in the valley that the Progs referred to as a lake. The valley lake was the terminus of a stream flowing out of the mountains, flanked by freshwater pools formed by natural springs; it had probably existed for decades, if not centuries. The swale only flooded, by contrast, when the beavers dammed a creek that bisected the meadow. The pond they formed was so new that in places the meadow's grasses still poked above the water in defiance of their watery condition.

But now all that changed back in an hour. When Wulff reached the pond at its south shore he was stunned.

Ninety percent of the water was gone, leaving a sea of mud in its wake. It was as though the tide had gone out, though where it had gone was a mystery since only puddles remained where the water had been A smell of peat and fish infused the air, the latter of which flopped in the puddles and gulped desperately for air along the shore. Frogs and salamanders, too – those not washed away – moved in the muck and tried to orient themselves to their new condition. Birds hopped everywhere, picking through the debris. An osprey circled overhead.

The creek appeared as a curving scratch that wound through the sludge. Its banks had long since eroded and the flow now worked its way across the sloppy surface in whatever direction offered the least resistance, reaching the destroyed dam as though by accident and then slipping through the breach to fall into the canyon. Around the edges of the old pond matted grasses pointed after the departed water.

"*Unbelievable*," Wulff breathed. He wondered not for the first time how destruction seemed to be the only talent of his dwindling band.

The camp lay across the swale from where Wulff stood. He saw Reed and the others huddled there. Jones, still amped up from the dam's demolition, was talking in an animated fashion with much waving of his arms. The native, the one they called Puff, was nowhere in sight. He had been with the valley party but had left before the ambush. Wulff wondered if the noise of that battle had now scared him off.

In fact, he wondered much about the Indian. Puff had lived with the Progs off and on for only a couple of months. He was reserved and silent so it was hard to know his motivations for befriending their group but Wulff suspected the Indian had an agenda. The man's eyes were keen; he watched and listened to everything. His speech was inscrutable but Elke and Reed had devised a sign language that communicated well enough. Reuben, too, of all people, had forged a bond with Puff, who was fascinated with his tattoos. The other gang member, Ray, also had tattoos but his black skin confused the Indians and they gave him wide berth. Puff's tribe did not have tattoos but the Indians sometimes daubed their faces with mud or berry juice. They also stuck feathers in their hair, with the number and type of feathers depending on the activity.

It was Puff who directed the Progs to the high meadow when the valley camp had begun to feel claustrophobic, though both locations were always understood to be summer solutions. If they were stuck in the wilderness for the winter all the Progs expected to move back down out of the mountains toward the hot springs. The springs were near the pass with all its issues but there was water there, there was fishing, and - most important – it was warmer. The warmth came from the elevation drop but also due to the thermal activity of the springs. The steam vents and hot water pools heated the air for a hundred yards around. That was critical. Though the wolves were more active in that area and forever a mortal concern, the cold would soon be 24/7.

Wulff had a feeling that Puff's friendship with the Progs was both tactical and strategic in nature. On the tactical front, he was pretty sure Puff wanted a gun. Despite the noise of a gunshot – or maybe because of it – Puff's tribe understood that the rifles and pistols were powerful and they wanted one. Puff really wanted one. He kept trying to touch or take one when the Progs were in camp, which is why Reed directed everyone keep his weapons on him at all times. And getting Puff to back off stealing was the first item of business once Reed started communicating with him.

Puff's strategic goals, Wulff believed, were equally straightforward. When the Progs had arrived in the region, the first natives they encountered were not Puff's tribe but a band from the plains, a group of maybe thirty adults who rejected any overtures toward trade or communication. That group – who the Progs called the Moons for the half-circle markings on their face – were, in contrast to Puff's tribe, quite intimidated by the Progs' weapons. It did not help that at their first meeting with the Progs – a chance encounter at the watering hole – Bern Jones had shot one of them. The same tribe had seasonal cliff dwellings in the pass and the Progs had had several run-ins with them, none positive.

Puff's band, who the Progs called the Arrows for their favored markings on rocks and trees, appeared later, coming down from the north. The two tribes' hunting areas overlapped and there was friction between them that had nothing to do with the Progs. Wulff himself, along with Aron Sorley, found two natives of the plains band dead at the base of the Tetons. They had been tortured and mutilated, and arrowhead markings on nearby rocks – like gang signs – had indicated that Puff's band was responsible. When told of this, Reed had seen the situation for what it was: a struggle for power and resources. Ever on the lookout for seams, he allied the Progs to the Arrows and between them they had effectively exiled the Moons from the foothills and the pass. Puff, in turn, along with one or two other Indians who the Progs had not yet bothered to name, occasionally scouted or hunted for the Progs and gave them information about the local area.

But if Puff's aims were strategic, Wulff believed Reed's motivations were equally calculated. The Prog leader wished to avoid dependence on Puff and thus ordered his group to avoid direct conflicts with the Moons in case they ever needed to switch sides. To date the Progs had largely succeeded in that. It helped that the land was vast and both tribes were small, so encounters were few. True, Mad Ben and Lace had helped the Arrows raid a Moon hunting camp, an event which resulted in the death of a Moon youth. Zee had also stabbed a Moon who snuck up to her at the hot springs camp and tried to steal her coat. But that Moon recovered, so with the exception of Bern none of the Progs had directly killed a member of the plains tribe. Reed was counting on that record to work in his favor should he ever need to double-cross the Arrows. Wulff loathed the man's cunning, his willingness to deal with anyone, to say and do anything to stay on top. But he also admired it in a way, perhaps because it was so far outside Wulff's own character. Unlike Reed he would not sell his own sister just to gain an edge. Then again, he reminded himself, that's why you're an out of work logger while Reed rose to command a nationwide political movement.

But Wulff did not trust the Indians, either, which is why he now wondered about Puff's absence. He looked for Puff by the pond but there was no sign of the man. It did not worry Wulff, exactly, but there was too much that they did not know about the natives for him to be at ease with the way they appeared and disappeared.

A shout came from the camp. Carlos waved to him. With a sigh Wulff turned to work his way around the shore of the pond. For no reason he suddenly wondered where Day was and if he had found his companion. In a way, he wished he could trade places with the Settler, though he still had mixed feelings about rescuing the man. If he had never seen Day trying to climb the rock wall he could have lived with knowing the Settlers had drowned. But once he had seen Day struggling to survive...well, at that point he could not stand by. Whose side are you on, he asked himself as he trudged along. Why do I have to be on anybody's side, came the answer just as quickly. Why has my whole life been spent wondering where the hell I am?

He spied a sizable cutthroat trout lying gasping and confused in a draining pool. I know just how you feel, Wulff thought. He chased away the swooping osprey and picked up the fish.

"Find a friend?" Bern Jones snickered as Wulff neared the camp. The Progs turned and watched him approach. Bern, Ruud, Carlos; Ray Williams, seated on a log running a fine-grain stone over his Winkler knife, looking pissed-off as always; Simon, on the grass being treated by Crazy John, who had heated water and infused it with leaves from a Rocky Mountain maple to wash out Simon's eyes; Elke standing at Reed's side; Heather nearby clutching her life's possessions – now reduced to a comb, a tattered book, and a broken toothbrush; and finally Nancy Peal, who huddled by a cold campfire holding her knees and staring at the ashes.

Another fire was still going but was down to embers. Wulff headed to it.

"I did," he replied. "Thought I'd invite him to lunch." He stoked the coals and fed the fire, then used a piece of split timber as a platform to gut the fish.

"You're welcome," Ruud called over in his usual provocative tone.

"For what?"

"That fish. You wouldn't have it but for us."

"Great work," Wulff muttered. "Next time burn down the forest to find a deer."

"What was that?"

"I said thanks."

Ruud mumbled something under his breath.

"There are probably more fish out there, by the way," Wulff announced to all of them, waving toward the mud expanse. "They won't stay fresh forever. You should all get some while the getting's good."

He hoped to avoid an interrogation by distracting the Progs with the prospect of an easy meal but his ploy worked only partially. Carlos took the hint, followed by Crazy John, who abandoned Simon and stumbled out into the mud to look for food.

"Where have you been?" a thin voice asked. It was Reed. The Prog leader was not distracted, not least of all by a search for food, which anyway he expected others to accomplish for him. He sat straight-backed on a log that was in turn perched on an eroded bank at the west end of the camp. His posture suggested the seat was uncomfortable but the position gave him a height advantage over the others as they stood below the bank a few feet away. Wulff had observed that Reed, a short man with a mane of hair and a heavy beard that seemed to weigh him down but gave him a brooding countenance he appeared to relish, rarely drew attention to himself until he had found a position of some elevation.

Today Reed sat wrapped in a long wool coat with hands buried deep in the pockets, the hood of a sweatshirt poking above the collar but almost hidden beneath the hair. A tweed skipper cap sat atop the hair, fighting a losing battle to keep it contained. The cap was black, so was the coat, and so were the pants the coat mostly covered and which were tucked inside a pair of black wellington boots. Karl Marx meets a gothic longshoremen's union, Wulff thought, though he guessed that few dock workers could afford Le Chameau footwear. His cynicism about the Progs had long since reached up to its leadership, including the remaining members of the band who trailed down and away from their leader in an oval formation as though they had gathered for a board meeting.

"Watching the show," Wulff replied.

Another thing Wulff noticed over the months was that Reed often timed his comments so they were oblique to any ongoing conversation, as if to suggest he was thinking more than anyone else. Even if the others were discussing the weather Reed – if he talked at all – would wait and then throw out an observation about the camp or the weapons or the intentions of the local natives, always changing the topic and always with a hint that there was more to the query than just the words conveyed. Probably a leadership technique, Wulff decided, but there could be a simpler reason: Wulff recognized an attention hog when he saw one.

"And what did you see?" Reed asked, his tone again mixing query with implied knowledge.

Wulff spitted the fish on a green branch torn from a willow and lay it carefully across the embers about eight inches up, using two rocks as supports. The others watched, mouths watering. He knew he would end up sharing, especially since Ruud was making no motion to prep his own catch. Still, it would be a good meal. He just wished he had some salt.

"A hell of a mess," he answered. "That's what I saw. The gorge is crushed. Don't expect to use that trail again."

"We don't care about using it," Ruud snapped. "That wasn't the point."

"It was Operation Johnstown," Reed added.

"Operation who?" Bern demanded.

"Johnstown," Reed repeated, pleased to demonstrate his knowledge. "A poor town in Ohio wiped out by a failed dam. In the 1800s. It was the fault of robber barons who didn't care about the workers below. Ironic, isn't it? Now the capitalists suffer the fate they once inflicted on others."

"I don't think these guys were that old," Wulff said dryly.

Before Reed could react, Heather spoke up.

"The robber barons blew up a dam?" she asked. She was a thin blonde with a long face who tended to stay in Elke's shadow but Wulff had noticed she occasionally showed a streak of independence. She sat in the grass propped against the small bluff, staring into the distance and asking the question of no one in particular.

"No, it just gave way," Reed answered.

"So it was an accident?"

"An accident caused by their indifference," Reed clarified. "It was inevitable because they didn't care, that's the point."

"Well, our dam wasn't an accident," Wulff noted. "Does that make us worse than the robber barons?"

Reed raised his chin so he could peer at the logger along the bridge of his nose.

"No," he said. "You surprise me, Eric. I would have thought better of you. Does anyone here look like an industrialist? We are the retributionists. The avengers of the people of Johnstown."

"The avengers?" repeated Carlos, returning with a fish. "Okay, I like that. I'm Thor."

Elke scoffed. "You're a dumbass," she told him.

"Uh-huh," Carlos replied. "Well, you're definitely the Black Widow, just not hot like Scarlett Johannson."

"That's right, I am a black widow," Elke hissed. "And don't you forget it."

Wulff concentrated on his lunch, ignoring the chatter. Crazy John came back, excitedly carrying two good-sized trout of his own. They were too much for him to eat alone but he nevertheless slithered away from the group to build a fire by his hut. Carlos showed off his own catch and then came over to Wulff's fire to prepare it for eating. Reed was annoyed by the distractions and tried to return their attention to the gorge.

"What else did you see?" he wanted to know.

"Nothing," Wulff answered.

"What about the bounty hunters?" Ray asked quietly

"The capitalists?" Wulff asked. "Well, they didn't look too wealthy to me but I only saw them for a few seconds. There were two. Plus a dog. A *huge* dog. It looks like a mastiff, or maybe one of those Irish wolfhounds. They went into the Narrows and came out the other side but I lost sight of them after that. Then the flood happened. They didn't have time to get anywhere..." – he chose his words carefully – "...so I'm sure they're dead."

Williams' peeved look froze and he paused his knife sharpening.

"You're sure?"

Wulff shrugged, guessing the gang member was disappointed not to have killed the Settlers himself. "Positive," he affirmed and gave a genuine shudder. "That water was something else."

Reed studied him but what he was thinking, Wulff could not tell. The Prog leader's eyes were cold. Not malevolent, just cold. Indifferent. Eyes that could rationalize anything. Wulff did his best to look back with a blank face.

"Did you see them dead?" Reed persisted.

"No. I told you, I lost sight of them after they came out of the Narrows."

"You didn't see bodies?"

Wulff tried to be patient. He gestured to the mud flats that flanked the camp.

"Bodies? Are you kidding? Do you have any idea what you did? Do you have any idea how much water just went down that gorge? How many trees washed over the side? How many rocks? Go look for yourself. You just caused a disaster that would be front page news for a week if we were back home. There won't be any bodies. Unless those guys can surf a twenty-foot wave, you'll be lucky if you find their boots."

"There was a dog?" Heather asked, her lips in a pout. "Was he hurt, too?"

"Wouldn't the bodies wash down into the valley?" Nancy Peal added in an absent voice, perhaps out of a professional habit to seize on loose ends.

Wulff shrugged. "I don't know about the dog. As for the bodies, they'll be crushed and buried. Part of the Narrows collapsed. Good luck getting through there again, by the way."

"We already said we're not going through there," Ruud reminded him. Spurred by Wulff's description, he gazed across the mud to the gorge as though wanting to check out his handiwork.

"And you saw nothing else?" Reed asked, still watching Wulff.

"No."

"He's not dead." The pronouncement came from behind Reed. It was Crazy John, hunched over his smoky fire. He spoke the words in a sing-song tone as though chanting.

"What did you say?" Ruud demanded.

Crazy John did not even look at them. "That Settler, the mean one. He's not dead. He's evil. Water won't kill him."

"Do you know something we don't, John?" Reed asked him.

"I know he's evil. And I will kill him." With that Crazy John turned his back on the group and went about cooking his fish. Reed turned his attention back to Wulff.

"Where were you when the gorge flooded?"

"At the overlook. Along that whole ridge but mostly there. All I saw was water."

Reed stared at him as though waiting for more, or perhaps just to make Wulff uncomfortable. It worked. When he finally looked away, Wulff breathed a quiet sigh of relief. The man's eyes were creepy.

"We'll need to check," the Prog leader decided.

"Check what?"

"We need to make sure the bounty hunters are dead. And see what they were carrying."

Wulff chose not to argue, deciding that might be suspicious. "One of them was carrying a nice rifle," he offered. "If you find that, I'd like to see it."

"If I find it, it'll be mine," Ruud told him. "You'll get to look at it from right there." He turned to go.

"I'll go," Ray Williams announced but Reed waved him to stay in place.

"No, we'll need you and Carlos to help move camp. Eric can go with Ruud." Reed looked again at Wulff, perhaps expecting an argument, but the logger seized only on the first sentence.

"We're moving?" he asked.

Reed nodded as though it were obvious. "Yes, for the same reason that finding another rifle is not our goal," he said, with a glance toward Ruud. "Those bounty hunters got here somehow and they have a way back. Remember, Aron told us the first killer had a device of some kind that he activated to disappear. A tube, he said. That's what we're looking for. The tube."

"But Sorley said the device disappeared, too," Simon protested, his eyes open now but red and watery as from a springtime allergy.

"Well, it must have come back, fool!" Reed snapped. "Otherwise how did these two new killers get here? The device, the tube – it's the vehicle, don't you see? It's the thing that allows them to come and go. If we get hold of it, we control them. And if Eric is wrong and these killers are not dead, they'll have no choice but to work for us."

Awareness dawned as the Progs realized they might have a way out of their nightmare. Even Wulff admitted to himself that he had not thought about the means by which the Settlers had arrived, only that they might be his ticket home.

"Oh, god," Nancy Peal breathed. "We could escape this madness. We could leave them in this wilderness and let them deal with the violence, the cold, the wolves, the Indians. Then the bastards would know what we've been through."

"Maybe we could make a deal with them," Heather suggested.

Silence greeted her suggestion. Ray Williams looked at her but said nothing. After a moment Reed did speak and his voice was cold.

"What did you say?"

"Well," Heather continued, still looking off into space, "they could have killed Nancy but they didn't. Maybe they would be willing to take us back with them."

The effect of her words on the group was fascinating to Wulff, as Nancy Peal at least seemed to ponder the idea. Even Ray Williams looked a little less pissed. But the others simply glared, hoping by looks alone to silence Heather's heresy.

"That might be a..." Peal started to say but Reed stood up.

"There will be no deal," he barked, staring down at Heather like a diminutive Old Testament prophet pronouncing sentence on the unworthy. "There is no negotiating with the enemy."

"But..."

"There will be no deal!" Reed shouted. He stared around at each Prog in turn to make his point. Only Ruud withstood his gaze.

"They're dead," Wulff insisted. "There's no way they survived the flood. But Nancy mentioned the Indians," changing the subject to something he hoped would be less controversial. "Speaking of our native pals, where's Puff?"

Reed ignored the question at first, continuing to stare around at his followers in case any chose to look up. Eventually he waved a dismissive hand.

"I sent him on a mission," he said.

"What mission?"

"Nothing to concern you," Reed replied in a tone that was either assurance or condescension, depending on how much one thought of the man. Wulff thought Reed was an arrogant sociopath so he took the answer as a snub.

"Alright," he replied. "It's just that if I'm looking around in the woods I want to know who else is out there."

"Your only concern is the capitalists," Reed instructed. "And you're our best man in the woods, which is why I want you to get out there and ensure they are dead."

"You can finish your fish first," Ruud added in a tone of expansive generosity.

"Gee, thanks," Wulff replied. "As a matter of fact, I'll finish my dinner and get a good night's sleep. Then I'll go."

"What? Why not now?"

Wulff poked the fish and turned it on the spit. The flesh was heating nicely and steam rose from the meat in a tantalizing aroma. Whatever else there was to say about this savage world, the wild game was excellent.

"Because it's late afternoon," he pointed out. "And the water in the gorge was still ten feet deep when I left. You say you don't care about the Narrows but if you're going to search for those guys you'll have to *walk* through the gorge, not swim. You can go now if you want but it'll be dark by the time you get there and there will be nothing to see. Morning will be better. But you do what you want."

"You're damned right I will," was the response but now Ruud looked uncertain. He kicked around camp for a while as Wulff ate his meal, then walked to the dam to look down into the gorge. He made no effort to go any farther and returned to the fires when it grew dark.

17

Day was too exhausted to run but as soon as Wulff departed he hurried back along the gorge as fast as he could, feeling sick at heart. There was no trail so he had to make his way through the forest, cutting frequently to the rim to look over the disaster below. Forswearing any risk, he called Roland's name again and again. There was no response.

In what was left of the Narrows the flood peaked but in other places it was hard to see much difference. The torrent no longer roared but it remained deep and strong and out of control, rolling against the walls and bouncing back on itself in the thinner stretches. In the few places where the gorge widened – in bell-shaped openings of eroded sandstone with pea gravel floors – the water spread out like a crowd exiting a theater. But even there the water was deep and choppy. As soon as the walls closed in again gravity pushed the current once more toward the valley and the blind stampede continued.

Day yelled himself hoarse, not heedless of the danger but willing to assume that all the Progs, just like Wulff, were at their hill camp now. He heard no reply. There was no sign of Roland: no body, no clothes, no weapons. By the time he drew close enough to the valley that he could look down into the cul de sac and see the aspen grove, he was so tired he could hardly stand. The sun had stayed behind clouds all day but now it was below the horizon and the temperature was dropping. His shivering, which had been intermittent, became constant.

He scanned the cul de sac, which now looked like a rice paddy. Most of it was under water several inches deep. The aspen, too, were in disarray. It appeared they had been hit by water exclusively, the thundering timbers and rocks being intercepted farther up the gorge, but a couple had been knocked down and the rest leaned this way and that after the sudden onslaught. Even now water poured through them as the gorge continued to drain. Day could make out nothing through their branches.

He wanted to continue out of the hills and down to the mouth of the gorge. From there he would work his way upstream and search for Roland. For all he knew the Indian was injured and trapped, and on foot in the gorge Day could probe every fissure. But as he watched the water drain into the cul de sac he knew further search was out of the question for several hours at least. For one, he doubted he had the energy to climb down the hill. For another, he realized there was no way he could explore the gorge while the water still flowed out of it. And worst of all, it was getting dark. He felt helpless: unable to see into the gorge due to its sloping walls and unable to enter it due to the water, he was leaving his friend on his own.

Frustration overwhelmed him and he dropped to his knees in despair. What an utter, utter disaster. He knew Roland was as resilient as they come but his companion had not been that far ahead of him in the race down the gorge. The wall of water would have hit him soon after it reached Day. The chances of Roland surviving the flood were miniscule. In his mind, Day was tormented by a vision of his friend drowned and trapped in the rocks of the gorge below.

And where is my damned dog?! he wanted to shout. Rarely had he felt so alone.

But after several minutes of anguish, Day began to get a grip on himself. If nothing else it was the shivering that brought him round. If he did not take measures soon to dry off and get warm, he would not survive the night.

Pushing himself to his feet, he pulled off his water-logged coat and hung it on the branch of a nearby spruce.

From an inside pocket he drew a wallet-sized package. Wrapped in wax paper as a small condescension to Shell's concern about biodegradable equipment, it was Day's fire starter kit. A quick glance around at the pine trees suggested he might not need it but most of the trees were still damp from rain. And since his only paper – the Corps of Engineers maps – was a sodden mass thanks to the flood, Day now took no chances.

With shaking hands and heightened awareness of the graying light, he gathered needles, twigs, and branches, methodically building piles for each in a dip in the ground just outside the trees. Satisfied he had enough material, he formed them into a teepee next to an old log that would be easy to roll onto the flames once they got going. Then he pulled from the wax package a swatch of dryer lint rolled in Vaseline. It was his no-fail tinder. Pushing it to the base of the teepee where the needles were thickest, he struck his steel on flint. It took several tries but the lint finally caught. Small flames licked across the Vaseline. They persisted and eventually coaxed the damp needles to light in turn. Soon the fire was underway and growing, and for the first time in hours Day enjoyed a small sense of relief. He would not freeze tonight.

He laid the fire in the open, at the top of the first hill that rose above the cul de sac. The trees were behind him while in front lay thousands of acres of the valley and the hills that ringed them. He wanted the fire to be a signal so he made it bigger than he would normally do. If Roland was out there, he would see it.

For a while Day sat with his back to the blaze, warming his body and drying his clothes and staring into the depthless night with its firmament of infinite stars. He listened, hoping to hear Roland call out, but there was nothing. He thought about the Progs, and what they would do next, and about Eric Wulff and whether he could be trusted. As he thought, he thawed, and as he thawed, he dozed. Finally he fell asleep in spite of himself, waking only once during the night to feed the fire.

As a rule Day did not dream; or rather, he had trained himself not to dream, waking as soon as the dreams started because they were never good. Tonight he must have been exhausted because a dream began and lasted longer than it should have. It was a dream of fire and confusion and many voices calling. Children's voices, though he could not see the children and though eventually they were drowned out by a booming horn, the wavering signal that schools in his youth had activated to warn of potential air raids or approaching tornados, and that in his adulthood had raised the alarum for more contemporary terrors. The sound, like the foghorn of a small but ambitious ship, circled the flames and rode the smoke as he told himself to wake up, wake up, before it was too late.

He awoke before dawn. The memory of the foghorn faded away but somewhere in the night, down in the vale, Day heard the howl of dire wolves. Three wolves, at least, maybe four. Not a full pack but enough to wake the dead. Their wail carried up the ridge and lingered among the trees, probing the dark. The fire needed more fuel so he rolled a new log into it but even with the flames against his back the sound of the howl chilled Day's blood. He cradled the Weatherby, peering into the night.

The howl was so different, so much more savage than the call of wolves back home. When it came to the North American gray wolf or even the timber wolves farther north, the call of the pack was to Day literally London's call of the wild: the sound of nature, of freedom, of defiance against the spread of civilization. With the dire wolves there was no defiance, it was simply a threat. Maybe it was a cultural perception, Day conceded, and maybe given enough time he would change his mind. But there was nothing about the melodic howl of a timber wolf that made him fear the apocalypse was at his door. Tonight's sound did just that. It was unearthly. It rose from the valley like lava from a crater, its tones originating deep on the chromatic scale and wavering in that range as though disdaining to rise above a low C. Deep and heavy and filled with dread, nothing in this howl celebrated freedom. It was all menace.

Then, in a moment that made Day leap to his feet, the dire wolves were met with an answering howl. Just as deep, it started low and then meandered all over like a bad jazz artist. This second wail shot into the night in blatant challenge to the wolves, a reckless portent of violence and death. It rose once, twice, three times, and then faded only to rise again farther north.

Day's blood warmed to hear the sound. It came unmistakably from his own damned dog. The beast had let loose with that cry the day it took on the black bear years before and even the mama bear then had been terrified. For a moment it seemed the dire wolves were similarly put on pause. But after a confused break they resumed, and this time they cried out with insane fury. Their sound moved, too, chasing the great dog's challenge. For the next hour Day listened as the call and response pursued each other around the ringing hills.

At first light Day descended the hill and worked his way across the sodden vale to the mouth of the gorge. By then the flood had ended. Water still flowed into the meadow but it was now no more nor less than the natural flow of the creek. The entrance was passable and most stretches inside the canyon were free of standing water.

Signs of destruction were everywhere, increasing as he moved up the gorge. Eroded walls, fallen rock, sand scooped and piled shoulder high, tree branches as well as whole trees uprooted and carried downstream; in places the sides of the gorge had even changed color as the current scrubbed them clean. Day encountered several animal carcasses: a deer, broken and swollen; a marmot, a fox, innumerable fish. Grass remained only in scattered clumps close to the walls. Elsewhere the surface had been scoured.

There was no sign of Roland.

He did his best to avoid leaving tracks, partly from habit but partly because he had considered that the Progs – with the exception of his rescuer – might think him dead. Sometimes it was impossible given the soft sand and then he tried to obscure what he could not erase. Moving with care and precision, he took an hour to reach the entrance to the Narrows. There he stopped. The passage had collapsed so to continue he would have to start climbing, but there was no need to explore further. He knew Roland had made it that far.

A scan of the walls above the rubble told him nothing. Maybe Roland had climbed out of the gorge just as he had but a quick study told him that was unlikely. Most of the walls here were steeper than what Day had attempted. Besides, he had had help.

He turned around and headed back. On the way upstream he had favored one wall of the canyon as he searched; now he stuck close to the other. He found no sign of Roland, and that in itself gave comfort. Up to now he had turned every corner with a feeling of dread, fearful of what he might find. But having found nothing, he allowed himself a flicker of hope. Only a flicker because Roland might yet be dead but hope nonetheless, and as he probed his way back toward the aspen there was still no evidence to turn it aside.

At the grove he had still found no sign of his companion. The soil there, soft with layered leaves the morning before, was now a mudflow carved into gullies. Day stepped through it looking for signs of life.

He continued out into the cul de sac, retracing the path they had taken the day before from the main valley. The going was wet but easy. Water had flooded their trail overnight but had since drained away. In only fifty yards he found his first clue.

One of Roland's moccasins lay in the high grass. The bear on the instep was unmistakable.

What did it mean? Had Roland made it this far and lost the moccasin here, or had the water carried it from the gorge? Day slipped the shoe into his pocket and prowled the area for answers. He even sloshed out into the middle of the cul de sac where the floodwater was knee deep. There he searched an acre or more but came up short.

He returned to drier ground and continued out to the main valley before turning back. It was when he reversed course that he finally saw evidence of activity, signs that made him despair at first. In the ground close to the cul de sac's wall were tracks of dire wolves.

Many tracks. He turned again and traced them toward the valley where the hairs on the back of his neck stood up. The wolves had followed the Settlers' trail.

Sometime in the last twenty-four hours they had picked up the men's scent in the valley and tracked it.

He reversed course one more time. Staying near the wall, he shadowed the trail into the cul de sac. The wolves had a light step despite their weight and Day had to work hard to stay on their path, but he was able to follow it toward a cut in the south hills that he and Roland had ignored the day before. From there the tracks went on almost to the gorge, then returned. Day guessed it was due to the water. Any trail or scent he and Roland had left in the gorge would have been washed away, scoured as completely as the ravine's floor. And the water itself would have been a hindrance. But at the entrance to the cut the wolves' tracks overlapped, coming and going. The wolves had lingered there. Why?

Several such carve-outs ringed the cul de sac. Maybe eighty feet deep, this one had a rock face for its back wall that Day could see from the entrance. It was unremarkable and empty. That was why it had not merited attention earlier.

But now it did.

He found a thin trail where at least one wolf had moved into the narrow entrance of the cut. As the walls closed in, Day stepped with caution, sensing that the terrible animal might still be lurking in the clearing inside. And it was, in a way. Where the tracks ended, almost hidden in the high grass, he discovered the wolf's carcass. Bloodied and ripped, it lay in silent agony as though stretched on a rack. The ground nearby showed signs of a vicious struggle.

This wolf was smaller than the ones they had encountered above the lake camp but that did not mean it was small. It was half again the size of a timber wolf. It had died violently, at the jaws of another animal, and as Day studied the scene and the carcass he he had a sinking feeling he knew which creature had done the killing. A clue was that one of the wolf's hind legs was crushed above the hock. The animal's throat was torn open as well but it was almost certain that the leg had been crippled first. Day had long suspected that his beast of a dog had a trace of pit bull in him for going for a hind leg was a favorite tactic of his in any struggle.

So maybe his dog had been here and had downed another dire wolf. But how did that come to happen? Had the wolves followed the dog, not the Settlers? If so, why did the scene indicate only one fight? Had it been one-on-one and the other wolves showed up later? And what was the great beast doing there in the first place?

Normally Day did not mind trying to divine what a trail told him but today he was working against the clock. He did not have Roland's talent for reading the land and now he felt the deficiency acutely.

He moved between the walls, studying the scene. There had been three or four animals, which would match the howl he had heard the night before. It looked as though the wolves had begun to move into the clearing but then backed off...and that's when the fight happened. As best Day could tell they had hurried away in the opposite direction, going directly across the meadow at a point outside the flood's reach. He glanced that way but made no effort to explore there. The wolves were of no importance so long as they were off his trail, and due to the flood it appeared they had lost his scent for now.

So then what to make of the moccasin? Day looked around, unsure what to do.

A crisp breeze rolling in from the Tetons fanned his face as he thought. He could imagine various scenarios but all lacked evidence for support. Finally, for lack of other ideas he went the rest of the way into the cut, even though from where he stood it appeared he could see everything it contained.

He was wrong. The view from the entrance was an optical illusion, the flat granite and sandstone walls obscuring a curve in both directions that yielded a larger clearing than supposed, an elongated teardrop of high grass growing right up to the rocks. Against the right wall the grass was matted flat.

Day scanned the hill above the walls. Short grass and shrubs, nothing more.

In a patch of dirt opposite the entrance he found footprints. Two were human: small and light, they almost certainly belonged to natives. A third was canine and he recognized immediately the print of the great dog. He knew his beast's tracks well – they were longer and narrower than those of the wolves – and it made his heart leap to see one here. Either the dog had been with Roland to provide support or he had followed the Comanche's trail. Either way both might be alive.

But the natives? As far as he could tell there were none of their tracks in the cul de sac and none in the entrance. If they had not passed that way, then how did they get there?

Day stared at the walls again. They looked unbroken but they had deceived him once already so he walked the perimeter to get a closer look. When he did that he kicked himself. *Thou blind fool,* he muttered. *What dost thou to mine eyes that they behold and see not what they see?* There *was* a break and another entrance, a trail that led up the south hill. It was masked by a rock outcropping, like a walk-out basement whose stairs rise behind an embedded wall.

In Day's mind a kernel of understanding began to grow. He went over to the matted grass.

The ground there showed no blood and no sign of a struggle. Yet someone had lain there. He found another track of his dog, the long nails dug into the soil. He knelt to look closer. When he did, his eyes glanced to the base of the rock.

There, scratched onto the andesite wall inches above the soil, was a crude figure of a waterbird. The tool used was a rock chard lying inches away. Tiny flakes from both lay in the grass.

Day let a wave of relief wash over him. Roland had survived the flood.

He stood and backed away, taking in the whole scene. Roland had made it this far. Exhausted or injured, he had collapsed in the grass. At some point he was concerned enough about his situation to scratch a sign on the wall to let Day know he was here. The great dog was with him. So far, so good.

Day looked from the grass to the hidden trail. Natives had appeared at some point. Was Roland still around when they did? Day guessed so. The question now was, did they help him or hurt him? Did they leave on their own or was he now a captive? There had been two natives with the Progs at the valley camp, he remembered. Were these the same guys? And how did they happen to find Roland, anyway?

Day realized he had never asked Eric Wulff about the Progs' use of the natives. That would have been good information, he chided himself.

The sun moved toward midday, hidden by overcast. Day pulled the last energy bar from his duffel and chewed it, considering his options.

Roland had to be with the Indians, he decided. Probably as a captive. That was the only thing that made sense given the information before him.

If so, then Day saw only two routes he could take. He could return to the hills above the gorge and assault the Prog camp on his own, or he could go after Roland. If he did the latter, he would have to intercept the natives who had taken his friend before they got him back to Reed.

Day closed his eyes and shook his head. He was closer to Reed than he had ever been and the desire to pursue the Prog leader was strong. Even if it meant going it alone, he was better armed than the Progs and – if Wulff could be trusted – Day was confident he could take them by surprise. If he could capture Reed, that action alone might prompt the others to throw up their hands. Wulff himself might switch sides.

But even as he plotted these possibilities, Day knew it was not what he would do. He had to follow Roland. Whether the natives were friendly or not, Roland's position with them would be precarious whether he was a captive or patient. Day could not leave him to face either situation alone.

"Alright," he muttered, with a last glance around the clearing. "I've screwed up just about everything up to this point. It's time to start digging out of this hole."

With that he slipped behind the wall and headed up the trail behind.

18

The natives' trail was easy to follow. Day deduced early on that they were carrying a heavy load between first two, then three, people, and no matter how light or agile the natives were on their own their footprints in the hills above the clearing could not hide their burden. He judged they were at least two hours ahead of him.

To his surprise the trail went south, paralleling in the opposite direction the valley he and Roland had crossed the day before. With every step he found himself moving away from the Progs' high camp. His working assumption had been that natives working with the Progs had taken Roland captive. It stood to reason, therefore, that they would head to the west, into the hills above the gorge. But that was not what they were doing.

So who were these guys? Curiosity mixed with frustration as Day traveled. He had to save Roland but he was moving farther away from Reed with every step. He could not help feeling that he was covering lots of ground to little purpose as far as their original mission was concerned.

The hills were as green as the valley below. The grass was shorter and the trees were younger. There were also scattered glacial erratics, great boulders left behind by an ice field that Day guessed was nearby. After an hour he topped a rise and his hunch was confirmed: the east wall of a glacier came in sight a mile away.

The way the mountain flowed he knew this could not be the retreating edge of the glacier. It must run north-south, which meant he was looking at a side wall that tumbled down a lateral moraine. But the wall was still forty feet high. Its ice, clean and pure, radiated a surreal blue that stood in contrast to the whitecaps of the Tetons some dozen miles behind. A breeze in Day's face brought the thick aroma of snow and ice. Water dripped off the wall and a thin stream flowed from beneath it into a course that Day could not yet see, but he assumed it found a way down into the valley and the marshes below.

From where he stood the trail veered toward the glacier. It must have turned south again, though, for in the distance, perhaps half a mile ahead, he saw highlighted against the ice four individuals moving in the same direction as he. He was surprised they were not farther along but then he realized they were no longer carrying Roland; instead they had taken the time to rig a travois, which they now dragged across the terrain.

Day watched their progress from the cover of a bitterbrush, trying to guess their destination. The glacier filled a gap in the mountains as it retreated to the west and south, toward the peak that he recognized would one day be called Mount Moran. Deep snow also spread south along the hills until reaching the pass that Crazy John had talked about. That meant the Indians were unlikely to go west from their current position. Their only options were to continue south or move east into the valley. But if they had wanted to be in the valley they could have traveled that way all along, so Day guessed they would continue south. That would keep them in the hills and parallel to the ice and snow until reaching the pass, at which point they would be obliged to descend.

Day was pondering his options when suddenly he felt he was being watched. A sixth sense told him he was not alone. There was no sound, no new scent, but someone was near.

Crouched, he slid his forefinger over the trigger guard of the Weatherby and readied his stance. Then he spun around.

The great dog sat ten feet back, mouth open and tongue lolling as though they had just played a game of fetch. Its red eye looked at Day with a sparkle while the brown one peered off to the right. The brown eye could have been searching the land behind the Settler or just wandering...it was hard to tell.

"Jesus, Mary, and Joseph!" Day growled. "One of these days you're going to do that and I'll blow a hole in you a mile wide."

The beast scratched its ear, unconcerned.

"You lose your buddies?" Day asked, scanning the land behind the dog. "Or did you bring the wolves with you? You had better not. I've got enough problems without being chased by Satan's kennel."

The great dog yawned. Not my problem, the motion said, but Day noted dried blood on the animal's coat. He had a feeling the dire wolves would continue to be a shared problem.

"Alright, then. If you're going to stick around this time our next challenge is up there. Three locals and your favorite redskin. We don't kill any of them, you got that? No killing! Save that for the bad guys."

The great dog made no commitment but when Day moved up the trail it followed at a respectable interval, perhaps confident that Indians or no Indians, there would be conflict soon enough.

Around the same time, Eric Wulff and Ruud Rohanson finally reached the Narrows. Their departure that morning from the high meadow camp had been delayed by two unexpected arrivals.

The first was Puff, the Arrow Indian, who emerged from the forest just after dawn with six tribesmen in tow. The warriors kept their distance from the camp, staying at the trees, but their sudden appearance – with painted faces and more than the usual number of feathers entwined in the hair above their ears – threw the camp into turmoil. Everyone from Wulff to Nancy Peal scrambled for a weapon, fearing they were being attacked.

Seeing the consternation his party provoked, Puff approached the long house with palms outspread, his face impassive but relaxed. He relayed through repeated hand signals that his group came in peace, that the warriors were loyal to him and therefore to the Progs. Blake Reed, in turn, was calm and composed and seemed to enjoy the panic among his camp mates. He informed everyone that he had expected the Indians' arrival, and that they came in response to his invitation.

His intent was to have the Arrows lead them out of the mountains and down to the watering hole and provide protection along the way, just in case either the Settlers or the Moon Indians made an appearance.

"And when the hell were you going to let us in on this secret?" Ruud demanded. "After my heart attack, or after we drilled a couple of these guys in surprise?"

"I'm letting you know now," Reed said.

"That's mighty white of you," Ruud shot back. "Why not yesterday, or the day before, or whenever you came up with this brainstorm?"

Grumbling among the others showed it was not just Rohanson who decried the early-morning shock. Reed did not apologize.

"I make plans and I let you know when it's time to put them into motion," he reminded them. "My plans change and so do the circumstances, and I won't waste time holding a committee meeting every time that happens."

"Uh huh. Well, from now on if you want my support for these wonderful plans of yours, then you start bringing me in at the start."

"You'll know when I tell you," Reed answered, his eyes burning into the Swede. But this time his hypnosis trick fell short.

"Then you can count me out of whatever the hell you're doing."

"You want out?" Elke asked. She stood off to the side with her arms crossed, as always never far from Reed, and now she shifted so the Rossi .38 snub nose revolver was visible in her right hand.

"Don't cross me, bitch," Ruud told her. "You think you're his enforcer but if you bow up on me I'll crush you like a bug."

Elke was unmoved. "I'm right here," she said, and pointed the barrel between Ruud's legs.

"What do they get out of it?" Wulff interrupted, eager to avoid a fight and unwilling to lose a man while half a dozen Indians of uncertain motivation stood only thirty yards away. He thought Elke was as crazy as Reed and from the look on her face she was ready to pull the trigger. "The Arrows, what did you promise them?"

"They think they're getting our weapons," Reed said, not looking away from Ruud but shifting so his back was to Puff. "And if we get the Settlers' device, I have no problem leaving them our guns."

"What if we don't get the device?" Nancy Peal asked.

"Then they'll get nothing and like it," Reed snapped. "The point is to use them to sweep the land before us and get rid of any threats. After that, I don't care what they want."

The second arrival was even more of a surprise than the first and it came just in time, for although Wulff changed the topic, Reed, Rohanson, and Elke continued their Mexican standoff. Aron Sorley showed up just then, limping into camp from the west over the rounded summit where the meadow swept down in a long slide to Jackson Hole. He came to the camp via the reverse of the route the Progs now intended to descend the mountain, carrying an M-4 carbine, a walking stick, and a Gerber hunting knife slung at his belt. He also bore a message.

"King's made a great alliance with the Moon tribe," he informed the others after filling them in with the details of his escape from the Settlers. "He found the girl he wanted and in return he promised to support them in their fight against the Arrows." Sorley seemed to expect a positive response to this announcement but his timing could not have been worse, and he received just the opposite. Reed's head looked ready to explode. The others pointed to the tree line where Puff had re-joined his tribesman.

"I'm surrounded by fools!" Reed erupted. "Morons! No-talent ass clowns!"

"Why?" Sorley replied. "King couldn't find his house but they ran across a Moon camp and they had food, so he did some trading with them. And he knows where we are."

"We all know where we are, you idiot! Knowing where we are isn't the goal, controlling our future is. And you don't do that by allying with the weak side!" Reed was angry enough that he forgot about Ruud and turned his gaze on Sorley, who was thoroughly confused. "You don't do that by teaming up with a bunch of foragers who have nothing to offer."

"Apparently they had something to offer King," Carlos chuckled.

Reed wheeled on him.

"You think it's funny? You think it's hilarious that instead of us dividing the Indians, they have divided us? And all so a washed-up actor can get laid? The only reason any of us are alive right now is because we stuck together. We stuck together in one group, with one leader, with each of us contributing to our survival. One group, one movement, one leader! That's the only way we'll stay alive and the only way we'll get out of here. King…" Reed was so contemptuous he had trouble finding words. "He made a 'great alliance?'" he said in disbelief. "That dumbass can't even make a decent movie! How did he talk to them? How does he know what they said? It'll fall apart in a week, if it hasn't already."

"But he has one of their women," Sorley reminded them in frustration.

"And that makes them loyal? What is this, medieval Europe? What did he trade for her? Don't tell us he gave them a rifle?"

"I don't know. I caught up with them afterwards."

"Where did you get *that* rifle? It's not yours."

"No, I borrowed it from Minh. I couldn't walk all the way back here unarmed."

"So what is our Vietnamese warrior doing to protect himself?" Reed demanded, sarcasm dripping from his words. "Has he made an arrangement with the Moons, too? You imbeciles!"

"Where are they?" Wulff interrupted again.

"Five miles south of the big canyon," Sorley answered, angry that his long trek was so unappreciated. "It's a straight shot from the bottom of this ridge. I made it here in a day, taking the same route you and I scouted that time we found the dead slants. King found a place to make a new camp on the Snake River – it's gotta be the Snake River, it comes out of the canyon where Jackson Lake was. But the lake's not there, at least it's smaller…"

"Enough!" Reed shouted, loud enough that the Indians turned and looked.

Reed leaned in close. Sorley backed up in response. The Prog leader's intensity could still cow some of his followers.

"Do you know why the Moons blew us off? Because they're weak. They're scroungers and scavengers, digging up clams and chasing rabbits. I gave them a chance to even the odds against the other tribe and they turned me down. So now we're with the Arrows. The Arrows have numbers, better weapons, and they're *hunters*," Reed emphasized, enunciating each word. "They're aggressive. They're also *here*. For now, *they* are our allies. Not the Moons. The Arrows. When we need to turn on the Arrows, we will. Then and *only* then will we talk to the Moons again, not before!"

So now Wulff, Rohanson, and Sorley were in the gorge, above the Narrows where there was nothing to see but fallen rock and washed sand and a new path carved through both by the persistent creek. Ruud was in a foul mood due to his confrontation with Reed and Elke. His frustration mounted the farther they hiked without finding the bodies of the Settlers. Sorley, to the contrary, was pleased. Despite his dressing-down by Reed, when he learned that Wulff and Rohanson were going to look for the Settlers he insisted on joining them. At least with the bounty hunters he could vent his anger by settling a score. He popped the blister on his foot, bandaged it with a strip of t-shirt and a honey salve that Crazy John gave him, and strapped on his boot. Then he wolfed down some fish and joined them on the trail. Unlike Rohanson he was just fine with not finding the bounty hunters dead: he wanted to find them alive so he could kill them himself.

Wulff knew searching the upper gorge would be a waste of time. He reminded his companions that the Settlers had passed the Narrows going up, but they would have had to flee *down* the canyon to get away from the flood. If the Progs descended into the upper gorge they would burn a couple of hours to no purpose. They would also have to climb back out the same rocky trail in order to go around the collapsed Narrows. But Ruud insisted on searching the whole gorge. Since his temper was already on a hair-trigger – and since a fruitless search might wear him down a bit – Wulff chose not to argue the point.

As expected, they found nothing. For Wulff, the only positive result of their exertions was Ruud's reaction upon seeing the destruction in the gorge. Wulff had told him what to expect but the Swede was nevertheless in awe at the scale of the damage, at the ferocity with which the water had roared through the ravine. This time he did not leap for joy or high-five as he had done with Bern Jones. He merely forgot his anger for a time and stared open-mouthed at the crumbled walls and piled debris.

"My bet is they're in there," Wulff said, nodding toward the mass of rocks and timber. "Buried. They never made it out the other side."

Rudd gave no sign that he heard. He just closed his mouth and stepped as close to the pile of rubble as he could. It was two stories high and some of the rock chunks were the size of school buses. His boots splashed in the trickling creek as he peered under and around the behemoths. Finally he backed away.

"We'll see," he said.

They climbed out of the ravine the same way they had gone in, using what remained of the old Prog trail that Day had spotted just before the dam blew. On Wulff's suggestion they split up after that. Wulff backtracked around the dam to search north of the ravine while Ruud and Sorley combed the forest above the south wall. Neither had Wulff's experience outdoors but Sorley had hunted and was no slacker in the woods, while Ruud had improved much since the spring. The three of them agreed to meet at the aspen grove.

Once out of sight, Wulff broke into a run and hurried along his appointed route. It took him an hour to get to the spot where he had hauled Day to safety; from there he continued east just as the Settler had done. There was no trail but on reaching the overlook to the cul de sac he discovered Day's campfire. Day had scattered the embers but the smell of ash lingered. The ground even had a hint of warmth yet, so Wulff stood on the ridge and searched the vale below for movement. He knew Day would have gone into the gorge first – the question was, was he still there? Wulff headed down to find out.

He arrived at the aspen grove a half hour before the others, giving him time to scout the area and look for anything he did not want them to find. Day had been good about hiding his tracks but Wulff nevertheless found two prints in the mud. He walked over them, taking comfort that they both headed out of the gorge rather than in.

"Holy crap," Sorley commented when he and Ruud arrived. "The water did a number on these trees."

Ruud ignored the battered aspen. "Any sign of them?" he demanded.

"None up top," Wulff lied. "None here, either. But I've gone only a few yards in."

"Well, then let's find the bastards," Sorley declared. He made toward the gorge but Ruud stepped in his way.

"You bring up the rear," the big Swede ordered.

"What? Why?"

"Because you stink."

Sorley flushed angry at the insult. "What the hell are you talking about? It's not like you've showered in the last six months!"

"I'm not talking about that. You stink of fish. Did you eat your breakfast or wear it?"

"I ate fast to keep you idiots from waiting!" Sorley protested.

Ruud was having none of it. "Just keep your distance," he repeated, and with no more comment strode into the gorge.

Wulff had wanted to go first so he would have a chance to cover up other signs Day might have left – as well as to get away from Sorley's fish odor – but Ruud beat him to it. With a shrug at the fuming Sorley he swung into second place.

They worked their way up to the lower end of the Narrows. Ruud's impatience overrode his caution and his pace increased the farther they went. With every bend they rounded that revealed nothing but rock and sand, he grew more anxious to get to the next one. Wulff's anxiety increased for the same reason. Despite the tracks he had seen, to him every section of the gorge that did not contain a

Settler meant that the next one was *more* likely to, and he kept fearing they would round a corner and come face to face with the barrel of that big Weatherby.

They did not. At one point they spooked a clutch of doves – almost giving Wulff a heart attack – but otherwise encountered nothing on their rapid journey up the gorge. Ruud went so fast that the others were obliged to follow in single file, but once they reached the Narrows and found nothing his haste fell away. They studied the collapsed gorge from the downstream side, then headed back down the canyon in a more desultory fashion, fanning out in the wider passages. This was to Wulff's regret. It was in such a bulging section, where the flood had spread and where the new creek now took a wide turn along one wall before returning to the canyon's center, that Sorley gave an excited shout.

It was a boot print. Alone and hidden above the stones by the creek, near one of the surviving stands of grass, the wet sand preserved its outline and tread clearly enough that Wulff could not explain it away. It was also pointing downstream.

"Never made it out the other side, huh?" Ruud grunted, looking at the logger. "Guess you're not such an outdoor genius, after all."

"I never claimed to be," Wulff replied, but his heart sank. He had hoped for a fruitless search that would end with the the three of them returning to the Prog main group where it would be easier to know everyone's movements.

"You seem disappointed." Ruud said, watching him.

"Damned right I am," Wulff admitted. "I was hoping they were in the Narrows. It would have been easier."

It was not clear if Ruud believed him but he let the matter drop. Sorley, in any case, could not have been happier. He prowled the gorge the rest of the way down to the aspen, looking for more signs of the Settlers. He did not find any but that did not dampen his enthusiasm.

At the mouth of the gorge they continued out into the cul de sac where it did not take long to find evidence of Day's passage there. His trail through the wet grass was recent enough that it was easy to see. Even Ruud could follow parts of it, marked by bent stalks and wisps of steam that rose from flattened blades warming in the sun. Not all of it was obvious, though, and for some time they were confused at the entrance to the cut where Roland had taken refuge. They even bypassed it just as Day had, convinced the surviving Settler or Settlers would retreat to the main valley. But after walking that way and losing the trail, they returned to the cut and explored there.

"Well, son of a bitch," Sorley whispered when they found the dead wolf, and again when they discovered the path hidden behind the rock wall. "This explains why we didn't see anybody above the gorge. If we had come down this way two hours ago we might have run into the guy."

Wulff doubted that, guessing that Day had a longer head start, but he kept silent.

"What do you think? He made camp here, maybe?" Ruud suggested, pointing to the matted grass against the wall.

"No camp," Sorley disagreed. "There's no fire or food. Maybe just rested. He was probably tired after escaping from the flood. Right?" he asked, looking in Wulff's direction.

"Yeah," Wulff answered. He was lost in thought, exploring the rest of the clearing. "Probably."

"You don't sound so sure," Ruud demanded. "What do you know that we don't?"

"Nothing. I think you're right that he probably rested here. But I'm wondering about the wolves."

"Why?" his companions exclaimed. "It's dead."

Wulff pointed into the grass along the entrance to the cut. "That one is, but he wasn't alone. Look at these tracks. At the entrance, and here, and over here, too," he showed them, including a track near the matted grass. "They don't look all that old. I'm wondering when they showed up and where they went, and what killed the dead one."

"What do you mean, what killed him? The other wolves killed him. They had a fight."

"Why?"

"Why?" Ruud retorted, as though Wulff was insane. "What, are you worried why wolves fight now? Who the hell cares? Maybe they were arguing over who got to eat the Settler first. It doesn't matter."

Wulff thought it did but he did not argue. "It's a weird coincidence," was all he muttered. He looked around the walls of the clearing as though expecting to see a pack of dire wolves glaring down at them.

The others studied the prints, tightening the grip on their weapons. Their rifles were M4 carbines looted from a California armory; a few of the remaining Progs carried them thanks to Lace and Reuben. They were sturdy and reliable guns but their .556 rounds did not carry the punch of the AK-47s that some of the Progs had, a fact which both Sorley and Rohanson now pondered ruefully.

"There were a few of them," Ruud admitted. "Did they go up the trail back there?"

Sorley returned to the hidden wall and examined the path behind it. "It's hard to tell. There's a lot of rock."

Ruud hefted his rifle and affected nonchalance, though he knew from experience that he would have to fire the M4 several times to stop anything larger than a coyote. Reed had distributed all the remaining ammo so their magazines were full but still, a bigger gun would have been nice to have.

"It doesn't matter," he insisted. "We'll find out for ourselves. If we need to shoot a few wolves, so be it. But if we're lucky they got to the guy first."

Wulff agreed that was a possibility but he was not so sure. They were doing a lot of guessing. He wondered if they were misreading what the clearing was telling them. Also – and this was not something he mentioned to Sorley and Rohanson – he spotted footprints in the sand by the far wall that did not correspond to Day's boots. They were certainly made by natives but which ones? Had Puff and his guys come this way or was it the Moons? If it was Puff and the tracks were recent, wouldn't he have said something that morning before Wulff and the others left camp?

Wulff knew the Arrows – with Prog help – had pushed the Moons out of the valley early in the summer. Seizing Moon territory was the main reason Puff's band had made the alliance in the first place. So the tracks could have been made by Arrow Indians. Then again, the Moons still made forays this far despite the risk of conflict with the Arrows. Wulff had seen them from a distance, tracking deer through the marshes or fishing in the valley streams. The game in the valley was too good for either tribe to ignore.

And how old were these tracks? Wulff could not tell. Were they there before Day, after him, or had the natives and Day encountered each other? If so, what did that mean? Had they killed him or vice-versa? Or were they now tracking him, too?

Things were getting complicated and Wulff did not like it. He did not like it at all.

19

Day was gaining on the natives. They moved at a steady pace but the travois held them back. The Indians steered toward the glacier to intercept a game trail and by the time Day reached that same spot he had cut the distance between them in half.

He wondered why the natives had taken Roland at all. As a captive, a prize, or a curiosity? Was Roland hurt, and did they intend to treat his wounds at another location? He remembered the native on the plateau, the one injured by the elk. Maybe that man had died and these people were his tribesmen who guessed that Roland was involved. Perhaps he had not died but still did not appreciate the aid given him. So did they want revenge? Maybe the natives were simply hostile to the Progs and anyone they assumed was linked to them. There were too many options and the trail gave him no clues. It only told him that he was getting closer, as the soil scatter in the footprints and drag marks had not even had time to settle. Unless the natives abandoned the travois, he would catch up with them by late afternoon.

The great dog moved off onto Day's right flank, prowling the land nearest the glacier. The temperature, already brisk, dropped the closer they got to the ice. Day watched in amusement as the dog stepped reluctantly across the glacier stream. Many times he had seen the beast dive happily into icy rivers that a Labrador would have shied away from, yet today for some reason he had muted enthusiasm for the water. Hunting in the Ice Age was a new thing for both of them.

Once across the creek their progress stalled. He had seen little game in the hills all day, mostly just tracks, including some type of bear, but now both he and the dog were held up by a pair of what looked like moose. A female and her calf appeared from a stand of trees upslope from him and browsed their way across his path. They were huge, with the build of moose but longer legs and heads like caribou. They resembled the single male he had seen on their first day – a stag moose, Roland had called it – though these lacked the expansive antlers. Antlers or no, even the calf was taller than Day.

Day kept his distance, waiting for them to move on. They were the only animals in sight but they were in his way. When they paused he grew frustrated and tried to work his way around them uphill. That almost ended in disaster. The cow lifted her head and stomped her feet. She locked him in a glare and snorted an alarm, then made a mock rush at him. He backed up all the way to the stream but now that she was alerted to his presence she kept him in sight. When he tried to go around the pair downhill she also moved to block his path. He had never seen a deer or elk be so aggressive, so relentless. Finally he gave up and held his position, which seemed to provoke the animals the least. The only good thing was that the big dog wisely stayed out of sight, busy as he was exploring a crevice in the ice wall.

After a while the moose moved downslope and left the trail open for Day to pass. By then the natives were out of sight. He pressed on, following the travois marks. The glacier wall fell behind though snow still lay uphill to his right, some of it deep. From the placement of the erratics and the young vegetation Day assessed the entire ridge was part of the retreating icepack. In a thousand years the glacier would be gone for good. He wondered if the natives obsessed about climate change the way residents of his own time did.

The great dog rejoined him at the end of the hills, where prevailing winds drifted the snowfield downhill. The beast carried a bone of some sort that was the size of a baseball bat. He carried it proudly, like a puppy tossed food from the dinner table, and growled when Day tried to take a look.

Pushed by the snow, the natives' trail now curved down into a spruce forest that filled the land above the southwest corner of the valley. The forest ran from the snowline to a series of cliffs overlooking the valley. The ground inside the forest was soft, with rivulets from melting snow running through the soil. Tracks indicated his quarry had picked up their pace.

The forest eventually thinned and gave way to a field of snow and ice that persevered in mountain shadows. The snow was powdery and several inches deep on top of the ice. While it was not difficult to cross, a false step could send a man sliding, particularly at the edge of the field where the ice brimmed upward like a pie crust. Day navigated the field with care and on the far side found himself once again on dry ground, beyond the valley and on the west slope of the pass toward which Crazy John had tried so hard to direct them days earlier.

Now the high plateau that he had been following merged with the pass in a mix of rockslides and eroded earth. Great stones jutted from the hillside as though waiting their turn to roll free. The natives' trail worked its way down to the bottom of the pass. There the land leveled and a thin stream wound its way through willows, more boulders, and tall grass.

To his left the pass curved into the valley. Day knew if he went that way he would in a few miles encounter the salt lake and artesian springs by the first Prog encampment. To his right the pass drove straight into the mountains. From his perch on the hillside he had a good view in both directions. There was no one in sight.

Yet the natives had gone down the hill. Day saw marks where they had dragged the travois across the stream. His rifle at the ready, he headed down after them. The great dog followed. At the bottom, the dog looked into the pass and cocked an ear.

"Wait!" Day whispered. "No killing!" Giving orders to the dog was useless but he hoped his tone at least would convey the message. The beast responded by feigning disinterest and wandering off in the opposite direction.

Day found cover behind a boulder and sat down to listen. The gurgle of the water and the cry of a pinyon jay were the only sounds. Wishing he had brought a small drone to fly over the land ahead, he finally rose and got back on the trail.

After a few hundred yards the walls of the pass grew steep. The stream still wandered and the grass grew thick. Day could see why bison would pass through here.

He had just stopped to listen again when a low call came from around the next bend.

"Day! It's alright. Come on up."

It was Roland's voice. Day's spirits leaped. He hesitated, though, fearing a trap, and when he did go forward it was with infinite care.

There was no trap. He found Roland lying on the travois beside the stream, on a grassy bank that was as lush and green as an Irish pasture. His bow and quiver of arrows were beside him, though Day noticed most of the arrows were missing. The stretcher was a deerskin tied between two aspen poles; the poles were propped on a marmot mound so Roland was in a comfortable position with his head higher than his feet. One side of his face was swollen and one eye half-closed, but he raised a hand weakly to signal for Day to approach.

"I need to teach you how to move in the wild," he mumbled. "Heard you while you were still on the hill. And I can smell that damned dog of yours. Tell him not to come too close. The natives are scared of him. They think he's a spirit."

"He's a pain in the ass, is what he is," Day replied. He took Roland's hand and held it, because it was not clear from the other Settler's gaze if he could see. "How bad are you hurt?"

"Could be worse."

"Doesn't look like it."

Roland ran his tongue over swollen lips. "Ever been to Rock Springs?" he countered. "Got in a fight there once with a couple of Arapahoe. I hate Arapahoe. Purple-eyed sons of bitches who smell worse than your dog. They can fight, though. I won but for the next week could barely get out of bed."

"Anything broken?"

"Don't think so. Just bruised." His words were slow and he pointed to his temple. "I would be on my feet now but for this. Got caught in the water and tossed around. Managed to surf it out of the gorge, then one of those aspen hit me and knocked me silly. Not sure how long I was out. Remember crawling so I didn't drown..."

Day checked the welt on Roland's head, on which the natives had smeared a poultice of smashed onion and wild ginger. He then examined him for other injuries. As far as he could tell Roland was correct: his body was turning black and blue almost everywhere but Day found no obvious broken bones. Roland's left foot was unshod so Day gave him the moccasin he had found.

"I found your trail in a clearing off the cul de sac," he told his partner. "You must have spent the night there. I was worried – the wolves made a ruckus and I was afraid it was over you."

Roland's eyes focused.

"The wolves..." he repeated. "Yeah. Yeah, they were close...but your dog was there!" he remembered. "I heard the wolves and thought: they're going to eat you, *taka suapu*. I could hardly move. Then that mongrel of yours showed up. Don't know what he did but they didn't eat me." Roland's voice drifted off.

"Where are the natives?" Day asked. "Where are the guys who picked you up?"

Roland did not answer right away. His eyes closed and he chanted softly, repeating a tribal phrase with quiet emphasis as though willing himself into good health.

"Sorry, my head is still spinning," he mumbled. "It's slowing, though. The chanting helps. But it'll be a day or two before I'm up."

"The natives?" Day prodded.

"Wouldn't be surprised if they're right behind you."

Day looked behind him but the clearing was empty. He backed away and searched the area, then scanned up and down the pass as far as he could see. There was no sign of anyone, nor were there tracks. He returned to Roland.

"It looks like they cleared out," he reported.

Roland could not shake his head so he lifted a hand to indicate he disagreed. "They're near," he said. "These guys are good. And they knew you were behind us."

"What do they want?"

"Don't know. Haven't gotten that far. But they have the same markings as our boy on the plateau. And they gave me this." He indicated the poultice.

"I've got Tylenol. You want it?"

Roland declined. "My head doesn't hurt that bad," he explained. "It's just the dizziness. Believe it or not this plaster helps. Don't know where they found ginger this far west but it's potent. Clears the head."

Day did not doubt it: the smell made his own eyes water. He realized there was not much he could do for his friend. The best thing for a concussion is rest, which meant that Roland was best off remaining where he was.

"I think they're okay," the Indian agreed when Day shared his thoughts. "I don't know what their game is but it's not to hurt me. I can stick with them a couple of days."

Day was uncomfortable with that plan but the only alternative was to make camp and sit with Roland himself until he felt strong enough to move. In that time the Progs could disappear or at least get such a head start that it would take the Settlers weeks to catch up with them.

"I've got news. The Progs have a new camp," he said.

He shared everything that had happened to him since they ran from the flood. Roland listened with his eyes closed. He could have been asleep. The soft drumming of a woodpecker replaced the cry of the jay, and the trickle of the stream played its gentle music behind Day's low voice. It was a peaceful place.

"This guy Wulff," he said when Day finished. "What does he look like?"

"Six foot, solid, black hair and beard. Carries a Henry lever-action, and he's missing part of a finger on his left hand."

"You think he's our mole?"

"Don't know. I didn't bring it up."

"But you think he's willing to help?"

"He already has. He pulled me from the flood. Didn't have to. He could have fallen in, I could have shot him, his own pals could have seen him. He could always change his mind but right now he seems to want to go home more than he wants to kill us."

"Maybe he wants to do both," Roland suggested.

"What do you mean?"

Roland opened his eyes but put a hand over them. When he spoke it was with great precision, as though he were afraid the words would fly off the spinning turntable in his head.

"The Progs must have figured out by now that they've traveled in time. They may not know how but they must know it happened, and they must know that Kurtz and we have done the same. They know Kurtz went back. So they should guess that all of us have something – a device or tool – to enable a return journey. Maybe they've realized they don't have to make a deal with us if they can kill us and take whatever that something is."

"Maybe," Day conceded. "But Wulff never searched me. He never mentioned wanting anything other than to go home."

"Well, he wants something now. He's on your trail."

"How do you know?" Day asked.

"Paleface talk, redskin listen."

Day was confused but then realized he had not checked his six in several minutes. He turned and sure enough, not ten feet away stood an Indian. The sight did not startle him as much as it should have; he reflected ruefully that he must be getting used to being snuck up on.

"Told you they were good," Roland said.

The Indian was around five feet tall with strong legs and a barrel torso. He had a small, expressive face and wore what looked like a deerskin kilt at his waist; a beaver skin hung over his chest. He carried a spear that was longer than he was tall and that appeared to be his only weapon. Behind him at his eight o'clock stood another native also clad in a kilt but with a heavy vest made of elk hide. That man carried a spear, too. Neither Indian raised his weapon but the way they stood suggested they could launch them at Day with no notice if he made the wrong move.

Roland looked at the closer native and put his hand on Day's arm. He held his other hand across his body, palm down. The Indian repeated the gesture, his face grave. Day noticed the man had the same half-moon markings on his cheeks as the native they had treated two days before. Small world, he thought to himself, and wondered if their patient had survived.

"Communication ain't good," Roland explained to Day, "but we've agreed on some sign language. They guessed you were my companion before you came down the hill. This," – he repeated the palm down – "is 'friend.' That's why they disappeared rather than confront you."

"Good to know," Day said, not taking his eyes off the Indians.

"I call this guy Ted," Roland continued in a quiet voice. "The other one is Bill. There's a third guy, Rufus, somewhere."

"From *Bill and Ted's Excellent Adventure*?" Day asked. "What an unexpected taste in movies."

"You have Shakespeare, I have Keanu Reeves."

"*Kupa*," the Indian called Ted interrupted, urgency in his voice. He lifted one foot and put it down, then looked away up into the hills.

"*Kupa*," Roland repeated. With a careful lean of his head he, too, looked toward the hills, then with his right hand pointed down toward the ground, like a boxing referee counting out a fallen pugilist. Ted's response was negative.

"*Hunh*," he grunted. He raised and lowered his right foot again, then did the referee point three times.

"Three guys on our trail," Roland translated. He let out a long breath and leaned back on the travois, spent. "And I can't help you."

Day pursed his lips. "How far back?" he asked.

Roland waved his hand. "I don't know how to ask that. We've gotten to 'friend' and 'enemy,' that's all."

"So you don't know how much farther into the pass they plan to take you?"

"I think this is it."

"What do you mean?"

Roland glanced across the stream. Day stood up slowly to avoid spooking the natives and looked where Roland indicated. Thirty yards behind the guy called Bill, the east wall of the pass rose above the grass and willows. Where the wall reached the level of a two-story building the limestone encountered a layer of schist that formed an overhang of several feet. Below the schist were four openings. Several feet wide and of varying heights, the holes blended so well with the rest of the wall that Day could easily have gone on up the pass and never noticed them. They were natural, not man-made, and deep enough to give cover from the wind and rain. Crouched in the opening of one of the holes was another Indian. That one – Rufus? – paid no attention to Day. His gaze was directed toward the valley.

"Thought you said there were no cave men," Day muttered to Roland.

"They're not caves," his companion replied. "These are cliff dwellings."

"Excuse me, I missed the distinction. You should be a realtor."

Roland looked ready to explain but Day interrupted.

"Nancy Peal said Indians lived in the pass before the Progs kicked them out. Maybe it was these guys."

Fading, Roland said, "Yup. Not all year, though. They're seasonal." He would have continued with a lesson on paleolithic hunter-gatherer habits but lacked the energy.

Day studied the holes. The wall was steep and it appeared Rufus had reached his position only with the help of a spruce pole leaned against the rock. An idea began to form.

"Roland, do you think these new friends of yours will continue to help?"

Roland had closed his eyes but he interpreted much from Day's voice. "Comms are limited," he repeated. "But they don't appear to be pals of the Progs."

"Okay, then." Day made ready to depart. "I'll go take care of the three behind us. If they give up, you'll see me again shortly and we'll use these caves as a holding cell. If they don't, follow my trail when you get better. I'll head for the top of the gorge to keep an eye on Reed. I'll give you two days. If you can meet me, great. If not, I'll work out a solo plan. The fallback will be to join up down at the watering hole."

Roland fought to stay conscious. "Day," he muttered. "Be careful."

"I will."

"Don't..." Roland's voice drifted off.

Day knelt back down to hear. "Don't what?" he asked.

"Stop showing mercy," Roland whispered. "It doesn't work with these guys."

Day touched his friend's arm. "I don't know about Keanu Reeves but Shake-speare might agree with you. *Nothing emboldens sin so much as mercy*, or so he claimed."

"Smart guy." Roland's eyes closed again and he fell asleep.

Day stood again and looked at Ted, who stared back with a mixture of defiance and uncertainty about what the Settler would do now. In answer, Day looked toward the hills and patted his rifle. If Ted understood the gesture his face gave no sign.

Day turned to go but as he did the second Indian, Bill, barked a warning and pointed up on the hill. There looking down on them was the great dog. The Indians raised their spears.

"Easy," Day said in as soothing a voice as he could muster. He pointed to the dog and then made the palm-down gesture he had just learned. "Friend," he assured them. He would have added that the dog was often more of a fair-weather companion than a reliable ally but the distinction was beyond him at the moment.

Bill and Ted were unconvinced. They kept the spears ready.

Day took that opportunity to depart. He backed away, then went downstream to the bottom of the hill to climb the same serpentine path he had descended. On reaching the great dog he muttered, "I suppose I should be grateful you didn't eat anyone." The beast did not look at him but swung in behind as Day went up the trail and into the forest.

20

E ric Wulff knelt beside the stream flowing out from under the glacier's toe. The water was frigid and opaque, colored by a flour of fine sediment ground beneath the ice. The silt and sand at the water's edge were just as cold. Gritty, too, speckled as they were with the crushed shells of fossilized mollusks from a pre-Cambrian past. In that broken debris were animal tracks, clear prints moist with the tiny seashells of ages ago pressed against their outlines.

"What is it?" Ruud Rohanson's voice came from behind him.

"I don't know."

The Swede looked over Wulff's shoulder. "Those are wolf tracks," he declared.

"Maybe," Eric admitted. "They had a dog, though. A big one."

"That's not a dog," Ruud snorted. "No dog's that big."

Wulff scanned up and down the stream. The temperature had dropped into the forties but water still rained off the glacier, pattering like a spring storm and throwing spray into the air.

"How about a bear?" he asked. "Is a bear that big?"

"What are you talking about?"

Wulff directed his companion's attention to another set of tracks that went in and out of the stream, massive prints the size of dinner plates. Visible only in the wet sand nearest the water, each print showed toes with claws. The largest toe was on the outside and the front claws were longer than those on the hind feet. Strangest of all was that the toes were straight. Bears he knew from back home always pointed inward. They prints disappeared where the stream bent as the owner crossed onto firmer soil.

"Holy s...!" Ruud exclaimed, interrupting his own hoarse exclamation to look around in panic.

"That's the reaction the dog had, apparently," Wulff decided, studying where the two sets of tracks converged. "Looks like he inspected the bear tracks and didn't like what he found because he then went the long way around."

"I still say that's no dog," Rohanson repeated. "No dog's that big."

"Six months ago I would have said no wolf was that big, either. Or a bear. Whatever it is, it's traveling with them so we should be alert."

Aron Sorley was downslope, reluctant to leave the main trail with its clear human tracks. He waved to them to hurry.

"You worry about your wolf," Ruud told the logger, turning to rejoin Sorley. "And the bear. We'll worry about the guys with the guns."

I'll worry about all of them, Wulff thought. His companions were too anxious to rush forward, convinced the Settlers were in retreat. Wulff was not so sure. He knew he was on the Settlers' trail but that was all he knew. He did not understand the drag marks, nor did he understand the native footprints beside them. Were the Settlers now tracking the natives? Had the Settlers found something that they were dragging back to a camp? Why were they dragging it, why not carrying it? And why was he seeing only one set of boot tracks?

About the time he reached the stream he began to consider a new explanation for what he saw on the ground. Maybe only one of the Settlers – and the dog – had survived the flood. That would explain the boot prints. It did not explain the drag marks or the natives. Maybe the lone Settler was following the natives, but why?

He searched the hills rolling before him. As if he did not have enough on his mind, now they had a bear to worry about.

The Progs had seen bears often since their arrival. It was impossible not to – food was everywhere so wildlife was everywhere, including bears. Wulff had never been in such a wilderness where every level of the food chain, plants and animals, appeared in such abundance. The very isolation the Progs were suffering, the total void of any form of human development, meant that the animal kingdom ruled here. Humans needed to be on their toes at all times.

Even when they were alert there still had been conflicts. Hitch had been killed by a bear, or so many of the Progs believed. Wulff agreed that was a possibility but Hitch had gone out on his own that day and what they found of him later was too scattered and devoured to know for sure. It could have been a bear, that was what mattered. The Progs had seen grizzlies and a couple of things that were hell and gone bigger than grizzlies, like whatever this was walking along the stream. But it was not just their size that made the bears and other animals dangerous, it was also their aggressiveness. Everything in this wilderness seemed to be itching for a fight.

Which meant the Progs were in good company, he reflected ruefully as he watched Rohanson and Sorley reunite on the trail and move to cross the stream. More and more the two men went ahead without waiting for him, impatient with his caution and intent on catching up to and killing the Settlers.

Wulff let them go on. He was not interested in killing. In fact, he was growing more uneasy the closer they got to the Settlers since any conflict was going to put him in a tough spot. Already he felt like a double agent: guiding the Progs with whom he had lived and suffered for much of the last year while at the same time getting nearer to at least one bounty hunter whose life he had recently saved. If push came to shove and they got into a shooting match with the Settlers, Wulff would have to make a decision about whom to support and he did not yet know what that decision would be. Or maybe it was more accurate to say, he knew what the decision would be but he was anxious to the pit of his stomach about having to make it.

He just wanted to get home.

Half a mile away Day eased through the spruce forest holding his rifle in a low ready position, grateful for the needles underfoot that muffled sound from his already careful steps. He had worked his way as high on the slope as he could, near where the trees gave way to tundra that spread uphill to the snow line. Going high on the hill would help to keep him from being outflanked. He also hoped the elevation would work to his favor if it came to a firefight.

The great dog watched Day move upslope but did not follow. He prowled through the trees of his own accord, sniffing both the ground and air and following whatever the scents told him. Several times he stopped, standing with his head held high to sniff and listen. Whenever he did that Day watched to see what came next: if the dog went back to prowling, Day relaxed; if he leaped forward, there was something to eat and he was going after it; but if the head came down and the beast made a deliberate move in another direction, Day knew a threat was near.

The hoot of a grouse from somewhere ahead brought his attention away from the dog. Day paused to ensure it was an actual bird, then continued forward. Sure enough, after fifty feet or so a dusky grouse jumped from cover under a blueberry shrub. The grouse was bigger than Day would have expected but he was getting used to that. Usually cautious birds that stayed under cover, this one ran several feet before turning to eye Day with a look the Settler could only take as a challenge. Even the birds here had attitudes.

He looked downhill to see if he could still see the great dog. Sure enough, the beast was stock still again, head erect, gazing toward the forest's edge twenty yards away. Day glanced that way but there were too many trees for him to make out anything. The dog could not see anything, either, but his floppy ear went up. After several seconds it went down again and the beast slipped to his right, slinking behind a leaning tree and heading toward the cliffs overlooking the valley. In no time at all he had disappeared.

Thus warned, Day crouched and moved toward his own end of the tree line. The grouse ran before him with clucks of disapproval. Afraid he would flush the bird, Day slowed, at which point the grouse stopped and eyed him. It cocked its head, debating internally as much as a bird can, then moved away, dropping into a tree well and disappearing under a net of spruce boughs.

Day reached the edge of the forest and looked out. From where he emerged the ground rose, obscuring his view beyond ten yards. Frustrated, he low-crawled through the brush until reaching a higher position where he could kneel and lift his gaze above the scrub.

His efforts rewarded him with an immediate view of Aron Sorley not fifty yards away. Galt's notes told him that Sorley had run a cannabis shop in Fort Collins before he jumped into the Prog movement. but today the man looked more like an Appalachian moonshiner than a Colorado businessman. His clothes were bedraggled and threadbare. His hair was jet black, matted, thick, and long enough to reach his shoulders where it curled forward and met an equally dark beard. His face where it was not hidden by hair was lined and drawn. Haggard, like he had not had a decent night's sleep in months. He limped through the scrub with an M4 rifle in his hands.

Sorley was alone at first but another man soon appeared a dozen yards behind him. This Prog was taller and heavier with another mass of curly hair – blond – that merged with a beard of the same color. As dirty as Sorley but with rugged, classically handsome looks, he resembled a Viking more than a moonshiner. Day guessed it was Ruud Rohanson. Galt's notes on Rohanson were few but Day remembered Eric Wulff's warning about him.

As for Wulff, Day did not see him. He searched the land back toward the glacier – nothing. Not good. The native, Ted, had been specific that three people were coming up the trail: someone must be out there.

The two Progs closed on the forest. Day had to make a decision. He could shoot one now but almost certainly only one: the other would drop and take cover as soon as he fired. Then it would be Day against the two remaining Progs in terrain where a man could be ten feet away and invisible.

On the other hand he could ambush them in the woods. He thought of a spot on the trail where he might be able to take them one at a time if the men maintained their current spacing. That still left the third Prog, Wulff or whoever it was, but unless he appeared soon Day hoped he would not be a factor just yet. Besides, he knew how the great dog operated. The beast usually attacked from the rear and picked off stragglers, so if Wulff or anyone else was out there he would soon have a bigger concern than sniping at Day.

Making his decision, Day ducked and reversed course. Regaining the cover of the forest he hurried across the slope before turning downhill. His preferred spot for the ambush was a bend in the Indians' trail where they had veered to avoid dragging the travois over a hummock. Trees stood on and below the hummock while branches littered the ground. Day reached the spot, guessing he had four to six minutes to set his trap,.

The canvas bag he had lugged along since their arrival was almost empty. The fireworks were gone, as were his food stores and the maps. All that was left were the medical kit, his night scope, a few piggin strings and zip-ties, and a hundred feet of parachute cord. Strong and light, the cord had been indispensable to Day in the past. Now he put it to work once again.

A short time later Aron Sorley swore as he spooked the same dusky grouse that had bedeviled Day. The bird nearly gave him a heart attack, bursting from the brush as though launched from a cannon. Jittery as he was, Sorley almost opened fire. That would have announced to the world that he was there, though what the grouse did now was almost as bad since it ran up the trail before him, clucking like a flustered maid.

He waited until the bird disappeared again, which it did after glaring at the Prog as though daring him to shoot. He hated this place, Sorley reminded himself for the hundredth time. He hated the remoteness, he hated the wildlife, he hated the remaining Progs, and most of all he hated not knowing if every morning would be his last.

He regretted ever joining the Prog movement, damn them. It had all made sense at the time but now looking back he could not remember how or why he allowed each event to lead into the next. After donating money to local rioters he had moved on to joining them in their nightly mayhem. It was fun at first, an outlet for his frustrations. And best of all there were no consequences! The cops, the prosecutors, the politicians…all stood around like idiots night after night, doing nothing and often even lending verbal support. The next thing he knew, he was not just joining riots but leading them, and from there everything spiraled ever more violent until the last twelve months was like watching a movie in which he had starred but that he did not recall making. Even now he was still in the movie, detached from reality, no longer connected in any way to a time not long ago when he ran a store and sold pot, and as bad as life was at least he had a roof over his head and understood his world.

Now he was lost in the forest and being scared to death by a feral chicken. He tightened his grip on the M4, wanting nothing more than to beat someone with it to vent his frustration.

The trail curved. The grouse turned off the path before then and vanished into some honeysuckle shrubs. Good riddance.

With the grouse gone the forest fell quiet again, excepting the *chirrup* of an insect and the gurgle of melting snow where it criss-crossed the trail.

For his own part Sorley made no more noise than a foraging squirrel. The needles on the trail helped, as did the trickling water which masked – he hoped – sounds he could not control such as his pounding heart, his nervous breath, and the drag of leaves on fabric as he squeezed through the brush. He tried to avoid touching anything but that was easier said than done. The bushes were fat with spreading branches, spruce limbs reached far from their trunks, and honeysuckle vines stretched across the trail. No longer flowering this late in the season, the vines still spread with abandon and perfumed the air like well-dressed ladies passing on the street. Sorley appreciated the heady fragrance, in part because it made him think of attractive women but also because it temporarily overcame his own fishy smell that Ruud had accurately noted. It would wear off, Sorley told himself in his own defense. In the meantime, the honeysuckle helped. It grew everywhere, its shoots and stems pointing this way and that like loose antennae. He pushed them aside.

In doing so, he dragged his foot through a trip line of parachute cord that blended with the waving stems. The cord yanked free a stick downhill of the trail, which in turn released a hefty branch that Day had suspended a foot above the ground. The branch fell onto the needles with a *whoomp* and then rolled several feet, making all the sounds of sudden, reckless movement.

Sorley almost jumped out of his skin. He spun toward the sound and squeezed the trigger on the M4...but nothing happened. The gun did not fire. To his horror he realized that although he had loaded a full magazine into the rifle the day before, he had never chambered a round. In panic he corrected that, yanking the charging handle and releasing it, and then lifted the weapon to his shoulder to peer in the direction of the sound. He was just wondering if he had not overreacted again, if the grouse had not created some other mischief, when a rustle behind him made him spin the other way. He was half way around when something hit him hard on the side of the head. He dropped senseless to the forest floor, the passing ladies offering up one last scent of beauty and possibility before fading to nothing.

* ~~~ *

Ruud stopped and cocked an ear. He was well behind Sorley and outside the trees but he heard the *whoomp*. It was muffled, like the forest itself had exhaled, but he heard it. Now he wondered what it was.

The tall Swede fell behind his companion after Sorley disappeared into the forest. They had taken spacing for safety and for the comfort of Ruud's nose, but Ruud was about to enter the trees himself when movement downhill caught his eye. He looked and hissed for Sorley to stop. Sorley did not hear him and continued up the trail.

So Ruud remained alone for a while at the edge of the plain waiting for the source of the movement to reveal itself. He stood with his rifle raised, his eyes and ears straining, his lungs breathing in the clear mountain air scented with sage. The brush downhill was taller than the scrub by him, fed as it was by water that backed up at the rocky ledge, and he saw the willow and woodfern bend as something tall moved through it. Wulff had unnerved him with talk of wolves and bears so he watched the brush with rising unease. Then he remembered it could just as easily be the damned Settlers. With that thought his confidence swung back. Let it be a Settler, he prayed, mentally urging the source of the movement to reveal itself.

When he caught a glimpse of what could have been a man's hat his spirits soared. He sighted down the barrel of his rifle, thrilled that he might finally – finally! – avenge his suffering of the last many months. Then the branches parted and it was neither a Settler nor a bear but a pair of stag moose that emerged, a doe and yearling browsing at cliff's edge.

Ruud stifled a curse, adding this disappointment to his already long list of grievances. If he had had sufficient ammo and no Settlers to worry about, he would have shot the moose out of spite. Instead, with effort he lowered the rifle and moved his finger from the trigger. The animals could wait.

And then he heard the *whoomp*.

"Sorley?" he whispered. There was still the faint whiff of broiled fish in the air but not a sound from his companion. The silence ratcheted up Ruud's nerves.

He glanced back up their trail but saw no sign of Wulff. Not that he expected to. The logger was too independent, too smug and self-satisfied to work with the rest of the Progs. Ruud suspected Wulff had plans of his own that he was not sharing with the rest of them. He vowed to resolve that mystery once the Settlers were taken care of.

In that dark mood the tall Prog pressed on into the forest.

He had not gone far before he decided he preferred the plain. The spruce were tall and their branches blocked the afternoon sky, leaving shade on the forest floor that muted colors and made objects seem closer than they were. Movement was easy: he could see the travois drag marks clearly. Yet undergrowth clumped between the trees, enough to hide anything that wanted to be hidden. Mountain ash and berry bushes crowded together, often next to trees where they made the trunks seem even fatter. Worse, honeysuckle draped itself over everything to create dark caves of branches that three or four men could hide within. Ruud moved with his head on a swivel, his eyes darting left and right. He wondered how far Sorley had gone.

"Freeze."

He froze. Not because he was told to but from the shock of hearing the word.

"Hold your rifle out to the side and drop it."

Ruud recovered somewhat. His frustration, already on a high boil, overflowed. There was no way he was giving up his rifle. There was no way he was giving up at all. He would die first. He said, "No."

"Your choice."

There was the click of a hammer being drawn back.

Ruud glanced over his shoulder. The speaker knelt on the trail fifteen feet behind him. He was shorter than average and stocky, with a heavy jacket and a wool cap pulled down tight above a camo-painted face. Against his right shoulder he pressed the butt of a large caliber rifle. Wulff was right, it was a nice gun, though from this angle much of its beauty was lost since the large bore opening of the barrel occupied most of the view. That gaping hole caused Ruud to rethink.

He dropped the M4.

"Keep your hands up and move up the trail."

Ruud hesitated again. He had a Glock 9mm pistol inside his coat and wondered if he could get at it.

"You're a dead man," he vowed.

The reply was that Day sprang forward and clubbed the big Swede with the butt of his rifle, hard enough to make him stagger. Ruud cursed him with a vengeance.

"I'm a man in a hurry," Day replied. "Move."

He was in a hurry. There was still a third Prog behind him. Though he wanted to believe the great dog would handle him, the fact remained someone was out there. Also, he had knocked down Aron Sorley and zip-tied his hands but Day had had to move so fast to circle back for Rohanson that it had been a slapdash job. He would not be surprised if Sorley was not already getting away.

Sure enough, as they moved up the trail they found Sorley dazed but on his feet. He stood with his back to a tree trying to cut the zip-tie that bound his hands by scraping it against the rough bark. He looked up in pain and fury.

"I'll kill you!" he shouted.

Day kicked Ruud, buckling his knees from behind and pushing him to the ground. With his rifle trained on Sorley he ordered, "Get back down. On your face, both of you. I..."

That was as far as he got. A crashing behind him cut him off. It was accompanied by a *huff* that sounded vaguely like the great dog but deeper. For a split second Day told himself it was the dog...but at the same time he knew he was wrong. He turned.

Twenty feet up the trail the branches waved and splintered as though a truck were rolling toward them. The huffing turned throaty and loud.

"Bear!" Day yelled. He looked to his prisoners just in time to see Ruud bring up a pistol and point it at him. Day ducked as the gun went off. The bullet missed his head by inches but hit something, for a roar of pain came out the woods followed by an explosive increase in the crashing. Ruud pulled the trigger again but the Glock jammed. He threw it to the ground and ran after Sorley, who had already taken off down the trail.

Day spun to bring his rifle on target but was hit from the side as though someone had swung a couch. Though cushioned by the canvas bag and his heavy coat, the blow was still terrific. The Weatherby flew from his hands. He himself sailed through the air as though thrown, off the trail and into the brush. He crashed through a thicket and rolled downhill, falling into a tree well upside down where he struggled to right himself and get the Colt from its holster.

On the trail, Sorley had the biggest lead notwithstanding his bound hands. He made it to the end of the forest and emerged onto the ice field. A quick glance in both directions told him straight ahead was his best option so he ran for his life. Ruud was steps behind. Together they charged across the slope, snow flying from their feet.

But the bear delayed only seconds on the trail after knocking Day aside. Now it burst from the woods in a rage. Likely it never even saw or felt the Settler as it barreled through the forest, following the scent of food that was richer and more delicious than berries. Then out of nowhere came the shock of an explosion and a painful sting that glanced off its skull. The brush where Sorley had lain unconscious occupied the massive carnivore just long enough to see that the occupant had moved on, and with a sound like a furnace roaring to life it spun to go after him.

Ruud looked over his shoulder. The bear was a hundred feet behind them and gaining. It was surreal in its size, as tall as him and as wide as a van. He heard its growl above his own frantic breathing as it threw itself across the ice in pursuit, its enormous paws scattering the snow and making a mockery of it as an obstacle. There was no way the two of them would escape.

"Go!" Sorley cried as he stumbled against Rohanson. "Go! Go! Get to the rocks!"

But Ruud saw there was no way they would make it to the rocks before the bear caught them. Even if they did, even if they were able to scrabble their way onto the stones that jutted from the hillside like giant steps, this creature looked powerful enough to come right up after them, or to knock the stones free and bring down the men on them.

He leaped in front of Sorley and then with no warning slammed on the brakes. Sorley crashed into him and stumbled. Ruud grabbed the other man by the shoulders, flipping him backwards off his feet.

"What the...?" Sorley screamed. He hit the ground, momentarily disappearing in the snow. As he scrambled to get up Ruud kicked him in the face.

It was a glancing blow but it knocked Sorley over again. Ruud then spun on his heel and ran all out. He would not make it to the rocks, he knew, but the ice field rose at its edge where blowing snow had collected and then slid downhill, smoothing the surface and forming a natural sluice. Whereas most of the field sparkled under dry powder, here the ice glistened like slick glass. It flowed downhill until the snow petered out, dropping into a culvert at the bottom of the ridge where it melted and drained to the pass. What was in that culvert Ruud had no idea but it could not be worse than a raging short-faced bear.

He dove at the sluice like a kid leaping onto a sled. The ice was as slippery as it looked and he rocketed downhill. Out of control, he heard a yell behind him but was unable to look back, and anyway the feeling that the bear was right on his tail made him want nothing but more speed. The ice curved and took him with it. Near the bottom it thinned. He skipped across dry patches, then the snow ended and he tumbled across grass. Unable to stop, his momentum took him up and over a ledge. There he fell off the hill and disappeared.

21

The Colt's holster caught on a branch and nearly tore free from his belt as Day rolled down the hill. He managed to get the gun out and pointed it upslope, unsure where he was or whether the bear was after him or not. His hand shook.

I need to move, he thought.

But he did not move. His heart raced and his head spun and his system was flushed with adrenalin that held him in place and let him not feel the bruises he had gained from the attack. Willing himself not to pass out, for a full minute he focused only on the Colt.

Water.

He needed water. The canteen had also torn from his belt but it hung on a bough a few feet away. With his free hand he reached for it, unscrewed the cap, and drank it dry.

He never even saw the bear. It had to be a bear, though. He stared over the barrel of the Colt, listening. It was quiet. There was no sound near him, at least.

He pulled off his cap and strained his ears. A distant roar came then, airy and blowing like wind in the trees. It came from somewhere uphill, off to the left. Then another noise arrived that was more clear. His brain did not register it at first but soon he realized it was a man screaming. That jolted him from his stupor.

He sat upright and felt himself for injuries. Finding none that would keep him immobile, he began crawling uphill following the trail of debris that marked his descent. He had to get his rifle. Whatever had attacked them was at least the size of a grizzly; if it came back for Day he would need all the firepower he could get.

Day knew little of bears besides the basics. They were big, they were strong, they were fast, and brown bears in particular were hard to kill. But why had it attacked them? Were there cubs in the area? Had they surprised it? Day remembered seeing the massive prints out on the plain but he had seen no sign of a bear in the forest, not even near the berry bushes. That did not mean a bear was not around since even the biggest ones could move with stealth. Still... He remembered what Roland had said about grizzlies having an incredible sense of smell. Sorley had reeked of something...he tried to remember what. Fish, that was it. Good god. Not the cologne to take into the wilderness with you. Had that drawn the bear to attack?

He found the Weatherby a dozen feet below the trail. Both the rifle and scope were undamaged so he grabbed it and scooted back downhill as fast as he could go.

The forest descended until reaching cliffs that rose above the valley. Trees and undergrowth went to the cliff's edge but he found the stones on the precipice clear and solid. The drop beyond them proceeded in steps so if the bear came at him he thought he could survive a jump over the side.

Not that he planned to do that. He wanted his prisoners back. He had been close to taking two of the most dangerous Progs alive and unless the bear had killed them already he still wanted them. With that in mind he headed south along the rocks.

It was not long before the cliff intercepted the ice field. From there it was a long way up to the trail but he could see the bear. Mostly he saw its upper half, a shaggy back leading to powerful shoulders with muscles that rippled and bulged as it moved in the snow. When the head appeared, as it did when the animal pivoted from one side to the other, it was massive with a snout that bore a resemblance to an overgrown Saint Bernard. The wind was off the ridge, behind the bear and blowing down into Day's face, and snow flew around the animal like talcum powder as it worked at something in the snow. Day guessed it weighed two thousand pounds if it weighed an ounce.

The bear appeared to be pacing, or maybe digging, plunging its head into the snow then lifting and turning to do the same several feet away. Day had a queasy feeling and raised his rifle to see better. His scope was a Leopold 3-9x, which was more than enough to close the distance.

He looked through the optic for a while and then lowered the rifle, his fears confirmed. At least one of the Progs was dead. Maybe both, though there was no way to know until the bear departed and allowed Day to take a closer look. He considered shooting the bear but then dismissed the idea. He guessed it would take at least three solid hits from the Weatherby to drop the animal; if he did not get them he would have wounded – and enraged – the largest predator since the tyrannosaurus rex to no purpose. Besides, whoever was on the trail was dead and could not be brought back, and Day did not have ammunition to waste. So he waited.

After some time the bear swung away from his kill and shuffled off down the trail. It returned once and dug some more, then departed a second time. It lingered at the edge of the ice field, smelling the air and pawing the snow, before finally going straight out onto the rock slide toward the pass. Day lost sight of him but for several minutes after he heard – or imagined he heard –the bear huffing and growling among the rocks.

That decided things. Day would check up on the dead man or men later. For now, he had the third Prog to find.

It was no trouble locating Eric Wulff. For one thing, the man waved to him. For another, the logger was perched atop the tallest boulder on the plain, one of a handful flanking the stream that flowed out from the glacier. On the ground below and not far away sat the great dog. The beast's eyes were locked onto Wulff and its face had a hungry look.

"I'm glad you showed up," Wulff greeted Day.

"Is that right?" Day answered. He did not exactly aim his rifle at Wulff but kept it pointed in that general direction.

"Yeah. Bullets are valuable. I didn't want to waste one on your dog. That's a hell of a dog, by the way. Where'd you get him?"

"At the zoo. What are you doing up there?"

Wulff gestured toward the glacier. "I came up because of a bear but then I saw your dog, who I'm guessing would have jumped me if I hadn't run from the bear first. There's a bear around, by the way. You might want to keep an eye out for him. He's huge."

"So I hear. How did you get up there?" The boulder was fifteen feet high with smooth sides.

"Let's just say I was highly motivated." Wulff held up his hands, palms outward, to show the abrasions.

Day sidestepped uphill to make sure no one lurked behind the rock.

"What were you going to do if the bear hadn't shown up?" he asked. "Help your buddies kill me?"

Wulff looked Day in the eye. "I told you, I'm not into killing. I hadn't worked out exactly what I was going to do but it would have been in your favor, not theirs."

"Wish I could believe that."

"How can I prove it?"

Day nodded toward the rifle Wulff held. "You can start by handing down that Henry," he said.

Wulff showed genuine pain at the suggestion. "I don't know about that. This gun hasn't left my side since we got here."

Day moved the Weatherby so it was now on the logger. "It wasn't a suggestion."

Wulff held firm.

"What if you need backup? I didn't hear shooting. What if Rohanson and Sorley come back?"

"I don't think that's going to happen."

"Are they dead?"

Day was noncommittal. "Not sure. I had them but your bear charged in and broke up the party. I went one way and he went after the other two. One of them at least is dead about a hundred yards the other side of the forest. Maybe both. The bear was still around and I couldn't get close enough to see who it was."

"So you came back for me," Wulff finished. "Alright, that's the way it is then. But don't get too fond of this gun, you might want me to take it back at some point." He held the Henry by the barrel and leaned down to pass it to Day.

Day reached to take it but just then the dog jumped to its feet and looked toward the forest. Not to the natives' trail but downhill at the cliff's edge where Day had re-entered the plain minutes earlier. The trees there shook. From between their trunks the short-faced bear emerged, bulldozing its way through the scrub with a swaggering gait that recognized few barriers. Once clear of the forest it sniffed the air, glared in the light, and drew a straight line for where Day stood.

"Damn, you brought him back," Wulff swore.

Day could not believe it. The bear had circled after him? A quick glance around told him there was nowhere to run, the plain was too open. Against his better judgment he would have to shoot this monster after all. He raised the Weatherby.

"Wait!" Wulff shouted. "You might not kill him. Get up here!"

Day glanced at the rock. Up close he could see small crevices but the nearest one was out of reach.

"Grab this!"

Wulff reached down again with his rifle. Day hesitated. He looked through the scope one more time – the bear was gargantuan. It filled the image in the scope, scarier than ever. It was less than two hundred yards away now and starting to trot, its nose in the air as wind off the ridge vectored it to its quarry. Day had a thought he had never had before: what if the .378 Magnum round was not enough?

He slung the rifle and jumped to grasp the Henry's stock. The logger pulled, bringing Day up enough that he could grab at the first niche and scrape a purchase for his feet. Day got his fingers in the niche but then slipped and fell.

The great dog ran at the bear.

Fear lending him urgency, Day grabbed the Henry again and scrabbled at the rock face. When he was high enough he released the rifle and slapped his left hand into a crack in the stone. From there he hauled himself the rest of the way. Wulff lent a hand and then slid sideways to give him room on top of the boulder, which was narrow but long and with just enough space for the two of them to lie flat. Day rolled over gasping and looked back.

The dog reached the bear, intercepting the giant carnivore twenty yards from the boulder and charging at him with nothing more than a snarl and insane courage. The bear was surprised but undeterred. It roared and lunged at the dog, who darted uphill just outside the swiping paws. The bear leaped after him with amazing agility. The dog was faster but the attack must have come close enough because once clear he decided he had made his point. He made a full circuit of the monster and then took off to the north at top speed. The bear went after him for all of three strides before giving up.

"That mutt's insane," Wulff observed in awe. "But he bought you ten seconds."

Breathing heavily, Day watched the dog run. "He didn't do it for me," he said. "He just likes a challenge."

Now that challenge came for them. With the dog gone, the bear swung toward the boulder with renewed vigor, swaying its massive head as it snorted and blew. Saliva flying, it launched itself onto its hind feet with a roar and brought its head within feet of where the men lay. Its paws came closer, inches from the summit, and stretched to reach the men. Day and Wulff drew back but could not go far – the top of the boulder ended at their feet. They had no choice but to face off with one of the largest carnivores North America had seen since the dinosaurs died out.

Blunted like a bulldog's and stained with blood, the bear's muzzle erupted with a roar that shook their bones. Hot breath hit them in a wave as 5-inch claws scratched at the rock. Day had never been so frightened in his life.

The bear roared a second time but that was all it could do. The rock offered no purchase and as big as the animal was its mass was nothing to the boulder. It pushed on the stone but was thwarted from even making it tremble. It tried again to knock it over, then once more. In frustration it dropped to all fours and circled the megalith, testing each side in turn.

"I'm not a bear hunter," Day whispered, "but I've never heard of one being so aggressive."

"Get used to it," Wulff advised. "Everything here will stick you, sting you, or bite you. Unless you eat it, then it will give you diarrhea."

"Yeah, but to follow you? I've heard of polar bears doing that but never grizzlies. That thing was hunting me."

Wulff scoffed, though there was no smile on his lips.

"You said 'aggressive' just now," he muttered, not taking his eyes off the bear. "I've been here six months. Aggressive doesn't cut it. Some of these creatures are murderous. The dire wolves are the worst. They'll track you, and even if you kill one the others don't always back off. It's like they've got nothing else to do. Survival out here isn't the same as it is in our time. I mean, back home predators worry about a loss of range, not enough prey, or being killed by us. None of that factors in here. They *make* the time to hunt us down. Just like this guy here."

For half an hour the bear prowled and growled and lunged at the rock. Twice it wandered away as though leaving, only to turn and rush the boulder again. The great dog stayed away and the men remained quiet but the bear could see them. And whenever it backed off it sniffed the air, too, tasting their scent and reigniting its rage. Its eyes were deep-set in bony sockets; small on the large pug face, they nevertheless sent death with every glance. Yet the boulder foiled the monster again and again. Only after thirty minutes did the bear concede. Huffing in denial it sauntered downhill, meandering at the cliffs until finally dropping over the side.

"You've seen that thing before?" Day asked, shaken.

"Unfortunately, yes," Wulff admitted. He was unsettled, too, but the experience of repeated danger and death over the last many months had made him resilient. "Well, I don't know if it's the same one but one of those things used to come through the pass a couple of times a week while we were living there. We learned to post watchers in both directions – it was a Chinese fire drill getting up into the rocks whenever one was sighted. We think a bear killed Hitch. They're all over down on the plains, too. At least it seems that way. Not all of them as big as that but they're all big. As far as I can tell this type is the apex predator here. The wolves are nasty and the bison are huge but nothing compares to that guy."

"I hope not. Have you guys tried to kill one?

"Hell, no. We run from stuff that big. Besides, Reed wants us to conserve ammo, to shoot only in defense or to eat. The only bear we killed was a black bear back in, oh, April maybe, and that was kind of both: he was raiding our camp *and* we ended up eating him."

They waited. When twenty minutes passed and the bear did not return, Day looked around to determine the best way down. The uphill wall had the shortest drop but the rock there was sheer. He slid his feet over the edge nearest him and felt for toeholds.

"So what's the plan?" Wulff asked.

Day nodded toward the forest. "I need to confirm your buddies are dead. If they are, it'll make my life easier. If not, I need to get them. Then I'm going after Reed."

"Alone?"

"If I have to."

"Where's your partner? Did you find him?"

"He's around."

Wulff thought about that. "He's hurt, isn't he?" he concluded. "I saw your tracks. You had a stretcher and were dragging him. Well, no. *You* weren't because your tracks were following it. The natives were up front. You have natives working with you?"

"He's around. Let's leave it at that. You asked for the plan and I told you."

"Okay, keep your secrets. But I did just save your life a second time. You might start to trust me a little."

"I do, a little. That's why I told you I'm going after Reed."

"But you don't know where Reed is, do you?"

"You told me the camp was at the top of the gorge."

"I did, and it was," Wulff acknowledged. "But as of this morning he's on the move. And he has reinforcements."

Day looked hard at the logger. "Go on."

Wulff told Day the saga of the Arrows and the Moons and of Reed's alliance with the former. He also relayed Aron Sorley's story of the second Prog band.

"So Reed is headed down to the plains to link up with Holden King?"

Wulff shook his head. "Reed doesn't care about King. I mean, he cares because King defied him and is now creating problems in Reed's grand scheme to rule the world, but that's not why he's going downhill. He wants whatever machine you guys have that will let you get home."

"What machine is that?" Day demanded.

Wulff raised his hands to show he meant no offense.

"Come on," he said. "We've traveled in time or space somehow. Even a dumb lumberjack can figure that out. Wherever we are, we got here via that contraption Ganesh put us in. That's the last thing I remember before being here. But our ticket was one-way while you guys have a round-trip. The last Settler that came after us, Trace said he saw the guy with some kind of white jug just before he disappeared. Then he was gone and so was the jug. Gone like vanished. And you didn't get here by bus. So there's something you guys use and Reed wants it."

"And you?" Day asked. "Are you after it, too?"

"I've said this so many times I'm beginning to sound like Dorothy in The Wizard of Oz: I just want to get home. I think my best bet to do it in one piece is with you."

Day debated how to answer. "There's a device," he said finally. "There's a device but I don't have it."

When Wulff looked doubtful, Day handed over the canvas bag. Wulff looked through it, pulling out Day's night scope which was now in three pieces.

"I'm guessing this was a night vision scope before you broke it," he said. "Too bad it's busted."

"Better that than my skull."

"I suppose."

Wulff handed back the bag. Day slung it behind his rifle and looked at the other man.

"My job," he said, "is to round up any Prog who surrenders and kill the ones who don't. If you want to go home, I'll do my part to get you there. What happens to you when we get there, though, is out of my hands. I'll vouch that you helped me, that's all."

"Fair enough."

"Between now and then, you had better not switch sides again. You do what I tell you and you back me up. One sign of hesitation and I'll kill you."

Wulff nodded. "That's fair, too. Does that mean I get to keep my Henry?"

"You can keep it."

The logger smiled and held out his hand. "In that case, Mr. Day, let me help you down."

22

It was Aron Sorley in the snow. They found him in pieces and identified him from his clothes.

"Aw, jeez," Wulff breathed. He took one look and turned away.

"Were you guys pals?" Day asked.

Wulff did not turn around. "No, but he wasn't all bad. He pulled his weight."

Blood was everywhere. Day found a leg and a pocket and gingerly removed a single AR-15 clip that held ten rounds. They now carried both Prog rifles in addition to their other weapons. He had thrown Rohanson's Glock into the forest: it held only one round – which he kept – but the chamber was so fouled with dirt he was amazed it had fired the one time.

Wulff moved off to look for signs of Sorley's companion.

"Ruud got away," he called back, finding footprints in the snow. "Running, of course, until..." He stopped at the end of the ice and knelt down. "Well, it looks like he fell...and slid downhill."

Day followed the sluice with his eyes, searching for a body. Not seeing one, he paused at the site of Sorley's demise. There was nothing else he needed, he just thought he should give the man another moment. This was a hell of an end for anyone. Day was raised Catholic and once upon a time might have added a prayer to his reflection, but prayer was no longer in him. In its absence he allowed Shakespeare to fill the void.

"*After life's fitful fever he sleeps well,*" he muttered. "*Treason has done his worst. Nor steel nor poison, malice domestic, foreign levy, nothing can touch him further.*"

When he finished he began to work his way down the slope. The snow was dry and slid from under his feet, but by the middle of the field it was deep enough that he could jam his boots sideways and get purchase. Wulff followed, stopping often to scan the hill.

At the bottom of the slide the snow petered out, revealing close-cropped meadow grass and stands of thistle vetch. At the corner where the sluice ended, they found scrapes in the dirt and drag marks that ended at a ledge. Day peered over.

Ten feet down the slope continued, but this time in a culvert filled with grass and snow melt. The grass was yellow and smashed flat. It led down and widened until leaving the culvert and blending with the rest of the terrain descending to the valley. From the ledge Wulff pointed away from the impact point to a trail leading out of the grass.

"He's alive and mobile. Looks like he hightailed it into the valley. I don't blame him."

Day moved along the ledge to get a better view. From where they stood they could see the valley floor but only a section of it heading north.

"Where would he go?" he asked.

Wulff considered the options. "Well, he's lost his rifle and his Glock. He could go straight across the valley to the ponds but we didn't leave much there. And he would be alone. My guess is he'll try to get back to our group. Ruud talks tough but he's not a loner."

"And he knows about Reed moving to the plains?"

"He does."

"So he would take the fastest route and go through the pass."

Wulff was doubtful. "He *could* do that," he allowed, "but I don't think so."

"Why not?"

"We've had bad experiences there," the logger explained. "Yeah, there's water and food in the pass but that's a double-edged sword. It's the easiest route up from the plains and it's got a lot of grass so wildlife is everywhere. That means predators go that way, too, including that monster bear. Well, bears as big as him, anyway. And there aren't many escape routes out of the pass. Once you're in there, you're in there. So it's a risk and Ruud's not a risk-taker. Being unarmed and maybe hurt, he's more likely to go the long way, back up through the valley. He won't go through the gorge now that it's a mess but he can take the north trail back to our camp. There's food and water that way, too. That would be my bet. Why don't we just track him? Then we'll know for sure."

Day shook his head. "It'll take too long. Besides, we don't need to. As you say, he's going to try to get back to the main group. So we can just go after the main group and meet him there. Or better, get to the main group before he does so there's one less guy with them to worry about."

"You want Reed, don't you?"

"I want everyone," Day reminded his companion. "But yes, I want Reed."

Wulff's gaze searched the valley again and then switched to the glacier. He rubbed his beard while he thought, though the habit was due more to dry skin than from any assist it gave his decision-making. He had never had a beard before this adventure and even after months of wearing it, it still itched.

"In that case," he offered, "we have two routes we can take. Either one will get us ahead of Ruud. As for Reed's group, it depends on how fast they got going and how fast they're moving."

"One route is the pass," Day guessed. "You've already made your feelings clear about that."

Wulff shrugged. "I'm not saying the pass is impossible, just that we'll have to be on our toes."

"What's the alternative?"

"We go across the glacier." Wulff nodded uphill. "There isn't a trail as such but above the trees last spring we found a way to get up to the top of the wall. From there it's only a mile or so across the ice. I went that way a couple of times with Lace Stevens. On the other side there's no wall, just a slope, so getting down is easy. There's more snow but it stops about the same distance downhill as it does here."

"What's on the other side?"

Wulff pointed to the southwest. "Hills that stretch that way another ten miles. The terrain is like here. But we won't follow the hills. We'll go straight west to intercept a slope that runs parallel to them. That's how Reed and the others will get down to the plains."

"How long will it take to get there?" Day asked.

"Half a day, maybe. We wouldn't make it tonight but by tomorrow noon."

"And the pass?"

"A full day to get through it, then we'll have to circle around the end of the hills to get where Reed will pop out."

"So Ruud's route – if we're right about him – is really the long way around," Day commented. "If he knows about this glacier shortcut, why wouldn't he take it?"

Wulff shrugged. "For one, he would have to climb all the way back uphill. For another, he probably got one hell of a scare from the bear. And it's not like the glacier is a paved road," he added. "It's ice and blowing snow. You can't move that fast. And it's open. There's nothing up there to hide behind. There are cracks in the ice, crevasses, but if you fall into one you're unlikely to get back out."

"Wildlife?"

"Not that we saw."

"No wolves? No bear?"

"When we crossed before, we didn't see anything but a few bighorn sheep."

Day frowned. The afternoon was passing and his fifth day on this hunt was almost done. If Wulff was right, they might yet cross the glacier before it grew dark but then they would have to make camp. Shell had told him he had just over nine days to finish his mission and it was looking certain he would need every hour of that to find and deal with the Progs. Time was of the essence, and it was running out.

"We'll go across the glacier."

Wulff nodded. "I figured you would say that. Okay then, bundle up. It's cold up there."

It took them an hour to get up to the glacial wall. They encountered a delay in the spruce forest when sounds of an animal moving through the trees caused them to hunker down, hearts pounding. But it was the stag moose that emerged, not a bear; the same pair of cow and calf that Day had seen earlier in the day. The moose did not see them and after a while the men were able to give both a wide berth and continue on their way.

The glacier's wall was not as sheer above the trees as it was on the plain. Its side sloped with the hill, flaring at the bottom so the men could hike upright until halfway to the top. From there it was a scrabble to climb as the ice they encountered fell away like crumbling steps. Still, they had no close calls and were able to reach the top with little difficulty.

The view from the ice cap was otherworldly. In one direction was a spectacular vista of the valley to the east. To the west, north, and south, all was ice. They could have been in Antarctica for as much as they could see, since the ice cap sat astride the highest land until one reached the Tetons twenty miles on.

Where they crested the ridge they were two miles south of the mountain's peak. Day's maps had not given him a name or elevation for the peak but he guessed it was over 11,000 feet. The slope on the peak's face was dramatic though it shallowed reaching their elevation. He noted with unease the snow buildup on a trio of cirques below the highest ridge. Bowl-shaped depressions carved into the mountain by the glacier, the cirques looked smooth and unthreatening from a distance. But Day knew better. It was summer on his calendar but these bowls were still buried in a late spring snowpack, and late spring snowpacks are notoriously unstable. He wondered why these had not collapsed during the earlier earthquake, and then considered how really shaky they must be now. Just hold out for another hour, he begged them silently. Just give me an hour.

They pointed west and started walking. As best as Day could tell they would be crossing from one ridge to another across ice collected in a long trough between. There was no telling how deep the glacier was over the trough.

The glare off the snow was blinding. Wulff tied a bandanna across his eyes to shield them. Day could not find his own scarf but he had a handkerchief that he tucked into his hat so it draped down over his face like a veil. He could see through the thin cotton but it blocked the brightest light.

"Watch your feet," the logger advised. "I almost walked into a crevasse the last time I was up here."

It was sage advice. With overcast above and ice and snow below, and the light fading as dusk approached, perspective weakened. Though the wall of the glacier had glowed blue, its roof bore no hue other than white. There were no tracks or trails, either. No dirt, and few rocks. Everything around them was frozen, with powdered snow blowing across the surface in constant reformulations of an infinite pattern. After stumbling twice, Day began scanning no farther than ten feet in front of him to watch for obstacles.

Slow and steady, they made good progress as evening approached. Day's habit in the field was not to wear a watch as it forced him to pay attention to the world around him for his time-keeping, but he had made an exception on this trip due to the importance of keeping track of the date. For that reason he knew it was just after seven o'clock when Wulff halted and waved him forward.

"We're halfway across," he said.

"How do you know?"

His companion pointed to a crevasse blocking their path.

"Because I remember this. It's kind of hard to forget."

The crevasse ran downhill, parallel to the flow of the glacier. It was twenty feet wide and stretched left and right as far as Day could see. He stood away from the edge, not interested in its depth.

"Lace threw a chunk of ice into it the first time we came here," Wulff said, reading the Settler's thoughts. "We heard it hit something but only after a long fall."

"So how do we cross?" Day asked.

Wulff pointed south. "That way. We tried to go upslope and couldn't find a way around so we went downhill. There's a bridge but the crevasse also stops in a quarter mile or so. We'll just walk to the end."

In a hundred yards he pointed out the ice bridge. As wide as a highway lane, it was two feet thick and flat as a board and stitched the two sides of the fissure as though sewn in place.

"You didn't cross here?" Day asked.

"No. Neither one of us was that adventurous."

"You don't think it'll hold our weight?"

"I don't want to find out."

They moved on, Wulff leading them downhill for another ten minutes until the crevasse made a sharp break and zig-zagged to the west. There it narrowed, narrowed some more, and finally shrank to a jagged fracture in the ice that the men could step over in one stride. Far below their feet the ground must have continued to be uneven, however, because a line of seracs now blocked their path, irregular columns of ice pushed up by shear forces in lower layers of the glacier until they emerged like house-sized teeth across the men's path.

"We have to backtrack," Wulff apologized. "There was probably a more direct way to get here but I didn't want to miss the turn and then waste time looking for it."

Day needed no apology. He did not like being on the ice or being out in the open, so whatever got them to the west side of the glacier soonest was alright with him.

The men hiked back uphill to the ice bridge, where they turned west again.

They had been trudging that way for maybe two minutes and were just going around the seracs when they heard a howl behind them. Turning, they saw the great dog far in the distance, uphill on the other side of the crevasse. He stood alone on the ice. As they watched he let out another howl.

"That sound is as scary as he is," Wulff shivered. "What's he up to now?"

Day shook his head but then movement back down their own trail caught his eye.

"Aw, crap. That's what!'"

"What?" Wulff demanded. He shielded his eyes and looked for himself. "Oh, you've gotta be kidding me..."

The short-faced bear was on the ice cap two hundred yards away, padding swiftly through the powdery snow in a direct line toward the men. Rangy and long-legged, he was moving fast though he had not even started to trot. The bear's breath formed clouds as he huffed along and his head swung from side to side in a menacing buildup to attack.

The men retreated but they were too far from any shelter to make a run for it. It was going to be a fight.

"What the hell did I do to this guy?" Day muttered as he threw down his bag.

"I don't know but you pissed him off somehow," Wulff replied.

Day lay the M4 he was carrying on top of the bag. He unshouldered the Weatherby and dropped to one knee, his heart pounding. *Of all base passions, fear is the most accursed*, or so the Bard told him. Day would not disagree. Then again, that line was spoken by Joan of Arc in Henry VI and she died before the play ended. Maybe she should have heeded her fear more.

Wulff hurried upslope twenty yards and set down his own M4 to bring his Henry on line. The spacing between the two men would force the bear to choose a first target and give the second shooter another angle of fire.

The bear reached the crevasse. Day waited, thinking the animal would stop, but the bruin did not hesitate. It found the ice bridge the men had disdained and leaped onto it as though it were a regular route – which Day now realized it probably was. In three strides the bear crossed the fissure and reached their side of the ice. Its pace quickened.

Day peered through the Leopold scope. He had sighted the Weatherby at 200 yards and now did not have time to make adjustments. He would have to aim and hope for the best. He prayed to the gods of ballistics that Ice Age bears were not bullet-proof.

The bear was a football field away and coming at Day straight on, the sway diminishing as the bear began to gallop. The men could hear the animal grunt and huff with each stride. The exhalations grew louder in a crescendo of inevitability that Wulff, at least, found scary as all hell.

Day picked a spot a foot below the the the bear's hump, just above where the left shoulder met the chest, and settled the crosshairs there. Taking a deep breath and letting it out slowly, he rested his elbow on his left knee, steadied his grip, and pulled the trigger.

The report of the Weatherby boomed across the ice. Looking calmer than he felt, Day chambered another round and aimed again.

The bear twitched at the impact. It let out a roar that shook the seracs but kept coming. Day fired again at the same spot.

To his left Eric Wulff opened up with the Henry, firing one, two, three shots in succession. The bear spun to its right. It noticed Wulff for the first time and for a moment seemed undecided about which man to attack. But its momentum was toward Day and that was where he continued. Day fired a third time when the bear was only 30 yards away, aiming this time a hair lower though careful not to go so low that the bullet would pass harmlessly through the fat and long hair that all bears carried in their belly. The bear closed on him another ten yards before it went down, its left foreleg buckling and throwing the animal onto its shoulder.

Only fifty feet away, Day pumped one more round into the bear for insurance, this time hitting the creature on its right side behind the neck. Wulff fired, too. Incredibly, the bear reacted by rising to its feet and letting out a roar that the men felt through their heavy clothes. The sound carried across the ice like thunder. But beyond that the giant did not move. Its bloodshot eyes glared at them as though willing them to come within striking range. The men did not, nor did they shoot again.

"What's the load on those bullets of yours?" Wulff whispered. He was breathing fast and stood poised to shoot again.

"300 grain, Trophy Bonded," Day managed to say. He did not take his eyes off the bear. "Why?"

"One shot of that should have stopped an elephant, that's why."

The bear stared at them, its eyes at least unwilling to give up the hunt. Eventually, though, confusion triumphed over anger and the animal looked away, searching the ice as if to determine what there was about this day that made everything so different. It was a creature not used to losing.

After a long moment during which the men wondered if they would have to shoot again, the bear sank down onto the ice. It was still not dead but it could no longer support its own weight. A red stain appeared on its flank. The bear sniffed at the blood once but then its eyes strayed back to the men. From then on they never wavered.

Now a new sound rose over the ice cap. The shooting had shaken the snowpack on the peak's face; the cirque on the far left was giving way. It tumbled, leaving unsupported the snow above so that shelf, too, now came loose and slid down the mountain.

"If it's not one thing it's another...time to go!" Wulff barked. He grabbed his M4 and ran. Their only chance to escape the avalanche's track was to get far enough to the west before it rolled out onto the glacier. How far that was, there was only one way to find out.

Day grabbed his pack and the other M4 and followed Wulff. Together they slipped and stumbled across the ice as the avalanche gathered speed.

The starting point of the cascade was ultimately what saved them. That and the fact that the failing cirque faced east so its momentum was away from the men. But the slide still had a thousand feet to build up mass and speed, more than enough to reach the crevasse and continue at high velocity out onto its runout zone. As the two men raced to get out of the way, a whirlwind of powder poured down the peak and crashed into the glacier where it shook everything loose from an already slick surface. Snow flew skyward in clouds.

A mile from the peak the avalanche bounced off an arete, a serrated ridge separating the first cirque from the second, and turned south. It curled over like an ocean wave and crashed downward with more force than ever. Gravity and momentum pushed everything before it. Even far into the runout zone snow slid as one piece like a loose cloth on a polished table.

It shifted below the men, too, and both fell off their feet. By then, however, they had moved far enough across the ice cap that the drift at their location was weak. The wobbly surface was more a nuisance than a threat. Not so behind them. When he regained his balance Day looked back and saw the short-faced bear being pushed unwillingly across the ice. The massive beast was still on its chest. It struggled but could not stand, its huge paws and long toes clawing uselessly at the ice. The slide moved the bear downhill and toward one of the zig-zags in the crevasse.

Wulff recovered his feet and sprinted for the western edge of the cap. He yelled to Day to hurry but Day was transfixed by the tragedy behind him. The great curl of the avalanche weakened and would not reach the bear but that no longer mattered. Its mass pushed all before it, shoving the top layers of ice across those below. As Day watched, the sliding surface shoved the great monster of a bear – more than a ton of nature's awful strength, a very symbol of the wildness and freedom of this primitive age – up to and over the edge of the crevasse. The bear gave out one last defiant roar and fell into the gap.

23

They made camp near a timberline lake west of the glacier. It was dark by the time they arrived and they went to bed hungry, but in the morning Wulff was up before dawn and caught a large cutthroat trout. In a stand of trees well back from the water they built a small fire and devoured the fish.

"How are they fixed for food?" Day asked, referring to the main group of Progs.

Wulff considered his answer, trying to picture who had stored what at the high camp. Food and shelter had been unending priorities for the Progs.

"There's some dried meat they'll carry with them," he remembered. "Vin Kimmel and John built a smoker. We use it for deer and goat." From his pocket he pulled a bundle rolled in aspen bark. From it he removed a pale rectangle of dried meat and handed it across to Day. "That's bighorn sheep."

Day examined it with suspicion. "Crazy John prepared this?" he asked.

Wulff snorted in derision. "No. I did. He just built the smoker. I wouldn't eat anything he gave me. He's smart on survivalist stuff, though. I'll give him that. You just have to catch him when he's not hating the world."

When Day still showed doubts, Wulff took a strip and popped it in his mouth. "It's tough," he admitted, chewing with vigor, "but it's better than starving."

Day bit into his. It tasted more like smoke than anything, but the meat had texture.

"It needs salt," he commented.

"Everything we eat needs salt," Wulff groused. "We've only found one salt lick so far and it's nowhere near our camp."

"So, smoked meat, then. Is that it?"

"For real food, yeah. There's other stuff we've gathered: pinons, cattails, wild onions, dandelions. If I ever get back to Oregon I'm going to spread weed killer on every dandelion I see, I'm sick of eating them. Huckleberries up by the high camp, some other stuff John found. We got to where we were eating okay in camp, either at the lake or up here in the mountains, but on the move it's hard to keep anything fresh. At the lake we had a spring back in the rocks where we were able to store things down to around forty degrees. It was a refrigerator for us. At the high camp we haven't found anything like that. It's been scavenging and hunting, day after day. Thank god for fish. They're easy to catch here."

"And everyone was able to do that? A bunch of city dwellers?" Day asked.

Wulff nodded ruefully. "Hunger has a way of concentrating the mind. Bill Galston's the only one who gave up. Mentally, I mean. Everyone else has tried to make it, one way or another."

"One cohesive group, is that it? All for one and one for all?"

"I wouldn't say that," Wulff replied. "Half of us hate the other half, and any-place else we would probably all kill each other. Opposite personalities, personal rivalries, jealousies, that sort of thing."

Day poked the fire with a stick and listened to a loon call from across the lake. "*Jealousy, the green eye'd monster, which doth mock the meat it feeds on,*" he mused.

"You spout a lot of poetry," Wulff noted.

"It's what I do. So, who hates who?"

Wulff shrugged. "Well, Ruud doesn't like me. Neither does Reed. I'm too independent for their tastes. Pettigrew also doesn't think much of me, but that guy has a temper so it's not clear who he likes. He pals around with Carlos but they've had blow-ups, too. Let's see...Ray, he's a mystery. He and Reuben were close but that makes sense since they're both gang members."

"Ray Williams?" Day broke in.

"Yeah. You know him?"

"No. Black guy, though? Tattoos?"

"Yeah."

"What's he like?"

Wulff tried to think of something but his mind drew a blank.

"I don't know," he admitted. "Like I said, a mystery. He pulls his load. I've worked with him but he's not the talkative type. He always seems pissed, more so now that Reuben's dead. You'll need to watch out for him. He wanted to come out after you as soon as he heard that."

"As soon as he heard Reuben was dead," Day asked, "or as soon as he heard there were Settlers here?"

"What's the difference?" Wulff asked. When Day did not answer, he continued. "Either way, watch out for him. He looks like a bad-ass with all his tattoos and maybe he is. Puff's afraid of him because of his skin. He likes the tattoos but black skin freaks him out."

"Has Ray ever said what he did besides being in the Crips?"

"No."

"So how did he get to know Reed?"

"Through the Crips, I guess. Reed seems to trust him, though."

Day was silent for a while, thinking. Unlike Reuben, Ray Williams was on the list Shell had given him. The two had linked up with the Progs somehow and found their way into the highest tier of the terrorist organization, but to Day the gang connection had always seemed weird. Unlikely. It might have been about weapons, or outreach, or a simple division of spoils – he did not know. He had never studied the politics of the Prog movement, only the violence. The groups involved had always seemed to him nothing more than a confederation of grievances.

"What about the women?" he returned to the conversation. "You told me before that Elke Neuberg is one to watch out for. Do you get along with her?"

"Only by avoiding her. As far as I can tell, she doesn't like anyone other than Reed. She worships him. She hates Ruud. There have been a couple of times I thought they might kill each other. And she has it out for Heather, too."

"Heather Westergard, the teacher? Why?"

Wulff raised an eyebrow. "Elke swings both ways. Heather doesn't. Elke took it personally."

"Ah."

They broke camp while steam still rose off the surface of the lake. The temperature was in the forties but for the first time in two days the sun broke through the overcast and rose behind them over the glacier. Day removed his hat and let the warm rays bathe his head and neck.

They made their own trail heading as straight west as the terrain allowed. The hills they walked through flowed on an angle away from the glacier. They were foothills, lower than the glacier ridge and dropping the farther the men traveled. A series of striking small valleys dotted the land between the hills, isolated but populated with meadows and lakes and forests as pure and wild as nature allowed. Even Day, alert as he was for an ambush or animal attack, marveled at the beauty of the scene. He knew in his head that he was in the Bridger-Teton Forest, just south of Yellowstone Park, but his eyes had trouble squaring even those classic landscapes with the incredible vistas before him. The lake surfaces were mirrors reflecting the bright sky as well as the peaks and their lattices of snow. The meadows were lush, scattered with blue forget-me-nots and white sky pilots as though they, too, wanted to replicate the heavens above.

There were animals everywhere. Beaver, deer, elk, fox... Day even spied a cougar in the distance, one that looked normal to him in size and weight. It was going up a hillside on the far side of a valley and paid no attention to them. Closer at hand, Wulff came around a bend and encountered a coyote that had just successfully cornered a pika. The coyote grabbed the rabbit-like creature as they watched and swallowed it in three bites. It then studied the men with curiosity – not fear – before trotting off. Most unusual to Day was a pond filled with trumpeter swans, at least a hundred of them crowded wing-to-wing among the rushes. He had never before seen a swan in the wild yet all of a sudden they were gathered here in scores.

Around noon they passed through a gap in the hills where limestone cliffs flanked a parade of whitebark pines. The trees stopped on the other side of the gap; from their cover the men looked out over a broad grassland that curved downward with the hills. Miles in the distance the open ground of Jackson Hole came into view.

A herd of elk grazed in the distance. Otherwise there was no one in sight.

Day studied the land. Once they left the trees they would be in the open, just like the elk.

"I came up this way once and I went down it once," Wulff offered. "Both times we were on the far side of the plain."

"Who was with you?" Day asked.

"The first time, coming up, it was Aron and Minh Tran. We were scouting west looking for a road, houses, anything. All we found was an abandoned camp and a couple of dead Indians." In response to Day's glance, he added, "We didn't kill them. It was clear there was a fight between tribes and these guys lost. There were a lot of markings from the Arrows."

"What kind of markings?"

Wulff described a basic arrow but with two heads.

"They put it on rocks but on the bodies, too," he added. "The Arrows are into torture."

"And the second time you came this way?"

"It was me and Lace. Reed sent us after that first Settler appeared. He was worried there might be more than one guy so we came over from the lake camp to scout this route."

"Why this far?"

To explain, Wulff drew two lines in the dirt.

"There are two ways to get up to the high camp," he said. "The pass and the highway. That's what we call this grassland, The Highway. We figured a Settler would go through the pass because all our tracks from the watering hole went that way and it was obvious we had spent time by the hot springs. He did. But just in case, Reed sent us down the Highway."

"His name was Kurtz," Day remarked. "Did you see him?"

Wulff shook his head. "No. I was hunting in the lake valley when he showed up. Once the weather warmed up we started splitting up into three or four groups to hunt and explore. My understanding is that he came across most of the group near the hot springs. Something happened and he killed Noah Abrams, then there was a running fight until he got away. He was gone by the time I made it down to Plymouth Rock."

"To where?"

"That's what we call the area where we all arrived. And I guess where you and your guy Kurtz zapped in and out. There's a big boulder near there. Plymouth Rock, get it? You know, arrival in a new world and all that? Why didn't he come back, by the way? Kurtz. He had enough of this place after only a few days?"

"You might say that," Day replied. He drew a third line in the dirt. "There's another way up to the lake camp, by the way. A canyon east of the pass."

Wulff nodded but drew an X over Day's line. "There is," he agreed, "but it's a hard slog, rocky and steep. Ruud and I started up that way once and we turned around after a mile. And not just because of the climb. We saw a lion there that scared the absolute crap out of us. After that, we never went that way again. Trust me, it was as scary as that bear."

"I can imagine," was all Day said. "How far is the high camp from here?"

Wulff pointed to the north. "It's up that way about two hours."

"So if your group left yesterday, they should be long past this point by now."

"Yeah, they should unless they were delayed again. There's an easy way to find out." Wulff gestured toward the plain. "I'm going to guess they stuck either to this side of the Highway or the other. They wouldn't go down the middle. If we head down there, we should cut their trail soon enough."

Day nodded but when he stood up Wulff put a hand on his arm.

"One thing," the logger cautioned. "Keep an eye out for the Indians. The Arrows. I don't trust them."

"Do you trust the tribe from the plains?"

"Well, no. But from what I've seen the Moons will avoid conflict if they can. Not the Arrows. The Arrows look for it. They kill first and worry about why they did it later. Every time that Puff guy came to camp he looked like he was just waiting for us to turn around so he could club us over the head."

Day nodded. "Got it. But my instructions are not to kill any Indians if we can help it."

"I'm okay with that," Wulff agreed, "but I'm just saying, watch the Arrows."

Four miles away the subject of their discussion stood in the shade of a cotton-wood, waiting. Puff wore two osprey feathers in his hair, a deerskin jerkin that went down past his waist, and deerskin moccasins. Otherwise he was naked, his skin wrinkled and worn from exposure and covered in ash drawings. He was impassive as he leaned on a short spear but his stance suggested impatience. Behind him the Prog band rested, scattered on a gentle slope on the east side of the grassland where it made its last turn before entering into the broad valley known in a later age as Jackson Hole.

Carlos Bardem was one of those resting. He sat sideways on the hill so he could keep an eye on Puff. Like Eric Wulff, he did not trust the Indians, any of them. Once the Arrows had gotten over the shock of encountering white men, they had become relentless about trying to steal from the Progs. They backed off a little after Reed and Puff made their alliance but stuff still went missing whenever they were around. Little stuff, like pocketknives or socks or an ammo can from the armory. Not big things like rifles but that was probably only because everyone kept a close eye on his weapon. But in a survival situation even little things mattered. It was not like anyone could replace a Leatherman once lost. So Carlos sat on the hill nursing his sore feet and watching Puff wait.

"Squanto seems to be in a hurry," a voice beside him said, reading Carlos' thoughts. It was Random, the tempestuous former school counselor whose real name was Simon Pettigrew. He was tall and gangly, an appearance heightened by bony wrists stretching beyond the sleeves of a dirty puffer jacket, and trouser legs that stopped short to reveal ragged red socks. He had scavenged both from fellow Progs who had perished; any concerns he might have felt about his fashion sense or wearing dead men's clothes had long since ceded priority to survival. "Does he know something we don't?"

Carlos answered, "I doubt it. It's just that he can walk for days and we can't, so he probably thinks we're weak."

"We are weak," Pettigrew said, keeping his voice low so only Carlos heard him. His eyes were still tender and he picked the occasional wood chip from his tear ducts, but thankfully he was able to see. Now he surveyed their companions, who lay around the slope in various stages of exhaustion. "That Indian knows that if we didn't have our guns, he and his pals could scalp us in a heartbeat." Pettigrew patted his AK-47, a well-worn weapon with a banana clip and a dirty piece of duct tape wrapped around the grip to keep his sweaty hands from slipping.

"You think they're that smart?" Carlos asked. "I can't tell what he's thinking, or if he's thinking at all."

"Oh, he's thinking alright," Pettigrew insisted. "He's simple-minded but he's plotting. I've seen that look on kids in school. You want savage, deal with a teenage boy. I don't know what this guy's plan is but he's got one. He wants a gun, I know that. Every time I turn around he's looking at my AK. Or yours."

"Well, he's not getting mine. And I doubt he's as smart as you give him credit for."

"Oh, he is," Pettigrew insisted. "He's clever, that one. The only question is, is he smarter than Reed? Which one of them is going to screw over the other one first?"

"Who are you screwing, Simon?"

Reed's voice came from behind them. The Prog leader had a knack for appearing where he was not expected. He approached them now across the slope, his face flushed from a fever he had been running.

"No one, unfortunately," Pettigrew said, unabashed. "And the name is Random, *Blake*," he added, knowing Reed hated anyone other than women using his first name. "We're wondering what your Indian friend is plotting, and if you're not trusting him too much."

"So again you're doubting me," Reed observed, using a grimy handkerchief to wipe sweat from his forehead even though the air temperature hovered in the sixties. "After all I've done for you, you might consider giving me the benefit of the doubt from time to time."

"After all you've done?" Pettigrew repeated. He looked around the harsh landscape and bit his tongue.

"As for the Arrows, I don't trust them anymore than you do," Reed went on. "They're violent, ignorant, conniving, and selfish – in other words, they're a lot like us. I expect he's plotting to murder us in our sleep and take our weapons at the first opportunity, so I recommend you sleep lightly."

"Wonderful," Carlos commented. "Then why are we letting them travel with us at all?"

"Because it's easier to keep an eye on them," Reed reminded them. "And because so long as they're working with us, even if they're plotting at the same time, we get some value out of them. They're scouting ahead and behind so we don't have to do it ourselves, and they're probably doing a better job. This way we don't have to worry about the Moons or the Settlers ambushing us."

"So the Settlers aren't dead?" Heather asked. She huddled with Nancy Peal, as she did more and more these days now that the female members of the Progs had declined in number. The only alternative was Elke, who Heather considered both scary and unstable. Besides, Elke now limited her companionship to Reed, considering herself his bodyguard. Right now, for example, she sat at the edge of the group, the better to keep everyone in sight.

Reed hesitated before answering. He closed his eyes as though to show great patience at the question, although in fact he felt light-headed and the motion helped him to steady. It was true that a day and a half had elapsed since Ruud, Sorley, and Wulff had left to explore the gorge. The group had heard what sounded like distant gunfire late on the day before but what it signified was anyone's guess. So the question was valid, but he was getting damned tired of having to explain his plans.

"Maybe they are, maybe not," he conceded. "Either way, the Arrows will help us avoid surprises. The sooner we get to the Rock, the sooner we can look for the device. If it's not there, then our men will get it off the Settlers once they find them and kill them."

"Yeah, right," Pettigrew muttered.

"What's that supposed to mean, *Random*?" Reed demanded.

"It means I don't have a lot of faith in 'our men,' " the counselor snapped. "Ruud's the only one who might get the job done. Sorley had a chance to kill them before and he failed, and I trust Wulff less every day. He'll turn on us the first chance he gets."

"He wouldn't!" Heather protested.

"Oh please, bitch," Elke spoke up. "You think because the guy brings you a fish from time to time he wouldn't flip you in a heartbeat? What are you, a trained seal?"

"Stop it!" Heather protested. "Why do you even say things like that?"

"Everybody, shut up," Reed ordered. "Stay focused. Our men will find the Settlers or they won't. If they don't, the Arrows will intercept them for us. We will concentrate on our objective, which is to get to the watering hole and find the device if it's there. That's the plan and it will work." He leaned toward Pettigrew and fixed him in a stare. "As for you, Simon," he said, menace in his tone. "The benefit of the doubt. Get on board and do it fast."

After resting, the group rose and continued moving down the long slope. They spread out in a ragged line, less from tactical considerations than because everyone moved at a different pace. One of Puff's companions led the way followed closely by Ray Williams. The Arrow leader himself brought up the rear.

Nancy Peal left Heather's side and maneuvered her way through the high grass to trudge next to Pettigrew, who lagged in a sullen mood toward the back.

"He's getting more short-tempered," she offered, sensing Random's grudge.

Pettigrew scoffed. "He's getting more nuts," he corrected her. "I don't know what planet he lives on – hell, I don't know what planet *we're* on – but he's lost all touch with reality. Did you hear him? 'After all I've done for you...' Are you kidding me? Look at us. Every one of us is here because of him. We're living a nightmare because of him! Half of us are dead, the rest are just waiting to die. We don't even get the benefit of a trial. Every day, we're just waiting for violent, savage death, and he wants me to be grateful?"

Peal waited, letting him seethe.

"You don't think Ruud and the others will succeed?" she asked

"No, I don't. And I don't care what Reed says, I don't trust Eric Wulff."

"I don't, either." She switched topics. "Have you noticed that Blake never talks about using the device?" she asked. "He talks about getting it, that's all."

Pettigrew said nothing, unsure of her point.

"The machine or whatever it is that let's us travel," she prompted.

"I know what you're talking about," Pettigrew replied. "He wants to get the device so we can get back."

"He has never said that," Peal repeated. "Think about it. All yesterday and last night we all talked about getting whatever this thing is and using it to go home, but not Blake. He kept saying we could use it to control the Settlers, or whoever sent them, or whoever. He never talks about going home."

"But what good is it if we don't use it to get out of here?" Pettigrew argued. "Of course, we would use it to leave."

"I would use it in a heartbeat," Peal agreed. "You would, Heather would, most of us would. I'm not so sure about Blake."

Pettigrew looked toward the front of their line where Reed and Bern Jones trudged close behind Ray.

"Well, I'm sure he's worried about being arrested the instant we get back to civilization. But come on, if the trade-off is to stay here that's insane, even for him."

Peal shrugged. She turned away from Pettigrew to head back toward Heather.

"I agree. But pay attention the next time Blake talks about it. You'll see."

They kept walking down the hill. Behind them Puff watched Peal end her conversation with Pettigrew and return to Heather. He had not heard the conversation, nor would he have understood it if he had, but he could read body language. He watched her go, his face giving nothing away.

Day paused when they reached the slope where the Progs had rested.

"What do you think, maybe two hours ahead of us?" he asked.

Wulff shook his head. "Maybe. I'm not that good a tracker," he confessed. "We're close, though." He found a twist of burned sweetgrass near a cottonwood tree and studied it.

Day did not like their situation. He would have preferred to be ahead of the Progs waiting for them, not following their trail. But following gave him the comfort of knowing where they were, whereas lying in wait required faith that they would show up where he expected them to. He believed Wulff had told him the truth about the Progs' intentions; the problem was, there was a lot of country between the high camp and the watering hole where Reed could change his mind. If for any reason the Progs went in a different direction – or if Reed had been lying to Wulff when he told him about his plan to go to the plains – Day could see himself wasting time setting up an ambush that the Progs would never get near.

He was also frustrated by the land. He had studied the Corps of Engineers maps enough to feel confident about where he was at the moment. Generally, anyway. Their angle on the Teton range got him in the ballpark. No more than ten miles southwest of their position, for example, was a peak that he was certain was Mount Moran. But the land between it and them was vast, which meant it was difficult to be precise about where he stood. Equally problematic was the difference that 14,000 years made: to wit, according to the maps he should be looking across the southern end of Jackson Lake right now. But there was no lake. Jackson Lake did not extend this far south until the early twentieth century, so instead of water Day gazed across an immense sagebrush steppe: miles of mountain big sage, though as it spread south he saw more color in the plants. It was an old outwash plain, rich with sand and alluvial deposits, but no lake. The only water he saw was a thin river that meandered through before heading south along the Tetons. The river came from a trio of tiny streams flowing off the plateau behind them and Day guessed it was the Snake, though its course – subject to change from decade to decade, let alone millennia – did not help pinpoint his position.

"Puff's with them," Wulff announced, breaking into his thoughts. "From the prints I've found, he's sticking with the group. So is one other Arrow. That leaves four unaccounted for."

"Scouting ahead?"

"Or behind. Or watching the sides. Or all three. Reed is worried about you but the Arrows are probably more concerned about knowing where the Moons are. Once we get out of the hills here, we're in Moon territory."

"Are the Moons fighters?" Day asked.

"Everything here fights."

"Are they *good* fighters?"

"Good enough. They won't start a war but they'll stand up if provoked. The Arrows are good at provoking."

"You said you found a Moon who the Arrows had killed?"

"Two of them, yeah."

"Did the Moons retaliate?"

Wulff exhaled, thinking. "We didn't see it but we think they did. They pushed the Arrows out of the plains and back into the mountains, which I think – this is just a guess – is the reason the Arrows were willing to partner with Reed. When we first ran into the Arrows they weren't as friendly as the Moons, but that changed and it might have been because they got chased uphill. The Arrows are more aggressive but we think the Moons are a bigger tribe."

"So the Moons are friendly?"

"They *were*," Wulff clarified. "Until Bern shot one of them. He didn't have to but he did. The guy's sadistic. That scared them off for a month. We ran into them again and Reed tried to patch things up but it didn't work. We've had to watch them close from then on. That was one of the reasons we left the hot springs and moved up to the lake valley. The Moons go there, too, but not as often because they run into the Arrows."

"Right. And the tribes fight over land?" Day said.

Wulff was disgusted. "Yup. Hunting grounds. That's what Puff told Reed, anyway. Can you believe it? Look around. It's not like this place isn't big enough for two small tribes. Or fifty big ones. It's depressing. I mean, if we've come back in time like you say, you would think everyone would get along better since what the hell is there to fight about? Everyone is just trying to survive. There's enough land and game for everyone, so why not work together? But it isn't like that."

"It never is," Day mused. *"Thy ambition, thou scarlet sin, robb'd this bewailing land."*

"What's that?" Wulff asked.

"Just one guy's commentary on greed."

At the cottonwood tree Day pointed to the twist of sweetgrass. "This is your guy Puff? And these markings are from a spear?"

Wulff nodded. "Yeah. The tobacco is why I'm sure it's Puff. And sometimes he carries a spear. The Arrows have a shorter one than the Moons." He held out his hand at chest level. "Both tribes are ambush hunters but the Moons live mostly on the plains so they have longer spears and the atl-atl. The Arrows are in the woods and mountains so they have to get closer. Some bows and arrows but mostly a short spear and a club is what they carry. They all carry clubs. About this long..." he held his hands out a yard apart "...with a chunk of rock in the head. They're good with them, too."

"You've seen them use it?"

"I've seen the results."

Day sighed. "Lovely," he said.

24

Two miles before the bottom of the Highway, Day and Wulff drew close enough to the Prog band that they caught sight of the stragglers. The group had turned east and was disappearing around the last of the foothills that flanked their progress down the mountain.

"What's down there?" Day asked his companion.

"Nothing much," Wulff replied. "These hills end and the ground goes flat, then there's the river and another hill and some forest before the valley opens up. There's a meadow where they'll probably rest again."

"Why do you think that?"

"Because it has fresh water."

"You've been down there?"

"Yeah, a few times. If you go south from there you're out in the valley. Jackson Hole, everyone says. I don't know, I've never gone past the river. But if you don't cross the river, if you just follow the mountains around to the east, you work your way back to the hot springs and the watering hole in a few hours. That's where they're going, or where Reed said they were going, anyway."

Day saw an opportunity. With the Progs turning it was a chance to cut the corner and approach them on their flank.

He studied the foothills. They had diminished with the elevation and now were only eighty feet or so higher than where the men knelt on the Highway.

"Can we get up there?" he gestured. "Can we go up and circle around to get in front of the group? Or at least into a position where we can hit them from the side?"

Wulff looked where Day indicated and thought about it.

"We can," he decided. "I've been up there. In fact, I tried to get us to move there from the hot springs but Reed said no, he wanted more distance from the Moons. Over this rise we should see a couple of small lakes. We can go between them and intercept a ravine that runs down the other side. It ends up close to the meadow where Reed and the others will stop."

"How far?"

"It's been a while but...maybe two miles to the ravine, another half mile or so after that. If we hump it, we're looking at just over an hour."

Day did not hesitate. Following the Progs was safe but it gave him few options. If instead he could take the initiative and surprise the group where they had few routes to escape, he might be able to round up half his targets in one go.

"Let's do it," he decided.

"You sure?" Wulff asked. "We've got a good trail to follow right now. What if I'm wrong and they don't stop at the meadow? Or they don't go that way at all?"

"You said they don't have much choice," Day reminded him.

"Yeah, but that doesn't mean they don't have *any* choice. Puff might take them another way, or Reed could change his mind."

"He won't," Day said. "What I know of him tells me that once he gets an idea it's his, and no one will change his mind."

"That's certainly true," Wulff admitted.

"As for their Indian guides, I don't know," Day confessed. "But one thing I do know is a basic principle of hunting men: do the unexpected. Get the surprise if you can. You say if we cut over this ridge we can get to that meadow first, so let's go. I want that surprise."

Wulff was right about the lakes. Just over the ridge sat two unassuming but attractive bodies of water, each a mile long and a quarter wide. The northern lake approximated a rectangle while the southern one bent south like a crescent moon. The land around them was a peaceful mix of woods and marshes, with bright tufts of red-yellow grass thrust above the water's surface in random displays.

The men found the shore of the second lake and followed it east and then south, encountering the ravine that flowed out of it just as the sun passed its meridian. The ravine was an ankle-buster, narrow and rocky, but they made good time descending by staying at its bottom where water flowed unseen among the stones. In half an hour the descent shallowed and the walls of the ravine opened, flaring like a grand staircase to reveal flat ground that ran perpendicularly across the mouth of the ravine.

"That's the bottom," Wulff whispered.

The stream they had followed down the ravine now appeared from under the rocks and ran in the open across the flat. Half a mile away it drained into the Snake River. A block-shaped hill covered in lodgepole pines loomed above the far shore of the Snake. Its bluffs flanked the water for a mile before the river looped around to run back in the opposite direction and cross over to the Tetons.

"Where's the meadow?" Day asked, frustrated not to see it already.

"Over to the right," Wulff said, peeking around a large rock. "Maybe a couple hundred yards from here. Sorry, I remembered it being closer."

Day crept forward to see around the ravine wall, then returned to brainstorm a plan. With two shooting positions widely spaced, he thought they might be able to ambush the Progs right here, outside the ravine. He began drawing lines in the dirt to show Wulff what he wanted. The logger listened but was unconvinced.

"That'll work if they're bunched up," he pointed out, "but they were single file coming down the Highway. And what if the Indian sees us? He'll let out a yell and they'll all scatter."

"Then we'll have to make sure he doesn't see us."

Wulff had his doubts. "I don't know. These guys can sense when something isn't right. They're worse than elk."

"These aren't elk," Day reminded him.

"No, they're worse. I'm just saying, if they scatter they'll be all over the place and we'll be playing hide and seek with both Arrows *and* guys with guns."

"What do you suggest?"

"Well, I thought the meadow was closer. I was thinking we could surround them there."

"It's not," Day said. "And we can't, not unless you know a way to get over these rocks without them seeing us."

Wulff looked up at the west wall of the ravine and shook his head.

"This hill is fine for cover," he explained, "but you won't get down on the meadow side without being seen." He frowned, debating internally. "What if I go out and talk to them?" he suggested.

"What do you mean?"

"Well, look. If you wanted us all dead, you would have been shooting from the moment you saw us. One by one. In fact, you and I could sit here right now and probably pick off the first two or three before they scattered. But you don't want to do that, do you?"

Day did not say anything.

"So, if you won't shoot them in cold blood," Wulff continued, "you're left with trying to capture them and that means getting as many as you can at once because otherwise how are you going to hold one group while you look for the others? That's it, isn't it? But even now you've still got that problem. What's your plan even if we catch all these guys today?"

"It's been a problem since day one," Day conceded. "And there has never been a good solution. But having you along now gives me options."

"How so?"

"We get these guys today," Day explained, gesturing with his rifle toward the outwash. "One way or another we'll chase off the Indians and keep just your Prog buddies. Then we herd them to the watering hole and wait. My partner will catch up with us either today or tomorrow. When he does, he'll ride herd on the Progs while you and I go round up Holden King's group and bring them back to join the others. Then we're all one big happy family."

Wulff listened. It was a plan. A vague one but a plan.

"You don't trust me to guard the others," he noticed.

"No, I don't. Not that I think you would turn on me," Day added. "But if you needed to shoot one of them, I don't know that you would do it. My partner won't have that problem."

Wulff could not argue that point. In part what motivated his willingness to talk to his former companions was that it might help him avoid shooting people.

"Look, I don't kid myself that if I go down there I'll convince Reed," he admitted. "But some of them will hear me out. And they'll put pressure on Reed."

"Reed is a fanatic," Day argued. "He worships himself and power. They can pressure him all they want and all he'll do is work out a way to divide them one from another, or have them killed. And you, too. You'll be wasting your time."

"Maybe, but you're my insurance policy," Wulff reminded him.

"How so?"

"If you cross over this wall you'll have a bird's-eye view of the meadow. You can't climb down the other side without being in the open but you'll have a clear shot at anyone there. If I make my case and everything goes to hell, you'll be able to take out Reed or anyone else."

"And if everything goes right? Let's say you're a natural orator and you convince them to give up. What happens then?"

Wulff held up his Henry. "In that case, I guard them while you come down and join me. You can still cover all of us while you hike down the hill. The way down on that side is wide open so you'll be in sight, but the upside is so will we."

Day did not like Wulff's plan but he admitted it had no more holes than his own scheme. And it had the advantage that he would be able to see all the Progs. After they discussed it some more he agreed to give it a try.

"With one change," he added, and held out his hand. "You're not taking your Henry with you. If everything does go south, I don't want to add to their arsenal."

Wulff sighed. "I figured as much," he said. With great reluctance he handed over his rifle. "Take care of it. If they don't kill me, I'll want it back soon enough."

Day now carried four rifles so once he was up on the ravine wall he stashed the M4s. With his Weatherby and the Henry he crept along the ridge looking for a perch from which to fire.

With the exception of a rattlesnake he encountered no wildlife as he scouted a position from which to cover the meadow. The rattler disappeared under a fallen tree, and in moving away from it Day found the perfect firing position. Two parallel outcroppings of soapstone leaned over the hill where it descended on the west side. Dark and smooth, the ledges were as tall as him and yards long. The uphill stone was taller than the lower, and on the lower one was a breach like an arrow loop on a castle wall. Standing back so he would not be seen, Day peered through the breach to the land below.

The view was as good as he could ask for. Sixty feet down and a hundred feet away from the base of the hill, a spring-fed meadow lay in plain sight. The bright green of the grass stood out from the dusky hues of the plains shrub. Nine Progs and two Indians were inside the green. The Progs clustered where the water flowed while the Indians stood apart, one at the west end of the meadow and the other the south.

Day's pulse quickened. An uneasy excitement grew inside him. It had been two years since the uprising began, two years in which the Progs and their follow-ers had wreaked violence and murder on the nation. Two years since Day's life had been ripped open and smashed, his wife and children taken, his friends scattered and his career destroyed. In that time he had grieved, cried, and plumbed the depths of self-pity; he had prayed and cursed and then prayed again; he had given up on life but not had the courage to die; and finally he had turned to vengeance as his therapy. That final journey had led him to this moment, where now the people most responsible for the carnage and misery were within range of his rifle.

The soapstone was thick enough that he could lay the rifle across it without the barrel sticking out the other side. Gingerly, he set the weapon in place and put his eye to the scope.

Two men in the center of the meadow he could not identify. They sat near the spring where water bubbled up out of the earth. One had his back to him while the other had a face Day just did not recognize. That was not a surprise since the photos Shell showed him before he left were all pre-uprising shots of clean-shaven, well-dressed people. Unless there was a distinctive feature to latch onto, he guessed most of the men would be hard to tell apart.

Near them sat the only black man in the group. Ray Williams. Mid-thirties, thin, medium-height, with a dirty ballcap covering frizzy hair. From his angle Day had trouble seeing the face but he made out a stubbly beard and thin moustache. Ray sat by the spring with one hand in it as though testing the water.

The next person down the line was Nancy Peal. She, at least, he knew. The lawyer had her shoes off and was massaging her feet. Next to her and huddled in close conversation was a woman who Day guessed – from process of elimination and her youth – was Heather Westergard, the teacher from Maryland. Heather clutched a bag of some sort, squeezing and pulling at it like it was a set of worry beads. Peal's hair was loose and long while Heather had chopped her own down to shoulder level. Even through the scope both women looked haggard.

After them Day saw Crazy John on knees scooping water into his mouth from the trickling spring. Behind him, away from the water and the others, sat a third woman who Day recognized as Elke Neuberg. He had ample information on her given her high public profile before the uprising. He remembered, too, that Wulff had warned about her being committed to Reed.

As for the Prog leader, Day found him ten feet past Elke, staring out at the plains and appearing to ignore the last man in the group – Bern Jones, maybe, from the broad shoulders? – who sat nearby and talked in Reed's direction.

Day placed the crosshairs of his scope on Reed's left shoulder and consciously fought to keep from squeezing the trigger. Reed sat motionless, one leg bent under the other, looking into the vast expanse of Jackson Hole. He had removed his wool hat but not the black coat. His hair, bushy and dark but showing streaks of gray, joined with the coat and pants to made the whole image an ugly contrast with the bright green grass, a brooding blot on a cheerful tableau. Day knew he should shoot the man. He knew that morally, legally, and in every other way he could kill the man with no regrets or remorse. His finger touched the trigger and then lifted away. Touched it again...and lifted again. Do it, he told himself.

As though hearing the exhortation, Reed's head turned. He looked back behind the meadow in the direction of the hill. He did not look up but the movement was enough to startle Day and make him wonder if he had somehow given himself away.

He was saved from possible discovery by a distraction. Up to then the natives on the perimeter of the meadow had stood motionless, sentinels on watch, but suddenly the one to the south raised a hand. The movement caught everyone's attention: the Progs grabbed their weapons and the second native leaped across the grass to join his fellow, spear at the ready.

The cause of the excitement was the approach of Eric Wulff. The logger came into view down and to the left, walking a path close to the river, which forced the occupants of the meadow to look south as he approached and away from Day.

Day heard Wulff hail the group. His voice, small in that vast space, faded even more before it bounced off the rocks of the hill. There were scattered replies. Wulff came within twenty feet of the first native and then stopped. After a moment he took another step forward but stopped again.

On the hill, Day divided his time between looking through the scope and over it, trying to determine the tenor of the meeting. He could not hear what Wulff said but from the man's gestures it seemed he was explaining the events of the last forty-eight hours. The logger pointed over his shoulder once, and twice behind the group toward the Highway. He spoke for a while, appeared to respond to questions, and then stood waiting while the Progs took over the conversation.

Day waited, too, wondering if Wulff had yet mentioned his presence and the fact that the Progs were in his crosshairs. He looked through the scope and decided the answer was no. Reed's face – now visible – was filled with suspicion;

he looked only at Wulff. Elke was behind him with one hand in a pocket. Now Nancy Peal moved up to say something. The lawyer spoke to her fellow Progs, not Wulff, and Day hoped that meant she was finally doing what he had wanted her to do: urging the others to surrender. Maybe Wulff's plan was not so bad after all.

Eric Wulff parted from Day in the ravine trying to divine – not for the first time – how in the hell he had ended up where we was.

He walked straight out across the flats, following the stream toward the river to make himself as visible as possible to anyone who might be in the area. The sun was bright and the air clear and everything from the plants to the rocks to the bluff and its trees stood out in sharp relief. No one with eyes could miss him.

When he was almost to the river he turned west, staying outside the cotton-woods that grew by the water. He could not see the meadow yet but he knew where it was. By approaching it from an angle he hoped to draw the Progs' attention away from where Day was climbing in the rocks. He picked his way with care, watching for snakes and gopher holes and trying to ignore how naked he felt without his rifle.

He saw the meadow before he spied the Indian standing at its edge. The Arrow looked like a sapling stripped of leaves but then the sapling raised a hand, signaling that he had spotted Wulff. Wulff raised his own hand in reply, then decided to raise both to show he was unarmed.

Behind the Indian the Progs converged. Even Puff was there, impassive as always. Wulff kept going and was soon close enough to recognize faces. Every-one was surprised to see him but he saw concern, too. Reed, especially, looked suspicious as hell, and Wulff heard him tell the others not to let the logger get too close.

"That's far enough," Bern Jones called out, dutifully complying.

"Far enough for what?" Wulff replied. He stopped and held out his hands to show they were empty. "Do I smell bad?" He stepped forward again.

"Stop where you are!" Reed barked. The Prog leader stepped forward and pointed at Wulff with a *J'accuse* intensity. As usual, Reed was not carrying a rifle though Wulff believed he only did that as part of his image of superiority, an effort to stand out from the sweaties around him. The logger knew Reed carried at least one pistol inside a coat pocket.

"What the hell's the problem?" Wulff demanded.

"Where are the others? Where's your weapon?"

Wulff dropped his hands. "Sorley's dead," he told them. "We ran into a bear."

That shocked the Progs and for a moment there was a sincere outpouring of disbelief and grief. But not from Reed.

"How did you get away?" he demanded. "And where's Rohanson?"

Wulff took a deep breath and began his story. He explained how he and Ruud and Sorley had found tracks in the gorge and followed them. He made no mention of the Moons but described how the men suspected one of the Settlers was injured, and how they tracked them into the hills overlooking the lake valley. They had known about the bear, he said, and spread out to cover each other as well as avoid an ambush.

"And you just happened to be in the back?" Elke sneered.

"I didn't *happen* to be there," he retorted, stifling his anger at her inference. "I was cautious while they rushed ahead. Sorley was in such a hurry to kill those guys he walked into a trap."

He continued with his tale, relating how he was cornered by the bear, then by Day, then by the bear again.

"Wait a minute," Carlos interrupted. "You were holed up with this guy and you didn't kill him? Why didn't you kill him? Why didn't you shoot him or just break his neck?"

Wulff shook his head. "Well, gee, Carlos, for one he had a gun on me. For another, we were a little busy dealing with a two-ton bear that was trying to rip us both to shreds."

"Where are they now?" Ray Williams asked with quiet firmness.

"Never mind that," Wulff said. He told the rest of his story quickly, never saying it outright but implying that Day had disarmed him on their first meeting. He also did not dwell on the second Settler's injury, suggesting instead that the bounty hunters had split up deliberately to cover more territory.

"Where are they?" Ray insisted when Wulff finished.

"They're near."

"You led them to us," Nancy Peal concluded. "You led them right to us. You bastard."

"That's rich coming from you, Nancy," Wulff responded. "The woman who practically walked them over to the gorge?"

"But you did it deliberately!"

"You're a traitor, Eric," Reed pronounced in his from-on-high voice.

"Really, Blake?" Wulff shot back, finally losing his patience. "You have one companion ripped apart by a bear, the other takes off for the hills, and you're trapped with a gun pointed at you. Would you have sacrificed yourself for the cause or would you have looked for a way out that might mean no one dies?"

"I would have sacrificed myself," Reed replied without hesitation.

Wulff laughed. "Oh, please! You don't sacrifice yourself for anything! It's all about you. All of this is about you. *We're all here because of you.* Thousands of people have died because of you and you're still acting as though you can judge the rest of us."

"You're a traitor, Eric," Reed repeated, dropping his hand into his pocket.

"No, damn it. I'm the one guy who's trying to give us an option for getting out of here alive. If these guys wanted us dead they would have been killing us from day one. You would be dead right now."

"What do you mean?" Simon Pettigrew asked.

"I mean, you're being watched. As we speak. If he wanted to start shooting, he could."

That caused consternation in the group. Everyone glanced around, clutching their weapons. Everyone, that is, but Ray Williams. Ray searched their surroundings like the others but to Wulff's surprise he then casually set his AK on the ground.

"You bastard, you did bring him to us," Bern Jones accused him. "We trusted you!"

"If we give up, they won't kill anyone," Wulff said.

"How do we know that?" Jones demanded.

"I told you, because he could have been killing us already. Look, he caught Sorley once and let him go. He didn't even kill him the second time. And he let Nancy go."

"That's true," Peal agreed. She said it reflexively, not intending to support Wulff, but then having spoken she stepped forward. "They're bastards," she continued, addressing herself to Reed. "But they didn't kill me and I don't think the one guy has the guts to, anyway. They could be our ticket out of here."

"They're not our ticket out of here," Reed snarled, his eyes ablaze. "They're a threat, a mortal threat, and they need to die. Our objective is the device they're carrying. How many times do I have to make that clear to you morons?"

"But we don't have the device!" Nancy yelled back. "And don't call me a moron, you sanctimonious son of a bitch. It wasn't me who brought us to Jurassic Park."

"He doesn't have any device," Wulff interrupted as Reed looked ready to explode. "Not on him, anyway. He said there is one but he let me search him to show he doesn't have it."

"Then where is it?" Reed demanded.

"I don't know. Either the other guy has it or they hid it somewhere."

"And that's the key!" Reed shouted, pointing his finger at each Prog in turn. "They hid it, just like the last killer did. So once we find it, they will have to answer to us."

"Answer what?" Peal queried him. "Answer how? Who cares about these guys if we can get out of here?"

"Getting out is not important. Controlling how it's done is."

That proclamation produced a chorus of outrage from the assembled Progs, who now shifted their attention away from Wulff. The logger watched their frustration grow with nervous satisfaction. He had suspected for some time that Reed had given up returning to the real world. Now it was becoming clear to the others how much their wants diverged.

"Don't you see?" Reed explained, his voice both a plea and an expression of contempt. "You're missing why those killers are here. They didn't come after us because of *who* we are, they came after us because of *where* we are. As our traitorous colleague keeps insisting, they're not trying to kill us. They're trying to get us to leave this place. Why? Because either there is something important about this location..." he looked around with scorn, indicating that was clearly not the case - ..."or about how we got here. How we got here is the device, so that device is the hinge on which this whole conflict turns. It is our negotiating tool."

"Negotiate what?" Carlos protested. "We either go back or we don't. What is there to negotiate?"

"What is there to negotiate?" Reed repeated. "You are an imbecile! How about what happens to you once you do return to the land of tyrants and bounty hunters? You don't think they'll kill you the instant you're back in their hands?"

"But how will having the device change any of that?" Carlos shot back. "Huh? Who's the imbecile now? Whether I hit the button or the bounty hunters do, I'll still be in the same situation."

"Which is why you should not be in a hurry to hit that button!" Reed shouted. "The enemy has given us an opening and we will exploit it!" He turned back to Wulff to continue but Simon Pettigrew cut him off.

"Just how did any of this even come up, anyway?" he wanted to know, also returning his attention to Wulff. "We're arguing over the device but why did you even say anything about it to the Settlers? Did you tell them we were looking for it?"

"Well, yeah."

"Goddammit!" Carlos snapped. "You *are* a traitor." The others joined in to agree with him and now, like any mob, their attention swung once again.

With increasing frustration Reed tried to regain control of the conversation but everyone was shouting at once, too emotional to pay him any heed.

"They were coming after you to kill you!" Wulff insisted to the group. "I convinced him to let me talk to you first. The only reason any of you are alive right now is because I bought you some time."

"By telling them where we are and leading them right to us?" Pettigrew shot back. "If you had done your job they would be dead or still up on the mountain trying to find us. I don't trust you at all. I think you made a deal with them to save yourself and it means turning on us."

"No!"

"Wait," Nancy Peal broke in. "Maybe there's a way to settle this. However Eric got here, these bounty hunters are still after us. If they don't have the device on them, they at least know where it is. We still outnumber them. We can make a deal."

"There's no deal!" Reed shouted.

"I agree with Nancy," Heather said. "We should make a deal,"

"Oh, you do, do you?" Elke spat at the younger girl. "The house bitch speaks up. You haven't had an opinion in six months, now all of a sudden you're defending your boyfriend and want to throw the rest of us under the bus."

"Screw you, you dyke!" Heather erupted, surprising everyone. "You're all arguing over power. Power, power, power! I just want out of here! I want to get away from all of you. You can all stay and die one by one but I'm going home!" She threw her bag at Reed, hopped across the trickling spring water, and ran toward Wulff.

Reed snapped. "No one is going anywhere!" he shouted. Elke raised her .38 but Reed had already lifted his own pistol from his pocket. It was also a revolver, a low-end Taurus, and he must have cocked it while still in the pocket because as he swung it up toward Wulff it went off.

Wulff saw Reed raise the gun. He threw up his hands and yelled "Wait!" just as the Prog leader fired. Whether it was that movement or because she had one last thing to say, Heather spun around to face the group just in time to get in the bullet's path. She caught it high on her chest, shrieked, and toppled to the ground.

Nancy Peal screamed. Others shouted in dismay. But whatever they might have done in the next moments never happened because at the same instant that the gun fired the Arrow Indian at the edge of the meadow, who had been distracted by the Prog infighting and thus not watching the plain, suddenly took a spear through his leg. Through his pain, he cried out a warning.

More spears flew through the air, along with other projectiles including stones. Two dozen Moon Indians leaped yelling from the brush and ran at the meadow. Puff threw his spear and dropped one of the attackers. He felled another with his club, then he turned and fled. Nancy Peal also spun on her heel. Leaving her shoes she ran to the top of the meadow where she struggled as the green grass gave way to rockier soil. Gunfire sounded as the Progs returned fire.

Wulff got his hands under Heather before she hit the ground. She was in excruciating pain. The bullet had hit her collarbone and shattered it on the left side. A piece of the bone protruded through her skin but there was no exit wound so it appeared the round ricocheted somewhere inside her shoulder or chest. As a Moon Indian raced by Wulff shielded Heather with his body, anticipating an attack, but the Indian did not stop. Someone shot a second Indian running up.

Wulff pulled Heather behind a sage and yanked the bandanna from around his neck to try to stop her bleeding.

"I'm sorry about this, Heather," he insisted as he plugged the wound. He felt her collarbone move as he did so. She had tears in her eyes and gasped for breath. Her face had already lost all color. "I really am. I was trying to stop anyone from getting hurt. Believe me, I..."

Something hit him hard on the skull. He rolled away, his head pounding. An Indian stood over him and Wulff lashed out with his foot, catching the man on the thigh. The contact was slight but the Indian fell nonetheless. Wulff tried to stand but felt himself losing consciousness. He got as far as his knees before everything went blurry.

The Indian must have recovered because once more someone loomed over him, a weapon raised. Wulff tried to kick again but he could no longer see clearly and his legs suddenly seemed a long way away. Out of habit, he reached for his Henry. *Where's my gun?* he thought, grabbing at the dirt. Then everything went black.

25

Day watched the scene unfold in the meadow through his Leopold scope. For most of the debate he kept the crosshairs on Reed but when the shouting began he moved them over to the two men who had been together near the spring. Reed, after all, was unarmed. The other two were getting increasingly agitated and pointing their rifles at Wulff.

Heather's dash surprised him as much as it did her companions. He held his aim on the two men but then heard the shot and looked over the scope to find out who had fired. Seeing it was Reed, he tried to re-establish a fix on the Prog leader. By then, however, everyone was in motion. Natives were pouring out of the sage as shooting erupted from all sides. Remembering that Wulff was his priority, he swung his aim in time to see the tall man from the spring raising his AK like a club over the downed logger. Day fired without hesitation, dropping the man in his tracks.

Bern Jones was on one knee firing at the attacking Indians. Ray Williams had knocked down one Moon and was grappling with another. Day searched for Reed and saw him retreat to the top of the meadow with his pistol in hand, Elke providing cover. Day threw away all doubts and drew a bead on Reed.

A sound came from behind him, the unmistakable scuff of leather on rock.

He spun around as an Indian leaped at him from the ledge above. At the same time a second native entered the passage and ran toward him with a raised club.

The leaping man held a spear. He dropped onto Day gripping it with both hands, aiming to drive it right through the Settler. Day jumped aside and just managed to avoid the blow. The stone point ripped through his coat, creased his hip, and snagged on the Colt's holster. The native's whole weight was behind the thrust and it tugged Day back toward the man. He responded by spinning with the pull and swinging the Weatherby to strike the man on the side of the face with a blow that made the Indian fall against the arrow loop.

The second attacker was now blocked by the first but with catlike reflexes he leaped over his partner to the soapstone ledge. As a bullet ricochets off a wall, he then threw himself at Day – too fast, as it turned out, for his strike with the club went long. The stone head passed over Day's shoulder instead of bashing his skull. But the Indian still crashed into the Settler and knocked him backwards. Day's coat ripped free of the spear, the native went over the top of him, and both men sprawled to the end of the passage.

The native was up in a flash. With a cry he launched himself again at Day. Day was slower but still had his rifle. He parried another blow from the club, head-butted his attacker, and after some grappling managed to get the man in a lock from behind. He lifted him off the ground but his opponent responded by planting his feet against the upper ledge and shoving hard. That pushed Day backwards into the lower ledge, which hit him just below the tailbone. His feet slipped in the sand and once again he lost his balance. Though he kept his lock on the Indian, the two now rolled sideways and fell to the ground.

Day had never fought anyone who moved so fast. The native was small and lithe and as taut as a cable, and the harder Day squeezed it seemed the harder it was to hold onto the man. He managed to get to his knees, thinking to slip the guy somehow into a chokehold, but then out of the corner of his eye he saw movement. The first native had recovered and was charging toward them down the passage, his spear again raised.

Day swung to face the attack as the man crashed into them. The Indian in his arms took the spear, which passed through his shoulder and pierced Day's coat. But again the momentum of the assault carried all of them off their feet. Day toppled back, clutching the first Indian and now pinned to the second. The three men rolled out of the passage onto the open hillside.

Even with a spear in him the injured native strained to bite Day's arms, while the other warrior held onto the shaft with one hand and gripped Day's collar with the other, trying to climb over his companion to get to Day directly. The battle now sprawled onto a thirty-degree slope. Locked in combat, the trio slid and stumbled downhill. Day fought to get his feet under him or throw an arm out to arrest his descent but every limb was engaged in a desperate defense against two clawing, stabbing assailants. There was no opportunity to control where they went.

In the end gravity decided the battle. Soon enough the free-for-all met one of the myriad channels of erosion that streaked the slope like lava flows. Unable to stop, the three men tumbled over the edge of the gully and dropped from view.

When Day came to it was dark. He was cold and lying face down on something cold, but he could not see a thing. He panicked, thinking he was blind. Then he realized it was night.

He tried to push himself up and felt something wet under his left hand. Reflexively, he yanked it back and rolled over, freeing his hand from the ooze but flopping onto his back in a rain-washed gouge in the earth that was not quite as wide as him. Now face up and jammed tight, he saw stars overhead. At least he thought they were stars. They were moving, shivering as though they were as cold as him. His head spun and he felt nauseous.

I need water, he thought. He tried to sit up. The effort, weak as it was, got him nowhere and drained him of the little energy he had. His eyes rolled back and his head dropped onto the dirt.

When he awoke the second time the stars were gone. Pale sky had taken their place. Sunlight touched the upper half of the gully wall. His head pounded and his vision was like peering through broken glass. He listened, studied what he could in the fragmented panes that his eyes gave him, and eventually worked himself loose from the dirt that pinned his shoulders. With great effort he sat up.

One of the his attackers lay next to him. The man's mouth was open and his eyes were wide to the sky. The other Indian lay ten feet away, downhill in the gully. The one downhill was face down and still had the spear in him though by this point it had gone almost clean through his chest and out his back. Now it leaned at a crazy angle, brushing the gully wall. A trail of blood led from Day to that man.

Day slid over so he could prop himself against the wall. He was numb with cold and hurt everywhere. He pulled his hat from his pocket and put it on, then opened and closed his eyes several times to try to clear his vision, with some success. The fragmented pictures decreased in number but the world still looked like a Cubist landscape.

There was no blood on the nearest Indian, at least none that appeared to be his own, but his chest was raised above the dirt. Day pushed on the body with his foot to reveal a rock the size of a softball under the man's spine. He saw also that the man's nose was smashed. The discovery coincided with renewed pounding in his own head and it was not hard to guess what had happened.

They had fallen into the gully in a scrum. The natives ended up on the bottom, with Day knocking himself out against the lower man's face. The second Indian survived and at some point freed himself from the pile to crawl away, making it ten feet before bleeding out.

Day held his head to ease the pounding and tried to ignore that he might just have killed not two men but thousands.

He felt for his canteen but it was nowhere to be found. To his surprise, his hand alighted on his Weatherby. It had slipped from his grasp during the struggle but somehow had slid into the ravine with them. Feeling the weapon from barrel to stock to note any damage, he tried to conduct an inventory. He had his rifle, he had his Colt...his duffel – he looked up and down the gully but it was nowhere to be seen. After a while he remembered setting it on the ground by the loophole, next to Wulff's Henry rifle. Damn. At this point the Henry was not essential to his survival but he had promised to safeguard it for Wulff. And the duffel still held his medical kit. He should not leave either of them for anyone to find. But the thought of crawling uphill to get them made his aches double.

He also felt like vomiting. After a while he did. He wondered if the nausea might be from internal injuries but decided no, it was more likely from the blow to his head. And dehydration.

He needed water. Water was downhill. Downhill was also easier to travel so he resolved to go that way and retrieve the Henry and the duffel later.

The gully ran more or less straight down, with a lean toward the south in deference to the elevation that sloped in the direction of Jackson Hole. Where it ended its bottom rose to meet the surrounding terrain. Day pushed himself to his feet and felt his way down the hill. He emerged in a sandy pitch that blended into scrub brush circling the meadow. He sat down again and rested, listening and watching.

The land was quiet. The meadow sat in the middle of an indent in the hills but none of those hills was higher than the one he had just descended so it was easy to scan them for danger. The meadow itself was not so obvious. From where he sat he could see only the tops of waving grass.

For ten minutes he waited. In that time the only movement was of the small bird and insect variety, with the exception of a massive vulture that swooped in and landed far down to his left, almost around the hill. Day knew that was where he had last seen Eric Wulff but he did not have the energy to go investigate the spot right away. He needed to get to the spring before he passed out. Pushing aside thoughts about what might be hidden in the high grass, he stumbled forward.

Spring water in the meadow burped its way out of the ground in three spots. They formed a triangle where water pooled before trickling away through the grass. Day dropped down, exhausted by his short walk, and again listened. For shouts, for footsteps, for the rustle of someone creeping toward him through the brush. For any reaction to his movement. There was nothing. Satisfied, he knelt and copied Crazy John's activity from the day before, scooping water into his mouth and splashing it on his face and neck.

The water was cold and fresh. Its effect was not so much invigorating as it was calming, a sense of relief in Day's body that it finally had fluid to replenish its systems. He drank, rested, then drank some more. After the second time his nausea returned and he moved away from the spring to vomit again, spitting up much of the water he had just imbibed. Then he went back to the pool and washed out his mouth.

He wanted to lie down. Sun was on the meadow and it felt good. He knew he was suffering from lingering shock and his body needed to reset. But here was not the place. Not out in the open with no idea who might be around. He did not know where the Progs were, where the Moons or Arrows were or what they were doing, and he still had to find Wulff.

So after another study of the hills and the land, he got to his feet and followed the trickling water toward the river.

Soon enough he spied blood in the grass. Drag marks, too, where bodies had been pulled away. Farther on he found shell casings. He pressed on to the meadow's edge.

The vulture was not alone. Day counted seven of the huge birds hopping around three spots just inside or outside the perimeter of the meadow. The raptors resembled species of his own time: red head, hooked beak, hunched shoulders. The big difference was size. More arrived to circle overhead and as one swooped in Day estimated its wingspan at a dozen feet. It was like watching a Cessna drop in to tear you apart.

At the first body he came to, three birds ripped at the corpse of a native. The man had taken a round between the eyes. It occurred to Day to look for a half-circle on the man's face but between the bullet wound and the vultures there was too much damage for him to see any markings for certain.

The second body was a dozen yards away. It was also a native but this time Day clearly saw the white clay sign that indicated he was a Moon.

He stopped to think back on the Indians he had fought. They had worn no face markings.

Beyond the Moon was a third victim, a lanky American male who probably had once had clothes that fit and a job to go to on beautiful mornings like this. Day guessed it was the man he had shot. Tall with a bony structure, the man sprawled backwards across a rabbitbrush with his long hair in the dirt and his feet pointing at the sky. His pants were too short and rose above his shoes, revealing thick red socks that stood out all the more among the twinkling clusters of the bush's yellow flowers.

There was no weapon in sight.

Two vultures were tearing at the man's chest when Day walked up. They watched him approach the way a diner views the arrival of a second course. Only when he threw some fist-sized rocks did they back off.

Day searched the man's clothes but only what he could reach easily. He found nothing in the way of identification. He glanced around for either a weapon or something to tell him who the man was, but found nothing. Lacking the energy or desire to search further, he made a mental note of the man's features and then turned away.

In another sign of his weakness and disorientation it took him a while to remember Heather. Once he did, the search for her was short.

Some animal had dragged her body to the bottom of the hill. Whatever it was, it must have been interrupted because besides a few teeth marks and the bloody wound near her neck Heather's body was thus far undisturbed. Day looked down at her and to his surprise felt a twinge of something he had not felt in years, and never for a member of the group that had destroyed his life. Pity. He wondered why. He had felt sorry for Sorley because of the way he died but not *that* he had died. Neither Reuben nor Lace Stevens nor Ben Maddox had given him pause so why did he feel different about Heather?

He that dies pays all debts... his Bard suggested. Maybe. But just because Heather was dead, should he forgive her for her role in fomenting a revolution?

She was pretty. Not a stunner but attractive. And young. Most likely it was her youth that touched a chord in him, Day realized. He looked at her face, contorted in pain but the skin still smooth, and the wastefulness of it all came back to him.

What might she have become had the Progs never happened? How else could her life have turned out? What could the world have done different that would have kept her from being so damned dumb? The questions came but no answers, and he turned away before his feelings turned maudlin.

But seeing Heather drained him even more. He thought of his wife...and quickly pushed those thoughts away. That way lay despair.

There was no sign of Wulff. He kept searching but the four bodies were all there was. He would have continued looking but could not muster the energy, and anyway the vultures began to eye him with more interest. He needed to get somewhere safe where he could rest.

Moving away along the base of the hill, Day headed east, paralleling in reverse Wulff's journey from the mouth of the ravine. He thought to return via that route to get the Henry but realized as he neared the ravine and saw all the boulders along its walls that the rifle and duffle would have to wait. He lacked the strength to climb the hill. Worse, every muscle in his body was stiff and his dizziness was not going away.

Giving in to the inevitable, he found a spot at the base of the hill that was blocked from view by junipers. There was a boulder for him to lean against, and soft, sandy soil. With a last look around, Day settled down.

He propped his rifle on his knee, pointed it back in the direction he had come, and stared out at the bluff across the flats. Within seconds he passed out.

26

"Well, what have we here?"

Day heard the voice from afar. Movement and noise descended on him as he struggled up from the depths of unconsciousness. Someone threw him down and jumped on his back. By the time he was awake enough to realize what was happening, his hands were bound behind him and his weapons out of reach.

"You snooze, you lose, bounty hunter," the same voice said.

This time the voice was closer. Day opened his eyes and blinked in the light. The sun was past its apex and behind the man talking, making him no more than an armed silhouette. But then the man moved and Day's vision cleared. Actually cleared. The fragments from earlier were gone and he could see normally. The nap had done him some good. Despite the circumstances that was a great thing.

"Something funny, bounty hunter?" the silhouette barked, mistaking Day's relief for humor.

"Not at all," Day mumbled. "Lately I'm just having a hard time getting a good night's sleep."

The silhouette turned and whistled, then swung back to monitor Day.

"Join the club, you bastard," the man said. He pulled Day to his feet and pushed him in the direction of the river. "Walk."

Day stumbled forward, letting the fog in his head dissolve and gathering his wits about him. It was afternoon, maybe six hours after he had passed out. He was so stiff he could do little more than totter through the alluvial soil that softened the terrain as they drew close to the river. His dizziness, however, had dissolved along with the corneal shards, and for that he was supremely thankful.

A figure approached them from the river. It carried an Indian spear, one of the long ones.

"Well, well, well," the new arrival called. "Nice job, Gromey."

"I walked right up on him," the Prog behind Day admitted. "Looks like he had a hard night. Random must have given him a fight before they killed him."

"Any sign of the other guy?"

"No. This dude is the only one."

The Prog from the river came nearer. Day saw he had Asian features and guessed it was Minh Tran. Tran was a wealthy businessman of some sort from California who had helped launder money for the movement.

Tran walked right up to Day and sucker-punched him in the gut. It was a good punch, so fast Day did not see it coming. If his heavy coat had not absorbed much of the blow, it would have dropped him. As it was it still doubled him over and made him gasp for breath. Tran clapped Day's ears, grabbed his head with both hands, and yanked him close.

"I could snap your neck," he hissed into the Settler's ear. "I could. And I might!" He jerked Day's head as though he was going to do it. Then he laughed, pushed Day back, and spat in his face.

"Go easy, man," the first Prog advised. "We can use this guy."

"We can kill him, too," Tran replied. He looked like he wanted to hit Day again but turned away. Day was grateful but this time kept it to himself.

"Random and Heather are the only ones I saw," Tran told his companion. He planted his spear in the dirt and glared out at the plain. "Them and two slants. Where's everyone else? Where did they go, and what were they doing here?"

Day straightened up carefully. As weak as he was, he heard Tran's comment and pondered the irony of a second-generation Vietnamese immigrant calling someone a slant.

"You killed Heather?" the first man said in disbelief. He slapped Day hard on the back of the head. "What the hell's wrong with you guys? What are you killing all the women for? Heather was freakin' stupid but now we're down one more clam."

"I didn't kill her," Day mumbled.

"Okay, your partner then."

"It was Reed. They argued and he shot her."

"He what?!"

Tranh turned back to Day.

"Don't lie to us, you freaking fed," he ordered. "If you saw Reed, then where is he? Where's the rest of our group? You didn't kill them all, not yet. That we can see for ourselves. So where did they go?"

"I don't know," Day admitted. "I passed out."

"What happened?"

"I don't remember."

"Bullshit. What happened?" Tran shouted in Day's face.

"I tracked them. I saw them fight. Then someone hit me. I don't remember after that."

Tran hit him again but pulled his punch this time. Day still doubled over. He was getting too old for this.

"I don't believe you!" Tran shouted.

"Hey, relax, man," his companion urged. "I don't want to have to carry his ass. Let's get him to camp and beat him there."

Tran stalked away, twitching and mumbling and punching the air. Day saw he would need to be cautious around him.

The men took him to the river where they sat him down and then removed themselves to discuss their plans. They did not go far and at least one of them kept his eyes on Day the whole time. The taller guy was having stomach trouble and disappeared into the brush for a while but they kept talking. Day heard only snippets of the conversation. As far as he could tell it was a simple debate whether to kill him and continue looking for the other Progs, or stop their search now and take him back to Holden King. While he listened, he tried with no success to loosen the bonds on his wrists. He could not see what they had bound him with but it was not rope. It felt like leather, it was wet, and it was as secure as if it had been soldered into place. He had made no progress by the time they returned and dragged him to his feet.

"We're going for a walk, bounty hunter," the taller man told him. He carried an old Ruger P-89 semi-automatic tucked into his pants and an AR-15 missing its magazine. He handed Day's weapons over to Tran. "You're not going to make a sound while we do it, you got that? Not a sound. And if anybody jumps us while we're walking, whether it's your buddy or the slants, you're the first guy I'm going to cap. So pray that no one jumps us."

"Your best chance to make a deal is now," Day replied. "Before..."

Tran hit him again. Damn, but the man moved fast. He was a martial artist of some kind because this time it was a palm strike to Day's chest that made him stagger and sent a shiver through his skeletal structure that he felt down to his toes.

Tran did the head grab thing again and snarled, "Not a sound."

He shoved Day away, mumbling and twitching, and moved off down the river. The tall man pushed Day to follow.

The Snake River where it wound past the bluff was a course still feeling its way. With its headwaters only a few miles to the north, its banks were low and the current was flush with the land, as though it were the remains of a flood rather the beginning of a thousand-mile tributary to the mighty Columbia. It wove in random channels around sand bars and islands so natural they could have formed the day before. The water level was down but there were signs that was not always the case. Some of the channels were deep and where the water flowed it was swift. Closer to the bluff the banks rose. Tran and the other man – who Day deduced was Josh Gromer, a professional gambler from Los Angeles – followed the shore almost a mile to the west before finding a spot where they felt comfortable wading across.

Where they came ashore on the south bank the land looked the same as the north side of the river: sage and willow with only scattered color from flowers like mule-ears and bitterroot. But as they moved away from the water the terrain evolved. The land began to roll. In the dips and hollows a richer soil developed, less sandy, churned by pocket gophers and burrowed by prairie dogs. Mixed-grass prairie took over from the sagebrush steppe. Grass and forbs flourished, as did blazing star, fernleaf, and the ragged white petals of mountain mint. Dogbane was in bloom; so were sunflowers that splashed yellow everywhere even as clouds moved in and darkened the sky.

The clouds were the fringe of a weather system the men could see building in the south. In the bottom third of the valley, twenty miles away, black cumulus buildups towered over the terrain and traded lightning between themselves. Columns of virga stretched down in floating columns, wispy precipitation that faded before touching the soil. Day hoped the storm would move their way. He needed a distraction if he was to have any hope of escaping; a lightning storm might provide one. But to his chagrin the storm stayed in the south and the clouds in his own part of the valley showed no inclination to produce their own. Their sole contribution to the afternoon was to replace the blue sky with a hazy glare that encouraged the men to keep their eyes down.

The distant lightning increased. For a while it provided quite a show as the men trudged south and east around the bluff. By mid-afternoon, though, the storm dissipated and moved west. Overcast took its place across the valley. The air tingled with static but in the end no more lightning emerged and no rain fell.

After walking for two hours, Day and his captors had gone all the way around the bluff. The back side of the escarpment boasted more trees but Tran and Gromer stayed wide of the bluff and avoided the forest. They did not appear to be following a trail, as far as Day could tell. Rather, they knew where they wanted to go and worked their way using landmarks. By tracing the forest perimeter they stayed in the clear until reaching the mid-point of the bluff on its south side. Then they turned their backs to the trees and headed straight into the valley.

Day gave the two men credit: for a couple of urban terrorists they seemed to have evolved into decent mountain men. They moved methodically across the land, watching their back trail, staying quiet and coordinating with hand signals as they walked. He guessed they had learned these lessons the hard way. Some Progs had failed the survival test but thus far Tranh and Gromer had succeeded.

They came to the Snake River again and crossed it. The terrain leveled out. Prairie stretched in a panorama of colors to the Tetons and points south. Looking ahead, Day could not see what their destination might be. Jackson Hole lay before them in all its stunning beauty but there was nothing in it that he could see. Nothing manmade, anyway. He spied animals grazing: elk or deer, maybe; some other shapes that could have been horses; and to the south a herd of what was probably bison. That was all. But he accepted that much was likely hidden in the terrain.

Random boulders dotted the landscape, ever-present remnants of glacial passage. Tran passed close to a few as he led the way and Day realized he was using the rocks to triangulate their position.

The technique worked, for when the river was a mile behind them the three men encountered a long berm that crossed their path from east to west. The rounded edge of some ancient uptilt fold, the berm was blanketed in grass and wildflowers and rose as a ripple on the land. Once close to it the men could no longer see down the valley but equally the berm blocked them from view of anyone to the south. Thus masked, Tranh turned right without climbing the rise. Instead he led the trio along the bottom of the ridge, following it to the west for another half mile. At that point the berm jinked south, and just beyond the jink was Holden King's camp.

27

The camp was basic. Day surmised the men had been there no more than a few days. Torn earth, burned grass near a campfire, a few rocks rolled close to use as seats since there was no large wood nearby. A seep farther down the berm, past the campsite, had taller vegetation but it looked ravaged already as the men tore up the bushes for fuel.

The fire was going and one man sat by it. Tall and well-built with of all things a battered Stetson on his head, he leaped up as Tranh came into view.

He was the only person in sight but Day heard voices, an argument, coming from somewhere. Scanning the area he saw movement off to the right. Someone was struggling in the high grass. Gromer laughed.

"The guy just can't stop," he said, aiming his comment at Tran. For his part Tran erupted in a torrent of profanity directed at the distant struggle.

The man by the fire picked up a stone and threw it at the wrestling match. Someone cursed and a head poked up. Day recognized Holden King. Even after months in the wild, with long hair, a straggling beard, and a few scars, the handsome face of the actor was unmistakable.

"What?!" he shouted. When he noticed the approaching trio he disappeared again into the grass, re-emerging with one hand on a rifle and the other pulling up his pants. Day was close enough now that he could see a woman on the ground, too, a native. As King stood up she tried to get to her feet but a vicious blow from his rifle knocked her back down. She did not move after that. He checked her, decided she was alright, then headed to the fire.

"Keep moving." Gromer gave Day a shove. "Watch him, Tran," he called. "I'll be there in a minute." He then backtracked to a cluster of rocks they had passed before the berm curved.

"Move it, dead man," Tran snarled. He feinted a punch at Day's face, then grabbed his collar and jerked him forward. Day fell into the camp.

"Well, what the hell?" the Stetson wearer inquired. He put a Ralph Lauren boot on Day's chest and studied him as though trying to remember if they had met before. It took no acuity on Day's part to guess that this man was Trace Johnson. A character actor and FOH – Friend of Holden – he rode King's coattails to get movie roles. The man had lost weight but still looked good, all things considered. A pale beard and tired face did not mask the strong features that made him popular on the set. From what Day remembered Johnson also was known for an explosive temper.

"A Settler?" King interrupted, bursting into camp.

"No," Tran snapped, throwing his weapons in the grass and sitting down, exhausted. "A Hollywood producer. He was driving by on the interstate and stopped for directions. Who the hell do you think he is? What do you think we were doing out there?"

"Relax!" King snapped back. "I just asked a question."

"Well, it was a stupid question. Quit screwing your bitch all the time and pay attention!"

Johnson decided he did not know Day so kicked him aside. "Where's Josh?" he asked.

"He stopped to take a dump. He's still having problems with his gut."

"Never mind about him," King said. "What was the shooting? Was it this guy? Did you see anybody else?"

Tran leaned back against one of the rocks glared at Day.

"There was a fight in the meadow. We found this guy not far away. Knocked cold. He won't say how."

King turned to Day. "How did it happen?"

"Hey, you want to hear my story or what?" Tran demanded. "Squirrel! Squir-rel!"

"Alright, already!" King apologized. "Go on."

"Well, thank you very much. You're so kind. Like I said, Josh found this guy outside the meadow. But *in* the meadow we found Lord Pettigrew of the High Pants, Simon Random X or whatever the hell he was calling himself lately. And Heather. Both dead. Yeah, I know," he added as the others reacted in dismay. "Random with a hole the size of a fist in his chest, I'm guessing from this asshole's rifle. Heather, I don't know. He shot her with something."

"I didn't," Day spoke up. "I told you, Reed shot her when she tried to give up."

"Give up to who? You?"

"Yeah," Day lied.

"Why would Reed shoot her?" King asked.

Tran scoffed at the question. Day looked at King and said, "Because she tried to give up. You know him better than me. He's a power-hungry maniac who has to get his own way."

Nobody argued the point.

"What else?" Johnson asked Tran. "Did you see anybody else? What were Random and Heather doing in the meadow?"

"I don't know," Tran replied. "That's where the shooting came from, though. It was the first place we went after crossing the river and we didn't have to go any farther. There were two dead Indians, too. And lots of blood and some shell casings. That's all. So they had a fight with somebody. But then Gromer found this guy so we came back."

"You didn't see Sorley?"

"What did I just say?" Tran barked. "I just said that's all we found. Do you listen when people talk?"

"Relax, damn it," King urged him. "I wasn't there, I'm just asking questions. You," he turned to Day and adopted a menacing tone. "What happened, and don't give us this bullshit that you don't remember."

Day was almost amused at the transparency of King's character. He could switch on a dime from angry to conciliatory to threatening, and none of it was believable. Nevertheless, Day had been beaten enough over the last couple of days and had had no luck working at the knot in the cord that bound him. He saw no harm in delaying more abuse by cluing in this group to their situation.

"Give me water," he said, "and I'll tell you everything."

Tran argued but King went to a battered ammo can at the edge of the fire that was full of water. He filled a wooden cup that someone had carved and brought it to Day. Day had hoped they would untie his hands to let him drink but no such luck. King poured the water into Day's mouth. Half of it went down his front but the rest tasted good.

"Thanks," he said.

"You're not welcome," Johnson retorted. "Talk."

"I tracked your buddies up to their high camp," Day began. "But they had already moved. They were on their way down the other side of the mountain, heading back to the watering hole."

"The watering hole?" King interrupted. "Why?"

"I don't know. I just know that's where they were heading. I caught up with them at the meadow and offered them the same deal I'll offer you. Give up and nobody dies. Anyone who wants to go back and face trial can do it. Anyone who refuses we hunt down and kill."

"Oh, is that right?" Tran leaped to his feet and made for Day but Johnson intercepted him. Fortunately for Day, Trace was big enough to restrain his companion.

"Who's we?" King asked. "Minh, did you see anyone else?"

Tran sat back down and ignored the question.

"We know there's another guy," King continued. "Aron told us that. Unless your pal's dead by now."

"He's not dead. He's out there and coming after you right now."

"Ooo, we're petrified," Johnson said, poking Day in the chest. "If that's so we'll make sure your body is the first one he finds. Where is Aron Sorley? Did you see him?"

"I did. He is definitely dead."

That provoked consternation all around. This time Johnson knocked Day down and kicked him. He was pulled back up, pushed around, and knocked down again. Aron Sorley may have made enemies elsewhere but he had friends in this particular group. After roughing up Day, Johnson and King dragged him back to his feet and demanded the details.

"I didn't kill him," Day started again, and had to persevere through a chorus of angry denials. "I didn't! He, Ruud Rohanson, and your woodsman guy Eric Wulff came after me as I was going up the mountain. But they ran into a bear first. The bear killed Sorley and Wulff. Rohanson got away. I don't know where he went."

"That giant bear we saw by the springs?" King asked in awe.

"Maybe. It was a monster," Day shrugged. "He hit them in the woods above the pass. I heard the attack and had to hide up in the rocks when he came after me next. Had to sit there for two hours. When he finally left, that's when I found the bodies."

They believed him. Either he was deft at weaving truth and fiction or, more likely, the memory of the nightmarish creature that had terrified them on more than one occasion was enough to lend credence to his tale.

"Sorley and Wulff..." Johnson muttered, conscious of the loss those two men were to all of them. Even Tran was pensive.

King recovered first. "And Rohanson? You said he got away?"

"He did. His trail went into the lake valley. I didn't go after him."

"Why not?" Tran demanded.

Day looked at his questioner. "Because that's where the bear went, too," he said. "And because I want Reed. The rest of you, sure, but I want Reed first and foremost. I know if I get him, the rest of you crumble."

"Is that right?" Holden King countered, insulted. He grabbed Day by the lapels. "Well, look around, tough guy! You don't have him and here you are, prisoner of a bunch of us who aren't even with Reed, so nobody is crumbling!"

"Yeah, thanks to me," a new voice said. Josh Gromer entered camp. He set his rifle against the berm and plopped down, his face pale. "What did I miss?"

"You look like crap," Johnson told him.

"I feel like it," Gromer admitted. "It's whatever I got from that deer we ate. But I think I just kicked out the last of it. Now I need to rest."

"Sorley's dead," Tran summed up. "So's Wulff. Killed by the godzilla bear. That's what the bounty hunter tells us, anyway. If we can trust him, we're down by four, not two."

"Damn. Sorley and Wulff? Man, Eric was a good guy to have out here."

"And Sorley, too!" Johnson protested.

Gromer held up his hands to show he meant no offense. "Yeah, yeah. Of course, Aron was a great guy, too. It's just that Wulff was our best hunter."

He asked for the rest of the story. Holden King relayed what Day had told them thus far. When he finished there was silence as the group pondered their new state of affairs.

"Why are they going to the watering hole?" Gromer asked no one in particular. He looked at Day and when Day shrugged, he repeated the question, adding, "Why there? Why now?"

Day maintained a blank face. King and Johnson did not think the question important but Minh Tran began to turn it over in his mind.

"Yeah, why?" Tran asked. "Reed doesn't do anything for the hell of it. If he's taking them there, there's a reason. What's there?" he demanded of Day. "Tell me or I'll put my fist through your chest."

"I don't know why he's going," Day repeated his lie. "I've only seen him once and that was from a hundred yards away when he was in the meadow."

"I don't believe you," Tran said.

"I don't care."

Tran leaped to his feet and rushed Day. He swung at the Settler but this time Day was ready and dodged the blow. As Tran's momentum carried him past, Day lashed out with his foot and caught the Prog hard at the knee. The boot raked Tran's leg. The businessman went down with a yell of pain.

For his trouble Day took a punch from Trace Johnson that made him see stars. He staggered and fell, hitting the ground in a position where again he had a close-up view of the Texan's footwear. Designer hiking boots. Even in his pain he could not help thinking how ridiculous that was.

More important, Day landed on some gear the Progs had piled near the fire. His hands touched what felt like a fork, the flimsy, flat kind included in camp cook sets. He grabbed it to use on his bonds but when Johnson pulled him back to his feet the metal slipped from his fingers.

"Hold it! Hold it! Hold it!" Gromer yelled as Johnson and King were about to beat Day senseless. "I figured it out! I know why Reed's going to the watering hole!"

Tran was crawling for Day's rifle but Gromer slid that away from him.

"Give me a reason not to kill this guy and do it fast," Johnson ordered. His own temper had him ready to keep swinging.

"The best reason!" Gromer exclaimed. "Because you want to go home."

"What?"

Gromer pointed to the northeast and then at Johnson.

"You were there when the last Settler got away. You and Sorley. Sorley said the guy had something in his hands before he disappeared, right?"

Johnson did not relax his hold on Day but he nodded. "Yeah. A tube of some kind. Or a box."

"But he didn't have it while you were chasing him," Gromer pointed out.

"He might have," Johnson argued. "He was running...he could have had it."

"But you didn't see it," Gromer insisted. "You didn't see it for sure, right?"

Trace shrugged but said nothing, waiting for an explanation.

Gromer held out his hands to indicate the answer was obvious. "Look, this guy and his pal got here somehow. They must have a box, too. But this guy isn't carrying one. Odds are his pal isn't, either. So that's why Reed is going to the watering hole. If they stashed it there, he wants to get it."

King's face transformed. He spun Day around and searched his pockets. "Where is it?" he demanded.

"I don't know what you're talking about."

Trace Johnson lifted Day off the ground and shook him so hard dust flew off his coat. "Talk, bounty hunter, or I'll break every bone in your body."

"You do that and you'll be stuck here forever," Day croaked out a reply. "Now's your chance to make a deal."

"Is that so?" Johnson growled. He shook Day even harder. "Then let me show you how we deal with guys like you in Texas."

King kept searching Day in between Trace's shakings. Not finding anything, he looked around. "Where's his stuff?" he asked. Gromer pointed to the weapons in the grass. King hurried over and examined the Weatherby, the Colt pistol, Day's knife, and the random survival items from his pockets. Not seeing anything of interest, he turned them over again as though he had missed something. Still dissatisfied, he picked up the Weatherby and returned to Day.

"Nice rifle," he said. "If you don't want me to beat you to death with it, tell us how you got here and how we get the hell out."

"Sure," Day answered. "Untie me, you guys put down your weapons and surrender, and I'll tell you as we walk to the watering hole."

King lunged with the rifle to strike Day in the face. Day got out of the way but ended up on the ground yet again, this time falling over one of the rocks the Progs used as seats. He felt like a yo-yo as King pulled him to his feet. The actor got the Weatherby across Day's neck and began choking him with it.

"Look out there," he hissed in Day's ear. "See that bitch in the grass? We took her from the Moons. They wouldn't sell her so I took her. Now they're pissed and looking for us but you know what I'm thinking? I'm thinking if we give them you and tell them it was you who kidnapped their whore, we can all be friends after that. Except you, of course. They'll stretch you out and kill you for days."

Day might have replied but he could not breath. Only when he was about to pass out did King release him. Day dropped to his knees.

"Hey, don't kill him," Gromer pleaded. "Not yet. We need him to get us out of here." He was going to say more but just then his stomach lurched. He cursed in frustration and hurried off, stumbling along the berm to make another visit to his chosen relief spot.

Watching Gromer run away doubled over tickled something in Trace Johnson's memory. He had a sense of déjà vu.

"Wait a minute," he drawled. He held up a finger and mentally stepped through what he had seen during the final confrontation with Matt Kurtz. "Gromer's right. The last guy wasn't carrying it when he ran. I thought he pulled it out of his coat but he didn't. He dug it up! Whatever they use, they don't carry it with them. Why would they? They could lose it or we could take it from them. No, it was in those rocks all the time. That's where their little box is."

"Does Reed know that?" King asked, excited.

"Why would he?" Johnson replied. "I just remembered it."

"Then we can kill this bastard," Tran proclaimed. He got to his feet and grabbed his spear.

"No, I still want to use him," King said.

"To get yourself another bitch?"

"To get the Moons off our backs, you idiot."

"Screw them. Kill this guy!"

Tran and King got into a shoving match. Day rolled over and found his voice.

"We moved the device," he managed to say.

Everyone looked at him.

"What did you say?" King asked.

Day got to his knees. "We moved the device," he repeated. "You won't find it without my help."

"You lie," Johnson barked.

"Everyone keeps saying that," Day complained. "But you'll feel damned stupid when you get to the watering hole and it's not there."

"I know where it is," Johnson insisted.

"No, you don't. And when I'm dead and you don't find it, you'll be stuck here forever following around this moron as he makes enemies for a hundred miles trying to satisfy his dick."

King swung the Weatherby. Day raised his shoulder to block it but the stock glanced off and struck the side of his head. He went down again, his skull ringing.

"You're the one making enemies," King threatened. "You want some more pain? I'll be your huckleberry. How about if we get medieval on you?"

"You don't even know what that means," Day mumbled through his haze. "You spout lines from movies you weren't good enough to be in. Val Kilmer doesn't know you and Tarantino would throw you off the set."

King kicked him, hard enough to remind Day to be more judicious with his insults. But King's blow knocked him over and his wrists landed on a sharp piece of shale. With fumbling hands he grabbed the rock and at the first opportunity wedged it into the leather cords.

Noticing the Weatherby for the first time, Johnson stepped forward and took it from King, who fumed from Day's putdown. The big man held out the rifle to admire.

"Well, look at this," he marveled. "This baby's a game changer. If we go back north, I could drop that bear from a thousand yards."

Day's head pounded and his ribs hurt. He could not take much more abuse. He closed his eyes to blink back the pain. When he opened them again, the pain was still there but he found himself staring through the grass at a familiar sight. Fifty yards away atop the berm the huge beast of a dog was slinking toward their group. True to form, he was arriving late but in a few seconds he would be close enough to rush the Progs and wreak havoc. Day worked faster on the leather.

"Give me that rifle," King demanded of Johnson.

"Go to hell," Trace replied.

Day saw the dog stop. The beast cocked its head, looked left, and stared. Then it turned and sprinted away.

"Hey, what's that?" Tran saw the dog and pointed.

Johnson raised the rifle. "Some kind of big-ass wolf," he said. "I could drop it, no problem."

Day was flabbergasted. The damned dog was always late, he was lazy, and much of the time he was pretty dumb, but he was afraid of nothing. Why had he run?

Then he felt it. Prone on the prairie floor he felt a tingle in his shoulder, a vibration that carried to his hip. Dogs felt earthquakes earlier than humans and the great dog had felt this.

Day twisted and looked behind him. The Indian girl lay where King had struck her. Twenty yards past her was a solitary boulder, yet another glacial erratic carried off and then dropped onto the earth like a Stonehenge reject. Beyond it was miles of open prairie before reaching the Snake River. He cleared his throat and ignored the pounding in his head.

"No, you couldn't," he said loudly.

Johnson lowered the rifle. "What did you say?"

Day spat blood. "You may have visited Austin once," he scoffed, "but a real Texan must have kicked your ass back to LA before you could buy a decent hat. You couldn't hit that wolf if it jumped up and licked your face."

Johnson put a boot on Day's chest and pointed the rifle at the Settler's right eye.

"Say that again," he growled.

"My niece can shoot better than you and she's three years old."

Johnson's face flushed. "I could hit you," he vowed.

Day felt the tingle in the earth turn to a rumble. He began to hear it, too, a low hum like a distant wind.

"Maybe you could, if I didn't move," he said. "But with thirty seconds head start I would be in the next county as far as you're concerned. Shooting that rifle would knock you on your ass."

Johnson looked ready to explode. "You think I can't shoot your precious toy?" he sneered. "You think in thirty seconds you would get far enough I couldn't blow you away? You might get fifty feet...I would be choosing which ass cheek to cut you in half."

"Get thee glass eyes, and like a scurvy politician, seem to see the things thou dost not."

"What?"

King found his voice. "Get his ass up, Trace, we're moving."

"Yeah, Trace," Day sneered, "we're moving so you don't have to prove what a crap shot you are."

Johnson's temper blew. "That's it!" he yelled. With one hand he yanked Day to his feet so violently the Settler's feet left the ground. The shale popped from Day's grasp. "You're moving alright," Johnson barked. "Run, smart guy. Run and get ready to have your leg blown off because that's where I'll be aiming. Then you can lie here and wait for the wolves to show up. And think of Sorley. "

"What the hell are you doing?" King demanded. "We need him." He pushed between Johnson and Day but Trace shoved him aside.

"No, we don't. We know where the box is. He dies here."

"No, damn it! The Moons..."

"Shut up! Run, smart guy. You won't be the first Settler I've killed."

"Thirty seconds," Day muttered. He turned to go but King pushed forward again. He swung his foot, aiming for Day's crotch. Day twisted and the blow landed instead on his thigh, where it was marginally less painful. For a moment his leg went numb.

Johnson swung the rifle and hit King in the ribs. The actor fell back.

"The clock's ticking," Johnson snarled at Day. "Move your ass."

Day staggered away, his head spinning and leg throbbing. He headed straight for the girl. Behind him Minh Tran asked, "Hey, what's that noise?"

With the shale Day had sawed through one loop of the leather but he stumbled across the prairie with his hands still bound. It was only as he neared the Indian girl that he managed to hook a thumb into the remaining loop and wrench his hands free.

"Ten!" came Johnson's cry. *"Nine!..."* Next to him, King and Tran finally felt the tremor. The air itself shook. Tran grabbed Gromer's rifle and limped up the berm to look around.

The Indian girl was conscious but motionless in the grass. Day grabbed her without stopping and dragged her along. Behind him he heard Johnson laugh and yell, *"Time's up, sucker!"*

The Texan raised the rifle to his shoulder. But then even he looked down at the ground as the whole prairie quivered like the surface of a drum. "What the hell...?"

Tran reached the top of the berm. He looked south and for a moment was struck dumb, unable to comprehend the sight. Then he screamed, a cry of primeval terror that rose above the thunder that now rolled from horizon to horizon under a dusky sky.

Day looked back. Behind Tran a wall of dust rose three stories high, stretching left and right across the prairie. From the dust emerged a line of bison, a mile-wide row of massive, panicked beasts running shoulder-to-shoulder with the inexorable power and momentum that only a herd can summon.

Tran spun on his heel but was overtaken and disappeared beneath the charge. The herd poured over the berm. Holden King threw his hands up either in surrender or a fruitless attempt to ward off the stampede; he was hit by a bull straight-on and thrown thirty feet before vanishing beneath ten thousand hooves.

Trace Johnson threw away the Weatherby and took off running after Day, who now reached the boulder.

The rock stood ten feet high with a conical formation and a trough running down the far side. Day shoved the girl into the trough and pressed himself against her, his hands gripping the pitted surface of the limestone.

The noise of the stampede rose to a deafening level. Above the din of pounding hooves were the bellows and grunts of the animals themselves, along with a cavernous hiss like a storm blowing across a ship's sail: the stampede generated its own wind, a hot breeze that blew above the shaggy humps of the bison and carried their power before them. Day thought he heard a voice cry out but then the herd was around him, rushing past the rock in a torrent. The boulder shook. Horns, some four feet across, scraped against the travertine surface in an ear-splitting rasp.

A minute went by, then two. The herd kept coming. Five minutes, then ten elapsed and still the tide of animals swept past. They pressed so tightly no individual animal could stop or turn; they just ran. If one went down it was trampled. The boulder forced the herd to part but as bison came around both sides they converged again only inches behind Day. A bull swung his head – the curve of its horn slammed into the Settler's back. The ground, too, tore away beneath his feet; Day felt himself losing purchase in the soil. He pushed closer to the girl but she was already almost suffocated against the rock. When would it end?

28

And then it did. With no warning the bison were gone, beyond the rock and flowing in a black tide toward the Snake River before bending west to parallel it. The bellows and grunts faded. Only the rumble in the earth continued. Day felt it through the soles of his boots, though he could have been shaking from the inside, too.

He stepped back from the boulder and fell over. The ground was turned over as though a plow had gone through. All grass had vanished, pulverized into the soil. Yards away the remains of a bison were scattered in the dirt. Another was on the berm. Day saw something that might have been a hand close to the far side of the boulder but did not bother to investigate. Trace Johnson was no more. Tran and Gromer were gone. And Holden King's Hollywood career had ended for good.

The Indian girl fell away from the boulder and collapsed.

After a while Day got to his feet and went looking for his Weatherby. He found it pressed into the earth about twenty feet beyond the remains of a Ralph Lauren hiking boot. The scope was crushed, the stock was fractured in two places, and the barrel was choked with mud. Yet being buried had kept the rest of the rifle intact.

As Day examined it, a scent reached his nostrils through the settling dust. Moments later a familiar figure jogged over the berm.

Roland stopped upon seeing Day. Dust coated him from head to toe. He had sliced the swelling over his right eye and drained the blood so it was no longer shut, but that side of his face was still a mélange of painful colors that showed through the dirt. The poultice of wild onion and ginger had spread to cover his neck. In one hand he held his bow. He had his tomahawk and knife, too, and a few arrows stuck up from the quiver over his shoulder. The bear amulet and leather necklace were visible through the hair splayed around his shoulders.

He stood tall and surveyed the scene.

"You don't look so good," he greeted Day.

"Says the pot to the kettle," Day rejoined. "*'Tis a goodly patch of velvet on's face. Whether there be a scar under't or no, the velvet knows; but 'tis a goodly patch.*"

"You're babbling, too."

"It wouldn't be the first time. At least I don't smell like a Thai restaurant. Stay upwind and the Progs will smell you a mile away."

Roland studied the ground. "Not these Progs," he remarked. "Is this all of them?"

"Almost. One went that way to take a dump. I have a feeling we'll find him still there. Or not."

The Indian eased down onto the berm. The breeze from behind him cleared the air but the musky smell of leather, sweat, and fear lingered. Cowbirds descended on the prairie, their brown heads bobbing across the broken ground as they picked through the detritus.

"How did you not get trampled?" he asked.

Day pointed over his shoulder to the erratic. Roland nodded.

"I didn't know you were here," he admitted, touching his fingers gingerly to his temple. "Or her. If I did, I would have tried something else."

"No worries. I was a late arrival. I'm just glad you didn't send mammoths."

Roland peered after the bison. The dust cloud turned again and crossed the Snake. It went as far as the west end of the forest before the stampede petered out. A black line appeared at the base of the cloud when the animals stopped running. The line spread as the bison separated, their heaving chests and wild eyes relaxing as panic fell away. The herd would settle down and soon be stretched again over miles of the valley.

"You got to see them run," Day commented.

"I did," Roland agreed. There was a spark in his eye.

After a long search Day found his Colt but it had suffered more damage than the Weatherby. The cylinder was broken clean off the frame. He found both pieces but the crane was irreparably shorn. What Prog weapons he found were bent and broken. He never did find his knife.

He climbed the berm and settled next to Roland. For a while they just sat, letting the quiet and calm soothe their senses. The Indian girl parked herself in the mud where she had collapsed. The great dog appeared from somewhere. It prowled the broken ground until finding a bison carcass, which it promptly set to eating.

"I saw smoke from their campfire yesterday," Roland explained. "Got close enough to see the Progs but decided not to take them all on. Then the bison moved in overnight so I figured to use some of them to scatter, maybe trap a few of these guys. It took me hours to get around the herd and upwind. They were jumpy after the storm so 'some' became all. Got a fire going...the grass went up and they took off, the whole damned herd."

"That they did." Day looked around for something to clean his rifle.

"Your neckerchief is on the quiver if you want it."

"I do," Day replied, retrieving the cloth. "You tracked me, then?"

"Started to. When did you see me last? Two, three days ago? Doesn't seem that long. I planned on laying up 'til today but heard shooting at sunset that first night. Got myself up next morning."

"Your boys give you any trouble?" Day asked.

"Bill and Ted? No. They left me food and then disappeared when they saw I was mobile. They gave you a name, by the way. *Awa-skan-aka*. 'Wolf Man' or 'Man Who Walks with Wolf,' something like that. Because of your dog. This is your sign." Roland brought his hand to his jaw and hooked his fingers, then brought them down and to the right in an L-shaped movement.

"Lovely. Did they give you a name, too?"

"Yeah. *Ro-land*."

"So you're Roland and I'm a werewolf?"

"You made more of an impression."

"Did you learn anything else?" Day asked. "Like how big their tribe is or whether they're going to keep being friendly?"

"No. Most of my attention was on how to get down from their cave. They hauled me up there after you left because of a bear – oh, I learned the sign for a bear, too," he remembered, opening his hand and running it up and down on his chest.

"What's the sign for big-ass bear?"

"You saw it then?"

"I did."

Roland exhaled. "I found a body. Who was that?"

"Sorley."

"And who got away?"

"Ruud Rohanson."

"Hmm. Then I'll guess you met up with your buddy Wulff? I found his tracks. Found your neckerchief, too. You must have dropped it climbing that rock. Looks like the bear tried to eat you."

"I did, and he did," Day said. He recounted everything that had happened in the last two days.

"Then I made the right choice," Roland resolved when Day finished his story. "I couldn't track you across the glacier. There was nothing to track. I saw the bear went up after you and figured that might explain the shooting."

"So you didn't cross the ice?"

"No. I didn't know if you guys went straight across or up or down – I would have been wandering and just hoping to cut your trail. Wasn't up to it anyway, and of course the bear was out there somewhere. So I tried to guess what you were up to. It looked like you changed your plan to go to the gorge and you had backup for now, so I thought, what can I do?"

"So you went after Rohanson?" Day guessed.

"Nope. Started to do that, too, but then your dog showed up." Roland gestured toward the huge canine, who had pried a bison rib from the mud and was gnawing on it with gusto. "He seemed to be trying to follow you but he went south, not north, following the glacier downhill. When I saw that I figured my best bet to find you was to trail him."

Day watched the great dog rip at the bison. "I don't know what goes through his head. But I suppose I shouldn't care. He has saved my bacon three times in as many days."

"He still seems ambivalent about me," Roland admitted. "But he let me follow him. Eventually we found another place to cross the ridge but by then we were almost out of the mountains. I took a route down to the plains well east of the pass. Then I got lucky...found some tracks. Boots. They went to the river where there was a trail. Somebody had used it recently and I guessed it belonged to the plains group, King's group. So knowing we were pressed for time, I came this way. Spotted their fire last night and you know the rest."

They talked more while Day cleaned his rifle, doing his best using the neckerchief and one of Roland's arrows. He had carried his cleaning tools on him and Gromer and Tranh had left them alone, but when King searched him he had thrown them aside along with all his extra ammunition. Now all of that lay twisted and broken in the mud.

"You say the Indians you fought had no markings?" Roland asked.

"That's right. One had feathers in his hair but no half-circle."

"But the dead guy in the meadow did?"

"One of the natives, yes. The other one I couldn't tell."

"And the other one was shot?"

"Very definitely."

Roland got up and went over to the girl in the grass. Day watched: the girl would not let Roland touch her but the two spent much time struggling through sign language. Roland gave her something from his pocket and sat with her a while.

"Anything?" Day asked when he returned.

"Her name is about all I'm certain of," Roland shrugged, settling down again. "Tu-san-ik-ani. And she was hungry. I gave her the pemmican that her guys gave me. Everything else...well, she could have been complaining about the price of mastodon steaks at the supermarket, for all I know. But she seems to be of the same group as the guys who helped me. She has the half moon marking. And her village is either over that way," he nodded his head to the west where the Snake River made its turn to parallel the Tetons, "or that way," he turned and indicated exactly the opposite direction, to the east and the foothills below Mount Leidy.

"Glad you cleared that up."

"Well, she's a typical woman. Once she started talking she wouldn't stop but none of it made sense."

"King said they kidnapped her and her tribe was after them to get her back," Day noted.

"You think that explains the fight at the meadow?"

Day pursed his lips. "It might. If they're all related, then we know her tribe – wherever they are – roams this way and more. Maybe they went looking for her and ran into Reed's band, who happened to have some Arrows along with them who had strayed into Moon territory."

"So they attacked because of the Arrows?"

"Because of the Arrows or maybe because they thought Reed had their girl. I don't know. We don't have time to work out tribal rivalries. We just need to stop dragging them into our fight. And we need to stop them from fighting because of things we do. Who knows how many innocent deaths King and his libido have caused..." Day trailed off, thinking also of his own contribution to future events.

"So what now?" Roland asked. "From what you've told me, we're down to eight Progs, seven if you still trust Wulff."

"I trust him," Day affirmed. "I don't know where he is right now but I don't think he has switched sides."

"Okay. Seven, then. What's your plan for finding them? The fireworks trick probably won't work again even if you have any."

"I don't."

"And we have a time crunch."

"Yeah."

Day looked down the barrel of his Weatherby. It was as clean as he was going to get it. His bigger problem was that he was down to four rounds, four bullets that he would have to fire from a broken rifle. He also had the one 9mm round from Ruud Rohanson's Glock, not that it would do him any good. Gromer and King had both missed it in their searches of him, buried deep as it was in a leg pocket, but he had no gun from which to fire it.

"They're going for the device," he resolved. "Ruud is a loose thread but Wulff said he's not a loner so he'll show up sooner or later. If we're lucky it'll be before we have to blast out of here. And before that happens we need to get Reed."

"So it's back to the watering hole," Roland concluded.

"Yes. If they know about the device, or think they do, nothing will keep them away from there now."

Roland stood and scanned the valley. It was stunning in its size, breathtaking in its beauty.

"Too bad. I like it here. Wide open and no white men to bother me. Well, except you. A fellow could survive here and do it without killing his fellow man. Not so once we go that way. Do you have any Shakespeare quotes for that?"

Day got to his feet and surveyed the stampeded land. The valley was indeed the biggest vista they had seen since their arrival. Its grandeur and raw innocence had a draw that even he felt. It was a savage land but savage only in the sense of untamed. There was no evil there.

To the northeast, by contrast, the open space contracted. The plains narrowed and ran between the hills and the bluff toward the watering hole. In that direction was a different kind of savagery, one concocted by design and deliberate in its purpose.

He would go that way. They had to stop Reed before their time ran out. Day had made it his destiny to settle with the Progs and he would not be swayed. Yet it was not just the setting sun that made his spirits sink as he considered their path forward.

"*Once more unto the breach, dear friend, once more,*" he offered his companion, gamely summoning a martial quotation. But in his heart he was feeling less Henry the Fifth bent on victory, than Edward the Fourth bowing to the inevitable.

"*What fates impose, that men must needs abide; it boots not to resist both wind and tide,*" he added. "One way or another, we're going to get this done."

29

They struck off to the east, following the berm for some distance before turning north toward the bluff. They passed the rock cluster that Gromer had used for his latrine but there was no sign of the poker player or his remains. Not that they expected to see anything; the ground around was as churned and torn as everywhere else.

The Indian girl watched them go. When they were almost out of sight, she rose and followed but made no attempt to catch up. She stayed behind them for over an hour until they neared the first crossing of the Snake River. Then she veered off on her own and disappeared into the landscape.

To save time Day wanted to pass the east side of the escarpment rather than retrace his path as a captive earlier in the day. To that end the Settlers waded across the Snake to get inside its oxbow, then followed the water upstream. After a mile they came around the bluff's east side.

The land inside the river's loop was flat and easy-going, a square mile of sandy soil and riparian plants. Cottonwood trees stood tall for hundreds of feet from the banks, while hackberry, Indian root, and snakewood occupied the understory. The men made good time working their way through this uniquely western ecosystem as shadows lengthened on the land.

The sun had long since dropped below the horizon by the time they found a safe spot to make the second crossing. Dusk came on and evening drew nigh. Day posed the idea of stopping for the night but Roland – feeling constrained inside the oxbow – wanted to get over the river right away. So, accompanied by the great dog, they slid down the banks and half-swam, half-waded across the water, moving from sandbar to sandbar and avoiding the deeper channels. On the far side another band of cottonwoods greeted them, joined by thickets of willow whose branches leaned over the water. The great dog scrambled up the bank and disappeared. The men followed, pushing on through the trees to set up camp on the forest's northern edge.

Roland's impatience was prescient. During the night the temperature dropped and the wind picked up as a cold front moved through. A powerful storm blew up over the mountains. Cold rain fell where they huddled under the trees, though the bulk of the storm's fury hit at higher elevations and turned to snow a thousand feet up. Wrapped in his coat, Day was grateful he was not still on the glacier.

The storm ended before dawn but only after hours of downpour. In the quiet that followed the men sensed a change in the dark landscape. The meandering Snake sounded louder...and closer.

When the sun rose they saw that the river had flowed over its banks in both directions. It had come up through the forest almost to their feet and was still rising. They gathered their things and moved uphill, finding a spot where they could look back over their trail.

The change in the river was something to behold. The lazy course of recent days had grown into a deep, rolling channel. It had flooded more toward them than toward the bluff, simply because the land rose more gently where they stood, but the tradeoff was that against the escarpment the water had carved new banks up to ten feet high. The flow everywhere was deep and strong. The current's speed was triple what it had been.

"Good call," Day complimented his companion.

Roland grunted and pointed. "In more ways than one," he said.

Day looked. So did the great dog, who leaped onto a boulder for a better view. Across the roiling waters a pack of dire wolves appeared atop the new bluffs. They came at a trot from the south, the same direction the Settlers had traveled, their dark shapes emerging from the brush one after another until there were seven in all. Ominous, loping creatures, they moved with a swaggering gait even with their noses close to the ground as they searched for a scent.

On sighting the men – and the dog – the pack went into a frenzy. Barred by the flood, some nevertheless leaped in place, baying in frustration. Others ran back and forth along the bluffs in fruitless efforts to find a way across.

All except one. One wolf, the largest, stood at the top of the bank and glared across the river. Even from a distance of several hundred feet the men could see its curled lips and bared fangs. Beside them the great dog growled and made to step forward, as though he would leap the river himself and launch an attack.

The wolf let loose a heart-stopping howl that rose above the noise of the water. The great dog answered with a wail of his own, a deep foghorn of a cry that – had it been from any animal other than his own – would have had Day locking and barring the door. His response drove the pack berserk.

"Looks like we got us a cock fight," Roland mused.

Day nodded. "I've been wrong about them," he realized. "Those wolves haven't been tracking us, they're after him."

"They probably ran across his scent early on. He's new. He's a challenge."

"And he's killed a few of them. They'll mix it up again if we let them. If my rifle was intact I would put a round into that guy and end this right here and now."

The wolf and great dog continued challenging each other until the wolf broke off and galloped away along the river bank, heading east into the oxbow. The pack followed.

"They'll find somewhere to cross," Day predicted.

"Not today they won't," Roland declared. "That river won't drop for a while. They'll have to go miles downstream to find someplace shallow and even then they might not make it. They'll quit before then."

Day was not so sure. "If there's one thing we've learned about this place," he reminded his companion, "it's that everyone carries a grudge." He nudged the dog with the Weatherby. "Come on, tough guy. You may get another chance."

The big dog rumbled deep in his chest as he watched the pack depart. It was with reluctance that he jumped down from the boulder.

A mile away Eric Wulff heard the howling and sat up. He took comfort that it was nowhere close. He wondered why the wolves were making such a racket now, after the sun was up. In the past he had heard the pack only during the overnight hours. Clearly something had gotten them exercised now.

He scooted forward and peered out between the aspen that masked his hide site. The thin trees with their quivering leaves clustered around a seep in the rocks that he had stumbled on the night before. The seep was on a slope well east of the ravine he and Day had descended before the fight. Wulff had found it by pure chance and had been fortunate to do so. In fact, he counted himself lucky to be alive at all.

Whoever had struck him at the meadow had not messed around. The blow to his head knocked him cold; he could still feel dried blood and a bump the size of a golf ball on his scalp. Yet somehow he had regained consciousness enough to crawl away while the battle was ongoing. At least he presumed that was what happened – he did not remember. But if he had not moved, then surely either the Moons or his erstwhile friends would have found him. If either group had, he guessed he would be dead right now.

All he knew was that later in the day he came to and found himself lying on some very uncomfortable rocks around a bend in the hills. All was quiet, his head hurt, and he gripped Simon Pettigrew's AK-47. The gun was empty, it did not even have a clip, but he knew it was Simon's because of the duct tape wrapped around the grip.

How Wulff had come upon the rifle, he had no idea. Looking back along his trail it appeared he had crawled to his position dragging it with him. Maybe Simon saved Wulff from being killed by the Moons. Maybe he and Wulff had fought. Wulff racked his brain trying to remember but came up with nothing. He remembered trying to help Heather...everything else was a blank. Not knowing what had happened or who was still about, he stayed hidden the rest of that day and night.

The next morning he tried to retrace the path he and Day had taken and make his way back up to the twin lake. There was water and food there, and he needed to avoid the plain. But the climb up the ravine was too much for his weakened state. Even with the AK to lean on he made it only halfway. Giving up, he reversed course to head downhill.

On the way down, however, a flash of light from the plains caught his eye and he spied Moon Indians moving around. He could not determine what caused the reflection but had no desire to find out. Instead he hid again. Descending to flat ground was out of the question for the time being.

With both north and south denied him, his only choice was to head east. He found a way over the ravine wall and spent that second day moving through the foothills, resting often, hiding frequently, always making his way in the direction of the pass. His body hurt and the going was slow. He had two pieces of jerky to eat but no water.

It did not help that his head still throbbed. The throbbing made him dizzy, the bright overcast hurt his eyes, and hiking tired him. He did not get far before the day was through. By nightfall he was parched and exhausted and seriously worried about surviving.

Then at dusk he saw steam drift up from a gully that crossed his path. He approached and found a tiny coppice of aspen clustered around a hot spring. Water seeped from the rocks and trickled a dozen yards before disappearing again. It was hot but it tasted good. It felt even better on his face and neck.

So Wulff crawled into the grove and lay down, allowing the warm earth and steam to soothe his wracked body. He chewed the last of the pemmican, drank water, and to his great relief fell fast asleep before darkness settled fully on the land.

On the morning that he heard the wolves his head felt better. The throbbing was gone, now it was just sore. He had trouble concentrating – twice he caught himself staring at aspen leaves for no reason – but jarring spasms of pain no longer shot through his body.

He had no idea what day it was. He had lost track of the calendar a few months into their wilderness ordeal and had long since stopped worrying about it, but now with two nights gone he realized it was forty-eight hours since he had seen his Settler companion. Where was Day? Was he alive? Had he captured anyone? Most important, how could Wulff link up with the Settler again? Day was his ticket home. Even in his confused state he had the mental wherewithal to know that finding the Settler needed to be his focused priority.

Less than a mile away Elke Neuberg plunged a threadbare scarf into a frigid mountain stream. When it soaked up as much water as it could hold, she carried it dripping to where Reed lay in the grass.

She had taken the scarf from a boutique store in Jackson months before. The Progs were racing through the night on their way to the ranch when she saw the place. Five of them were packed into a Land Rover Discovery that JP had stolen near Rexburg after their first ride broke down. It was cold: the dashboard thermometer said 26F. Snow was blowing across the hood and hurtling toward them in the headlights. Elke was unprepared for Wyoming in winter; all of them were. It had been in the sixties when they fled Silicon Valley for Oregon, and even Klamath Falls had not been too bad. But then they fled east into the mountains and the temperature kept dropping. When she spied a window display of woolen clothing among the abandoned, boarded up, and burned-out buildings flanking Jackson's main square, she yelled for JP to stop.

It was a nice place, somehow untouched by the looting and burning, and right up at the front window were stacks of tartan scarves and hats and sweaters. They broke down the door and ransacked the place. It was one of the best things she had ever stolen, she realized now as she wrung out the scarf over Reed's fevered face and then lay it carefully on his forehead. Since that night she had used it to keep warm, carry food, and shade her eyes; as a splint and a tourniquet; even as a napkin. After all that abuse it still retained enough fibers to soak up water from an icy stream. Aside from her Rossi revolver the scarf had become her most prized possession, reminding her of more comfortable times. She wondered if the store was still there. She hoped it was. If she ever got the chance, it would be nice to go back and take something else.

Reed sighed on feeling the cold compress. He patted her hand. It was the closest he ever came to saying thank you.

"How many?" he mumbled.

Elke looked around the clearing. The stream flowed from a canyon behind them and leveled out for a dozen yards before disappearing into nearby trees. The sliver of grass where they rested was cropped and peppered with elk droppings, but it was flat and comfortable. Besides Elke and Reed, Nancy Peal, Crazy John, Bern Jones, and Carlos Bardem were gathered there. Nancy was soaking her feet in the stream. Crazy John was in the water, too, poking among the watercress with a homemade spear and muttering to himself. Bern was cursing in frustration as he inventoried their weapons. Carlos was on guard, watching back the way they had come.

"Six," she told him, and then added before he could ask, "Ray's not here."

"Where...?"

"I don't know. He was with us but then went off."

Reed opened his eyes and stared up at the sky with his piercing gaze, as though trying to intimidate the heavens into cooperating with his plans.

"Fool," he said with sudden energy. "We need to be together. He needs to follow orders."

"I'll tell him."

"We need to move together, stay together, fight together. That's how we'll survive."

"I'll make it happen."

Carlos overheard them and grimaced in disgust. *That's how Reed hopes to survive*, he thought to himself, *by keeping everyone around him for protection*. And who the hell was Elke with her arrogant *I'll make it happen*? It was clear to all of them that she had long since nominated herself as the group's second-in-command but she had another thing coming if she thought he was going to take orders from a power-hungry dyke.

As for Reed, Carlos respected the Prog leader and everything he had accomplished to build his movement but until they arrived in the wilderness Carlos had never realized how self-centered the man was. And what a whiner. Reed handed out compliments from time to time like a monarch dispensing titles but mostly he criticized others' work. No matter what the rest of them did, he always found fault. This with people who were just trying to survive one disaster after another. *Move together, stay together*...what a bunch of crap.

Carlos did not know where Ray had gone but he was not worried. The Crip was weird and hardly ever talked but he was dependable. He had pulled his share of the load and more ever since they arrived. Besides, he and Reuben had always been going off exploring, since the very beginning, so it was safe to assume he was out there now trying to figure out where the hell they were, or if the Moons or Settlers were about. That was something Reed never bothered to do. And where the hell was Puff? Where were their damned Indian guides?

Reed lay staring at the sky, his mane of hair bunched around his head like a grubby pillow. He stayed like that as long as Elke ministered to him. When she turned away to adjust the laces on her boot he sat up.

"We can't wait," he declared, and tossed aside the scarf. Elke retrieved it from the grass and folded it into a careful square. Carlos glanced over at Reed but the others went about their business. The Prog leader repeated his announcement, this time louder.

"What about Ray?" Nancy asked.

"He's not important."

"Why not?"

"If he cared, he would be here," Reed said. He stood up and looked around. "We need to focus on our goal. That is to get to the watering hole and find the device."

Nobody moved. Carlos shifted his weight and looked back over the hills they had crossed since escaping the meadow. It was rough terrain but colorful, with dark spruce towering over the greens and purples of lower growth. He was getting accustomed to the wilderness despite himself. He still wanted to get the hell out, of course, but the forests and the mountains no longer terrified him the way they did when he had first seen them. Was it because he was stronger now, he wondered, or was he giving up? Becoming more fatalistic about his future? Galston had given up and he was dead. Maybe he was the smart one. After all, how much more could they take? How many more close calls could they survive? He wished Eric Wulff was still with them. Carlos did not like the logger but he felt safer with the guy around. Now especially, when they were being whittled down to nothing.

Suddenly he remembered where they could get some help. "Hey, what about King?" he asked loudly. "Holy crap, I forgot all about those guys. How can we link up with them?"

"We don't," Reed barked. "We go to the Rock."

But Bern Jones entertained the idea for a moment. "Hang on," he said. "That's a good point. We could use four more guns. Sorley said they weren't that far. He said what, five miles south of the river?" Then he reconsidered. "But good luck getting there. Those plains are crawling with Moons now. I'd love to have the extra firepower but we didn't make it past the meadow. If we're going to join forces, they're going to have to come to us. Reed's right, we should head to the Rock."

"Oh, I'm right, am I?" Reed said, sarcasm dripping from his voice. "How good of you to agree with me, Bernard. I'm so relieved. For a moment there I doubted myself. Is there anything else you want to comment on?"

"Hey, relax, your highness. The guy had a good idea."

"No, he didn't," Reed argued. "He didn't at all. Holden and the others abandoned us, have you forgotten that? Whatever happens to them is on them. They're dead, as far as I'm concerned. Dead! But perhaps you don't agree?

Perhaps you would like to take charge of the group and direct us from here on out?"

"I couldn't do any worse," Bern muttered.

"What was that?"

"I said I couldn't do any worse!" Bern shouted. He racked the slide on his AK-47 and pointed it at Reed briefly before slinging it over his shoulder. "Breaking news, chief – you don't exactly have a track record of success. You've failed at pretty much everything since you crawled out of your basement at Berkeley and this situation right here is no exception. So don't get all holier-than-thou on us about leading! You're still in charge but that's only because you've cocked it up so bad that nobody wants to clean up your mess. I sure don't. I'll go to the Rock. I'll follow so lead the way. But you know why I'm going? Because look around, jackass – we've got no other choice! At this point there is nothing, *nothing*, left for us to do but go to the Rock and try to get our asses out of here."

Reed's face grew red. He looked ready to self-combust, so angry he trembled. Elke moved to steady him but he waved her away. He took a step toward Bern and pointed his finger at him.

"One leader, one movement, one goal," he said slowly, grinding the words out. "If you can't handle that, get out. Go surrender to the bounty hunters."

"I'm not surrendering to anyone," Bern said. "I'm not surrendering and I'm not taking orders anymore, either. You go ahead and lead this circus if you want but don't assume I've got your back. You want my loyalty, from now on you've got to earn it."

"Don't talk to him like that," Elke threatened.

Bern did not even look at her. He stared back at Reed with a light in his eyes Carlos had not seen before.

"Alright, guys," Carlos intervened. "Let's calm down. Let's just get ready to move."

"I'm ready," Bern said, his voice calm. "Waiting on the great master here."

"You will not talk to him like that," Elke repeated. She moved her hand toward her pocket but Bern was faster. Still not looking at her he whipped the AK off his shoulder and leveled it at her chest.

"You don't scare me anymore than you did Ruud," he told her, finally deigning to glance in her direction. "Go for your little popgun. Reed will need a new lapdog when you do."

For several seconds everyone held their breath. Nancy Peal was frozen in place. So was Crazy John, though his expression was not nearly as concerned as the lawyer's. He seemed to find the conflict amusing. Carlos wanted to say something but in the eight months he had known Bern Jones he had never seen him this angry. He worried that if he tried again to mediate his companion might swing the rifle his way.

To their surprise it was Reed who dissolved the tension. A smile broke over his face. A real smile, as though he had finally seen behavior of which he approved. He chuckled.

"You're right," he said. "He is right! Every leader needs feedback and now I've had mine. Relax, Elke."

At his side Elke did not relax but she did remove her hand from her pocket.

"You are right, Bernard," Reed continued, "that nothing has gone according to any plan I've made since we arrived here. Since before that, in fact. I admit it. I didn't see this coming and have been reacting to our situation the best I could. Clearly, not well enough."

His followers in the clearing were flabbergasted. This was unprecedented. Never had they heard Reed admit to any shortcoming.

"But now," the Prog leader added, "whether due to my ineptitude or sheer fate, we don't have many choices available to us. The elements and our implacable pursuers have diminished our numbers to what we see before us. We can't fight the bounty hunters, not with what we have. You can vouch for that. You've been checking our weapons – how many bullets do we have left?"

Bern remained calm but Reed's magnanimous admission of failure caught him off guard. He answered with caution, suspecting a trap.

"24," he said. "Not counting whatever you and Elke have in your pistols."

"I've got four," he said. "Elke?"

"None of his damned business," she replied. She was as surprised as anyone by Reed's behavior but that did not stop her from glaring at Bern. She would kill him, she decided. It was just a matter of time but she would kill him. Her hand continued to hang at her side, not far from the pocket in which she held the Rossi.

"Let's say she has six," Reed offered, not wanting to argue. "That gives us 34 rounds in total. Plus whatever Ray has with him."

"He's out," Bern said. "He fired his last rounds at the meadow."

"Well, then. There we are. We have hardly enough for another shoot-out like the last one."

At which you didn't fire a shot, Carlos thought, remembering that it was he, Ray, and Bern who had held off the attacking Moons. Simon, aka Random X, too. The former counselor had killed one Indian and then charged forward but Carlos lost sight of him after that. Ray told him later that he had seen Random dead.

"So what do we do then?" Nancy brought him back to the conversation. She swung her feet out of the stream and rubbed them to get feeling back. "You're saying we can't fight, so what do we do?"

Reed held his hands up, palms out. "We can fight," he corrected her. "We just can't shoot it out with them. Here's how we defeat them: we get the device. Give me this one last chance. If we get the device, we won't need our guns. The Settlers will have to come to us, deal with us, surrender to us."

"What good is that?" Carlos asked. "I don't care about them."

"You do care," Reed insisted. "They're trying to kill you. Or at least they're trying to catch you and return you to the authorities under their control. If you go back – and you want to go back, don't you? – you want to do it on *your* terms. You want to go under your own control. With the device, you can deal. You can call the shots, as it were."

The others listened. It was a variation on a theme they had heard before but the new twist was important. Reed was not just talking about control, it was control with a purpose. Here was a chance to get home without having to surrender first.

"The bastards will have to negotiate," Nancy concluded, picking through the logic. "They wouldn't before but now they'll have no choice. We can use them as our bargaining chips to control how we go back. Not if, just how."

Reed nodded, though it was not clear if he agreed with her or was simply acknowledging her thinking.

Carlos considered it. Bern seemed to as well, though he did not lower his rifle. Crazy John processed the conversation in his own way. He had gone silent as the showdown reached its climax but now he giggled to himself, alternating his private mirth with quiet singing. *"Bad man soon he dies...bad man soon he dies...he brought a rope but him I'll choke and gouge out both his eyes..."*

Bern made up his mind. He swung the AK back over his shoulder.

"Okay," he said. "You're right. At this point the device is the only hope we have to get those guys to back off. And we're running out of time. So let's get down to the Rock and find this damned thing. Lead the way." He added, "I'll bring up the rear, if you don't mind."

Everyone breathed a sigh of relief. Reed tilted his head in a slight bow as though Bern had done him a great favor – which he had. The Prog leader motioned for everyone to follow and turned upstream. Then he hesitated.

Classic, Carlos thought. The idiot has no idea which way to go. He got up with a sigh and hopped over the stream to head toward the trees.

"I'll take point," he offered.

Reed, followed by a sullen Elke, swung in behind Carlos. Crazy John climbed out of the stream and splashed along, accompanied by a limping Nancy Peal. With Bern at the back watching Elke and Reed as much as he scanned the forest for threats, they picked their way through the aspen and along the banks of the winding gulch behind. Tired as they were, it was with renewed purpose that they worked their way downhill. The device and all it promised gave them hope – if not for redemption, at least for an end to the savage purgatory in which they had been living for so long.

30

In combat as in policy, there are few clear choices.

Day contemplated that as he and Roland debated whether to go back and retrieve the rifles he had stashed above the meadow. The argument for more firepower – and what remained of his medical kit – was obvious. On the other hand, he felt the press of time with each passing hour. From what Shell had told them, the buried canister would activate somewhere around dawn on Monday morning, possibly earlier. At most that was 70 hours away. It would take them much of the morning to get to the guns and return, more if they ran into trouble. Then they still had to trek to the watering hole. He was not sure they had the time to spare.

But in the end the decision came down to simple math: they had more hours than bullets. Roland's three arrows and Day's four rifle rounds could be enough if everything went perfectly, but nothing ever went perfectly. And they had no idea how well armed the remaining Progs were. The M4s had full 20-round magazines; they had to go for the guns.

With the decision made, they turned west again and backtracked into the narrow plain between the river and the foothills, heading for Day's former perch above the meadow.

It took them ninety minutes to get there. When they arrived, a surprise and a mystery awaited.

The M4s and ammo were still there, hidden where Day had left them. Wulff's rifle was gone. The canvas roll that contained the med kit had also disappeared but some of its contents were strewn in the passage between the soapstone ledges.

They found Tylenol capsules and other painkillers scattered in the dirt. A syringe was crushed on the rocks, while the needles on two others were bent as though someone had tried to stab the soapstone. A dirty gauze bandage trailed out onto the hillside where more bandages had blown and then been soaked with rain.

"You fought how many natives?" Roland asked as he prowled the lane.

"Two."

Roland frowned and climbed up on the rocks. He was still frowning when he came back down.

"Who else knew you were up here? Just Wulff?"

"Just Wulff." Day studied the passage, remembering how close he came to being pinned to the rock by a spear. "But he could have told the others."

"Does he wear Keens?"

"No. A Carhartt boot with a thick heel."

Roland crawled around some more. His eyes narrowed. "Well, someone was up here after your fight," he concluded. "A couple of somebodies. Maybe more. Native and gringo. What I can't tell is who got here first. I'm going to guess the native because the Progs would not have thrown the med kit to the four winds." He found a package of sutures in a crevice of the soapstone and tossed it to Day.

"No, but they would have taken the rifle," Day said, dropping the sutures into his pocket. His spirits sank as he realized that not only was he killing the natives, he was now arming them as well.

"Probably. I suppose we can consider that good news. The locals aren't likely to know how to use it. Can't say that about the Progs."

Day bent down and collected any pills he could find. There were pieces of the plastic pill bottles but nothing usable. He studied the one shoe print that was clear in the dirt.

"A guy?" he asked.

"I'd say so." Roland pointed to the distinctive lug pattern and its distance from the next nearest print. "Judging from the size and spacing of the prints. Wide toe box, thick tread, the mid-sole is coming apart."

"Someone from the meadow?"

"Maybe, but if so he didn't come from there directly. There are more prints up there, along the ridge. They depart the same way. Could be your boy Rohanson."

Day shook his head. "No, Rohanson wore boots, too."

"Maybe he has another pair of shoes. Or it's another maverick. Someone who doesn't mind going off on his own."

"More likely the second. The Progs were retreating uphill when I last saw them. They might have decided to avoid the plain once the fight was over. Regardless, whoever it is didn't come up here by accident."

"No. This guy was looking for you. He stopped here, and again over here, before coming to these rocks. Listening, checking things out."

"Wulff might have told them I was up here covering them. Or they saw me shoot. Either way, that rifle's gone. Damn. I just gave a gun to a caveman. God knows where that will lead."

"Maybe he'll scare himself with it and drop it in a hole somewhere," Roland offered.

"Not with my luck." Day sighed. Well, we'll have to make do with these. At least this detour wasn't a total waste of time."

He gave one of the M4s to Roland and kept the other. The Weatherby's strap had been shredded by the bison but the carbine had one that was intact, so he shouldered that weapon and pointed the way downhill with the other.

"You want to follow this guy?" Roland asked.

"No. Let's stick with the plan. Surprise will be our best advantage if we can get to the watering hole before the Progs. Which I still want to do."

Roland grunted his agreement and turned back the way they had come. "Then let's go. Try to keep up, shorty."

Back down on the plain they went east again, preceded around the outside of the oxbow by the loping, sniffing, great beast of a mutt. They saw no signs that the Progs had moved that way after leaving the meadow, lending support to Day's hunch that Reed was now taking a more arduous route to the watering hole. He hoped so. He and Roland needed all the time they could get to reach the wash and set up an ambush.

A steady but unassuming stream ran into the Snake River at the bow. It flowed from the south and then east, coming down from the continental divide up near Togwotee Pass. Day guessed this was the Buffalo Fork or a precursor to it. If they followed it, it should lead them to the grasslands below the watering hole. He said as much to Roland.

"That might be the way to go," the Indian suggested. "It's not a straight shot but it'll keep us away from the foothills. That way, we won't run into the Progs until we're ready. And we can come up to the wash through the forest."

"That's what I'm thinking." Day said. "It'll keep us out of sight until the last possible moment. If they look for the device where they last saw it, we can be there waiting."

So they set off, not following the Fork exactly but cutting the corner inside its arc and working their way to where they deduced it would be in a few miles.

Ahead of them the landscape rolled, a mix of meadow and forest. The great dog ran ahead to explore on his own but otherwise Roland led the way. Nothing invigorated him more than a long walk under open skies. Any lingering effects of his injuries seemed to drop away as he strode across the virgin land.

They saw deer, elk, and a herd of llama along their route. None of the animals got in their way and the men did not pause to observe them, not even the llamas. In other circumstances Day would have stopped and marveled at it all but by now he had accepted that the ancient world was a circus and carnival attractions waited round every bend. Though he watched for anything that would eat him, he doubted anything could still surprise him.

He was wrong. After two hours they encountered the Buffalo Fork again when it turned across their path. The land sloped to the water's banks, presenting a ribbon of lazy blue as it wound through several curves. Fallen trees showed signs of flooding but today the stream drifted inside its channel. By the farthest curve the brush gave way to pebbled stone and grass, indicating an access point. The Settlers directed themselves there.

But then the great dog went to ground.

"Wait!" Day hissed.

The dog hunkered and then backed up. Day kept an eye open for the telltale sign of the beast either bounding forward or turning aside for a flanking attack but it did neither. It seemed confused.

Roland nodded to movement by the river. At the forest's edge a dark shape stirred.

The dog rose and looked...and then sat down, cocking its head to one side.

A long arm swung out and a body followed. Another arm moved out and down, touching the ground. There were too many shadows for Day to see colors or flesh. His first thought was that it was another mammoth because the movement of the brush suggested a wide body. But then the shape rose up as if on hind feet, growing half again as tall as Roland. A branch snapped and leaves rustled. A whole tree shook. Still the men saw nothing definitive. Only when the animal finished browsing did it move out of the treeline and into the light. And when it did, Day found himself as mystified as the dog.

"What the hell?"

The creature was almost as large as an elephant, nine feet long and surely tipping the scales over two thousand pounds. It had a blunt snout, massive jaw, and comically-long knuckle-dragging arms. The fur was thick, shaggier even than the mammoth's, with brown and gray mixed in. Day's jaw dropped.

"Megalonyx," Roland murmured in awe. He did not move. They were thirty yards from the animal and it was not clear whether the creature had seen them.

"It looks like Bigfoot."

The creature stopped. Whether it heard Day's comment or smelled the men or the dog, it paused for a moment leaning on all fours. Then it reared up on its hind feet and looked in their direction. The long arms hung to its knees, flashing scythe-like claws. An oval face and dark-rimmed eyes gave the animal an impatient, even imperious, glance as it looked down its nose to where they crouched in the grass. Day revised his opinion: Bigfoot was a pipsqueak compared to this.

The men held their breath. The dog, remarkably, just stared at this weird apparition.

The creature held its stance long enough to decide that whatever was out there was of no concern. Then it flopped forward again, landing on the fist-like forelimbs with the claws curving back and out of the way. It moved with flowing, unhurried steps across a sun-drenched clearing to browse at the next group of trees.

"Giant ground sloth," Roland whispered. "Shouldn't be a problem. The books say it's an herbivore."

"The mammoth was an herbivore, too," Day reminded him.

"Good point."

"Aggressive?"

"Shouldn't be. Sloths are usually slow."

"They're usually small and cuddly, too."

"True. We'll give this one his space."

So they moved downstream of their planned crossing point. The sloth paid no more attention to them but they went far enough to get out of its sight, anyway. The great dog was the most reluctant to leave.

It was because of this move that when they finally crossed the Fork they ran into another delay, one that was more dangerous than the sloth and potentially disastrous.

The stream was no problem: the waist-deep water hardly pushed against them as they waded across. It rippled over a sandy bottom with a soft hum that masked nothing from the world around. But when they reached the far side and stepped beyond the brush hugging the shore, another unexpected apparition appeared.

A hundred twinkles of light erupted at them like sparks thrown off a flint. They emerged from all over the meadow that stretched from the Fork to the next stretch of forest. It was as though the men had triggered an alarm.

Day and Roland hit the deck, thinking they were under fire.

But no gunshots accompanied the flashes. There was no noise at all beyond the normal sounds of the plain: the trickle of the stream, the chirrup of insects, and the nasal trill of a red-winged blackbird as it rode the stem of a cattail behind them on the shore. Only when the bird took a break did they perceive a metallic rustle rising somewhere in the midday air.

The dog had disappeared so they did not have him to interpret the scene. The Settlers exchanged looks of confusion and then moved apart to avoid presenting a common target. Day retreated to the treeline while Roland vanished into the high grass.

The sparks faded away. Seconds later they erupted again as a breeze swept over the meadow.

The third time it happened, awareness dawned. Day saw one of the flashes ignite and then retreat, and in its wake he spied a strip of metal flutter where someone had tucked it into the stalks of wheatgrass and alpine timothy. His eyes widened in surprise.

By this time Roland had worked his way forward to the closest strip of foil. He stood up. Day went out to join him.

Neither man said anything as Roland lifted the shard of aluminum from the grass and rubbed it between his fingers. They surveyed the other pieces scattered across the meadow, placed to catch and reflect the sun in haphazard outbursts of yellow, orange, and white.

They moved through the field looking for anything to explain the display. There was nothing until they passed the last shard, a long piece that was tied to a clump of grass. The clump abutted a hillock that blocked sight of the back of the meadow. In two steps the men were on the hillock, and from there Roland, being taller, spotted a dwelling. Immediately he ducked.

An Indian camp sat tucked into the corner of the meadow close up against the trees. It was a large camp – Roland did not bother to count but there were at least a dozen structures and numerous fire pits. People moved by the huts. Roland backed down the hillock and gestured for Day to retreat. But it was too late.

A shout went up, not from the camp but off to their left, in the direction they wanted to go. A dozen natives of various ages appeared there, a foraging party returning to camp. They saw the Settlers and cried out.

More shouts rose. People at the huts jumped up. Suddenly natives ran everywhere. Men wielding spears and bows poured out of the camp.

The Settlers ran for the Buffalo Fork. The high grass slowed them and the shortest route to the water was quickly cut off by three warriors from the foraging party who raced along the edge of the meadow. Roland veered left. As he did one of the Indians launched his spear. It flew behind Roland and in front of Day, close enough that Day got a good look at the javelin as it soared past. He pointed his rifle at the thrower but did not fire and did not stop running. Other warriors raced through the meadow behind them to close off escape to the west. Their options for escape dwindled.

"No use," Roland barked when he saw they would have to kill someone to get away. He stopped and faced the closest natives. Raising his long bow over his head, he held his other hand across his body, palm down.

It was a sight to behold. Roland was tall to begin with and his bow stood just as high. His black hair dropped over his shoulders, bright against his dusty clothes. Even the bear amulet at his neck stood out. The natives pulled up short, momentarily awed. None lowered their weapons but neither did they attack. Day saw no one carrying a Henry rifle, which was both a relief and a disappointment.

The man who had thrown his spear retrieved it from the grass and took his place in the ring that enclosed the Settlers. He waved it as did the others but for now Roland's majesty kept him in check.

"*Kamaati ya-suu*," Roland announced to the crowd, looking at none of the natives in particular. "*Nana tawak awe.*"

Day kept silent, his pulse racing. He held his rifle low and pointed at the spear thrower. The guy was impulsive.

The natives did not respond to Roland's words, nor did he expect them to since they were in Comanche. But he saw curiosity on a face or two – faces marked with the now familiar half-moon – as though some of the natives at least wondered if they should take meaning from them. But what they would do once their curiosity wore off was a mystery.

Fortunately for the Settlers they did not have to find out. Just as the impulsive warrior was getting agitated again someone said something from the back of the crowd. The Indians turned. It was the girl from Holden King's camp.

"Tu-san-ik-ani," Roland greeted her when she moved to the front. He lowered his bow.

The girl looked at him and at Day but did not reply. Instead she turned and spoke to the man next to the impulsive warrior. Like all of the Indians he was short and wiry with taut brown skin. Like many of the men he had a shred of the space blanket woven into his hair, a strip that glittered and flashed as he turned one way or another. Unlike the others he had a broken nose that bent to the side in a manner impossible to ignore. It was difficult to guess the man's age. His deerskin kilt seemed to be standard wear but the elk hide over his shoulder was not, and Day wondered if it conveyed status.

The girl spoke and her audience listened. No one lowered any weapons but as her story went on Day thought he detected a relaxation of tension in the crowd.

When the girl finished, the Indian in the elk hide turned and said something to the Settlers. They did not reply so he settled for the *friend* gesture. Roland and Day dutifully repeated the motion.

That was where things stood when another party of natives appeared on the scene. A half dozen men arrived in the meadow from the east. Two carried a deer slung on a pole, one carried a brace of ducks. Seeing the gathering by the Buffalo Fork they hurried over. Among them Day spied familiar faces: Bill, Ted, and Rufus. He hoped that was a positive development.

It was, though it took a while. Whatever one might say about the Moons they were not rash in their decision-making, the one warrior being a notable exception. Either that or it just took a long time to say anything in the Moon language. The trio who had assisted Roland in the mountains joined the crowd and shared their experience with the others. None approached the Settlers or offered a hand or made any friendly gesture beyond the standard palm-down movement. As the discussion went on, though, the spears came down, and that went a long way to calming Day's nerves.

After they had been standing by the Fork for half an hour, the Moons came to a resolution over what to do with the intruders. Ted and the other Indian with an elk hide vest motioned for Roland to follow them. Day, though not ignored, was clearly regarded as a hanger-on. In a gaggle the whole crowd moved over to the camp.

The huts there were conical structures reminiscent of teepees. Formed with aspen and birch poles and thatched with grass, they had solid doorways, smoke holes in the roof, and a low profile. Even Day had to duck to get inside the one they were invited to enter. Once inside, they were greeted with a sight that suggested they might not be killed by the Indians, after all. At least not today.

Half-lying, half-sitting on a reed mat and smoking a twist of some awful-smelling grass was the Moon native they had treated in the mountain clearing days earlier. His space blanket was gone, shredded and spread across the meadow. In its place was a beaver skin that covered him from the waist down. His chest was bare, revealing scars from the lion attack and others that pre-dated it. His right arm and shoulder appeared to retain the stitching and bandages from the Settlers' treatment but it was hard to tell for certain because everything had since been encased in an additional coating of clay, charcoal, and flaxseed. The side of his head, too, was suffused in a poultice, this one of the ever-present wild onion and ginger. But the man looked up with clear eyes as they entered. After a quick explanation by Ted he offered both Roland and Day a drag from his smoke.

The gathering passed the next several hours in arduous cross-cultural communication. It was not just the language that gave them trouble, though that was inscrutable enough. Day had been a classics major before he taught Shakespeare and was conversational in both Latin and Greek. Thus trained in multiple almost unemployable skills, he nevertheless had some insight into linguistics. Language has structures, not just words, and he understood that if one could grasp the structure that was part of the battle toward comprehension. The problem here was that he had no sense at all of the Moon language structure.

And that was not all. Beyond words and structure, there is culture behind communication. A glance alone can speak volumes, so too can tone or humor or nuance or slang. The meaning of a grunt now might mean different things depending on something said five minutes before. But grunts and nuance and everything else meant nothing to Day regarding the Moons because he knew nothing about them to begin with. The setting was ripe for misunderstandings. The only good thing was that everyone seemed to realize it, Settlers and Moons both. So the arduous efforts continued.

More than arduous. Messy and slow, Day thought. *Sprinkle cool patience upon the heat and flame of thy distemper*, Shakespeare counseled him as his frustration grew, but he also recalled Lawrence of Arabia's observation on counterinsurgencies: *like eating soup with a knife.* That's what this whole conversation is like, he thought as they grunted, glanced, spoke, and sighed along with the Moons. Like eating soup with a knife.

That said, Day did little of the eating. He sat quiet for the most part, allowing Roland – who was the star attraction, anyway – to do his best to convey friendship, peace, and a shared enemy in both the Progs and the Arrows. Roland was happy to take the lead in this, for though a warrior at heart he was an anthropologist by vocation. Pressed for time as they were, he was nevertheless elated to have this opportunity with a clear head to connect with an ancient culture.

In contrast, Day felt the passage of each minute as though a gong was sounding beside him. *How poor are they that have not patience?* the Bard insisted. *What wound did ever heal but by degrees?* True enough, but their wound – their need to get to the wash by the watering hole – did not have time to heal by degrees. They needed to get there before the Progs.

The hut was filled to capacity with fourteen individuals crammed inside. All sat since the only place to stand upright was in the center where a fire pit lay. No one made a move to light a blaze in the pit, for which Day was grateful. The press of native bodies and the smoke from the cigarettes was enough already to make breathing a challenge.

He heard the girl's name mentioned, as well as his own. *Awa-skan-aka*. Wolf Man. The name seemed to convey to him a bit of celebrity status, though whenever the natives spoke it and looked at him he had the impression they were awed more by the great dog than Day himself. Other conversation devolved into drawing in the dirt, where Roland took a stick from the fire and scratched a crude map.

"What's the symbol for the Arrows?" he asked Day. "You said the logger guy told you he saw something?"

"A basic arrow but with two heads," Day replied. "One on top of the other."

When Roland drew that in the dirt it caused a hubbub among the locals. Roland took pains to calm the uproar, indicating again through an elaborate game of charades that the other tribe was a common foe. He found a way to convey that Day had killed two Arrows in hand-to-hand combat, which generated an appreciative response from the assembled warriors and seemed to improve *Awa-skan-aka*'s status.

Yet after hours in the hut it was not clear to Day how much they had accomplished. The natives had not killed them and that was good, for staying alive was his first priority. But even that did not appear to be settled. More arrows were drawn in the dirt. Many arrows in different locations. There seemed to be a debate going on between the natives, with Ted and the man they had saved arguing one way and the elk hide wearer from the meadow arguing another. The assembled Indians voiced support for one or the other with grunts and sighs and the occasional remark, not unlike the British Parliament. And just as in the British Parliament sometimes it was hard to tell what was being resolved. Day did not know for sure that their lives were under discussion but either way he and Roland were literally in the middle of the dispute. And anyway, his second priority was to get on their way.

"Roland," he said under his breath as Ted lighted more smokes and a native by the door added his opinion to the conversation, "we need to get moving."

Roland lowered his head to show he had heard.

"I don't think it's going to happen tonight," he replied.

"Why not?"

Roland paused as two natives behind the fire directed sharp words at each other. The elk hide wearer, who Day decided to call Bent Nose, said something through the smoke that encouraged the two to back down.

"In the immortal words of Keanu Reeves," Roland continued softly, "I believe our adventure through time has taken a most serious turn."

"How so?"

"I believe..." Roland drew out the verb to indicate his uncertainty, "they understand our situation. More or less. But they don't care. It's not their problem."

"Then what was Bent Nose going on about for the last twenty minutes?"

"What he said and what I got out of it could be wildly different," Roland admitted. "But the gist of it seems to be that they have their own issues. One is the Arrows, one is us. To sum it up, life was bad enough before we – the Progs *and* us – showed up, and it's worse now. More competition for game, more killing, the girl's kidnapping...Tu-san-ik-ani's his daughter, by the way..."

"Naturally. Trust Holden King to aim high."

"So some of these guys think they should just kill us all. All the Arrows, all the gringos. Kill us all and get it over with."

Roland said this in a murmur, showing no emotion. Day listened, equally stoic. For the most part the natives ignored them as they carried on their own discussion. One exception was the man on the mat, who watched the Settlers with a steady gaze as though hoping by sheer intensity to understand them. Another was Bent Nose, who – though his eyes studied the smoke – appeared to listen carefully to the Settlers, perhaps trying to divine through their tones what he could not comprehend through their speech.

"It's a simple solution," Day conceded. "Not elegant, but simple."

Roland grunted. "I've tried to make clear that once we – you and I –get the others, we will return to our own hunting grounds. Never to be seen again. Ted supports us on that, I think. But that leaves open the question of the Arrows. If I understood something that Rufus said, the Arrows are on the move."

"Where?"

"I don't know."

"How many?"

"I don't know that, either. To be honest, I'm only seventy percent sure that anything I've just told you is accurate."

Day practiced his inner sigh and struggled to keep his frustration in check.

"How about getting out of here?"

Roland waited while Ted said something to the group. There was much murmuring in response. A few of the natives crawled out of the hut but others took their place. Bent Nose spoke again and more smokes went around the circle. Day puffed on one and wanted to gag.

"I don't think so," Roland whispered. "They're going into another round of talking. I think they're debating their options."

"Have we started a war?"

"I doubt it. There was war before any of us got here. If anything, the Progs may have delayed its resolution."

Just then Bent Nose stood. He was short enough that he could do so near the fire pit. Looking at his audience through the haze that filled the hut, he spoke in a confident, level voice that more than any aspect of his appearance hinted at advanced age. He held his arms across his stomach the whole time, except for the occasional gesture with one hand as though he were ticking off items on a list. His voice droned on. Day had a sense the man was telling a story.

When at long last the speech ended, Bent Nose sat and stared at the fire pit. There was a long silence until Ted, hunched over his cigarette, grunted and nodded. Then everyone else made various sounds of agreement and the meeting was over. The men and women in the hut – there were women, though they had not spoken – one by one made their way to the exit.

Day did not move. He sat with one leg bent under him and both rifles in his lap. The natives had never tried to disarm the Settlers so Roland, too, still carried all his weapons except for the giant bow, which he had been obliged to leave outside due to its size. Day wondered if now they would need to fight their way out of the camp but when he looked to Roland for guidance his companion merely stretched his long legs and patted his stomach.

"Now we eat," he said.

31

Eric Wulff left the thermal seep when the howling stopped. Going north along the gully he worked his way up and around the last stretch of foothills, looking for level ground that would take him east toward the hot springs and the pass.

He struggled through a canyon choked with fallen rock and emerged onto terrain that was both flatter and greener than anything he had seen since leaving the meadow. The ground remained uneven but mixed stands of deciduous trees and swathes of switch grass were making inroads across its surface, civilizing the topography and facilitating passage. Wulff's gaze traced the land as it spilled down to the south. His eyes picked out a rock formation that looked familiar. For the first time in days he thought he might know where he was.

From the canyon he watched for signs of danger. Seeing none, he moved into the open and across to the first stand of trees.

There he practically walked into Puff.

In fact he almost backed into the Arrow warrior. Reaching the trees, a score or more young oaks and maples with exposed roots and layers of fallen leaves, Wulff went through them to the far side where he paused again to watch for movement. He had just stood up with the intention of glancing over his backtrail when he sensed someone watching him. He turned...and was startled to the point of a heart attack to see Puff standing only ten feet away, staring intently at the AK-47 Wulff held in his hands.

"Whoa!"

The exclamation burst from him unintended. Whether the native had been there all along or had crept up on him, he had no idea. But what startled him even more was what Puff carried. In his right hand was the ever-present club with its triangular piece of flint buried in the head. In his left was Wulff's Henry rifle.

"Where the hell did you..."

Before Wulff could finish the question, Puff dropped the Henry and leaped at him. With a martial cry he took two strides and vaulted himself upward, throwing his arm high and then swinging it down at the logger's skull. Wulff barely got the AK up in time to parry the blow. There was a *thock!* as the club met the gun barrel, sending a shock through Wulff's arms.

Puff was fast and swung again, this time from the side. Wulff was slower to react and the club caught him on his left arm below the elbow. He felt and heard a crack as the bone there broke.

"Son of a bitch!"

In a rush of adrenalin he looped his right arm around Puff's waist and hip-threw the Indian against a tree.

"What are you doing?" he yelled. "Get away!"

The fall must have hurt but the Arrow was on his feet again too fast for Wulff to press his attack. Puff rushed him again. The logger blocked two blows and shoved Puff away but then he stumbled on a tree root. Off balance, he did not get the rifle in front of him as Puff rebounded and brought the club across, aiming again for Wulff's head. Wulff's only defense was to raise his broken arm so again he received a crushing blow that sent a wave of nausea through his body. *Damn it*, he thought. *This caveman is going to beat me to death.*

He managed to avoid the next strike by ducking under the branch of a maple tree, and even got in a decent blow against Puff's ear with the butt of the AK. But the Arrow had more tricks up his sleeve. Recoiling from the strike, with his left hand the Indian scooped a handful of leaves and threw it in the air. He scooped another, swung around the trunk opposite the first toss, and threw that in Wulff's face. In the moment it took for the logger to turn away, Puff hit him with a backhand blow. This one caught Wulff's good hand against the rifle, breaking a finger and knocking the weapon free. As the AK dropped to the ground, Puff reached to grab it.

Wulff responded with a shout of pain and two savage kicks that caught Puff in the shoulder and the chest and threw him back against a nearby oak. The AK slipped from the Indian's grasp.

Wulff kicked a third time but this time Puff spun clear: the boot clipped the trunk instead and sent bark flying. The Indian countered by swinging his club backhand again, this time hitting Wulff on the knee. A second blow landed on his back. The back blow hurt the most, striking the kidney. The logger went down unable to breathe, his right side numb.

He rolled over and held up his good arm for protection. He was about to die. He knew it. He could not get up and even if he tried Puff would be on him before he could do anything. Sure enough, the Arrow Indian appeared directly above him, the club raised high.

Wulff glimpsed Puff's face through his bloody outstretched fingers: feral, indifferent, mouth open, teeth bared. In that instant before death when time seemed to stand still, the logger reflected on the horrible absurdity of it all: this primitive warrior from an ancient world was about to bash in his skull, and his poor daughter would never even know where her father had died.

But just then there was a crack like a branch breaking. Puff's head jerked and he fell against the oak. He let go of the club, which dropped to the ground next to Wulff's broken arm. Wulff scrabbled for the weapon but there was no need. The Indian leaned on the oak for a moment, staring straight ahead. Then his body rolled around the trunk and crumpled. He fell into the leaves and did not move. Through the thick, matted hair above his right ear, blood trickled into view.

The soft crunch of footsteps came from uphill. Ray Williams appeared between the trees, holding a small semi-automatic in the Weaver-ready stance as he stepped with care over the ground. He kept the gun trained on Puff until he was close enough to kick the body and be confident the Indian was dead. Then he dropped the pistol into a pocket and knelt to help Wulff.

"Ray...where..?"

"I've been looking for you," the gang member explained. "Went back to the meadow but you'd gotten away. You're a tough guy to find. And kill."

"Apparently not," Wulff mumbled. He could not close his right hand. Two knuckles there looked broken and were swelling. His left arm hurt so bad he fought back tears. "That bastard broke my arm."

"Let me see."

Williams examined him and there was no doubt the arm was broken. The bone was not sticking through the skin but both men could feel the fracture.

"Goddammit..."

"Where's your bandanna?"

"Lost it."

"Hold still."

Williams pulled a rag from his pocket and tore it into strips. The Progs had learned not to throw anything away and for months had carried old socks, t-shirts, and underwear to use for bandages when they became too worn for their original purpose. Using bark from the oak, a couple of straight sticks, and Puff's club, within minutes he immobilized Wulff's arm. Then he took the AK strap and used it and the remaining strips of rag to jerry-rig a sling that he looped over the logger's shoulder. The getup did nothing for the pain but the first aid alone gave Wulff a chance to steady himself.

"Damn, that's neat work. Were you an Eagle scout?"

"I was, actually."

Wulff stared at him. "I was kidding," he said. "Are there many Boy Scouts in L.A. street gangs?"

"Don't know. I didn't ask. Can you stand?"

"Not yet. Give me a minute."

Williams helped him to sit up and Wulff scooted to put his back against a tree. He examined his right hand, which by now was twice its normal size and hurt like hell.

"That son of a bitch," he muttered. He was now helpless. It would be difficult or even impossible to shoot a gun even if he had one.

Williams wore a checkered wool coat that had belonged to Sly Marchetti before that unfortunate salesman froze to death. It had a faux fur liner that was soiled and gray but still soft. He produced a pocketknife and cut a strip out of the liner from the armpit down to the hemline, which he then wrapped tight around Wulff's hand. Again, it did nothing for the pain but it would protect the knuckles from being damaged more.

"I think I'm going to keep you," Wulff joked even as he fought to ignore the agony in his arms. "I never knew you were so handy."

"You're going to keep me alright," Williams agreed. "Or rather, I'm going to keep you now that I've found you." He moved over and checked Puff again to reassure himself the Indian was dead. Then he picked up Wulff's AK-47.

"No bullets?"

"No."

"Where's your other rifle? The lever-action? I saw Puff had it."

Wulff looked around but did not see the Henry. "Uhh, somewhere."

Williams got up and prowled through the trees. He returned with another empty AK-47 and the Henry. He threw the AK aside and checked the magazine on the Henry before laying it at Wulff's side.

"Mine's empty. Yours has three rounds. Three? Is that all you have?"

"The others went to good use," Wulff said, not apologizing. He caressed the Henry like an old dog.

"You didn't use them on the Settler, did you?" Williams asked with concern.

"Hell, no. I gave him the gun."

"You gave him the gun? When? Why?"

"Before the meadow. So you guys wouldn't get it. I don't know, a few days ago?"

"Then how did Puff get it?" Williams demanded.

"Damned if I know," Wulff shook his head. "I told you, I left it with the Settler. I didn't see it until just now when..." He stopped, realizing the logic of what he was saying. "Aw, crap."

"Where's the Settler?" Williams asked, reading his thoughts.

"I don't know. I haven't seen him since the meadow."

"Well, he's not there. I looked. Are you supposed to meet him somewhere? Is he looking for you?"

Wulff shook his head again. "The plan was for you guys to give up at the meadow. We didn't count on the Moons showing up. There was no plan after that. Is anybody left besides you?"

Williams swore and did not reply. He stood with his hands on his hips looking around as though the grove of hardwoods would suggest something. When the trees stayed quiet, he started to say something but then noticed the distress on Wulff's face. He snapped his fingers.

"Don't move," he said. "I'll be right back."

He returned in a few minutes with water, collected in a plastic intravenous fluid bag that said "Sodium Chloride" on the side. It leaked at its base but the hole was small enough that the bag was still almost full when he offered it to Wulff, who struggled but was able to hold the container with three fingers long enough to swallow half of it in one go.

"And here," Williams said, digging in his pockets and coming up with a handful of red and white capsules. "Take a couple of these."

Wulff looked at the pills and his jaw dropped.

"Tylenol?" he gasped. "Where did you get those?"

"Tell you later. Just take them. You're getting white as a ghost. Don't go into shock on me because you've already tapped out my first aid skills."

Wulff swallowed the pills and washed them down with the rest of the water. Part of him wanted to puke and there was a warm feeling of nausea building in his throat, but just taking the pills reassured him.

"I'll stay with you," he promised.

Williams sat down against a tree opposite the logger and fixed him in a steady gaze. The wool coat hung open and Wulff saw a tattoo in stylized gothic script creeping up the man's neck.

"You're not a Prog, are you, Wulff?" Williams said. "You never have been."

The question was unexpected but the logger was straightforward in his answer. "I never claimed to be," he replied.

"So what are you doing here?"

Wulff shrugged. "Paying for my sins?"

It was an attempt at humor but when Williams did not laugh, Wulff added, "I don't know. I was broke and dumb and did a favor for the wrong people. Next thing I know I'm dodging bullets in a garage in Wyoming."

"Wrong place, wrong time?"

"Pretty much."

Williams kept staring at him. He had intent eyes in a round, brown face. Where it was not covered in beard his skin was pockmarked from youthful bouts of acne; there were even dimples on his nose. The heavy build that had given him a resemblance to the rapper Ice T had diminished over the months as he went through the enforced paleo diet. Still, the man was solid. He had an intimidating gaze to go with the build, though as he stared at the woodsman Wulff realized for the first time that the guy was not in fact pissed off. He was just keenly focused. Maybe, he thought, you have to be if you are going to survive in a gang.

Right now Williams appeared to be debating something internally. If so, his next statement showed he had reached a decision.

"I know what that's like," he announced. "Being in the wrong place at the wrong time. Here's a shocker for you, Wulff. I'm not a Prog, either. I'm not even a Crip. I'm a DEA special agent undercover inside the gang's Long Beach set."

Wulff was taken aback but did not react. He might have displayed surprise if he did not hurt so much but the Tylenol was taking a while to kick in. For the moment the pain in his arms occupied all his attention. Williams seemed to expect some response, though, so after a moment Wulff said, "You're a long way from Long Beach."

"I've been telling myself that every damned day for six months," Williams assured him.

"How did a DEA agent end up here?"

Williams looked around. They were as alone as they could get but he still hesitated about telling a story he had not told anyone ever.

"The short version...I was undercover in Long Beach trying to track fentanyl smuggling through the port. The set there..." When Wulff looked quizzical, he explained, "Set, that's a local gang. The Crips are a franchise. They're broken up into local gangs called sets. Like a lodge for the Elks Club or a chapter of the Sierra Club."

"If the Sierra Club smuggled fentanyl," Wulff quipped.

"If they did, I would be hugging trees," Williams promised, and it was easy to believe him. "Anyway, I was there for the fentanyl, what the street calls dance fever. All I cared about was fentanyl and the port. But then my set got involved with some Progs because half of them were buying drugs the Crips were smuggling. Not just fever but heroin, coke, marijuana out of Mexico... My boss told me to work that angle, use the Crips to get friendly with the Prog network, find out who was who and how they were funded, all that crap. Then bam! The uprising kicks off and the next thing you know I'm on the run with that crackhead Tran and a few others."

"And Tran introduced you to Reed?"

"Not intentionally. Tran didn't know Reed. I think only Elke, JP, and a few others knew him before Wyoming. Tran, Reuben, and me were all just hiding in a safe house in Walnut Creek when Reed walks in unannounced. He was on the run, too, and we ended up crashing in the same place. But then once we're with him he wants us to stay. He needs an entourage, you know that. People around him telling him twenty-four hours a day how brilliant he is. You can't be a messiah if you don't have followers. So every time we moved we picked up more people until we got to you in Oregon. I didn't mind. I had stumbled on the biggest Most Wanted case since bin Laden and I couldn't just walk out. My problem was, we moved so much, so fast toward the end there that I had no time to get word to my boss."

"So you were stuck."

"Yeah. The networks were down, phones were out... I didn't know how things were going to play out so I couldn't leave. I was afraid if I did I wouldn't find them again. Reuben wouldn't flip – I didn't try but knew he wouldn't – and for all I knew I would need my Crip cover later. So I stuck with Reed and tried to alert the authorities as I could. I got a message out when we passed through Chico, and again one night in Utah. That's how the whole damned army surrounded us outside Moran."

Wulff thought back to that night. It was surreal. One minute they were feeling secure in this palatial home below the Tetons, the next there were helicopters, trucks, bright lights, and orders shouted through loudspeakers for everyone to surrender. He himself had been looking for a way to crawl outside when Reed came through telling everyone to get to the hangar and onto the weird stage.

"I tried to get away that night," he confessed. "Why didn't you? You could have let the cops in and just surrendered."

Ray snorted. "Easier said than done," he said. "It could easily have been a massacre. None of those guys outside knew me – I was just another Prog. Same with you. I'm not into massacres, especially when I would be on the receiving end. Besides, I wanted Reed alive. I've gotten over that, by the way, but back then I wanted him alive. And the only reason I got onto that damned platform was because I thought Ganesh was insane and there was no way the contraption would work. I figured if we all just went along it would give me time to come up with a plan, time for the guys outside to break in. If we had had just five minutes more..."

The two men were silent for a moment, thinking about what could have been.

"So what now?" Wulff asked.

Williams snapped out of his reverie. "Now we find your buddy the Settler," he declared.

"He might be dead," Wulff said, glancing over at Puff's body. "Otherwise how did Puff get my Henry?"

Williams nodded but then switched to shaking his head. "Yeah, could be. But no, I don't believe it. Even if he is, he's got a buddy, doesn't he? You said there were two of them."

"There were, though I haven't seen him since before the flood. Tall guy, long hair. Day said he was still alive but I don't know that for sure."

"Day? That's the Settler's name? First name or last name?"

"I don't know. It's just Day."

Williams thought for a minute. "I don't think he's dead," he decided. "I mean, yeah, he could be but I don't think so. I found where he was shooting from up on the hill. There was no body there. No body and no other rifle. It looked like there had been a fight. There were pills and bandages everywhere. That's where I got this stuff..." He shook out his pockets, revealing a trove of loose bandages, gauze, hemostatic dressings, and a tourniquet. "But he had his own gun, right? If he was dead, Puff would be carrying that one, too, wouldn't he?"

"I suppose," Wulff agreed. "Unless he gave it to another Indian."

"Maybe," Williams conceded. "But why would he do that? And where's the other Indian?"

Neither man had answers to those questions and they lapsed into silence. Changing the subject, Wulff asked, "How did you find me? Did you track me from the meadow?"

Williams returned to his intent stare. "Track you?" he deadpanned. "I'm DEA, not a Texas Ranger. I wasn't tracking you or Puff."

"Then how did you find us?"

"Luck. I ditched the others yesterday to find your boy Day. When he wasn't on that ridge I tried to guess where he would go from there. There was no reason to go downhill if we went up, so I figured he was somewhere between us and the plain."

"So you went cross-country like I did."

"I guess. Spent last night in a tree, if you can believe that. Not having any rounds in the AK made me feel pretty vulnerable."

"I know the feeling."

"Thought maybe it was paranoia until I heard those wolves this morning. You heard them, too? Well, that got my ass up and moving. I just humped it over the hills and lo and behold, two hours ago I caught a glimpse of Puff doing the same thing. I wouldn't have cared except he was carrying your rifle. That got my attention so I followed him."

Wulff traced his swollen fingers along the Henry's stock, reflecting on how close he had come to dying.

"I'm glad you did," was all he said.

"You're welcome. Now you can return the favor by helping me find the Settlers. I want out of here as bad as you do."

"But I don't know where he is."

"No, but it ain't like he's got a lot of options. We know what he wants: us."

"He wants Reed more than anyone," Wulff clarified.

"Okay, so he wants Reed. And we know Reed's going to the watering hole. Does Day know that?"

"Yeah."

"In that case, we can figure out what he's up to. Maybe even get an idea of his plan. Tell me what you know about him. Tell me everything."

32

Day was a light sleeper. He always had been. In addition to having an internal alarm clock that would wake him before dawn, he was sensitive enough to open his eyes when even the smallest noises or slightest movement happened nearby.

Or so he thought. When he awoke the morning after they encountered the Moon camp, light was touching the eastern sky. There was frost on the ground and on his coat. He turned his head and saw Roland standing at the edge of the meadow, a silhouette against the stars. Roland was looking off toward the Buffalo Fork where water burbled as it slid by in its course. The camp was quiet except for a boy who poked at a fire outside one of the huts.

He sat up, sore and cold. His neck was stiff and his left hip felt like he had been kicked. Sometime during the night he had rolled onto his side and onto a stone.

Orion's belt was bright in the southeast where the black horizon was melting into deep blue and purple, but Roland kept his attention to the north where the night still held sway. Day joined him as two figures emerged from that blackness. It was a pair of natives returning to camp. They went past the Settlers in silence, one to a hut and the other farther on into the trees.

"What's up?" Day whispered.

Roland did not turn.

"Strange things are afoot at the Circle K," he replied.

"And for those of us who don't speak Keanu Reeves?"

"They're gone."

"Who?"

"The men. Most of them. They're going after the Arrows. Or to another Moon village for reinforcements. I'm not sure."

Day looked around. It was too dark to see much but he did notice that the Indians who had been sleeping on the ground near him were gone. Even the boy by the fire had disappeared now, perhaps to find wood. The camp looked and sounded deserted. He had counted forty-one natives the day before, with sixteen of those grown men of fighting age. Two had just walked past so that meant fourteen had departed?

"A war party left and I slept through it?" he asked, furious with himself.

"Yup."

"Which way did they go?"

Roland nodded toward the Fork. "They crossed there. After that, no idea. Nobody was into conversation this morning. Or last night."

That was certainly the case. The Moons had apparently talked themselves out during the extended discussion inside the hut the day before, for afterwards they had gone almost silent. They remained friendly and generous, sharing the deer, some ducks, and fish for the evening repast, but any interest in the Settlers expended itself by nightfall. The only attention the men showed was to Roland's bow. They gathered around it in twos and threes, took turns holding it, and grunted among themselves as they examined the new technology. But even that interest petered out. In the end the men decided it was nothing they could use since the bow stood a foot taller than even the tallest native. They dropped it in the dirt and walked away.

"So we can leave?"

"I think they would prefer that."

"Nobody's going to stop us?"

"Doubt it," Roland said. "My impression is the sooner we leave their camp and their world, the better off we'll be. If we stick around and keep messing with their game and their women, we may find there are limits to their hospitality."

His voice was level but Day sensed disappointment. Time was not on their side and although Roland had learned much from his interaction with the locals so far, that window of opportunity was closing.

— ⚜ —

They carried on them everything they possessed. All it took to leave was to go. Day was ready but Roland had one more piece of soup to eat with his knife.

While Day stood in the grass watching Sirius drift toward the horizon, his companion sat down, crossed his legs, and began to sing in a soft voice barely audible above the gurgle of the Fork. There was no melody that Day could discern, just a gentle current of Comanche words that rose and fell in irregular waves. He had no idea what it all meant but it was soothing. His impatience dissipated as he listened.

Roland stopped abruptly after a few minutes. He stood up and collected his weapons.

"It shows gratitude," he muttered, inferring from Day's silence that his companion wanted an explanation. "They were our hosts, we were their guests."

"Very polite. Maybe they'll invite us back."

"Don't count on it."

With that the men moved out into the darkness, across the meadow toward the break in the trees where the hunting party had appeared the day before. The grass there flowed into a field on the other side and then into an extended stretch of prairie that rolled out into the night.

Behind them in the camp the boy returned with an armful of wood. If he noticed the men were gone he gave no sign. Only one person observed their departure, sitting in the opening to the closest hut where she had listened with interest to Roland's song. Tu-san-ik-ani watched their figures disappear into the morning gloom, and continued watching until the last sound of their movement faded away.

Finally moving again, the Settlers made good time. Day felt liberated – and in a hurry. The land cooperated by being soft underfoot and presenting no major obstacles. They stayed in the open as they walked, sticking to the swath of grassland that passed between forested hills on their right and smaller woods that spread north along the banks of the Buffalo Fork. The grass was miles wide in places and narrower where the trees pushed in, but it never stopped. Day guessed it linked the vastness of Jackson Hole – which had disappeared behind them – with the endless prairies on the other side of Togwotee Pass, and that enough grazing herds roamed this way to keep the corridor open.

They saw hundreds of such grazers as they covered the remaining miles to the watering hole. Large stretches of prairie had been mowed and ground up by bison, though only several dozen of those massive creatures were in sight today. And as had happened before, the few delays they encountered came from having to circumvent creatures they came across. Besides the bison there were elk, deer, antelope, horse, more llama, a family of stag-moose and two animals that looked like stag-moose except with different antlers, grouse everywhere, and a pack of coyotes. They spied a trio of elephants that were smaller than the woolly mammoth they had seen and not as aggressive. Roland spotted them at the edge of the forest while still at a distance so the men felt no need to increase their spacing. They also saw two black bears – for which the men did increase their spacing – but no grizzlies or anything larger.

It took time to work their away around some of the herds depending on how the animals reacted when seeing the men. The stag-moose, in particular, looked ready to run them over if they got too close. Another time the Settlers returned all the way to the Fork to circumvent a kill site at which a pack of gray wolves was feeding. The wolves had brought down a young bison. There were ten of them, ghostly shapes that flitted through the high grass as they ripped at the flesh and then pulled away to gulp it down. They paid no heed to the men but there was no point in taking chances by getting too close.

The men also slowed when they wandered into an enormous prairie dog town, one a mile long where burrows were everywhere and the chances of twisting an ankle or worse increased. They could not find a way around it so just plodded through, watching their steps. It was there that they ran across the great dog again. It sauntered into view with a prairie dog the size of a pig in its mouth, then disappeared again.

The day remained bright until just after the sun reached its zenith when scattered clouds appeared overhead. Thereafter the random breeze that had played across the land switched to gusts from the west. Day glanced over his shoulder and saw more clouds building again over the Tetons. Any weather they portended was hours away but the temperature began to drop nonetheless.

Roland saw the clouds, too. He knelt and scanned the land in every direction, then motioned for Day to join him.

"There's the glacier," he nodded, indicating a ridge on the northern horizon that was split by a streak of white. The land rose between them and the ridge, making it seem closer than it was. Still, it was not more than four miles away.

"You sure?"

"Yup. That's Mount Leidy behind us, and see those woods in front of the ridge? That's the forest by the watering hole. I stood there and looked this way the day we arrived."

"I hope the Progs don't do the same thing. It's pretty open between here and there."

"Unlikely. If they've even made it to the watering hole they'll be looking for the canister, not exploring."

"Alright, then let's get up there."

They turned north and in short order encountered the Buffalo Fork again. The stream had split into two channels so they had to cross it twice, once in the grassland where it meandered through the prairie like a wayward canal and again in its normal course. After the second crossing the men were faced with a mile of open ground before they reached the forest. They took spacing and moved out, with Day expecting at any moment to come under fire.

That did not happen. The world seemed deserted of all other human life. Moving steadily upslope, they approached the forest and took comfort from the cool air that wafted out to meet them.

"There are some trees knocked over up there," Roland pointed to his right. "I'll guess the mammoths pass that way to get to the grass on the other side. That's as far east as I went last week but I didn't see any sign of Progs."

"Wulff never mentioned coming down this way," Day confirmed. "It sounds like they went to the hot springs as soon as they arrived, and then to points north after that."

They were about to move into the trees when Roland, glancing back, touched Day's shoulder. Far in the distance the kill site they had passed was still in sight. Having gained elevation they could look down on it now and onto the gray wolves who were suddenly scattering in dismay. A new pack had moved in, dire wolves whose size and dark coats stood out against the wheatgrass and grama. The gray wolves protested, retreating and then loping in ever widening circles around the newcomers, who occasionally whirled and gave chase. Gusts of wind rippled and waved the grass around the site, creating hypnotic patterns through which the combatants pursued each other. But soon enough the gray wolves moved on, resigned to the law of size and strength.

"You might be right," Roland murmured. "We just can't get rid of those guys."

"You think it's the same pack?" Day asked.

"Yup."

Day no longer had his rifle scope so he shaded his eyes with his hand and just peered into the distance. It was hard to tell but one wolf seemed to be giving hell to the others as they claimed the carcass for their own.

He glanced down at the great dog who, having finished his lunch, lay stretched in the forest's shade, catching a nap.

"You had better be on your toes," he warned him. "I may not have enough bullets to take out that dude for you."

The beast heard Day's voice and opened one eye to look at him. Then he closed it again and went back to sleep.

The Settlers took spacing once more and entered the forest. They encountered no surprises. The woodland slumbered in an afternoon daze, lulled to tranquility by a gentle soundtrack of bird calls and rustling leaves.

Near the northern border the men dropped to their hands and knees and crawled to the treeline.

It had been eight days since their arrival but little had changed on the juniper plain. The wash and the moraine leading to the glacier looked the same as they had on the first day. The boulder that the Progs called Plymouth Rock squatted like a misplaced asteroid next to the wash, and not far from it leaned the old cottonwood tree. Most important, a limb from that tree still leaned against a bush where Day had left it.

The boulder pile and the watering hole were also in place but unlike on their first visit the area was now crowded with wildlife. An adult mammoth was in the middle of the hole, sunk beyond its belly, splashing water at a swarm of flies. A juvenile mammoth, possibly the same baby they had seen on the first day, was also in the water close to the muddy bank. Around the water's edge, drinking, jostling, or rolling in the mud, were more than a dozen camels, a larger group of antelope, and a collection of long-nosed peccaries.

Day studied the scene before backing up and moving to where Roland lay behind the cover of a rotting log.

"Rush hour at the hole."

"Yeah."

"Anything else?"

Roland gave a slight shake of the head. "Nothing I see," he said. "But if I were coming from the hills and wanted to get to where Kurtz hid the canister, I would get east of the moraine before coming into the open. Lots of broken ground and the juniper is higher."

"Maybe even go all the way to the hot springs by the pass," Day said. "From there it's the shortest distance to the watering hole."

"Right, but you wouldn't go to the hole. No reason to. The wash extends this way so that would be the best way to stay under cover. If you skip the hole, you can get all the way up here while staying out of sight."

"Which they would do if they suspected someone was up here in the trees. But they think we're behind them, or at least coming from the west."

"Maybe. We don't know what they're thinking. Either way, that wash is the best way to move."

Day rubbed his chin, considering their options. Roland was right but even without the wash, there was enough space on the plain to hide an infantry division.

"They're short of time, too," he pointed out, returning to basics. "And they'll assume we arrived the same place they did so when they come looking they'll search over there." He pointed around the trees to their left.

"If they got here first, they already know by now the canister isn't there," Roland commented. "They'll have to look elsewhere."

"I don't see anyone out there looking."

"No. They might have done a quick search and pulled back when they didn't find it. If that's the case, you can forget about setting a trap."

"But they might not be here yet."

"I think they are."

Roland retreated into the shadows where he could stand and stare out at the vast field between them and the glacier. To the east and north the juniper stood like a silent crowd, filling most of the space between the watering hole and the north hills. To the west, across the wash, the juniper gave way to sage and smaller brush of a paler green. To the north-northwest, the glacial stream and moraine provided a welcome clear space, like the wake of a great ship retreating up into the mountains.

"Why do you think they're here?" Day asked, his own eyes watching the plain. Roland shifted to stand next to a lodgepole pine.

"A hunch," the Indian said. "Remember the first day when you said you could sense there were Progs close by? I've got that feeling now. Something tells me we're not alone."

Day respected Roland too much to question his sixth sense. But the clock was ticking. If there were Progs out there, they needed to find them and do something about it.

"I had hoped to get here early enough to set a trap," he admitted. "Maybe you're right, maybe it's too late to do that. There's a chance that Reed beat us here."

He stopped as there was a brief commotion at the watering hole. The mammoth was climbing out of the water, scattering the smaller animals. The beast's giant feet plopped in and out of the mud with giant sucking sounds that sounded like gunshots.

"If they've been here and searched," he continued, thinking aloud, "we can't wait for them to show themselves again. We need to find them. Or at least know where they're not. They would have gone to the old arrival site so we'll see tracks there if they did. But before we look there, we need to sweep the high ground here."

"I was going to suggest that. If we go out onto that plain, I want to know no one is going to shoot me in the back from up here."

For the next hour the Settlers crept through the woods looking for signs of the Progs. They started by moving through the forest to their right, paralleling the treeline and the open stretch beyond it that led downslope to the watering hole. They crossed a trail evidently used by the mammoths: the track on the ground was narrow but from the waist up it was a swath of wreckage through the younger trees. Unlike mastodons who lived in woodland areas, mammoths saw trees as obstacles rather than a source of food and treated them accordingly. The Settlers crossed the trail and explored until they reached a point where they could view the back side of the boulder pile. Satisfied that the Progs had not ventured into the forest, Day signaled they could reverse course.

They retraced their steps in the other direction, crossing the mammoth trail again a few minutes before the party at the watering hole broke up. The wind now blew strong enough to rattle the herds, relying as they did on sound as much as sight to detect predators, so they were moving on. The Settlers did not see where most of the animals went but the pair of mammoths lumbered up the hill and entered the forest just after the men had exited the trail. The colossal adult and its growing behemoth of a baby swung onto their boreal path with purpose, as though they had someplace to be. Day was surprised how little noise the great creatures made, all things considered. As massive as the adult was, for example, with its great girth and sagging belly carried along on legs that were the diameter of trees themselves, it nevertheless placed its feet with precision and in such a way that minimized any din from its passing. With the baby close at its heels, the heavyweight of the ancient world passed behind the concealed Settlers with barely a sound, not looking left or right, moving with the lumbering confidence that prodigious size confers.

When the pair was gone, the men dared to move. Day led the way, continuing through the forest to its western edge. There they ran into the great dog again when it trotted across their path. Day urged the mutt to join them, anxious not to have it interfere with the mammoths. The dog, as usual, looked at Day as though he were mad, and continued on its way.

At their western edge the woods narrowed like the prow of a ship, with one side shaped and guided by the wash that ran past Plymouth Rock. The Settlers halted to observe the wash from under cover, then Day slid down into the streambed to inspect it up close. Since the M4 had twenty rounds in it, he swapped out its sling and slung the Weatherby over his shoulder. He held the carbine at the ready while Roland covered him from the trees.

This stretch of the wash was empty. The bottom was churned by the recent passage of some herd and cow pies littered the sand. Downstream he was able to see a good distance since the wash flowed along the edge of the forest and out to the prairie on the far side. Upstream – toward the glacier – he could see only a few score yards. Beyond that the bed curved toward the juniper field. He crossed to the far wall, climbed up into the brush, and then covered Roland as his companion followed.

From there it was a short distance to the jumble of rocks that bordered the original arrival site. Neither Day nor Roland had investigated the location before but they knew it from Kurtz' description. Sure enough, they found clear evidence of recent activity. Footprints were everywhere, and the weeds and grass growing at the base of the pile had been ripped up and dug away. The Progs had excavated several holes that remained unfilled. They had also pulled or pried away stones from the pile in the desperate hope that the device lay hidden inside.

"Well, that decides it," Day said, only loud enough to hear above the restless wind.

Roland bent over and studied the ground.

"Yup," he murmured. "Two people. Men. And not more than eight or nine hours ago. Since the last frost, anyway. We haven't missed them by much."

The tracks spread away from the rocks in rough concentric circles as the Progs had expanded their search. At some point, though, the circles stopped, and the prints converged again in one trail heading back to the north. The Settlers followed. In a short while they found themselves once more overlooking the wash.

"So they look, don't find anything, then run away," Day summarized, interpreting the trail. "Why? Did something scare them off?"

"Maybe," Roland said. "They were definitely running. No sign of anything chasing them, though."

Day scanned the wash from the western wall. There was nothing to see but sand, rock, and tufts of needlegrass that sprouted from cracks in the dirt. The sand was deep and heavily trampled by whatever herd had passed through – bison or musk ox, judging from the dung. The herd had foraged the grass, too, cropping it short everywhere like relentless landscapers. In the process they exposed more crannies in the wash walls. From one such fissure a different shape caught Day's eye. A bone. Near it was a strip of cloth. He realized they had been there before.

He lifted his gaze to see the dried-out cottonwood tree leaning over the wash from the far side. Close by was the bus-sized boulder, Plymouth Rock. Roland had guided him into the wash here the first day to see the skeleton he had stumbled on after their arrival. Which meant they were almost directly across from...

His stomach tightened. From this angle he could not see the cottonwood limb that marked their arrival location. He knew it was there – they had seen it from the forest only an hour before. He had leaned it against one of several juniper bushes that crowded the boulder on its east side. Regardless of which one it was, they were close. So was it just a coincidence that the Prog tracks led where they did? Maybe the Progs were not running *from* something, but to something.

He turned and whispered his thoughts to Roland. Roland's expression remained stolid but his impassivity only encouraged Day's fears.

They conferred and agreed on a plan. They had to check on the device, even if they left it where it was.

Roland put aside his bow and quiver. With the M4 as his primary weapon and Day covering him, he dropped over the wall of the wash and crossed to the far side. In seconds he was up the other wall and out of sight behind the boulder.

He was gone several minutes. Day waited, growing anxious. He watched up and down the wash and peered over the tops of the scrub but there was too much that he could not see. The wash bent twice to his left, preventing him from clearing it more than a hundred feet. He re-positioned to see past the first curve but to go any farther would make him lose coverage downstream. Normally that would not bother him because he could listen for anyone approaching but the wind removed that option. It swirled over the plain like a fidgety child, gusting loudly one moment and pulling back the next, and seeming to come from three directions at once. The storm clouds over the Tetons were expanding. Something in their makeup produced downdrafts that now roiled the foothills and lowlands beyond. Day did not care about the meteorology. He just wished they would stop so he could hear anything beyond ten feet away.

When Roland reappeared on the opposite bank Day breathed a sigh of relief. But the Indian bore bad tidings. With his hands he shaped an imaginary cylinder and pointed behind him...and then shook his head. A few additional efforts at pantomime signaled that the Progs had discovered and dug up the device. The squeeze on Day's stomach quadrupled.

Roland had been right all along. They could forget about laying any trap. The Progs had gotten there first.

33

Eric Wulff sat down to slide over a ledge a quarter-mile west of the glacier's toe. The geology of the foothills had forced them ever lower as he and Ray Williams hiked toward the juniper plain; now that descent brought them across someone else's trail. The ledge ran above a timbered slope where the surface was easily dislodged. Someone – several someones – had climbed down the ledge, scraping lichen off the rock and hopping onto the grass below.

"It's them," he said, pointing to one mark in particular. "That's Reed's boot."

"How long ago?" Williams asked.

"Twenty-four hours, at most."

Williams looked downslope, trying to see between the trees.

"Alright. We had better be heads up. I don't want them to know we're here until after we find the Settler."

"You think they would shoot at us?" Wulff asked.

"They'll shoot at you," the agent said matter-of-factly. "Maybe me, too. I don't know."

"They might think you're bringing me in."

"They might." Williams held the Henry rifle in a patrol-carry position across his chest. He and Wulff had decided it made sense for him to keep the weapon for now since Wulff would be unable to fire it effectively. As compensation, the agent gave Wulff his M&P Shield pistol. That, too, would be a challenge for Wulff to employ but it was better than nothing.

"It's only got one round," Williams had told him. "And it's a .380. So don't waste it on a grizzly. In fact, don't waste it on anything larger than a gopher. If you get attacked by a bear, just let him eat you and I'll collect the gun later."

They worked their way through the timber and emerged at the top corner of the glacier's terminal moraine, the broad field of unsorted debris that marked the farthest reach of the ice. On their left, the retreating wall of the glacier rose ten stories high and exuded a blast of cold air that they could feel while still in the hills. Where sunlight struck the ice water dripped, making the wall gleam as though polished. The water collected in a kettle pond close to where the men knelt, a depression formed from ice that had calved off the glacier and dropped into the sediment below. The pond stretched away in a long oval that eventually overflowed and fed a thin stream that ran south through the glacial till. The moraine was empty of life except for a scattering of dippers along the stream's edge, and a large, lone wolf in the distance who seemed to be stalking something in the frigid water.

Wulff crouched and studied the land, unsure what to make of it. Far off he could see the watering hole with its accompanying pile of boulders; beyond that lay the south forest. There were animals at the watering hole but nothing in between.

"Well, we made it," he said. "Now what?"

Ray Williams sat beside him. He, too, surveyed the landscape with a doubtful eye.

"It's too damned big," he growled.

"Agreed. But we don't have to search the whole thing. There are only a few places anyone will go."

"Where will your bounty hunter go?"

"Wrong question," Wulff countered. "He'll go where Reed goes, so the better question is, where will Reed go? If Reed wants the device, he'll go to where we arrived, won't he?"

Williams stared at the plain, thinking. "No, I don't think so. That's not Reed's way. He doesn't do anything himself, not if there's risk involved. If Day is alive, he might have gotten here first and laid a trap. He knows Reed wants the device and the arrival site is the first place Reed will look. So he'll ambush any Progs there. But Reed will guess that, too, so he won't go near the place. He'll send someone else."

"Carlos?"

"Yeah, or Bern. Or both. He can't trust Crazy John not to get distracted, and Nancy's falling apart day by day."

"What about Elke?" Wulff asked, but then answered his own question at the same time Williams did: "She won't leave Reed's side."

The men lapsed into silence, mulling over the situation. The wind picked up, spinning a dust devil that whirled among the rocks before heading west. The wind whistled across the ice wall, too, making it hard to hear as well as pushing the temperature down. Wulff could not see the Tetons from their position but he guessed a storm was building there. From what they had experienced, it seemed to be a typical pattern for this time of year. There would be snow by nightfall, maybe mixed with a thunderstorm. The weather in this place was strange. Summer or not, in the Progs' experience it never really got warm.

"I might know where Reed is," he declared.

"Where?"

"The hot springs."

"The old camp? Why?"

"Two reasons," Wulff said. "One, there are tracks that head that way." He nodded toward footprints in the sand that skirted the top of the kettle pond. "And two, it's warm at the springs. There's water and maybe shelter, too, if our huts are still standing. Look, it's getting cold. Like you said, Reed won't go in the open if he thinks it's dangerous. Even if he does, he won't stay there. None of them will. Not with snow on the way. They'll all go back to the hot springs for the night whether they find the device or not. It's either that or they freeze in the open."

Williams did not argue but he did not look enthusiastic, either. He remembered the hot springs with ambivalence. Yes, the springs were warm but they were also right next to the pass, and the Progs had had many unpleasant wildlife encounters there as a result.

"So we can head across the plain looking for the Settlers, or follow our buddies to the springs."

"That's the way I see it. I vote for the springs."

"Why?"

Wulff tried to wiggle the fingers on his right hand in the hopes that a little blood flow might get the throbbing to go down. "Because I'm more confident that we'll find someone there than I am that we'll find Day out there," he said, nodding to the south. "Even if Day is out there, the only way we'll make sure he sees us is to walk in the open. And if we walk in the open, we'll also get seen by our buddies, as you call them. To tell the truth, either one of them might shoot us so I would rather stay out of sight until we can pick for ourselves when to come out."

Williams agreed with the logic. From what Wulff had told him, the Settlers were trying to capture the Progs, not kill them, but the fact remained there were now three armed groups wandering in the wilderness trying to bump into each other. At least three, not counting the Arrows and the Moons. That created a lot of potential for accidents to happen. Williams did not like accidents. He was a planner, and since he could not control anyone else he tried to control his own actions whenever he could.

Control meant staying under cover, not wandering to the watering hole or the south forest. He looked across the moraine to where the hills picked up on the far side. It was a half mile to cross in front of the glacier face, a half-mile in which they would be more or less exposed. Then another half-mile to where the hot springs bubbled out of the ground. That second stretch, the fringe along the bottom of the hills, offered plenty of cover. There was the ever-present juniper but also dense stands of lodgepole pine, both of which popped up quickly in the wake of glacier drift. Williams considered the thick vegetation both a blessing and a curse. The Progs had traveled through it plenty of times so they knew it well, but so did predators.

"Let's do this," he suggested. He sounded pissed-off again – which told Wulff just how worried he was. "Let's go for the springs but stay out of that mess at the bottom of the hill. We'll get above it. Get above it, stay above it, and find a way to see down into the camp. If Reed's there, great. Like you said, Day has to come to him eventually. If we're lucky we can keep a visual on the plain at the same time and maybe help him when he does. Either way, when those Settlers show up, we'll know."

"Sounds good."

Wulff cast his own nervous glance out in front of them and got ready to move. He had taken another dose of Tylenol so the pain in his arms was less but both still throbbed with an ache that was impossible to ignore. The broken fingers bothered him the most. Whenever he tried to use the hand it felt like Puff's club was crashing into his knuckles all over again. Both injuries weighed on his mind. He was a walking cripple in a land that thrived by killing off the weak.

"Ready?" he asked through gritted teeth.

"Ready."

They set off, picking out the path of least resistance that lay as close to the ice as Wulff dared. The Progs' trail was easy enough to follow but it strayed too far into the moraine for the logger's comfort.

Stepping with care, the two men moved out onto the rock-strewn ground and passed like ghosts across the glacier's face.

"How the hell did they find it?" Day whispered when Roland returned from across the wash.

"Don't know but they did. There was digging all around the clearing and they got it. Left a message for us scratched into that flat rock, too. Nothing repeatable."

"I'll bet they did."

Day was floored by this development. Not just floored, scared. Reed now had their only means of getting home. He could not use it – yet – and might not understand how to, anyway, but he could destroy it. To do so would be insane but Day doubted that a man who would destroy society itself to gain power would have any compunction about remaining in an *un*civilized world to do the same.

"Crap."

"Yup."

"Crap, crap, crap!"

"That's not very Shakespeare like."

"Shakespeare has too many commentaries on fools to choose from, and they all apply to me right now."

Day felt stupid and ashamed. But feeling stupid was not going to fix the problem. He urged himself to concentrate, to relax so he could focus on the problem.

"Okay. There's a way to deal with this. There has to be." He thought for a while and then looked at his companion. "I've got an idea but I've screwed up so much already why don't you give me your thoughts first?"

Roland lay in the dirt and peered across the wash, picturing the clearing from which he had just come.

"There were more than two sets of tracks," he remembered. "Four, maybe five. They came in from different directions but they all left the same way." His eyes shifted to the north. "That way, toward the pass. I'm thinking they split up to search different spots. Somebody stumbled on our clearing and found the canister. When they did, the others came running. Then they left together."

"So they're all in front of us now."

"Should be, unless they circled back. No reason to do that, though. They have what they want."

"They had a camp by the pass," Day remembered. "At the hot springs. Nancy Peal and Wulff both said so."

"Uh-huh. Maybe they tried to do something with the canister here but when it didn't work, they just took it with them."

"Knowing we would follow?"

"We don't have a choice, do we? As you keep saying, the clock is ticking."

Day grimaced. "No, we don't have a choice."

"So what's your idea, white man?"

Day listened to the wind blow over their heads, bending the sage and making the juniper quiver. Sprinkles of rain fell while the Settlers conversed but the winds were the bigger nuisance. Wind carried sound but it also masked and distorted it. It made everyone jumpy, hunters and hunted alike. And unfortunately for Day, these winds were not leaving the area anytime soon. As long as those clouds towered over the Tetons the winds would play havoc in the open areas.

The old cottonwood would have agreed with Day. Its gnarly branches waved in the gusts and looked ready to part from the tree at any moment.

"They know we're coming for them. Hell, they're giving us no option. I'm going to guess this is Reed's way of making us negotiate. How he expects to meet up with us, I don't know, but if they're watching for us it makes sense they'll expect us to come from the west. Right?"

"You said that before. Maybe."

"Let me put it this way: we could come at them from any direction but the last one they should expect is the east, isn't that true? Why would we?" When Roland nodded, Day continued, "So we either go back to the woods and hike to the far side before turning north, or we follow this wash as far as we can go and then cut over into the north forest. From there we approach the hot springs from behind. And we need to do it all now, before they get too many bright ideas and the weather gets worse."

Roland turned it over in his head.

"The wash will be faster," was all he said.

"Then let's go."

They slid forward and scanned over the wall. Trying to hear anything above the wind was difficult but the streambed was clear to the eye. Roland dropped down, followed by Day.

At the bottom of the wall they paused. It was less windy but the gusts were still above them.

Roland took the lead, crossing to the inside of the first curve where the bits of skeleton lay. He glanced around the corner, gave a flick of his hand to indicate it was clear, and moved on. Day stayed twenty feet back, clearing their six o'clock.

The wash turned again in thirty yards. The Settlers were halfway there when a gust caught the longest limb on the old cottonwood and tore it free. There was a *crack* that made them spin around, followed by a crash as the branch dropped into the juniper and cartwheeled into the wash.

His heart in his throat but relieved to see the commotion was only a branch, Day turned forward again just as Bern Jones and Carlos Bardem appeared around the turn. They were hurrying, their AKs held low, and they were as startled to see the Settlers as Day was to see them. But they recovered fast.

"Down!" Day yelled, and fired as he said it.

Both Progs fired at the same time as Day, Carlos from the shoulder and Bern from the hip. Roland was hit and went down. Carlos went down, too.

Day squeezed the M4's trigger twice but it jammed after the first shot. The chamber was clean but the spring in the magazine, subject to the elements for months, did not push the next round up. Day threw the weapon aside and swung his Weatherby on line as Bern fired again.

Bern had his AK on burst, firing three rounds, and damned if that rifle's magazine had no malfunctions. Day felt a round rip through his coat as he leaped to get out of the way. He aimed the Weatherby and fired but the stock collapsed as he did and the bullet went wide. Bern retreated around the corner at a run, leaving Carlos behind.

Day rushed to Roland. His friend had pushed himself up but was bleeding heavily from a wound above his left hip.

"I've got it," Roland snapped when Day tried to help him. "Go!"

Day jumped up and ran down the wash. Carlos was crawling away but he sat up and raised his rifle when he saw Day coming. Day slammed the butt of the Weatherby against his gut and fired from only twenty feet. Carlos' gun went off but he shot high, whereas the Weatherby's round caught him square in the chest. Day did not even pause to examine the body. He sprinted past and stopped only where the wash twisted again, this time to the left.

Dropping prone, he leaned out to look downstream and instantly pulled his head back. The quick glance showed him Bern crouched and pointing his AK back toward the corner. Sure enough, Bern fired the instant he saw Day. The rounds exploded the wall, spattering Day with dirt. He moved farther back. Bern fired again, then once more. The last time it was a single shot. Day wondered if Bern was out of bullets or simply realized he was wasting rounds and switched to single-fire.

There is a time in any gunfight to stand fast or move, and Day decided this was a time to move. He did not want to get stuck in a standoff where he could see clearly in only two directions. He grabbed his hat and did a couple of cheap fakes with it around the corner, trying to get Bern to fire again, but nothing happened. He listened but could hear nothing reliable above the wind. He climbed up the wall and peered over, trying to no avail to see between the juniper into the streambed beyond. Finally, in desperation, he ran forward and threw himself past the corner, landing flat in the middle of the wash with his rifle pointed to Bern's last position.

The wash was empty. Bern had pulled back.

A quick study showed a half dozen spent cartridges and a hurried retreat by the Prog. Day retreated as well, backing up until he was around the bend. He picked up Carlos' AK and ran to help Roland.

But when he got to where he had last seen his companion, Roland was gone. There was blood in the sand but the lanky Comanche and his weapons had disappeared.

"Roland!" Day called in a hoarse whisper. "Roland!"

There was no response.

He crept downstream, searching. There were no tracks and there was no sign that anyone had climbed either wall. How the hell could he just vanish with a wound like that, Day wanted to know?

A rustle in the sage buoyed his hopes but it was the great dog that appeared, not his fellow Settler. The beast carried a fish tail at the corner of his mouth which he shook off and dropped into the wash as though bragging about a catch.

Day was so furious he could barely speak. The damned dog should have been reconnoitering in front of them, not out on a fishing trip.

"Roland!" he snarled. "Find him!"

He stepped forward as though to swing at the dog and the animal took off, disappearing back into the sage. His quick retreat gave Day a modicum of grim satisfaction: like Desdemona in Othello, the mutt understood the fury in the words if not the words themselves.

Day tossed the AK, M4, and his own Weatherby into the scrub behind the giant boulder and climbed up after them. Just off the clearing where they had hidden the canister he did a quick inventory of the weapons.

He had two rounds left in his own rifle. Carlos' AK had three. The M4 had the most, nine, but using it would involve a fight with the magazine after every shot. He decided to take it with him, anyway. He slid the AK under a juniper to get it out of sight, keeping the bullets and slipping them into his pocket. Then he ensured a round was set in the M4, swapped slings again, and shouldered it, keeping the Weatherby as his primary weapon.

It was late afternoon and would be getting dark soon. He needed to find Roland before it did. Their best hope was that Roland could hold out while Day went after the remaining Progs on his own. If not...well, at this point it did not matter much. The only option for either of them to survive was to get back the device as soon as possible, before Reed and the others could make things even worse.

He crouched below the boulder, out of the wind but listening to it whistle around the rock. More raindrops pelted the sand. The clouds had moved closer and he could see the sky darkening to the west of the glacier, but as yet there was no thunder or lightning. Maybe they would get lucky and it would pass them by, he thought.

On that thread of optimism he stood up, thinking to backtrack along the wash wall to find Roland's trail. He stepped around the boulder...and looked right into the barrel of an old Ruger P89.

"Drop everything," the man holding the pistol said. "Do it, or I'll blow your head off."

34

The storm clouds swept in a forty-mile arc from the Tetons to the Absaroka Range, a dark mass that rolled outward along its entire front. The western sky's fading light could not compete with this wall of shadow, so night came early as Josh Gromer led Day at gunpoint across the juniper plain.

Day's spirits should have been crushed but they were not. He was distraught, to be sure. One plan after another had fallen apart as soon as he put them into action. More than half a dozen Progs were still on the loose, Roland was injured and possibly dying, and he had as little as twelve hours to recover the device before their only chance to escape the Pleistocene availed itself. And now here he was a prisoner. Things could not get much worse.

Yet he felt something akin to relief as they trudged through the high brush. All alternative courses of action had been stripped away; paradoxically, that meant there was no longer the stress of choosing between them. Planning was over. He would have to respond to the current situation somehow and fast, and whatever happened would happen.

Day was no fatalist – he was not giving up. Far from it. Nor was he whistling past the graveyard. But his options for getting out of this fix were dwindling. He pinned a faint hope on being able to divide the Progs somehow so they would turn on their master. He pinned another on his damned dog, though that wish might be more dubious than ever since the beast could very well abandon him now out of spite. What he was counting on more than anything – assuming the other Progs did not kill him off the bat – was that they did not know what to do with the device, and he did.

And it was clear Gromer was leading him to the other Progs. Otherwise he would have killed Day the moment he saw him. Instead of shooting him, the gambler had stripped Day of his two rifles and then forced him to head northeast on a track parallel to the wash. They had spent the time since moving across the plain, east of the glacier and the forest that lay beside it. They were now coming abeam the pass.

At this point the wash turned in front of them so they approached it again. Day saw more tracks in the earth, game trails started by small animals and taken advantage of by larger ones and then eventually humans. Here Day saw it was jackrabbits who had forged the way, since their trails went in every direction, splitting off from one main path the way capillaries diffuse from an artery. Gromer made Day intercept the most-traveled track and head for the wash.

Gromer said little after Day's capture and nothing about where they were going, though that was obvious enough. Across the wash the ground rose into a clear space between two forests: the large one on the right where they had captured Crazy John, and a smaller band of trees on the left that stretched back to the glacier's moraine. The clear space sloped up to the pass. In the twilight Day saw steam billowing in great clouds west of the pass, above the neighboring hot springs. When they had crossed the wash, Gromer broke his silence and ordered Day to head that way.

How in the world had Gromer survived, Day wondered? The gambler astonished Day by showing up at the rock. It was incredible that he had avoided the bison stampede. From the looks of him – and the smell – his continued existence owed something to whatever cavity in the berm he had used as a latrine. His clothes were soiled, almost black, and encrusted so deeply with dirt and muck that they had the stiffness of cardboard and the odor of an outhouse. He had a gash on his forehead and another on his face, his left arm moved with difficulty, and he leaned to the left, too, as though he had taken a punch. More queerly, there was a remote look in Gromer's eyes – a thousand-yard stare – that Day did not remember from before. But the man was alive.

And how had he hooked up with the Progs so fast? By all rights he should be dead, or at least behind the Settlers, not lying in wait for them on the plain. Again Day cursed the delay he and Roland experienced at the Moon camp. They had gained nothing from the visit; in contrast they had lost a vital twenty-four hours, a full day that ceded the advantage to the Progs.

"How did you escape the stampede?" he said over his shoulder.

Day spoke in a loud voice, in part to be heard above the wind, in part to make noise on the off-chance that Roland might be out there somewhere.

"Shut up," came the reply.

"I'm just asking. I'm impressed. You're a survivor, Gromer. You've got skills. You don't deserve to be here."

His comments were met with silence so Day tried again.

"How's your stomach doing?"

The attempt to build rapport earned him a sharp poke from the Weatherby's barrel at the base of his skull, which hurt like hell.

"Talk again, bounty hunter," Gromer snarled, "and I'll shoot you in the leg. Then I'll drag your ass to Reed so he can finish the job."

So much for rapport. Day kept quiet after that.

Eric Wulff and Ray Williams were past the glacier and climbing the hill on the far side when they heard the shooting in the wash. The reports were muffled, like explosions underground, but there was no mistaking the sound.

"That's an AK," Wulff whispered after the second group of shots.

"But that other one wasn't," Williams replied, and the words seemed to energize him. They strained their ears for more but heard nothing.

They were above the forest that Williams had wanted to avoid. Their goal was to get to a narrow ledge of sedimentary rock that bisected the hill. From there they planned to travel the rest of the way to the pass. They made it onto the ledge, a thrust fault from which rocks eroded and rolled down into the trees, but just as they began to move across the hill they had to drop below it again and lie still. A black bear and her cub emerged out of nowhere directly in their path.

Williams stifled an oath. This was precisely what he had feared. There were too many damned animals near the pass and the woods around it. He and Wulff were above the forest but there were still trees on the slope and for whatever reason a couple of bears were exploring among them. He peeked over the ledge: mama was shoving on a fallen tree, then pawing below it. Whatever she found made her happy. Both bruins dug in and began to feed.

He looked at Wulff for suggestions but the logger shook his head. There was not much they could do besides hug the ground. If they moved in any direction they would be seen and that meant they would be attacked. The only factor working in their favor was that the wind swept down the slope rather than across it. If it stayed that way – and they did not move – the bears should not catch their scent.

Damn, Williams thought. Damn, damn, damn.

"Reed!"

The shout came from below the springs. The Progs around the campfire grabbed for their weapons. Bern, standing watch, pointed his rifle out into the dusk, searching for the source of the voice.

"Reed!"

The voice sounded familiar.

"Who is it?" Bern yelled back.

"It's Josh! Josh Gromer! I've got one of the Settlers and I'm bringing him up!"

Gromer, of course! Bern recognized the voice now and his heart leaped. King's group from the plains was alive and had showed up to help. He raised himself to tell Gromer to come in but Reed cut him off.

"Stay where you are!" the Prog leader shouted into the darkness. He took a position next to Bern and tried to see into the gloom. "Where is he?" he asked.

Bern pointed to the high grass, which was visible for about ten yards. Beyond that was an amorphous tableau of black and gray that leaned and shifted in the wind.

"It's me!" the voice called. "Come on, I've got one of the bounty hunters."

Bern believed the voice belonged to Josh but he absorbed Reed's caution. He turned to Crazy John and the others and pointed around the clearing. "Watch the sides!" he whispered. "Watch for anyone coming in from the sides."

"And keep quiet!" Reed commanded. "Don't give away your position."

Crazy John took his spear and hopped away into the bushes leading to the pass. Nancy Peal and Elke crouched on the other side of the fire facing the woods, Nancy with her AK and Elke with her ever-present pistol.

Reed's eyes danced across the dark landscape as he tried to see the speaker. He did not have a weapon in his hand but he cradled the white thermos like a baby in his left arm, as he had done since Nancy Peal had dug it up that afternoon.

"Where are the others?" he called to Gromer.

"Oh, Jesus Christ!" came Gromer's exasperated reply. "I'm not going to yell a goddamned conversation out here. We're coming up."

"Stop or we'll shoot!" Reed demanded but Gromer was having none of that.

"Fine, shoot! Just hit the first guy, not me."

For a minute nothing happened. Cloud covered the western half of the sky and only a few stars were visible elsewhere to give a backdrop to the slope below the camp. The juniper, branchy and unkempt, and the feathery bluestem and hairgrass that surrounded it all swayed in the wind like a crowd listening to music, making the slope seem alive. It did not help that most of the plants reached the height of an average man. Nor did it help that the same wind, swirling among the trees and bouncing off the hill that rose behind the camp, pushed steam from the hot springs in all directions to float as ghostly vapors until they dissipated. Altogether it was difficult to impossible to see or hear anyone approach.

"Shoot the first person you see," Reed hissed to Bern.

"Oh, shut up," Bern replied.

Then suddenly there was someone there in the darkness. A stocky man, medium height, wearing a heavy coat and with his arms raised, materialized out of the gloom. He walked closer, moving with reluctance. Moments later a second figure appeared: taller, favoring his right side, and carrying three rifles, all pointed at the first man. Bern leveled his AK at the pair.

"Okay, stop," he called when Day reached the outskirts of the camp.

Day stopped. Behind him Gromer stepped to the side.

"Jones, is that you? Bern?"

"Yeah, it's me, Josh. Who else is with you?"

"Nobody. Just me and the bounty hunter here."

"Where's Holden King?" Nancy Peal yelled from her position behind the fire. Reed cursed and told her to shut up.

"He's dead," Gromer called. "They're all dead. King, Trace, Minh...all thanks to this guy."

In the silence that followed, Day felt the anger directed his way from anonymous stares in the darkness. He glanced around, trying to see who was where. Steam rose behind the camp, wispy exhaust from pools at the base of the hill. It rose ten feet before the wind divided it and pushed the pieces sideways in all directions. Some of the vapors reflected orange light from the fire, illuminating the camp enough to give Day a decent fix on Nancy Peal and someone else near her. The two men who shouted were in that direction, too, but hidden.

"So there is no one else with you?" Reed inquired.

"No, just us."

"Okay, come on up," Bern told Gromer, pre-empting Reed who was going to give more complex instructions. "You," he pointed his AK at Day as the Settler came closer, "on your knees. Now!"

"Do you give the orders here?" Day asked. "You don't look smart enough to be in charge."

Bern stepped around the boulder he had been using for cover and moved toward Day, but before he could do anything Gromer hit the Settler from behind, swinging the Weatherby against the back of his legs and folding them under him.

Day stumbled, and when he did Gromer put his boot on the Settler's back and shoved him to the ground.

"Anybody got any rope?"

"No."

"Then keep your gun on him. Keep every gun you've got on him. I need a rest."

Gromer limped to the fire and sat down with his back against a log where he could still point the Weatherby at Day. The other rifles he dropped in the dirt. His face was drawn and his eyes distant. Between the loss of his friends and the near-trampling, the last few days had exacted a heavy emotional toll.

Reed pulled a pistol from his pocket and stepped over to look at Day where he lay on the ground. The Settler pulled himself into a sitting position and stared back. His whole body flushed warm. Some of that came from the ground itself, being so near the springs, but the rest was bottled anger. He knew this must be the Prog leader. The bringer of death, the destroyer of his family, the instigator of all the madness that had happened in the last two years.

He could not see Reed's features in the dark, only the thin shape of a man even shorter than himself, one who sported an incongruous skipper's cap atop an oversized mane of hair. Day was disappointed. Though he had seen pictures of the man from years before, in his mind he had conjured Reed to be massive, an oversized bully with a bullhorn voice who compelled people through strength and fear to do his murderous bidding. Yet the man before him was a veritable midget. His smallness was depressing. What did it say about his followers that they let a pipsqueak such as this lead them into chaos?

"What happened?" Reed said over his shoulder, keeping an eye on Day and the gun at his side. The pistol was profiled against the curling flames. Day saw it was a snub nose revolver, probably a Smith & Wesson from the shape.

Nancy Peal brought Gromer some pine nuts she had gathered on their trek through the foothills. All the Progs were famished and Gromer was no exception, but he took the food with no enthusiasm. Eating had lost its attraction.

"You guys had a fight," he summarized. "We heard it, took a look the next day, and found this guy. Hauled him back to our camp but then…" His voice trailed off.

"Then what?" Bern asked.

Gromer chewed the raw seeds. "Buffalo," he mumbled.

"What?"

"A stampede," Day said when Gromer refused to say anymore. "There was a storm in the valley and it set off a buffalo stampede. They came through camp."

"How is it you survived?" Reed wanted to know.

"I don't know," Day temporized. "Maybe the same way he did - luck. Everyone ran, some got run over and some didn't."

"So you're a lucky man?" Reed asked.

Day looked back and said nothing.

"Do I know you?"

"No."

"What's your name?"

"Day."

"Day what?"

"Just Day."

"Well, Mr. Day, I don't know you, either. So if I don't know you and you don't know me, why are you trying to kill me and my friends?"

"You don't have any friends. And I'm not trying to kill anyone else. Just you."

"Whoa-ho-ho!" Bern cackled. "He's got you pegged, Blake!"

Elke did not find it funny. She already had her pistol out and now she strode toward Day ready to use it. Reed stopped her. He stared down at the Settler.

"I would say I have more friends than you right now, Mr. Day. But you did bring a friend with you, didn't you? Where is he?"

"Yeah, where's your partner?" Bern echoed, kicking Day's legs.

"Dead."

"Yeah?" Bern looked across the fire to Gromer. "Did you see the body, Josh?" he asked. "The tall guy? In the wash?"

Gromer shook his head.

"I dropped him," Bern insisted. "I saw him go down. Right there in the wash. You didn't see him?"

"I didn't come through the wash," Gromer replied. "I spent last night out there..." he gestured vaguely to the sage plain, "and then came through the woods. I went to the arrival spot looking for the device but saw you guys had already been there. Was working my way over to the watering hole when I heard the shooting. Got there too late to help but found this guy hiding by the Rock."

"You did well, Josh," Reed said, still staring down at Day.

Day guessed the Prog leader was trying to intimidate him but it did not work. It was too dark for either man to see the other's face clearly so the stare-down was pointless. Day began to think Reed was stalling, unsure what to do.

"Damned right, he did," Bern agreed. "Thanks for the backup, Josh. I nailed the one guy and would have killed this one, too, but I ran out of ammo."

Hearing that, Gromer managed a smile. He set the Weatherby aside and held up his battered Ruger. "I captured him with this," he said, then before anyone could stop him he pointed it at Day and pulled the trigger.

The hammer clicked on an empty chamber.

"I was out of ammo, too," he bragged. "But I've got a good poker face, don't I, bounty hunter? I fooled you."

"You did," Day agreed. People had pointed guns at him before and it never felt good, but on this occasion he was little moved. He had Reed within his grasp. What frightened him now was failure, not death.

"I haven't had any bullets in that gun for over a month," Gromer admitted. "How are you guys fixed for ammo? Anybody have some 9mm?"

When nobody answered, Gromer threw the Ruger aside and put the Weatherby back across his lap. He lapsed into a sullen silence.

Reed tried to get back control of the conversation. He raised his pistol – not at Day but as a way of getting attention. But before he could speak he was sidetracked again, this time by a shriek that came out of the darkness. Crazy John leaped from the shadows and thrust his spear into Day's leg.

"Die!" he yelled in triumph, and pulled the spear free to lunge again. "Die! Die! Die!"

Day did not see the attack coming and pain shot through his leg like an electric current, but once the spear was clear he spun on his butt and kicked John's legs from under him. John was skin and bones and had no weight to him – he flipped sideways and crashed to the ground. Day followed up with a left hook to John's face that knocked him senseless. He would have done more but Bern recovered from his own surprise and jumped in to club Day over the head. Day fell back.

"John, goddammit!"

Like Bern, Reed recoiled at Crazy John's assault. Now he exploded at his own team. Rashness and undiscipline plagued the Progs and once again they had ruined his moment. With Nancy's help he dragged John away from Day and dumped him by the fire. Reed hurled the crude spear into the brush.

"Everyone back off!" he screamed. "We'll kill him when I say so, not before!"

It began to rain. Day lay in dazed agony, one hand clapped to his head and the other clutching his leg, as cold drops spattered the camp and hissed into the fire. John's spear had glanced off his femur and the sensation was nauseating. The hole in his thigh was jagged – he guessed the spear lacked a steel or stone head – and in the dark he felt blood run over his leg. No one bothered to help him but no one hindered him, either, so he pulled off his neckerchief and tried to staunch the bleeding. He prayed it was not coming from the artery. He would know soon enough if he passed out and died.

"You brought this on yourself, bounty hunter," Reed declared, watching him struggle.

Day gritted his teeth and pushed the neckerchief into the wound. It hurt like hell – everything from his hip to his knee felt like it was in flames. He used his belt to hold the cloth in place, not confident either would stay put if he tried to stand or move.

"No, Reed, you did," he said loudly through the pain. "You did this to me just like you did all this to everyone here. Everyone is here because of you. Everyone is hungry because of you, dirty because of you, and miserable because of you. Everyone who's dead is dead because of you. It's all about you."

"No!"

Reed thrust his gun forward and fired a single shot that just missed Day's arm. Whether he meant to hit Day or not was not clear. Everyone jumped in surprise except for Day, who froze.

"We are here," Reed shouted, "because of people like *you*! *You* are the cause of our problems, not us!"

Day held his tongue. He had heard that the Prog leader was all about control but for the moment he seemed to have lost it.

"Go ahead and kill him," Bern broke the silence. He sensed Reed's confusion and enjoyed it. "We don't need him. We have the device."

"Shut up," Elke said.

"You shut up," Bern retorted. "Your master here has been going on for days about how once we have the device we'll be fine. Well, we have it, so what now, Reed? Are you going to move the goalposts again?"

"But we don't know how to use it," Nancy Peal spoke up. "We don't know how to turn it on or what the procedures are."

"Ah, well, that's a bit of a problem, isn't it?" Bern said with derision. "Too bad someone didn't think of that in advance, huh?"

"I did think of it!" barked Reed, his voice as taut as a piano wire. "Which is why we don't kill the bounty hunter until he tells us what we'll face when we push this button."

"Not a damned thing," Day muttered. He had transferred his attention to the bruise on his head but as he had no more neckerchiefs he was left with applying pressure with his bare hand.

"What do you mean?" Elke demanded. She came from behind the fire to stand by Reed, still in a position to watch everyone. "Are you saying the device doesn't work, or that no one is waiting for us if we activate it?"

Day saw an opening.

"Both," he said. "Nobody cares about you. Sorry if that disappoints you, lady, but all anyone wants is Reed. Give him up and you'll walk."

"That can't be true!" Nancy Peal protested, but beside her Day saw Bern Jones cock his head in interest.

"That's not even a good try, bounty hunter," Reed interrupted. "You won't divide us."

"I don't care if it divides you or puts you in a group hug. The reality is we didn't come here for them. Just you. The rest can go back to smoking crack in Portland, for all anyone at home cares. Your neighbors might bump you off soon enough but that'll be on you."

"He's a liar," Elke snarled. "Kill him."

"Oh, now you want to kill him?" Bern laughed. "A minute ago, I said kill him and you all jumped on me. So do it, already. Cap the bastard and push that damned button!"

It was Day's turn to chuckle, a mirthless laugh due to the pounding in his head. "You can punch on that button all day and it won't take you anywhere," he said.

In the consternation that greeted this pronouncement, Gromer noticed for the first time what Reed was holding in the crook of his arm.

"Holy crap!" he exclaimed. "You have it! You did find the device. What are we wasting time for, let's get the hell out of here!"

Once again the camp devolved into bedlam as the Progs argued among themselves about the next step to take. The only one quiet was Crazy John, but the commotion awakened him and he began to stir. He stirred even more when the light rain that was pelting all of them turned into a downpour.

The Progs kept yelling at each other but retreated to two wooden shelters that stood at the back of the camp. They were not much more than lean-tos but someone had lashed branches to the front, leaving a small opening behind which the occupants could hide from the wind and rain. Bern kicked Day to get him to move closer to the shelters where they could keep him in sight. Day cried out, exaggerating the pain in his leg, but Bern dragged him anyway. That was what Day hoped would happen, for it left his hands free to sweep the dirt and feel for the Ruger Gromer had thrown away. His left hand touched the pistol just as Bern dumped him by the fire. Hooking a finger around it, he slid it under his left leg, groaning in discomfort.

"Shut up, you whiner," Bern snapped. "You want suffering, try spending six months out here! Try going to sleep every night thinking you're going to be eaten by the L.A. zoo. You know what, that's what we oughtta do. Forget wasting a bullet on you, we'll just leave your ass to get eaten by wolves. They'll smell your blood soon enough."

Bern crawled inside the nearest structure and sat at the entrance with his AK pointed out.

"Enjoy the shower, bounty hunter!" he called above the rain.

Day did at first. He wrapped his coat tight around him and turned up the collar, and let the rain bathe his head wound and wash away the blood. The cold drops assuaged the pain from the blow, which he was sure would leave a lump. After a while he pulled out his wool hat and carefully put it on. It was soaked in seconds but would still keep him warmer than no cover at all.

With his injured leg straight out in front of him and the fire smoldering behind, he sat in the thunderstorm while the Progs watched from the comparative comfort of their ramshackle accommodations. Crazy John and Nancy were in one hut, the rest crowded into the other. He heard talking from both but could not make out what anyone said. From time to time there were taunts from Bern and an epithet from Crazy John, but eventually all that died away.

Minutes turned into hours. The rain remained steady. Day found an opportunity to slip the Ruger into his leg pocket but decided to wait until later in the night to load it with the single 9mm round he carried.

Steam from the hot springs continued to drift through the camp, warming it above the surrounding air. For a while it lent an ethereal cast to the already otherworldly setting but soon the night grew so dark that it, too, disappeared into the blackness. The fire had long since drowned. Day could no longer see inside the huts to determine who was on guard or awake, but two rifle barrels remained visible and their owners shifted often enough that it gave him pause about trying to get away.

Not that he gave escape serious thought. The fire in his leg abated but that was only while he sat still. The wound still hurt like hell and all the muscles around it were stiff – his quads had seized and his hamstring was as rigid as a bone. Combined with the thudding pain in his head he was not sure he could get far even if the Progs fell fast asleep.

His best hope was to wait out the storm and the night. Stay alive, sleep if possible, and flex the leg from time to time to keep it from getting unusable. Before dawn he would have to try something but not right now. Let the storm blow, let the Progs sleep.

He hunched over his injured leg and closed his eyes. Above him lightning flashed inside a massive cloud. Thunder rolled out of the wreckage and shook the land, while the wind continued to swirl like the current of a swollen river. The rain fell in sheets, and the night grew blacker and colder as the hours ticked by.

35

Day was not the only one enduring the elements.

Wulff and Williams were both patient men but as the afternoon wore on they had begun to despair that the bears would ever leave.

Even more chilling was Wulff's fear that the bears *would* leave – and come down to the ledge where the men were hiding. To forestall that outcome, he suggested they back up and work their way downhill into the forest. That almost led to disaster. They had withdrawn only six feet when the mama bear raised her head and looked in their direction. The men froze again and changed their minds, giving up any thought of retreat.

The bears wandered off after a few hours. By then it was getting dark and the storm had moved closer. Clouds that had masked the peaks all day pushed downhill, bringing the sweet smell of snow and wet sage but also spits of rain. Once the bears were out of sight – uphill, thankfully – the men rose and hurried across the slope, lest the bears change their minds.

The ledge eventually tapered and disappeared. By then the slope had begun to level. No longer sliding uninterrupted into the forest and down to the juniper plain, the hillside suddenly turned horizontal and ended in a cliff-face, thirty feet of igneous rock that had resisted erosion when the glacier pulled back from the plains and into its current trough. Trees and bedrock atop the wall offered shelter from the elements so the men, chased by the wind and desiring a lookout point, headed that way.

"I smell smoke," Wulff whispered.

Williams did not but when they reached the cliff they both spotted the Prog campfire down and to their left. Its flames were partly masked by trees and by steam rising from the springs beyond, but the men recognized their old camp.

Wulff realized now where they were: this spot was where the depressed Bill Galston had tried to kill himself. The logger peered over the ledge and shook his head. The writer had picked a bad spot to attempt suicide. The cliff was steep but not quite vertical and there was enough brush along the face to interrupt one's fall. But then, Wulff remembered, Galston was never a bright man and by the time he jumped he was ready to try any way out.

"Did you hear something?" Williams asked.

"No."

"I thought I heard a yell."

They listened but a roll of thunder rumbled down the mountain just then and overrode other noise. As it faded it began to rain, the drops raising a din of their own from the terrain.

Wulff said, "I say we..."

A shot rang out, coming from the camp. The men crouched at the cliff's edge and tried to see between the trees.

"Pistol," Williams said when the view yielded them nothing. "Could be your guy."

"Or Reed or Elke," Wulff reminded him.

They waited but heard no more. The wind increased. Soon after the drizzle became a torrent. In the dark and the rain it was foolhardy to move so the men found a tree well that offered decent shelter and hunkered down.

Wulff was miserable. With the exception of some juniper berries he had not eaten in twenty-four hours. He was running on empty – and Tylenol. Even with the drugs his left arm throbbed while his right hand shot stabbing pains to his elbow whenever he moved it. He had threaded a thin stick between his fingers to try to lock them in place, or at least to remind him not to use that hand. It helped. But in the cold and the dark and the rain, that was poor comfort.

What kept him going was knowing that Ray Williams was just as bad off. Misery does indeed love company and if the DEA agent was not complaining, Wulff would not, either.

Another thought that sustained him was the feeling that they were nearing a climax to their ordeal. Wulff believed Day was still alive – he had to be, for otherwise any last hope of the logger getting home was gone. And if Day was out there somewhere, he was bound to be close on the heels of Reed. Reed was in that camp below, Wulff was sure. The tracks, the pistol shot – all signs pointed to that conclusion. So at first light if not earlier they needed to get down there to get a closer look at what was going on. Tomorrow would bring answers, he convinced himself. Tomorrow would be a big day.

With those encouraging thoughts in his head, he drifted off to a fitful sleep. Beside him Ray Williams dozed. The Henry lay across the agent's lap. His finger rested on the trigger guard while its barrel pointed out into the stygian night, a night where nothing moved but water and the only sound came from the sky overhead.

36

Bern Jones woke before dawn. He had not wanted to fall asleep but could not help himself. He had no energy. It had been days since he had had a decent meal...hell, it had been months...and he was running on a desperate mix of adrenaline and fear. He did not expect the Settler to escape, not with the wound he had in his leg; still he wanted to keep an eye on him. But by midnight he could not keep his eyes open. He shook Reed awake and told him to take watch. Then he closed his eyes.

He had a vivid dream while he slept. There was a storm and he was lost in a forest. Every way he turned there were more trees and more rain – he could not get out. Then suddenly there was a cabin and he knew if he made it to the cabin he would be safe. More than safe, he could eat. He stumbled toward the building, picturing the kitchen inside. It was loaded with food: food on the table, food in the oven, and food in the cupboards. And on the stove was a kettle of boiling water to make coffee. He burst in the door and it was all as he imagined. Even the kettle was whistling. But the whistle was not a normal whistle. It was a deeper tone, a horrible yowling that made him back right out of the cabin. No, he shouted. No, no, no...

He awoke with a start. The yowling was still in his ears but it came from outside. Somewhere in the distance the wolves were in full chorus. Bern knew what the noise was about – the pack had found Carlos. Maybe the Settler, too. Even as he listened they were ripping both men apart. The thought sickened and terrified him. He had a feeling of impending doom that it was just a matter of time before the same thing happened to him. Why? Why did he have to end up that way? Frustration and rage tore at his insides.

But then it occurred to him why he could hear the wolves at all. Because it was quiet.

Quiet*er*, anyway. The rain had stopped. The thunder had moved off to the east. Even the wind had died down. In place of the cacophonous storm, light winds pushed through the camp while snow fell silently from a black sky. It had already accumulated on the ground outside the camp, beyond the reach of the thermal vents that kept the surface below them a warm and muddy brown. Even with the fire extinguished Bern could make out the snow, since its white brilliance imparted an illusion of light.

And in that false illumination Bern saw that Day was gone.

"Dammit!"

He followed up with several choice epithets and felt around for Reed. The Prog leader leaned on the doorpost across from him, fast asleep. Bern kicked him and then pushed his way past to get out of the shed. He tripped and fell into the clearing but was up in a flash, pointing his AK in all directions as he searched for the Settler.

"What? What?" came confused calls from inside the huts.

"He's gone!" Bern said, his voice husky from the early hour. The deep silence of the plain kept him from shouting but in a hoarse whisper he barked orders for someone to start a fire. Crazy John leaped to the task. He was their premier survivalist, better than Wulff, and had an astonishing ability to get a blaze going even in the wettest surroundings. This particular morning tasked his abilities but still, within ten minutes he had flames crackling over the previous night's ashes. The fire threw a circle of light against the nearby trees and out onto the nearest grass, where wet snow bent the stalks in tired arcs.

"How did he get away?" Nancy Peal demanded. "Weren't you watching him?"

Bern fought the urge to club her over the head.

"I was," he growled. "I turned it over to Reed and he fell asleep."

"You did not!" Reed protested.

"Don't start with me, dude," Bern warned him, searching the perimeter of the camp for signs of travel. He found a muddy trail that led to the plain.

"Here! Over here! Bring a light!"

It took a few minutes for Crazy John to rig something they could carry, but soon the Progs had three usable torches to light their way.

"He's not walking," Gromer whispered, joining the hunt. He held a brand down to the drag marks in the snow. "Looks like he crawled the whole way."

"Then he won't be far," Bern muttered.

Behind them Crazy John continued to apply himself to the campfire with gusto, hauling up wood until the flames rose six feet tall. The blaze threw its light wide against the trees and reflected off the snow weighing down their branches. It also stretched shadows across the juniper, nervous shades that quivered and jumped as the Progs searched. Added to the cold breeze and the never-ending steam clouds that floated like spectral observers, the whole scene was unnerving.

"Wait!" hissed Nancy.

Everyone stopped.

"What is it?"

"Listen."

The wolves were moving. Their howling rose and then died away. It rose again but turned to furious yips and barks when there were two shots from somewhere on the plain. More shots followed, and anguished cries from a wounded animal carried on the night air.

"What the hell?" Gromer asked. "He couldn't have got that far."

Bern swore. He knew where the shots had to come from.

The pack now broke up. Howls and barks and more tortured cries moved left and right from where it had been.

"Forget it," he insisted, sounding more confident than he felt. "Find this guy."

The searchers tried to ignore the distant racket but it was impossible. Something was going on with the wolves and every time they heard a new howl it was closer. Then one of the torches went out. The Progs began to divide their attention between the ground at their feet and the clamor out on the plain.

Gromer was about to suggest they retreat to the fire when he glimpsed Day's boots.

"Here!" he yelled. He shoved his torch low with the barrel of the Weatherby right behind it. In the wavering light Day's mud-caked form emerged, stretched in the high grass. In a few more minutes the snow would have covered both him and his trail but for now he was hard to miss.

"This is the third time I'm bringing you in, bounty hunter," Gromer growled as Day raised an arm to show he would not resist, "and it's the last."

He threw the torch in Day's face and delivered a savage kick to his mid-section. Bern hurried up and piled on with blows of his own. Day did not resist. He had crawled out of the camp only seconds before Bern awoke and knew from the noise behind him that he did not have a chance to get away. He could have stood up and run – his leg felt good enough to hobble, at least – but knew he risked being shot if he did.

The two Progs dragged him back up to the camp. There they dropped him in the mud and subjected him to another beating. Day put his arms over his head to ward off the worst of it. The fire towered over him and in the hellish vision of orange and black the Progs loomed like demons, the same screaming, running figures that had terrorized his dreams for two years in the wake of his children's deaths. For a moment he toyed with pulling out the 9mm and shooting one of them – Reed, preferably, if he could identify him in the crowd. The others would kill him, he knew, but with a round in him it was certain the Prog leader at least would die. But Day did not. Instead he cowered, shielding his head and doing his best to conceal the pocket with the Ruger. If he killed Reed, he wanted to see the man die. Besides, he had heard the shots out on the plain. They meant Roland was alive. Alive and probably fighting off wolves. He would need Day's help so Day could not sacrifice himself just to see Reed fall. He had to persevere and watch for another chance.

Light was touching the horizon and the snow still falling when Reed yelled for the others to stop. He stepped close and stood on Day's right hand.

"Enough games, Mr. Day," he said. He was exhausted but his voice oozed menace. "You're wasting our time."

"Yeah, thanks to you," Bern muttered, out of breath himself.

"Shut up," Elke snapped.

"Stuff it, bitch."

"I'm warning you..."

"Yeah, warn me again," Bern turned on her. "Go on, do it."

"Stop it!" Reed barked. "Both of you, stop it! We are on the verge of winning this. Wait until we get this done. You!" he turned back to Day and held up the device. "Tell me how this works."

"Get off my hand," Day replied, tasting blood in his mouth. Despite his efforts, someone had struck him in the face.

"You are in no position to give orders," Reed snapped. "I'll..."

Day rolled to his right and struck Reed on the kneecap with the flat of his hand. The blow was not as hard as he would have liked but Reed cried out and fell over. Gromer grabbed Day and yanked him back. What came next might have been fatal for the Settler but suddenly there was a shout that stopped everyone in their tracks.

"Freeze!" it commanded. "Drop your weapons!"

The voice came from the trees leading to the glacier. It was deep and authoritative and familiar.

"Who is that?" Gromer demanded.

"I can see all of you against the fire," the voice said. "Stand up, drop your weapons on the ground, and raise your hands."

Elke was the first to catch on. "Ray?" she called. "Ray, is that you? What the hell are you doing?"

"I'm going to tell you one more time," Williams replied. He was braced against the trunk of a birch twenty feet away with the Henry trained on Bern. Now he levered the cocking handle, methodically and loudly, letting the noise carry into the night. Wulff normally carried a round in the chamber but Williams had reloaded the gun specifically in the hopes he could use the sound to intimidate the Progs before he was forced to shoot.

It did not work.

"That's Wulff's rifle," Bern said, confused rather than intimidated. "Is Wulff with you? Eric, you lying son of a bitch, where are you?"

"I'm here, Bern," Wulff called from the gloom behind the huts. "I'm here and I've got another gun on you. So do what he says, drop your weapons."

It was a measure of their exhaustion, confusion, and sheer desperation that none of the Progs complied. They looked at each other, then out into the dark. Some turned to face one voice, some the other.

Wulff was afraid this would happen. Still, he and Williams had planned for it. Per that plan the DEA agent would now shoot one of the Progs. Probably Bern, but there was another guy in the crowd he did not recognize and had not expected so maybe Williams would shoot him instead. Wulff waited, expecting the shot any second.

But it did not come. Instead there was a *thud* and the sound of branches breaking over at Williams' position. Then finally there came a shot. All the Progs by the fire dropped to the ground but it did not appear that any of them was hit. Instead, to his horror Wulff heard a new voice launch a victory cry, a voice he had not heard in days.

"Take that, you traitorous son of a bitch!" The words came from where Ray had been standing. Then, "Reed, Carlos, is that you? It's me, Ruud."

"Ruud!" Reed yelled back. "What are you doing?"

"I just saved your ass, that's what! Get that bastard Wulff, he's out there somewhere."

Wulff's heart froze. Where had Rohanson come from?

He ducked and moved as fast as he could, cutting behind the huts to the trees on the far side of the springs. The fire was so big he could see to avoid major obstacles but that meant he could be seen, too, a reality confirmed as two shots sounded and bullets tore into the brush behind him. He fell to his knees, lunged up, and sprinted into the darkest patch of woods, with another bullet striking a tree just as he got behind it. A fourth ricocheted across his path, creasing his chest. That doubled his panic and his speed. He dodged right, then left, and ran another ten yards until he could not see to run anymore. There he dropped and crawled, stopping only when he bumped into a tree. He stayed still then, worried he might do the Progs' work for him if he impaled himself on a branch or worse, ran into a bear. He tried to hold his breath to keep quiet but it was impossible, so he shoved his mouth down into his armpit to muffle the sound.

Someone was after him. More than one person. He heard shouted instructions, then whispers, then movement in the brush he had passed through. There were more whispers, and yelling from the fire.

The camp was out of sight but light from the blaze reflected on snow-covered pine boughs overhead. Wulff rose and stood between two trees, trying to make out anything in the black woods. He doubted anyone could see him; there was a glow in the sky but it was faint. The only real illumination was behind his pursuers. His eyes strained to look down his trail, picking out trees and the spaces between them. There! A shadow moved.

He raised his right hand to his mouth and took the stick there between his teeth. With his fingers free to move – as much as they could – he reached into his pocket and drew out Ray's .380 sub-compact. He did not want to shoot if he could help it: he still did not want to kill anyone. It was also too dark, and he had to use his fourth finger on the trigger. Unless the person was right on top of him he was unlikely to hit anything. But the gun was all he had. If he tried to run he would only draw their fire.

The shadow merged with another and disappeared. A branch swayed. He heard snow plop onto the ground. Wulff's nerves tingled: he began to imagine he was surrounded. Though his heart pounded in his chest, he scarcely breathed.

Then a twig cracked close by. Off to his right someone stumbled but it sounded as though they were charging through the brush, coming right at him. Wulff whirled, ducked, and pulled the trigger. The .380 popped in the night.

A cry of pain answered and whoever it was turned and ran. At the same time someone in the direction of the camp fired an AK several times. The rounds cut a limb overhead that fell on him, making him panic and cry out in turn.

He heard Nancy Peal yell, then Bern Jones shouted Wulff's name followed by a steady stream of threats. Wulff dropped prone and lay still. There was movement again but now it was going away. More yelling...then silence.

Minutes ticked by. The Progs had evidently decided to give up chasing him in the dark. He was left alone.

He fought the urge to vomit. He had never been shot at before. A bear had tried to kill him but never a person. Well, maybe at the meadow but that was unclear. There was nothing unclear now about what they had just tried to do. They had tried to kill him! It was a feeling unlike any he had ever felt.

Now he was alone. Really alone. It was dark, it was cold, he was injured and exhausted and hungry, and people he had lived with for half a year had just tried to shoot him dead. He felt like closing his eyes and doing the job for them by just dying. Giving up. That was probably what they would expect him to do now, anyway. Either that or keep running. Who wouldn't?

Do the unexpected.

Day's observation suddenly came into his head. *One thing I do know is a basic principle of hunting men,* the Settler had said before the fight at the meadow. *Do the unexpected. Get the surprise if you can.*

The Progs expected him to run or give up. So what if he didn't? What would be the last thing they would expect him to do, he wondered?

The last thing *he* would expect himself to do is go right back where he had just come from. Back to the camp, back on the attack. That was not like him at all. He recoiled just thinking about it.

But the more he considered the alternatives, the more sense it made. After all, the Progs thought he was dead or wounded, or just plain scared and getting as far away as possible. They would not expect to see him again anytime soon. But what choice did he have? He had to help Day. It was the right thing to do and besides, the Settler was his ticket home. Not to mention Ray Williams, if he was still alive.

Having made the decision to go back on the offensive, Wulff stood up straight and gathered his confidence. You can do this, he told himself. You're still the best man in the woods. You can bring the surprise to them.

The woods around him were still. There was some light now, a reflection off the clouds that made the forest shimmer. Fat flakes continued to fall through this hazy vision. They swirled in the lingering wind, masking everything more than ten yards away.

That was fine, Wulff thought as he moved back up his trail. Dawn with its muted colors was the best time of day to travel unseen, so if the snow wanted to cooperate by camouflaging him even more, he welcomed the assist.

Making no more noise than the flakes themselves as they merged with the forest floor, the logger from Oregon slipped between the trees and headed for the thermal springs. The only sign of his passage were footprints but in minutes they, too, faded from view.

37

D ay looked up as Ruud Rohanson dragged the body of Ray Williams into camp. The Swede threw an Arrow club at Reed's feet and stood over the corpse like a hunter posing with a trophy elk.

"You're welcome," he told the assembled Progs.

Day had never seen Williams except through the scope of his rifle and now it was too late to make his acquaintance. He had suspected that the man was the mole Gault had told him about: this appeared to confirm it. Damn. Williams had lasted this long only to fall at the end.

For his part, Ruud looked like hell. Day thought so, anyway. He was hardly one to talk, lying beaten, bloody, and coated in eight layers of mud; still, when he had seen Rohanson on the mountain the guy had looked wild but human, even carrying a bit of mountain man charisma behind the cruel swagger. Now he was a mess. His eyes were sunken and his face drawn. His clothes were in tatters. In only a few days it looked like he had lost twenty pounds and run three marathons. Being on his own in a Pleistocene wilderness had not been good to him.

"What happened?" he heard Reed ask.

"It's obvious, isn't it? I killed him."

"But why Ray?" Elke asked. She knelt down to look at the DEA agent, who the falling snow covered in a white layer so he looked as though he were wrapped in a sheet. "Why did he...?"

"He was stalking you idiots. All of you. I spotted him and Wulff yesterday up there," Rohanson pointed to the cliffs over the springs.

"Where did you get the club?" Reed asked.

Rohanson looked down at Ray's body as though challenging the dead agent to answer the question.

"Off Puff," he said. "He's dead."

"What?!"

"These guys killed him. I found him back that way about three miles with a bullet in his brain. I heard the shot, that's how I found them."

Reed was more upset to hear about Puff than he was about Ray Williams.

"Did you see other Arrows?" he demanded. "There should have been more. Puff was supposed to bring the rest of the tribe to help us."

Rohanson scoffed. He shook his head.

"Do you get anything right, Reed?" he asked in wonder. "Anything? I wish I had known what a screw-up you were when this whole thing started." When Reed protested, he yelled, "They're dead!"

"Who's dead?" Elke said.

"The Arrows. His redskin relief force. Yesterday morning, before I found Puff, I came across a massacre. There must have been thirty of them..." Rohanson's voice choked, revulsion welling up as he remembered what he saw. "The Moons must have ambushed them. I missed it by maybe three hours. God almighty, they were in pieces. Their heads..." He stopped and refused to continue.

Now Day understood why Rohanson looked shaken. He had walked through a killing field.

Reed was thunderstruck. He could not believe what he was hearing. His plans for the Arrows evaporated before his eyes. Still, to the power-hungry mind every disaster creates an opportunity. The gears in his brain began to turn as he revised his opinion of the Moons. In seconds his shock turned to calculated nonchalance.

"No matter," he dismissed the news. "We don't need them now."

"But how did Ray and Eric know about that?" Elke was still confused. "Were they working with the Moons?"

Rohanson looked at her in disbelief.

"You must have sucked as a lawyer," he told her. "No, sister, they weren't working with the Moons. They didn't plan the massacre. I don't know how they hooked up with Puff or how they even got together with each other. All I know is the slants have gone berserk on each other, while these two came down the mountain as far as the cliffs and stopped. From there they watched you and waited for dark. I would have jumped them then but the storm hit – it was so bad they didn't know I was only fifty feet away. And I could tell they were planning something." He kicked Williams' body and yelled into the night: "Traitors!"

His cry was sucked up by the darkness but in its wake came a burst of gunfire in the woods, followed by a series of shouts. Gromer headed that way but before he got far Bern, Nancy Peal, and Crazy John returned. Bern was furious, Nancy looked hysterical, and Crazy John clutched his shoulder where Wulff's bullet had grazed him.

"You get him?" Ruud demanded.

"Yes," Nancy blurted but Bern gave her a look that would cut glass. He shouted at the sky in frustration.

"I don't know," he admitted when he calmed down. "Maybe. Maybe wounded him."

"Why don't you make sure?" Reed said angrily.

Bern whirled on him.

"Why don't you?" he shouted. "He's armed and you can't see a thing in there – go right ahead, jackass!"

"He's hurt," Crazy John said confidently in his nasal voice, talking to his shoulder more than the others. He leaned toward the fire and tore at his raggedy shirt to inspect his wound. "I heard him yell when he got hit. He's bear food now."

Bern was unconvinced but he had bigger problems. In the rush to go after Wulff, Nancy had grabbed his AK instead of her own. In her panic, she had fired all six of his remaining rounds into the darkness. Now he had only the two rounds left in her own magazine. Bern wanted to beat her to death – or cry. Or both.

"But why did Ray turn on us?" Elke persisted, still looking at Williams' body.

"It doesn't matter," Reed said. It appeared to be a conversation he wanted to avoid.

Rohanson did not feel the same way. "Wulff must have got to him," he said. "I never trusted that lumberjack. He was never one of us and never wanted to be."

"But Ray *was* one of us," Gromer reminded them. "I don't get it."

"You turned on us," Reed reminded him in turn. "Why not Ray?"

"Are you serious?" Gromer barked. "You're going to bring that up after I just brought you the Settler?"

"My point is, people are weak," Reed pontificated. "And weak people lose faith."

Gromer looked ready to take a swing at him. Elke put her hand in her pocket but at the last moment Gromer turned his back and went to sulk on the other side of the fire.

"Here's a wild guess," Bern snapped, watching him go. "Maybe Ray just got tired of being stuck here. Maybe he figured the only way out was to try something other than the *failure* we've been following for six months."

Elke glowered at him across the fire. Bern scowled back but any escalation was cut off by a ghastly howl that erupted down at the wash. Everyone spun to scan the slope. By now gray light was creeping across the plain, revealing expanding waves of sage and juniper standing like armies on the inches of accumulated snow. Flakes continued to fall, making it hard to see far even with the light. But the howling came from the streambed so it was closer than before. Crazy John stopped worrying about his scratch and threw more wood on the fire.

"Then Ray was a fool," Reed returned to the topic. "He should have waited one day more. I told you we would find the device and we have."

This was news to Rohanson. He gazed in wonder at the canister Reed held out and then pulled back when he reached to touch it.

"Holy crap," the Swede exclaimed. "You found it! You guys found it! Freakin-A, how did you do that?"

Reed swelled but affected more nonchalance.

"We found it because we stuck together," he lectured.

"We found it because Nancy has a photographic memory," Bern scoffed. When Rohanson looked confused he added, "Nothing changes out there on that plain. It's the freaking ice age. But Nancy noticed the Settlers had propped up a branch over by the Rock. As Doc Abrams used to say about turtles on fence posts, it couldn't have gotten there by itself."

On the ground, Day muttered something.

Rohanson laughed. "What's that, bounty hunter?" he said, giving Day a kick. "You screwed up, huh? You're not so smart, after all."

"Never claimed to be," Day mumbled.

"Well, good. Because it looks like it's your turn to have a vacation in the wild."

"I don't think so." Day rolled over and struggled to sit up. "You still don't know how to use it."

"If you did, we can figure it out," Rohanson declared. He turned to Reed. "Let me see it."

"No," Reed replied.

"What do you mean, no? I just want to look at it."

"No! I will keep it and I will activate it when the time comes."

Rohanson's face flushed. He stepped close to Reed and looked down at him.

"When the time comes? What time would that be? When we're all dead? The time is here, genius. Right now. Let me see it."

"No. We don't know what we'll go back to."

"Who the hell cares? We'll get out of here!"

Now it was Reed's turn to get angry. "How many times do I have to tell you?" he shouted. "Only a fool acts without knowing the consequences."

"The consequences will be that we get out of here," Rohanson argued, incredulous that he even had to make the point.

"That's what I've been saying," Bern piled on, "but the grand master here is afraid."

"It has nothing to do with fear," Reed retorted. "What good does it do us to jump back to the same stage we left if it's surrounded by fascists who are waiting for us?"

"I don't care anymore!" Bern shouted back. "At least I'll get a shower in prison! And besides, according to the bounty hunter here, it's you they want, not us."

Reed tucked the canister back under his arm but did not see Crazy John sneak up behind him. The pharmacist must have had quiet frustrations of his own because he hit the back of the device hard and knocked it right out of Reed's grasp. It shot over to Rohanson, who caught it in surprise.

"Ha, ha!"

Reed whirled on John, who leaped out of the way. Elke pulled out her pistol but Bern knocked it out of her hand and stomped his foot on it, covering both her and Reed with his own weapon. Shouting erupted in the clearing as Rohanson backed up to study the device. Gromer came around the fire to join the fray. Day, forgotten for the moment, slid his hand down to his pocket, thinking a gunfight was about to break out. But before it could get to that Rohanson snapped back the cover on top of the device and pushed the button beneath.

"No!" Reed shouted.

Nothing happened.

The Progs went silent. Even Day had to put his heart back in his chest. He knew the device was supposed to be inactive until the light flashed but still, as far as he was concerned the canister was a loaded weapon.

"What the hell?" Rohanson said, looking around. "Why didn't it work?"

"You damned fool," Reed seethed.

Rohanson looked at the canister in confusion. He hit the button several more times.

"Leave it alone!" Nancy urged. "You don't know what you're doing."

"Why doesn't it work?" Rohanson demanded.

"Just hope you didn't break it," Day said quietly.

The Swede leaned down and pulled Day to his feet. "How does it work?" he demanded, holding the device in the Settler's face. "Tell me, or I'll beat you to death with it."

Day believed him. "It's on its own cycle," he said. "Not yours."

"What cycle?"

"Not for another two days at the earliest," Day lied. He looked over at Reed. "Unless Rohanson here broke it. That button sends a current to the charger. If it gets a current out of cycle it can delay the schedule as much as a week."

"Auuugghhhhhh!"

Reed yelled unintelligibly in his fury and frustration. He shoved Bern out of the way and grabbed the device from Rohanson's hand.

"Brilliant!" he screamed in the big man's face. "Moron! This is what your stupidity costs us!"

Ruud was confused. Even Bern was in shock, grasping that his escape from hell might just have been extended.

Gromer now asked to see the device but Reed's response was to pull out his own pistol and glare around at everyone with murderous eyes. He backed away, covered by Elke who retrieved her own gun.

"No one touches this but me," he vowed. "No one."

"Oh, come on," Gromer argued and the others joined in. But suddenly their protests were replaced by a collective gasp. Nancy Peal pointed to the device.

"Look!" she squealed.

The gas in the tube atop the canister began to glow. Normally clear, it now gained color, a pale blue like the horizon on a lake when dawn approaches. As they watched, the blue sharpened and began to pulse in a slow rhythm. Reed held the device in outstretched arms as though fearing it would explode.

Day felt a stab of panic. From what Galt had said, he now had forty minutes – maybe – to get the device back to its arrival point.

The Progs erupted in consternation.

"What happened? What's it doing?"

Rohanson had released Day but now he grabbed him again and shook him.

"Tell us, bounty hunter!" he yelled. "What's it doing?"

Day did his best to look frustrated. It was not a stretch.

"I warned you," he replied. "Every time you hit the button when the device is out of cycle, you can add days or weeks to its schedule. Make yourselves comfortable."

The Progs' alarm turned to anger. They gathered round the device again, blaming each other and arguing what to do. Reed tried unsuccessfully to shout everyone down. Only Rohanson kept his head. He maintained his hold on Day and stared at the Settler.

"Wait!" he yelled. "Everyone shut up!"

The others quieted down..

"When is it in cycle?" he asked the bounty hunter.

"When the blue light turns red."

Rohanson continued to stare at him and then abruptly shoved Day backward into the fire. Day fell and sent up a shower of sparks but rolled out quickly.

"He's lying," Rohanson announced. "He's lying. It's not broken. It's working."

"What?" said Bern.

"That guy can fool the rest of you but not me. That thing in your hand is working, it's working right now. There's no delay. Hit the button. Hit the button right now while the light is on."

Everyone looked at Reed, who looked at the device and then at Day.

"Well?" he demanded. "Tell us."

Day grabbed a handful of snow to press against a burn on his neck. "I told you already. Suit yourself."

"He's a liar," Ruud snarled. "Push the button."

"But we don't know," Reed insisted. "We can't control..."

"We'll never know!" Bern shouted in frustration. "You and your damned need to control – push the damned button!"

He made a grab for the device and missed. Reed recoiled and for a moment the gesture allowed him to recover his haughty manner.

"I am in charge," he barked at Bern. "I will decide."

"You're in charge of nothing!" Bern yelled, and lunged again.

Elke shot him.

She aimed at his face but Crazy John jostled her from behind as he reached for the device himself. Her arm dropped and the bullet struck Bern in the middle of his chest instead. Bern fell back in shock and horror and sat down heavily in the mud.

"You bitch," he gasped. "You crazy bitch."

Everyone fell back. Elke had finally lost it. She swung her pistol around at Rohanson, who froze, and at Gromer, who had the good sense to back up.

"You want this?" she said with cold fury, her eyes wide and her flushed face looking infernal in the light from the fire. "I am sick of you! All of you! You'll follow orders or I will kill you right now. How about it, huh? Either of you? How about you, bounty hunter? You're the one who caused all this. Why don't we just deal with you now?"

She pointed the gun down at Day but whether she would have fired or not he was fortunate not to find out, for just then a blunt *thupp* broke the silence. Elke spun a complete 360 degrees and almost fell down. At first it was hard to see what had happened. As she righted herself the others saw feathers suddenly blossom out of her coat above her right breast. The arrow had struck with such force – and she was so emaciated – that it had gone almost through her. Most of it stuck out her back and had almost penetrated into Crazy John, who as usual reacted faster than anyone else and now jumped away from Elke as though she were on fire. Still, the former state attorney general kept her feet – and her hold on the Rossi. She looked down at the feathers in confusion.

"What the hell…" she said.

Her confusion did not last long. Bern Jones, on the ground in pain of his own, now lifted his AK and fired it point blank at Elke. The round did what the arrow could not, hitting her in the stomach and blasting a hole right out through her back. With a scream Elke doubled over and dropped.

Pandemonium now ensued. Bern screamed at the dying Elke while Nancy Peal held out her hands and called for everyone to "Stop! Stop!" Reed retreated into the darkness, limping between the huts while the remaining Progs came to their senses and looked around for the source of the arrow. Momentarily forgotten in the middle of the fray, Day crawled toward Elke's dropped pistol.

But then the chaos spiraled exponentially higher as a cacophony of howls and barks erupted from the juniper. They had forgotten about the pack on the plain. Clearly it had been on the move for now the great dog burst from the scrub and charged into the clearing, a dozen dire wolves hot on its heels.

"Look out!"

Gromer fired one shot that hit nothing and went off somewhere into the dark. The great dog leaped through the fire, over Day's crawling form, and knocked Crazy John sprawling before disappearing again into the woods on the far side of camp. Right behind him came the wolves. In their frenzied pursuit, the wolves may not even have seen the camp until it was too late to avoid. Now they barreled through, adding to the bedlam. Howling, baying, and snapping, they rushed among the Progs like feral wraiths.

Well out of the way by the hot springs, Eric Wulff watched the Progs devolve into turmoil. He had crept up to the pools with the idea of getting to where he had last seen Ray Williams, but stopped when he saw Ray's body by the fire. Uncertain what to do next, he suddenly found Reed backing up right to where he crouched hidden in the clouds of steam. In a spontaneous rage, Wulff curled the good fingers of his right hand around a rock and advanced to meet the Prog leader.

Reed had his pistol out and fired several shots as one of the wolves cut toward his position. The bullets missed but the wolf changed course, darting off past Crazy John, who screamed and lifted a piece of wood from the fire to protect himself. Reed kept pulling the trigger until the hammer fell on empty cylinders. Then he turned to run just as Wulff swung the rock.

The impact hurt Wulff almost as much as it did Reed. A bolt of pain shot to his shoulder as the rock met Reed's skull. He dropped the stone and fell back in agony.

But the blow knocked the Prog leader sprawling. The device and pistol flew from his hands.

Day was almost at Elke's own gun when out of the darkness the canister bounced into the dirt and rolled into view. Forgetting all about Elke, he lunged for it.

A rifle shot almost blew out his eardrums. He dropped onto the canister but the bullet was not intended for him. A few feet away Bern Jones lay on his side, shooting at a dire wolf that had passed too close. He should not have pulled the trigger but being wounded and then seeing the wolves reignited his nightmare of being eaten. The 7.62 round ripped a hole through the wolf's hindquarters; now instead of disappearing into the woods the animal writhed in agony at the edge of camp. With its anguished yowls adding to the chaos, Day saw his best chance to make a break for it. He grabbed the device and ran.

Nancy Peal found Reed behind the huts and helped him to his feet. The Prog leader picked up his empty gun and waved it in confusion.

"The device...where is it..?"

"I thought you had it."

He pushed her away and bent over, holding his head. In the camp the last wolves disappeared except for the one wounded animal. Relative calm returned.

"The device!" he shouted. "Where is it?!"

Elke was dead and could not answer. Bern was dying. Crazy John stopped yelling and looked around as though seeing the clearing for the first time. Gromer and Rohanson emerged from where they had taken cover. Neither had the canister. Gromer was the first to notice Day was gone.

"The Settler!" he yelled.

"Forget him!" Reed ordered. "Find the device!"

But it took only a few seconds of frantic searching to put two and two together. Reed screamed his frustration.

"He went that way," Bern whispered in the aftermath of Reed's outburst. With a weak hand he pointed to the bottom of the clearing. "Help me..."

No one paid attention to him after that. Grabbing every weapon they could find, the remaining Progs charged down the slope in pursuit of the Settler.

The clearing went quiet except for the tortured whines of the wolf. The fire, too, still crackled but it had lapsed from its peak. When Day fell into it he scattered the logs so now the flames licked lower from several places. With the spreading dawn their orange light looked less hellish, though they still reflected off a savage scene. Ray's body remained where Rohanson had dropped it. Elke was across from him. Opposite both Bern Jones lay gasping for breath.

"Don't leave me..." he called after his departing companions, but his voice was weak and they were already gone. All his pleading accomplished was to attract the attention of the wolf, which discovered it could still stand. The bullet had torn a chunk from its flesh but the wound was not mortal. With difficulty the creature staggered to its feet and looked about.

"Oh, no..." Bern mumbled. "No..." He pointed his rifle at the wolf and pulled the trigger but the hammer fell on an empty chamber.

The wolf turned at the sound.

Bern dragged himself backwards, searching for a weapon, but the only objects within reach were a fist-sized stone and the empty pistol Reed had thrown away. He threw both at the advancing wolf but they landed at its feet. The wolf sniffed at them, bared its teeth, and kept coming.

"No," Bern begged. "Go away. No!!"

38

Halfway down the slope Day cut to his right, hobbling as fast as he could between the juniper trees in a direction parallel to the wash. He could hear the Progs behind him but doubted they had found his trail yet. He guessed they would go straight downhill all the way to the wash, hoping to overtake him. So he cut to the right.

Where would they expect him to go, he wondered? Out onto the plain? To the watering hole? They did not know it but he did not have time for either of those options. He had to find Roland and get to their arrival spot. Once there he would make all the noise he could and try to lure the Progs to him. At this point that was his only shot at salvaging the mission. It could still work – if he had the time to do it.

Beneath his coat the blue light of the device shone brighter than ever. It pulsed once every two seconds, like a tiny lighthouse launching a beacon into a storm. He was immensely relieved to see the light still worked, given how the canister had been tossed around. He prayed for it to remain flashing, *an ever fixed mark that looks on tempests and is never shaken.* For this was a tempest alright, Day reflected grimly as he hobbled through the brush. And it was one he wanted to survive.

***

"Where did he go?" Nancy Peal shrieked. She waved Puff's battle club and dashed through the brush like a harpy. The desire to recapture the device invigorated all of them with energy they had not felt in months. The blue light and the fact that

Day had grabbed the canister and run dissolved all their doubts about its viability. The device worked. All they had to do was get it back.

"Shut up!" Rohanson snapped from his place at the end of the line. "You'll give away our position."

"You shut up!" Nancy screamed back. "It's too late for that. He knows we're here and we're going to kill him!" With that cry ringing in the wind she plunged forward.

Stupid bitch, Rohanson thought. *She'll get us all killed.* Nevertheless, he moved forward at a jog, reluctant to fall behind and as anxious as any of them to retrieve the canister before Day could get too far. He weaved through the scrub, looking for any sign of the Settler's passage.

Suddenly, through a break in the juniper he glimpsed someone fifty yards ahead on the far side of the wash. It was not a Prog – none of his companions had even reached the streambed yet. But it was a man. Either the Settler or...no, it must be Wulff! A snow flurry obscured the figure briefly but the coat, the dark hair... Rohanson ran forward, raised his rifle, and when the snow cleared he fired. The figure across the wash stumbled so he levered the Henry and fired again. Whoever it was went down.

"I got him!" he yelled, forgetting his earlier caution. "Across the wash! Straight ahead!"

Whooping, Rohanson cut around a nearby sage and sprinted downhill.

Ten steps on, something hit him hard at the knees and sent him tumbling. The Henry slipped from his hands. Coming to rest spitting sand, he pushed himself up just in time to be kicked in the face and knocked flat. The world went blurry.

"I'll take my rifle," he heard a voice say. Then he passed out.

Day was moving better than he had expected. His right leg hurt like hell but it still allowed him to hop with a limping gait. He was not moving far or fast enough, though, for only thirty or so yards after he made his turn a horrible scream reached his ears. It came from the camp and sounded much closer than it should have, given as far as he thought he had traveled. He realized he could not deviate any more to the west. He had to head for the Rock. With a clumsy shuffle he turned and pointed himself downhill.

Whoof!

Out of nowhere someone cut across his path and collided with him. Day was already off balance so he went down hard. The other man did the same. Both came up swinging.

"Day!"

Day stopped, his fist raised. Eric Wulff's face was pale and strained. His eyes were not quite as wild as Rohanson's but the splints on his arms made up for that. His Henry rifle was strapped across his chest.

"What..."

"Never mind, move!" Day whispered.

"But the device..." Wulff insisted. "I tried to get it but..."

Day opened his coat to show the canister. Wulff's agony changed to rapture.

"We have to get it to Plymouth Rock," Day hissed. "In the next twenty minutes. It will only work where they dug it up. If this light goes out before we get there, you are *never* going home."

That was all the guidance Wulff needed. He grabbed Day's sleeve.

"The wolves went that way," he panted, pointing to the east where the wash flowed out of the trees. "Reed and the others are between us and them. Your buddy," he swung his hand toward the southwest, "is down there." In response to Day's surprised glance he added, "I saw him. Just a glimpse. He can barely walk but it looked like he's trying to flank them."

Day jerked his head for Wulff to lead. The logger stepped past him, listened for a moment to the shouts off to their left, then the two men hurried downhill.

Rohanson came to after a minute. In his head he could still hear Nancy's reckless yelling. As it faded he tried to get his bearings.

The Henry was gone.

"Son of a..."

He realized what must have happened. It was not Eric Wulff he shot. The logger had blindsided him.

Rohanson crawled to his feet and looked around. He was still upslope from the wash so he turned that way. But just as quickly he stopped.

Something moved in the brush. To his left, between the boughs of juniper and sage, he glimpsed a flash of color that was out of place. The wolves had gone that way, he remembered, but this was not the color of a dire wolf. Besides, now that his head cleared he could hear the wolves farther out, baying and running and rallying themselves on the plain. This was something else.

He still had Elke's pistol tucked into his pants and now he pulled it out. He pointed it toward the sound of feet padding in soft sand.

A gray form raced downslope. Rohanson fired. A *yip* of pain in response was followed by an angered growl.

"Aw, crap."

It was an animal, not the Settler. Rohanson looked to his right for help but the rest of the Progs had advanced without him. He backed up and tried to move in their direction but the animal below him moved the same way. The form dashed back and forth in the brush.

He looked behind him. Upslope was the camp but he did not want to retreat that far. To the east, then, was the only option. There the forest bottomed out. Some trees were within range and he might find one to climb. That was all he needed, then he could continue the chase. He began to back that way.

The animal darted again toward the wash. Rohanson once more saw gray so he fired again. Hearing what he thought was an impact, he pulled the trigger a third time in the same direction. A terrible howl rose from the brush in response, a savage cry that drained the blood from his face. He turned and ran.

Day and Wulff heard the shooting as they reached the wash at their end of the hill. Then came the howl of the great dog. Day listened – it did not sound as though the beast was injured. Not that he could help. He had to find Roland.

The logger jumped off the low wall and crouched in the wash, listening. He motioned to Day, who tried to hop down but stumbled and fell. Wulff helped him up and together the men hurried along the sandy bottom.

Ahead of them a spot on the wall had crumbled, creating a ramp from higher ground. As they neared it two dire wolves leaped onto the cascaded dirt and slid into the wash. Whether they already knew the men were there or were escaping something else, they spotted Day and Wulff soon enough and reacted as though they themselves had been cornered. The wolves planted their feet wide apart and arched their backs, lips curling to reveal alarming rows of teeth.

"Give me the rifle," Day barked.

"It's empty."

The men retreated but it was no use. The wolves snapped their jaws with a violence that could be heard through the wash, made some feints, and then sprang.

But in mid-air one of the wolves twisted and spun, yelping in pain as an arrow pierced its shoulder. The second wolf tore at Day's arm but he knocked it away with a desperate punch to the side of its head. It turned to him again but then choked as a second arrow impaled its throat. The wolf forgot about the men as it danced in pain and tried to shake the shaft loose.

Roland knelt above them on the opposite wall. His left side was wet with blood, there were teeth marks on his chest, and a new wound dripped from his right arm. His normally sharp eyes mirrored the opaque skies above.

"That's all I've got," he mumbled, with a nod to his empty quiver. Then he fell over onto his bow.

Day scrambled up the bank and pulled Roland away from the ledge. Wulff followed, surveying the Indian's injuries.

"Oh, god," he said. He looked helplessly at his own injured hands. "I can't do anything for him."

"Neither can I," Day grunted. He stripped off the quiver and grabbed Roland's coat at the collar. "The only thing we can do is get him to the Rock asap and get the hell out of here. Help me drag him. Pull!"

With the Rossi in hand, Rohanson sprinted past the fading treeline. Nothing in the forest looked like something he could climb fast enough to escape the animal chasing him. He knew what it was now: it was the damned dog the Settlers had brought with them. It had to be. It was no wolf and he remembered Eric saying their dog was freaking huge. Well, damn it, this one was huge and it seemed determined to tear him apart.

He still had two bullets but he needed a clear shot to use them. The juniper plain offered none, he could not get down to the wash, and the camp was now too far behind him. So he ran.

The forest stretched down from the hills like a blunt peninsula. It was not wide and in a short distance it stopped where the ground collapsed into an eroded bluff that led down to the same creek Day and Roland had ascended on their second day. The bluff was covered with fallen trees and old timber. Normally this was an obstacle to skirt but the Swede leaped onto the first toppled trunk and ran down its length. From there he jumped to one log after another, making his way down the bluff like a man taking several stairs at a time. He would never do this under other circumstances – the risk of injury was too great – but adrenaline and desperation got him to the bottom of the pile in one piece. He leaped from the last trunk and rolled into the turf bordering the creek, rising in one motion with the Rossi pointed back uphill.

He was alone. At least it seemed that way as his heart pounded and he fought to catch his breath.

In fact, though, the great dog had merely gotten lost, pursuing its quarry into the timber where the mesh of broken branches and upturned roots blocked the way. After a few moments Ruud saw the beast again, cutting back and forth around the fallen trees to find its own way down through the maze.

"Gotcha," he snarled, and aimed the pistol.

He fired his two shots but the great dog moved too fast. Its matted hide blended with the tree bark and as big as he was his image blurred and faded against the background of arboreal waste. Instead of ripping through the beast's flank, the first bullet thudded into a lodgepole pine while the second disappeared entirely, sucked into some dark gap of the collapsed stockade.

Out of bullets, now Ruud was really scared. He dropped the gun and ran, splashing through the creek and stumbling up the embankment on the other side. He could not outrun the beast, he knew, but he had one more card to play. He knew where he was. The Progs had been this way before and he had one last hope for protection if he could find the trail he wanted.

Great boulders crowded the land on this side of the creek. There was no avoiding them but to enter this maze of rock from just any angle was to ask to get lost: from inside, the boulders all looked alike and it was impossible to get a bearing. But Ruud knew a path that would take him through the labyrinth. Not just any path, but a path that held a weapon he could use against the mutant hound chasing him.

He glanced back – the great dog was nowhere in sight but Ruud heard movement in the timber as the beast sought a way down the hillside. His heart pounding, Ruud sprinted along the edge of the boulder field. There! The cairn they had built months before was still standing. Capped by snow and almost hidden in tall grass, it marked an entrance into the jumble of giant stones. He ran forward and slipped past the cairn into a corridor of rock, disappearing and – with luck – leaving his pursuer behind.

The boulder field was a playground for giants. Most of the stones were too tall even to climb. They were so big it would be easy to believe they had stood in place forever but the truth was more prosaic: their faces were scored and etched with deep grooves, reflecting how they had been ground by the ice sheets and assaulted by interminable cycles of freeze and thaw.

Ruud hurried between them looking for the second cairn. It was supposed to be just beyond the second right turn but when he rounded that boulder there was nothing but another gap of high grass pressed down by snow. He panicked. Where did it go?

With a herculean effort he took a deep breath and re-traced his steps, every moment expecting the rabid beast to leap into view and tear him limb from limb. Every boulder looked the same now. The paths between them had identical twists and turns. How was he supposed to get through the maze if he could not find the second cairn?

He went back to the entrance and re-entered the field again, going straight as he was supposed to and then taking the second right...crap, that was it! In his earlier haste he had missed this opening in the rocks and taken the third right instead. Now he slipped into the correct gap and saw the second cairn. It had been knocked over but the base was still there. It marked another opening in the boulders, one that ran through a twisting tunnel until opening in a clearing. Beyond the clearing was another corridor, then another clearing and another. Like ponds in a forest the clearings dotted the boulder field, tiny meadows now covered in white, linked by portages of stone passageways. Ruud dashed from one to another. Now there were pale arrows to guide him, markers scratched into the granite months before when the Progs had first found this warren.

The boulders became closer, denser, forming walls all around, but the arrows showed the way. Just when it seemed the stones would close in for good he saw what he was looking for: an X chiseled into a slab beside a crevice only wide enough for a man to slip through. Ruud scrambled into the gap, slithered along for twenty feet, and emerged into the final clearing, the one he sought.

This one was lush with grass that the fresh snow did not yet conceal. It was compact like a druid's henge, round and rimmed by an almost unbroken circle of ten-foot-high monoliths. There were signs of browsing and animal tracks galore, and the tracks ran in a clear trail to the only exit, a gap across the clearing at the one o'clock position. The exit was wide enough for one man – or animal – to pass through, which was what made it perfect for a trap.

Ruud hurried to the exit. The beauty of the opening there was that the boulders on either side bulged in the middle, obscuring two birch trees growing close behind. One tree was tall and thick in the trunk, while the other was younger and supple, growing at an angle tailor-made to leverage as a weapon. Eric Wulff had spotted them months earlier. He recognized the site for the opportunity it was and together he and Ruud had returned to take advantage of it. They built a version of a feather-spear trap, using both a counter-weight on the older tree and the springy nature of the younger birch to create a powerful killing device. A quick glance told him all the elements of the trap – three spears, the log weight, the twisted grass ropes – were still in place, ready to be set. Their plan had been to skewer a random deer but now Ruud would use the trap to finish off that mangy wolf hybrid once and for all.

A trigger lay hidden in the grass but Ruud could also release the spears by hand. That's what he would do: expose himself to attack, get the dog to come at him, then yank on the cord and watch the three spears – sturdy jack pine sharpened to needle points – spit that damned creature like a pig at a barbecue. They were set at knee, waist, and chest level and any one of the three would inflict a lethal injury. He set to work.

Snow continued to fall from a leaden sky. The flakes grew wetter as the sun rose behind the overcast and the air warmed above freezing. They dripped now as much as floated, plopping onto the surface as though resigned to melting even before they landed.

Despite the overcast and the snow, light flooded the clearing with only a sliver of shadow on the south side. Ruud watched that shadow closely as he labored to set the trap. Sweat poured down his face. He worked fast, knowing his life depended on it.

Minutes later the great dog arrived. Ruud heard sniffing, then the scratch of nails on stone. He set the last spear and looped the rope over the trigger, then slipped behind the gap just in time to see the beast emerge from the gloom of the opposite crevice.

The huge dog was wary. Its bloodshot eyes roved in opposite directions as they scanned the clearing for an ambush. Not seeing a threat, it moved into the grass, its nose following the clear trail that led straight across. Only when it got to the middle of the clearing did it glimpse the tall Prog standing beyond the next gap. A fearsome growl rose as it bared its teeth.

Ruud trembled seeing the beast this close, wondering if he had made a mistake. Half mad with fear but also with anger and desperation, he gripped a rock shard in one hand while the other rested on the branch of the stout birch, inches from the rope trigger.

"Alright, damn you," he snarled in a challenge of his own. "This is it. You want me? Have at it! Come on, let me tear your guts out!"

The dog slunk forward.

"That's it...come on, you bastard...a little closer..."

The dog hesitated. Ruud saw him study the gap and the rocks. They were now less than twenty feet apart.

"What are you waiting for?" Ruud shouted. He hurled the shard, the size of a coffee cup, at the animal. The dog ducked but the shard bounced off its back. The blow got its attention. It crouched and a bottomless rumble erupted from its chest.

"Come on! You want to kill me, then k..."

The dog sprang. Ruud yanked the trigger rope and dove left as the counterweight dropped and the feather-trap snapped left to right into the opening between the rocks.

"Hahhh!!" Ruud yelled in release and triumph.

But the great dog had seen this movie before. Its explosion into motion was a feint: it leaped but not nearly the distance it could have. Instead of going up it went straight forward and as soon as its front paws touched down the dog flopped into the dirt, feet splayed as its chin drove into the grass between the boulders. The feather-spear swept overhead, the lowest spike skimming its back and ripping off pieces of the matted coat but nothing more. Rather than driving through the dog's throat and impaling its chest, the lethal trident whipped through its arc unimpeded and slammed against unyielding granite.

Ruud spun around expecting to see the beast mortally injured. Instead his last sight of this world was a rushing mass of gray fur and yellowed fangs beneath bloodshot eyes.

39

Day wanted to draw a straight line to the Plymouth Rock – which he could see if he stood up straight and peered over the juniper – but that was easier said than done. Though the Rock was at most only two city blocks distant, between it and them were patches of dense scrub brush, a couple of gullies, and still more wolves. For reasons he could not fathom, the wolves had spread out across the plain. The pack had broken up – or was in disorder.

"He's chasing them," Roland mumbled, reading his thoughts.

"The dog? He's chasing the pack?"

"Yeah. Picking them off one by one."

"How do you know?"

"I saw him do it."

Roland fainted after that comment, but a short time later the three men came across the body of a dire wolf that had two arrows and Roland's bowie knife sticking out of its side. Near it was another wolf that the great dog had mauled.

Soon after that the men broke out of the juniper and found themselves in the smaller sage and greasewood that predominated as the plains closed on the south forest. They were also at the wall of the wash again, half the distance to the Rock. Off to their left they saw four of the Progs making their way to the watering hole, thinking Day had headed that way. He wished they were even farther away, for once he and Wulff moved into the open they would be seen and then it would be a race to the Rock. He cursed, feeling exposed and helpless. He was unarmed, exhausted, and pulling an injured man. Where was his damned dog to run interference?

No sooner had he asked himself the question then the beast appeared, climbing up out of one of the gullies as though he had been taking a nap. Clearly he had not been, since he sported gashes on his flank, half of one ear had been chewed off, and a strip of fur was missing along its spine. But the animal's spirit was undaunted. He sauntered by like a model on a runway, called out to display his scars.

"Nice of you to drop by," Day growled. "How about taking out a few Progs while you're at it?"

The opportunity soon arose to do just that. Day rose and leaned into his good leg. With Wulff on Roland's other arm, they emerged from cover and pushed out into the sage.

As he predicted it was all of twenty seconds before the Progs spotted them. Their shouts carried across the snow-blanketed plain as Reed and his companions turned to intercept them.

"Now's your chance," Day panted to the dog, and the beast rose. But he did not move toward the watering hole. Instead he looked in the opposite direction and his good ear bent forward. Day glanced that way and his spirits sank. Wulff looked, too, and exclaimed in awe.

Across the wash and standing on the opposite wall was the largest dire wolf they had seen yet. It was even bigger than the great dog. It was alone, and it came out of the brush looking for a fight. With a growl that reminded Day of the short-faced bear, it stood on the wall and bared its teeth.

The great dog responded in kind but did not move right away. Day looked at the dog, then at the Progs, then back at the massive wolf.

"Alright," he muttered, knowing he had no choice and sensing this was their final parting. "I know you want a shot at the champ. Go on, then."

The beast hesitated. For a moment, just an instant, it turned its eyes toward Day. But if the Settler expected any maudlin farewell – and he did not – there was none. With that last glance the dog was off like a shot. It leaped into the wash as the wolf jumped down from the far side. Instantly came the sounds of mortal combat.

"Right flank's clear," Day snapped. "Come on, pull!"

The men turned their attention forward. The Rock was so close.

The Progs closed in, running as fast as they could across the plain. Day and Wulff hurried from the south, rounding the last gully and turning straight toward the Rock, now only a few dozen yards away. Day could see the cottonwood branch sticking above the scrub. It had betrayed him before but now he saw it as a shining light that marked his goal. But could they get there before the Progs caught up?

"Stop where you are!" he heard Reed yell.

A glance back showed the erstwhile Prog leader racing through the brush like a crazed Beethoven, his mane of hair flying around his head while his long coat flapped behind. The other Progs were close beside. Reed waved a pistol while Crazy John had his spear, Nancy Peal a club, and Gromer – to Day's dismay – wielded the Weatherby. The thought of being shot by his own gun impelled him to strain even more as they dragged Roland through the dirt.

"*Sweet are the uses of adversity*," he muttered through gritted teeth. "So use them!"

"What?" Wulff gasped, tugging the best he could with his three working fingers.

"Just move!"

"Stop! This is your last warning!"

Day's foot slipped in the sand and he fell.

"Get up!" Wulff urged. "We're almost there."

It was no use. They would not make it. Day's lungs were on fire and his bad leg was ready to fold under him. He needed to stop. Wulff, though struggling mightily with his bandaged hand, could not carry them both. Day let Roland drop to the sand and in the same movement shoved the canister under Wulff's good arm.

"Go," he ordered. "Get to the clearing. But wait for us!"

"What..."

"Just do it! If we can't get there, flip the tab and hit the button."

Wulff cradled the canister like a football and took off. Another flurry blew up, a gust that whirled snow sideways through the air, but he stumbled through the juniper with determination.

"Stop or I'll shoot!" Gromer yelled.

Day turned to face his pursuers and put himself between them and Wulff. Gromer aimed around him but Day jumped to block his view, waving his arms. In desperation, Gromer spun right and fired. The kick of the Weatherby knocked him off his feet while its blast ripped the morning air.

The round missed Wulff by ten feet but he heard it zip past. It took the crown off a peachleaf willow before striking chips from the Rock itself. Then it caromed off into the plain.

"Don't!" Nancy Peal screamed. "You'll hit the device!"

A huff from the forest sounded as the echoes of the blast reverberated. Day heard it but had more immediate problems. He threw up his arms again as Gromer got back to his feet.

"That's right! If you hit that canister you're here forever," he shouted.

"Don't believe him!" Reed ordered. "Kill him! Just kill him and go." He had found another pistol but this one was empty, too, and he waved it in frustration.

Gromer turned his rifle on Day but Day lifted the old Ruger from his pocket and pointed it back at the tall Prog.

"My turn," he warned. "You pull that trigger, I'll blow your head off."

Gromer looked at him in surprise and laughed. "Nice try, bounty hunter!" he shouted. "That's my own gun. It's empty."

"It was, but I had one bullet on me. A parting gift from Ruud. How do you feel like gambling now?" He swung the gun toward Reed and then back toward Gromer.

Gromer hesitated. Reed also stopped, uncertain. Crazy John dropped to a crouch, almost to all fours, and slunk behind Nancy. His eyes bulged from their sockets, his face was bright red – as red as when Day had had him hanging upside down from the tamarack. He's the wild card, Day thought. If he charges me, the gig is up.

"You're bluffing."

"Then shoot, Gromer! Pull the trigger. We just saw how that rifle's too big for you. You'll miss and I'll spread your brains all over Crazy John."

A hundred feet behind him Eric Wulff reached the cottonwood limb and slid into the clearing below it. He set the canister upright and then scrabbled around, pushing away twigs and leaves and smoothing the dirt. He did not know what else to do and panicked urgency drove him to action of any sort.

"Day! Come on!" he shouted.

Day did not move. If he tried to back up, Gromer would fire. And there was no way he could get away from them dragging Roland. They would be on him in a second. It was a standoff.

The blue light on the canister suddenly skipped a beat. Wulff glanced down in horror.

"Day!" he shouted. "It's slowing down!" He jumped up and held the canister overhead. "The flashes are slowing down!"

The Progs stared at Wulff, panic in their faces. Reed gripped his gun until his hand went white. His last chance at control was slipping away.

"THAT'S IT!" he yelled. "Enough of this. Charge him! He can't kill all of us. Come on, bounty hunter! You want me! I killed your kids, now I'm going to kill you!"

He lunged forward. His companions needed no encouragement. Nancy Peal screamed and ran at him. With a savage yell of his own, Crazy John burst from behind her and hurled his spear. Day ducked to avoid it but stood back up and pointed the pistol from one to the other, uncertain what to do.

Behind Nancy the aspen waggled and another huff reached Day's ears, a small one, like the contented sigh of an overweight infant. The trees parted and the baby mammoth burst into view. It trotted toward the watering hole, paying no attention to the drama taking place yards away. Day guessed it was the same rash juvenile they had seen twice before, including when it almost ended the Settlers' mission before it started. When it rains it pours, he thought. He's coming to finish the job.

But suddenly he knew what to do. He aimed for the gap between Nancy and Reed and pulled the trigger.

The 9mm barked, its report half that of the Weatherby but still sharp enough to cut the air and bounce off the trees.

Day was a dead shot with almost any weapon but his muscles ached and the gun was dirty: he missed by a mile. He aimed at the baby's foreleg and instead the bullet barely hit the animal at all, glancing off its skull. To his great fortune, the effect was still dramatic. The baby let loose a heart-wrenching scream that went on and on as it shook its head, trying to expel the pain that had just struck out of nowhere. A bellow from the forest responded instantly to its cry. Seconds later, the adult mammoth burst from the trees.

Day dropped the pistol and grabbed Roland with both hands. Terror lending him strength, he pulled his friend over his shoulders and staggered away.

The Progs whirled in confusion to see the mammoth charging down the slope. They reacted with a moment of paralyzed shock followed by a starburst.

Gromer had the presence of mind to pull the trigger on the Weatherby but where the bullet went was anyone's guess. If it hit the mammoth it changed nothing. He then threw the rifle and ducked right, betting it would distract the beast long enough for him to dodge its charge. But the wager was his last one and it went wrong. The rifle bounced off the mammoth's nose like a toothpick. The monster did not even break stride. It slammed Gromer broadside with its swinging tusks, breaking his back and sending him flying through the air. He sailed over the heads of his companions and landed in a pile at the wall of the wash.

The mammoth next turned toward Crazy John, but the wily hermit ran behind Nancy Peal who was screaming and backing up as fast as she could, too panicked to turn. The mammoth knocked her over and stomped on her, wheeling and bellowing. Thus occupied, it missed John as he slipped aside and sprinted for the forest.

John was in the clear and had almost reached cover when he was bowled over by the baby mammoth, which was running upslope in a blind rush of its own. The panicked creature plowed into John like a minivan striking a pedestrian. It never slowed down, but carried John uphill in a frenzy until both crashed headlong into a stand of birch. There the animal shook John loose, fought to get free of the bramble, and with one final squeal ran off into the woods, trampling the one-time pharmacist in the process. John lay in a crippled heap half-buried in the thicket. Had anyone been close enough to hear, they would have caught him in his last breath mumbling about someone named Mary.

Reed instinctively took off downhill but then realized there was no point in escaping the mammoth if he did not get to the device in time. He changed course to sprint directly at the waving logger. Strategically that was a prudent move, but in the short run it put him in the pachyderm's line of sight as it finished with Nancy Peal. With a roar that shook the surface of the watering hole, the mammoth came after him.

"Day, hurry!" Wulff yelled. He left the clearing and ran to help the Settler as Day's right leg buckled for the last time, dropping him to one knee and spilling Roland into the dirt. Wulff hooked his good fingers around Roland's collar and dragged him off Day's back. Day lurched onto his good leg and hopped forward to grab Roland's other arm. Together they pulled the unconscious warrior the final few yards.

Behind them came a tortured cry but it was drowned out by another bellow from the mammoth. Day and Wulff drove forward, not bothering to look back. The ground shook, the smell of the raging creature was everywhere, but they had no time to spare.

They spilled into the clearing, knocking the canister rolling. Wulff lunged and tried to pick it up but could not. Knowing it was useless, he swept it to Day who let go of Roland and grabbed the thermos in both hands. The blue light was still there but faint, a flicker of color through the dirty lens. Day fumbled to flip up the cover.

"Aauggghhah!" came a scream of agony from right behind him.

Day rolled over and saw the mammoth almost on top of them. Reed was impaled on its curving tusks, being waved left and right as the animal covered the remaining feet to where the men lay on the ground. Hair flying, ears waving, the enraged giant barreled into the clearing just as Day slammed his hand down on the switch.

40

In the hastily-built shed north of the hangar, the recovery team had been on alert for eight hours. Knowing the switch was due to cycle, Don Galt had had everyone on station since the night before. But as the minutes ticked by and the canister on the stage remained quiet, hope faded.

The guards held their weapons in a low-ready stance, while the ambulance crew left the vehicle and sat anxiously on folding chairs along the wall. Twenty people stared through the plexiglass panels, waiting for the thermos on the table to energize. Waiting for something to happen. But the tube remained dark. The buzzer stayed quiet.

Doctor Saks himself monitored the main console. The researcher was consumed with signals on his screen, affecting an academic objectivity. Neal Davis sat behind him but there was nothing objective about his posture. He was the poster child of apprehension as the cycle weakened and nothing appeared on the stage. He shifted his weight once in half an hour. Otherwise he was a statue.

One man not sitting still was Don Galt. He stood facing the stage with his arms crossed, rocking on the balls of his feet. His face was flushed, the veins at his temples protruded.

"The signal is almost gone," Saks said to no one in particular.

The announcement was met with absolute silence. One of the paramedics by the wall turned to look questioningly at Doctor Campbell but he simply patted her hand and kept watching the stage.

Saks cleared his throat. "If we shut down now, we..."

"We wait." Neal cut him off.

Saks nodded. For a moment he pretended to study the images on his screen, flipping from one window to the next although he already knew the data by heart.

"I'm just saying that if we shut down now, we might preserve enough power for another..."

"We wait!" Galt shouted. He turned and slammed his fist on the table so hard a coffee mug bounced to the floor.

Saks swallowed and nodded. He said no more.

Two minutes later, with no warning the blue light on the canister flared. At the same instant the stage buzzer sounded. Everyone leaped but before they could do anything a brilliant light burst from the enclosure and an explosion rent the air.

The flash blinded the waiting group but that was nothing compared to the detonation that accompanied it. In past time swaps the plexiglass wall around the stage had funneled the explosion upward and out through the hole in the roof. This time the wall failed catastrophically. Something massive struck the panels nearest the ambulance and blew them outward as though they had been shot from a cannon. The detonation escaped through the breach and the whole structure collapsed like a burst balloon, filling the building with smoke and dust.

The lights went out. Several guards went down, struck by debris. The hospital corps barely escaped annihilation even as the ambulance was thrown halfway through the shed's wall. Its lights flashed and the siren triggered, wailing as though in pain as studs toppled and part of the roof fell onto the cab.

Don Galt was thrown across the console. Most of the tables collapsed and Doctor Saks and his technicians struggled to get out from under them. The servers escaped immediate damage but a loose cable struck Neal Davis in the face and knocked him to the floor. Blood streaming from his cheek, he was nevertheless the first back on his feet.

"Doors!" he yelled. "Open the doors!"

He could hardly see anything through the dust and smoke. Still, something felt odd. He touched his hands to his chest – he was wet across his front. It was water, though, not blood. And there was a chunk of what looked like frozen snow melting rapidly on one of the keyboards.

"Someone get the..."

His order was drowned out by a roar that shook him to his heels. Then another, and then the earthen floor itself quivered as though struck. In a horrified instant he realized there was an animal of some kind in the room. He heard the sound of bending metal, then another roar, and finally the siren's wail was choked off in a cacophony of smashing glass.

Someone got the door behind the servers open and light streamed in, joining shards that filtered through above the smashed ambulance. Neal spied Galt struggling under an overturned desk and went to help him. As he got Galt to his feet, another deafening bellow shook the building and a massive form loomed out of the dust, coming right at them.

Neal pushed Galt aside, leaping after him just in time to escape the charge of the mammoth. Crazed, confused, and now injured, the massive beast obliterated the computer drives that bestrew the floor and crushed the servers as it plowed into and through the west wall of the shed. Its mad rush carried it outside as timbers splintered and sheets of corrugated tin ripped apart as though made from paper mâché. The mammoth stumbled into the Wyoming landscape and kept going. Inside the building, the ground shook less as it raced away, but for several minutes they could still hear its roars – thunderous, triumphant peals ringing in the open air.

The dust began to clear. Doctor Campbell was up and helping his team to their feet. Three were injured, the rest wandered dazed, rubbing their ears. But soon enough they recovered and swung into action. They found each other and the new arrivals; Campbell barked orders and delegated teams of experts to each.

"Day!" Neal cried, seeing the Settler sprawled by the east wall. He helped the doctors pull him into the light. "Day, speak to me."

To Day the world was a blur. He heard Neal's shouts but could not make out the words. His eyes struggled to focus. There were people in white coats all around him. More were nearby, tending to Roland. His friend looked dead, a gawky corpse with limbs thrown wide. Wulff was nowhere to be seen.

He saw his leg, the injured one, with a piece of plexiglass sticking from the calf. Just can't catch a break, that one, he thought. He wondered why it did not hurt.

Galt came over and touched Neal's shoulder. When Neal looked up, Galt jerked his head for the other man to follow. Neal put his hand against Day's cheek and said, "You're okay now, Day. We've got you." Then he went after Galt.

A helicopter spooled up and hovered over from the main compound to wait outside the shed, but moved away again when the wall over the destroyed ambulance collapsed. Care paused while everyone was hurriedly moved outside. Doctor Campbell already supervised the equivalent of a regional trauma center so there was no urgency to transport any of the arrivals, but with the additional staff casualties there was the risk they would be overwhelmed. He told the helo pilot to stand by.

Day found himself lying on a stretcher in the grass, blinking in the light. His head began to clear. He saw Eric Wulff some yards away, stripped to the waist, head bandaged and both arms being tended to by EMTs. Behind the EMTs were guards with rifles. Beyond them lay a figure in the dirt, covered with a blood-soaked sheet.

Someone touched his hand. He looked over and saw the doctors laying Roland beside him. His companion wore an oxygen mask. Multiple tubes ran into one arm, while the other and much of his torso were covered in Celox, bandages, and gauze. The docs were shaving his scalp over one ear to treat a wound there; they had also cleaned and bandaged his earlier neck injury. A whiff of ginger still wafted over, though, and Day wrinkled his nose. Roland squeezed Day's fingers to indicate he understood.

The helicopter returned, settling into the grass and dropping its rotors to idle. The medical team loaded two injured guards and then came to get Roland. Campbell, Galt, and Davis were huddled in conversation by the boulder but now the last two hurried over to the Settlers.

"Hang on a second," Galt ordered as the EMTs prepared to lift the Indian. "Take a break."

Reluctantly the med team retreated out of earshot. Neal knelt down between the stretchers.

"You got him," he said simply, looking down at the injured men. "He's dead. Lasted maybe two minutes. Long enough to know he had failed and we had him. Thank you."

Roland closed his eyes. Day said nothing. What was there to say?

"The other guy," Neal continued, nodding but not looking in Wulff's direction. "Is he the mole?"

"No," Day replied.

"Then who is he?"

"Not on the list. And not a Prog."

"That might not help him," Galt grunted.

"It had better," Day said firmly. He fixed Galt with a hard stare. "You wouldn't have Reed without him. Or us."

"Serious?"

"Serious. Debrief him and let him go home. He deserves it. And he won't talk."

Neal thought about it, looking at Day the whole time.

"Okay," he said. He tapped Roland's arm. "We're getting you to a hospital." To Day, he added, "Doc says we can keep you here. We'll get you well, then talk, then everyone goes home. Good?"

Day nodded. "Good."

Neal stood up and motioned to the med team but Galt remembered something.

"Wait," he ordered, and fixed Day with his own stare. "Where's that damned dog?"

Day's eyes fell. He had forgotten about the great beast and now he felt a sense of real loss. The stupid mutt had been the last link to his family.

"Didn't make it," he mumbled.

The EMTs returned and prepared to lift Roland. Day gave his friend's hand one last squeeze and murmured, "*Farewell, good friend. If we do meet again, why, we shall smile; if not, then this parting was well made.*"

With effort Roland pushed aside the mask.

"Party on, dude," he whispered back. With that they carried him away.

41

The sun dipped early below the hills, leaving the sage in shadow and letting patches of snow that had accumulated by the cabin survive into another day. Now only the holly grape still showed color near the clearing, the low evergreens glowing orange like embers in the fading light. Many of the aspen still had their leaves but they had turned pale with the shortened days, while cottonwoods by the creek were already bare. It was autumn in the Rocky Mountains but winter was knocking at the door.

"The childing autumn, angry winter, change their wonted liveries, and the mazed world, by their increase, now knows not which is which."

Day said this to himself as much as anyone else as he settled into his porch chair and propped his leg on the rail.

"And in plain English," the woman prompted, watching him from the doorway.

"The seasons are changing," he replied.

"They have been," she informed him. "You missed two months. We had snow in September, then an Indian summer, and then the snow began again last week. It's going to be a cold winter."

Not as cold as it might have been, Day thought. Ever since he had come back to his own time, he had had nightmares about being stuck in the Pleistocene. Then again, perhaps it was unfair to call them nightmares. He dreamed of being stuck there, of the device not working and bringing him back, but even in his sleep the experience was not all bad. In his dreams he breathed the incredibly fresh air, he saw stars by their billions, and he glimpsed wide-open vistas untouched by modern sprawl. And he heard the quiet. Even now in the mountains the world was not as quiet as what they had experienced in the ice age. Though his cabin was five miles from his nearest neighbor there always seemed to be something at some point during the day that sounded...unnatural. He missed the quiet.

"How's your leg?" his companion asked. She sat in a rocking chair at the end of the porch and looked at him with genuine concern. She still wore her cargo pants and combat boots, but today donned a fleece pullover to ward off the chill. Her Beretta carbine leaned on the doorjamb within close reach, just as Day's shotgun rested by his chair. Habits.

Day rubbed his thigh. "Good. The brace helps."

"That's good."

"Yes, it is."

His debrief at Shell lasted a week but by the time it ended the doctors had discovered sepsis in his system due to the leg wound from Crazy John's spear. Not surprisingly, John had wiped the spear point in his own feces to impart that extra touch of evil to his attack. The leg became infected so Day had spent another five weeks in the ICU undergoing antibiotic and fluid treatments, as well as two surgeries to remove infected tissue. The bastard swore to kill me, Day reflected, and he almost succeeded.

A chipmunk appeared from under the porch and ran across the driveway to the woods. It returned a moment later carrying a pine cone in its mouth. When the woman stretched the chipmunk froze, then decided it was safe enough to pry at the cone right there in the open. Watching him, Day could not help thinking of the huge dog. The beast had never been fast enough to catch the munks but he had never stopped trying, and the munk population had always avoided the cabin. Clearly that had changed.

"You miss that mutt of yours?" the woman asked, watching Day's face.

"I do."

"You should forget him."

"Should I?"

"Yes. You can get another one."

"Not like him."

That was a dumb thing to say, Day chided himself. Why had he said it? Maybe it was because he had not 'gotten' the big dog in the first place, it had found him. At one particular point in time, on one very specific occasion, the great beast had come into his life. And now it was gone. Most likely dead. Most likely killed by the alpha dire wolf or the rest of the pack. Day wanted to believe the mutt had survived the fight in the wash but he would never know. And anyway it did not really matter now. One way or the other, the dog had been dead for thousands of years. There was nothing left of him but a memory.

Day was not against getting another dog. It was just...go on, admit it, he told himself. The memory was not enough. He wanted that link to the past.

The light faded and dusk came on. The temperature dropped. The woman turned up the collar of her fleece while Day stretched out his leg and propped it again on the rail.

Up the gulch there was movement in the shadows. A timber wolf appeared. Day watched it nose about in the scrub and mark its territory. He expected the wolf to turn away as they usually did but this one kept coming down the gulch. That's another change, Day noted. When the great dog was around the wolves, like the chipmunks, had kept their distance. Even as a pack they had feared the great beast. Now, apparently, they sensed his absence and their nerve grew.

Day lowered his foot and sat up as the wolf worked its way closer down the gulch. There was something unusual about its profile. Its shape...and how it moved.

"What is it?" the woman asked.

"Wolf."

"Oh. They've been around more."

"I gather."

He watched the animal come closer. It reached the bottom of the gulch and turned to parallel the clearing inside the treeline. From time to time he got a good view of it between the trees.

"Well, I'll be...

Timber wolves have a triangular face, blunt ears, and smooth, short fur. Day had seen them countless times in the surrounding mountains.

"Does that wolf look strange to you?" he asked.

The woman sat up and peered over the railing. The wolf was digging under a log but after a minute it climbed up on the wood and stood there, looking around.

"No."

"It doesn't seem unusually big to you?"

The woman looked again and shook her head. "They're all like that."

Are they now, Day wondered?

He studied the wolf. This animal had a snout that leaned toward the rectangular, with a sturdy, squared-off jaw. Its ears were pointed and the right one bent down in the middle. The fur was gray trending to black – normal enough – but it curled. It even looked matted on the flanks. Most of all, this wolf was the beefiest one Day had ever seen. Not huge, but wider across the chest than any gray wolf and heavier. If this one tipped the scales less than 120 pounds, then Day needed to have his eyes checked.

"What are you smiling about?" the woman asked. She looked from Day to the wolf, which hopped off the log and trotted down the driveway. Day watched it go.

"Time," he said.

"Time?"

"Yes. Shakespeare was right, as always. *Time is like a fashionable host that slightly shakes his parting guest by the hand, and with his arm outstretch'd, as he would fly, grasps in the comer.*"

"Which means, exactly?"

Day settled back in his chair.

"It means I don't have to forget anything," he said.

Above the canyon a star appeared. For a long while Day sat and listened to the night, and watched a crescent moon rise into the sky.

AFTERWORD

Thanks for reading **Bad Day in the Late Wisconsin.** If you enjoyed the book, please leave a review at your favorite distributor or website. In particular, I'm on a mission to get 500 reviews on Amazon as soon as possible and would appreciate your help.

Also, if you liked this adventure, please check out my other titles listed at the front of the book. Thank you.

ABOUT THE AUTHOR

D. M. Sears worked as a cowboy and backcountry packer in the Sierra Nevada before joining the United States Air Force. In his military career he flew a variety of aircraft and also worked as an attaché.

He began his author career writing memoirs of his pilot life. Published under the pseudonym Michael Bleriot, *Flying Naked* and its sequels capture the adventure and excitement of flying counterdrug missions in South America during the 1990s War on Drugs.

Later, Sears published a highly-successful adventure trilogy for younger readers called *The Untimely Journey of Veronica T. Boone*. A mix of time-travel and historical fiction, the books are a dramatic and educational journey through the United States in the late 1800s and early 1900s.

www.ingramcontent.com/pod-product-compliance
Lightning Source LLC
Chambersburg PA
CBHW061507020726
47502CB00006B/1966